MERCENARY CALLING

LAURA MONTGOMERY

ACKNOWLEDGMENTS

I want to thank Tim Gray and J.M. Ney-Grimm for their help, observations, expertise and insights. Thank you.

All mistakes are solely my own.

For Jessica

CHAPTER 1

CALVIN TONDINI HAD TO SQUINT against the glare to see the motorcade of starship captains exiting the spaceport gates. With not just the sun and the water, but the air itself blindingly bright in the Florida afternoon, the world felt hot and alien for a January day. Coming to Canaveral Port from Washington, DC in winter he had almost forgotten his shades, but now he dug them out of his pocket and placed them on his face. He didn't want the sunglasses to obscure his view of the commanders of the USS *Aeneid*, the starship that had discovered Earth's twin, but he needed to be able to see, and his parents had spent no money on his eyes.

Calvin and his companions stood on a causeway over the Banana River between Merritt Island and the peninsula that held the spaceport. He could make out three figures still inside the spaceport in the pale green uniforms of the old ship: Aldo Contreras, the real captain, and Felicity Orlova and Paolina Nigmatullin his second and third, respectively. Everyone recognized Nigmatullin. She was tall, and had sharp pale features set off by black hair and brows. Her hair was long, and she wore it high in a horsetail that made her look even more severe than her impassivity already suggested.

Strangely, it was Nigmatullin who had appeared in the bulk of the broadcasts about the new planet, Elysia, from the starship. The population of the entire United States, if not the world, recognized her.

Calvin was pleased with the vantage he and his friends had attained.

They had crossed the causeway over the Banana River the night before on foot, and found a spot next to the road right outside

1

the spaceport gates. Sean Han had agreed to come for the captains' landing, since it was a Saturday. He lounged by Calvin's side and played with the recording functions in his palm. His parti-colored face was intent on his goal of capturing every second of the historic event. Tri Marlin, who was younger and browner without the many hues that marked Sean's epidermis, did not lounge. He leaned forward hard, intent on everything. Tri, who had learned the landing date a month ago, bought his ticket, and found them all rooms as soon as he heard the announcement, had brought three friends from college.

Tri and the other students made Calvin, who was twenty-seven, feel old. Tri's group had made it through all of one semester of college, but Tri understood the bubble drive that had powered the starship, and two of the others were at least able to pretend they did. The third was quiet and just shone with the same inner excitement that glowed from Tri and that Calvin admitted he felt himself. Not aloud, because that would only invite ridicule, but he felt it.

The commanders of the *Aeneid* were on course to pass within ten feet of them. He could see them standing in the back of their vehicle, Contreras in the center, one hand holding the roll bar and the other waving at the mob who'd come to see them. Women talked a lot, too much, some might say, about what a handsome man he was. Even at a distance, his grin flashed white. The women to either side of him stood very straight and proud, and somehow managed to look as happy, if more quietly. They'd been gone from Earth a decade in their personal time. It had to be good to be back.

A guard sat in the front seat of the vehicle, and military police walked at its side, easily keeping pace with the vehicle's stately progress. The police presence was not absurd. The starship's popularity was not universal.

Calvin and his friends stood on the lavender side of the road, to the right of the gate. The division was not official, but when the supporters of the settlement the *Aeneid* had left on Elysia showed up and pitched their campsite on one side of the road, and people with the green flag of a disaggregated Earth saw them and took the other side, those who came later felt more comfortable following suit.

Calvin spared a quick look behind when he was jostled. The

crowd stretched back to rocks leading down to the water. Those not wearing purple shirts had purple hair or armbands, and one fellow with a tail had a lilac ribbon tied to its tip.

Calvin looked away from the tail. Odd birth gifts could make him uncomfortable on a visceral level. Growing up mostly overseas, he was still not used to them. Calvin himself lacked the genetic enhancements of his cohort because his parents had left him natural. As a result, he had some height, but not enough to have had any chance at going pro in basketball. His coloring was neither brown nor blond, and his eyes were too long and his jaw too pronounced for the genetic fashions of his generation.

Contreras and his senior officers drew closer. They had yet to exit the gates, but the crowds there mobbed the car. The spaceport had reserved the space inside the gates for its employees and their families, and they had taken full advantage of their special relationship. The spaceport, with its demure single story buildings and modest walks and lawns from a time long gone, was packed. Calvin was envious, although he had no reason for it. He and Tri stood right at the front. The others had insisted. Tri, one of his classmates had explained, was very good at standing in line, and Calvin got points for his patent exposé the year before.

Calvin tried not to act pleased that three college freshmen he'd never met knew of his very minor triumph of administrative law in the service of humanity's settlement of outer space, but he agreed that he should get a spot at the front purely on the basis of his advanced age. The others found this arbitrary and capricious logic acceptable, and Calvin got to watch the approach unimpeded.

Captain Contreras was close enough now for a good look. The interstellar traveller, one of humanity's first, caught his eye and gave him a grin and a wink. The older man was dark, with olive skin and black hair, and the world's whitest teeth. His eyes were dark, and, looking into them as he pulled closer Calvin was struck with how this man had seen other suns, had walked on another world, breathed alien air and lived to come back and tell the world.

Contreras had travelled forth at a time of great peril, the spearhead of mankind's response to its brush with extinction, and now he was back in the normal world. Calvin's was not the studied, cynical response of a seasoned attorney, and it wasn't as if he shared it aloud with anyone else, but he very much wanted to follow this man back to the stars.

The vehicle drew closer, and Calvin found his eyes turning to the women. Orlova was nothing special to look at, and she lacked the magnetism that Contreras shed so freely. Nigmatullin was a little more alarming than the smaller woman. Were it not for the smile playing on her lips Calvin would have agreed she looked cold.

He realized he must have been staring like a slack-jawed rube, for Contreras's attention returned, and Calvin could see the other man laughing at him. There was no malice, and it did not change Calvin's opinion about following him from the planet, but he had no chance to share this thought, even though the slow-moving vehicle was now within thirty feet.

There was no warning. Calvin would remember it later as an unsettled blot of time, where everything was wonderful and not all at once.

There was a noise, a piercing crack, and Contreras' head jerked in response to a sudden, sharp collapsing of his torso. The air around him filled with a red darkness, a disbursed liquid that had no place in the brightness of the day.

It wasn't real. It couldn't be happening, not to anyone, but not to this man, not on this day.

"No," Tri moaned at Calvin's side. "God, no."

Felicity Orlova spasmed. Her hands flew skywards as if pulled by wires, and her chest collapsed, too, as her face vanished in the same spray of darkness that marred the light of the day.

The crowd had started screaming. Calvin couldn't see Nigmatullin. Surely, Calvin thought, they couldn't all three be dead. He had no doubt about the condition of the first two.

Tri, who was an idiot, was running toward the vehicle. Calvin knew this because he was at the boy's side doing the same. He saw two of the MPs fall, and it occurred to him that he was maybe in the wrong place and going in the wrong direction.

Some of the military police stayed with the convoy, but others rushed in pursuit away from the port, up the causeway, toward a curve where anyone could have blended back into the crowd. How the people in the crowd hadn't seen or stopped someone was hard to say, but someone had managed to get off enough shots to kill.

Nigmatullin lay on the ground, blood flowing dark and red from her leg. The MP crouching over her looked up at Calvin and Tri. "Get out of here," he said, right before a bullet grazed his helmet. The next one caught him in the neck.

It was nightmarish. Calvin had never seen anything approaching this level of violence, and the thick smell of the blood and other odors, the viscous coating on human flesh, turned his stomach. He breathed through his mouth as he pulled the purple bandana from his arm and took the spot at Nigmatullin's side. She appeared to be unconscious, but her eyes opened as he began to wrap the bandana high up her leg. "It's not an artery," she said, as if she would know.

Tri picked up the wounded MP's weapon, and stood between Nigmatullin and the causeway, sighting down the road to the west. Calvin hoped no one decided to shoot him. He liked Tri.

The other vehicles in the convoy looked to be untouched, but the remaining police clustered around the one that had preceded the captains' ride, as if it contained someone more important. A woman with olive skin and black hair was trying to get out of the car. The MPs were aggressively discouraging her.

"Calvin," Tri said. "Watch out."

The scene to either side of the road had changed, too. It had all been so fast, but he could see the difference in the crowd. Where people had run from the car earlier, they were now returning, and the ones on Calvin and Tri's side of the road were angry and screaming, "You killed them," at the carriers of the Earth flags.

Calvin saw a blur of faces under the Earth flags, and one hollered, "You know we didn't," and shouted something foul.

Tri and Calvin were the only two in the road near the vehicle. Calvin noticed something strange about that. There were dead and wounded MPs. The shots had been indiscriminate, it looked like. But there were plenty of MPs crowding the vehicle with the politician or whomever she was up ahead.

5

"No one's helping anymore," Calvin said. "We've got to get her out of here." He tried the vehicle's ignition, but it wasn't keyed to his bios. He'd always heard it wasn't wise to move a wounded person. That was fine in the abstract, but someone had killed two starship captains and tried for a third, and the mob on the Earth side of the road was straining closer. He looked toward the spaceport and saw only a packed crowd of horrified port employees.

Tri stood guard, his weapon aimed at anyone who looked to be stepping into the road. "I'll cover you. Over here," he finished, calling to his friends, who approached at a tight dogtrot. Two sported the close buzz cuts universal to ROTC youth throughout the country. One of them had enough mass on him to look useful.

"We're taking her back inside," Calvin said. He shifted his stance and tucked his arms behind Nigmatullin's back and knee before draping her, as gently as he could, in a fireman's carry. Whatever medical finesse he lacked, he figured she'd be safer if she weren't between the parti-colored crowds.

The edge of the road seemed to serve as an invisible barrier to the now angry people packed to either side, but the pushing of those from the back pretty much guaranteed that, like most invisible barriers, it would eventually fail. The din was loud and the air hot, and still Calvin's neck hairs prickled as if with cold as he began to walk Nigmatullin to the spaceport gates.

"Elysia!" a high voice, a girl's, called to his right, and someone else picked it up.

"Earth first!" came an answering cry to his left, and he saw it was another girl, slim and furious.

"Elysia," screamed the girl on his right again. She was also slim and furious, and looked as if she could have been the other's sister. Maybe, Calvin thought, they were.

He moved in his own screen of young men, the four of whom had apparently decided the threat of shooters came from the west, and guarded his back.

What the girls had started didn't stop, the syncopated screaming substituting for any desire the onlookers might have had to rush each other. Picked up by the male voices in the crowd, the screaming

6

changed to a roar and reverberated drum-like through the heated, shimmering air.

Nigmatullin's weight slowed Calvin even as he tried to move quickly. She wasn't a small woman, but he had his own mass and used it to maintain his pace. His shirt grew tacky with her blood, and he prayed that someone inside Canaveral was sending help. The roared chants sounded prayer-like, but they were a different kind of prayer, and there had been enough blood sacrifice for one day.

He had a dim notion that a thigh wound could lead to a very bad outcome, and the woman he carried was the one who knew the way back to the new planet. He scanned the crowd inside the port for any sign of something useful like an ambulance as his feet pounded in rhythm to the roar and counter-roar.

It was as if he now jogged atop a giant drum, and the sweat ran into his eyes and the blood was too warm and there was too much of it.

Someone threw something, and it hit him in the shoulder, just missing Nigmatullin. His arm hurt.

"Tri," Calvin muttered. "To my left."

"You," Tri called, pulling up level to Calvin and letting the weapon's muzzle travel across the green Earth crowd. The surge of people rippled back and lost the rhythm of their calling.

This made the crowd on the right, no longer using the cry of "Earth first" as a moment to gather air, lose their own pacing. The cries of "Elysia" picked up in speed, and with too much war vid in his youth, Calvin was convinced the change in pitch presaged an advance from what had been his own side of the road.

"To the right," he called out to the youngsters behind him.

One of them had acquired a weapon somehow, and made the same slow fan that Tri had used. It had the same effect. It shouldn't have been necessary. The right side had the same interest in not trampling Nigmatullin that Calvin did.

They were closer to the gates, and, sure enough, through the sweat that clouded his eyes, Calvin saw that an ambulance worked its way slowly through the parting crowd.

He felt Tri stumble against him, but he had his left arm wrapped around the woman. He tried to turn and catch him, but one of the other young men did. "Help her," Tri said, when he saw that Calvin was pausing.

Calvin looked, and two men and a woman, all clutching rocks, were coming at them from the Earth side of the road.

Ray Hillman had meant to watch the landing of *Aeneid*'s crew from the comfort of his home with a feeling of quiet elation. The starship had accomplished the goals it had been set, however subtly those goals may have been conveyed and to however limited a number of personnel.

Ray had achieved his first goal. As he occupied the center of the couch in his spacious home in Virginia outside of Washington, DC, he watched the starship crew return to Earth. His wife sat at his side, and had been holding his hand since the start of the broadcast. They used full holo, so they could see everything and everyone, from the crew's exit from quarantine to their happy, joking boarding of the open-topped convertibles. Many, many of them raised their faces to the sun like so many flowers, and the captains entered their vehicle looking proud, as if they had done something important, which they had.

Ray had contributed to that mission, and was happy to see it bear fruit. The *Aeneid* had discovered blue-green Elysia, with its oceans and continents of arable land, air that humans could breathe, and a colony left behind and populated by volunteers. Ray had had a hand in picking those people, to ensure that there would be those who would have the desire and courage to stay should the opportunity arise.

When the first shots were fired and all three captains went down, the transmitter on the vehicle cut off, but not before it had shown the watching world the two shattered bodies of Contreras and Orlova. Nigmatullin herself, with whom Ray had had several careful conversations those long decades past, could not be seen.

All elation fled Ray Hillman, and he found himself on his feet, hands clenched at his side. He despaired for Earth all over again, but at least the last time he had felt such fear it had been caused by a pair of large asteroids on a deadly trajectory. There was something more horrible about watching the brutality and idiocy of your own kind. It was worse than the inexorable advance of mass and momentum.

The mid-range optics picked up what the editors had cut, but at a more tasteful and litigation-averse distance. The holo no longer showed a vantage of walking with the vehicle, but of being back in the crowd somewhere and elevated maybe ten meters.

He blinked, awakening to the realization that his emotion had blinded him. What looked to be a converging mob was closing on someone who had picked up Captain Nigmatullin and was attempting, with a small escort, to reach the spaceport's gates. He saw no police, and he knew they had been there earlier.

"What the hell is going on?" he demanded, but Ellen just squeezed his arm. She was on her feet as well. She, too, had lived through the asteroid scare and the fears of, if not extinction, which had been the most likely outcome, complete civilizational collapse.

Three people were at the front of the mob on the left, and it looked as if one of Nigmatullin's escorts had fallen. He was light brown and young, almost a boy.

Ray turned away sick.

He forced himself to listen to the caster. "The police have abandoned the captains' vehicle and are protecting the one up ahead. We are still trying to find out who's in it, and no one knows why they left the crew. Captain Contreras appears to be dead, and Orlova as well. We are working on obtaining more information, but if the police have left them, perhaps all three are dead."

To his complete and utter shame Ray Hillman felt the faintest sense of relief.

Calvin had no intention of leaving Tri, not with the three idiots racing toward them with rocks and what looked like the broken pole off an Earth flag. They looked possessed of a manic stupidity. Another rock hit him again in the same arm.

One of Tri's crew-cut friends picked up Tri's weapon and aimed it. The trio didn't even slow.

It was instinctive, Calvin's decision. He handed the unconscious starship captain to the smallest youth, the one who had spent the most time talking about the *Aeneid's* bubble drive. He was wiry and could have passed himself off as a high school student. For all Calvin knew, the guy was the sixteen he looked to be. "Take her," was all Calvin said, and the boy collected the long woman in his arms without staggering.

The quickest of glances showed no blood on Tri, but Calvin had time for no more than a glimpse before the woman launched herself at the youth carrying Nigmatullin, and they all three went down.

The other two went for Calvin, dodging the projectiles that shouldn't have missed them, the one attacker carrying the ragged pole readied for an overhead strike. Calvin slammed into him, his stance low and long enough to get a knee high up the other man's thigh, the bones of Calvin's forearms meeting the other's arms before they could start to bring the wooden pole down. His attacker screamed and dropped his weapon, and a student with a crew cut brought the butt of his gun across the other man's head.

The last student was grappling with the third attacker, but Calvin had no time to help him.

Calvin and his ally turned to the three on the ground. Calvin picked up the pole and brought it down on the back of the woman's head. He made sure not to strike with the ragged end. If the ROTC kid could refrain from shooting any of them, the adult could control his visceral desire to do far worse. The Earth Firster fell away to reveal the smaller youth who had been trying to keep her from the starship captain.

It had all happened very quickly, and several men from the purple side of the road reached them. One plucked the attacker off Tri's friend, and another bent over Tri. He looked up at Calvin, his face pale. "This one needs a doctor, too."

Calvin finally saw the blood. It ran down the back of Tri's left side, and Calvin knew that if he never smelled blood again it would be too soon.

One of the ROTC youths gave Calvin a nudge. The crowds were very close to each other, forming shallows arcs around the wounded. The spaceport gates were so close, and people were starting to pour out. He saw the lights of the ambulance. With a great wave of relief he realized they wouldn't have to move anyone again, with whatever risk of damage that might have.

Calvin Tondini was not a drill sergeant. He was a regulatory attorney with the federal government, and did not command platoons or engage in politics. He had, however, refereed more than one pick up game of basketball.

He lifted his arms, threw back his head, and shouted, "Time!"

A nation that grew up on sports understood him. There was silence. The heated air stopped ringing, and the sounds of water and gulls replaced the lost voices. A seahawk mewled. There weren't enough of Tri's friends to form a ring, but they'd settled into point positions.

He'd never had a jury trial, just administrative hearings, but one didn't shout. He knew that. But a strong voice could carry if pitched right. "Everyone. Back to the bench. We need room for the ambulance."

"You," he said to a large woman with Earth's flag. "Get your folks back." He turned, assuming she would do as requested, and laid down the same request to a man in a purple shirt. "Both of you, start checking if anyone's hurt."

It didn't work at first. The people in the back wanted to see, but, when the ambulance finally leant the sound of its siren and the distant chopping sound of a helicopter made itself heard, the crowd began to recede. The humming in his head wasn't nerves or anything, but it went away when he heard the woman shouting at her side of the road to back off.

Calvin knelt by Tri. The boy's chest rose and fell, but his eyes were glassy and staring.

CHAPTER 2

THE PORT HOUSED A SMALL hospital. The hospital employed burn specialists and could handle anything from a collapsed lung to a broken ankle. Its employees regularly tended lacerations, puncture wounds, and any other form of blunt force trauma short of a bullet wound. They had experience with the occasional bullet, and they called on that experience for the influx of wounded MPs, starship captains, and overeager university students.

Tri had been shot through his left side. He had been operated on the day before, and was allowed visitors. Calvin, who had been waiting for an hour in the hall, didn't want to disturb Tri's time with his parents.

Calvin leaned back against the glass wall, and tried to focus on his reading, but the constant rush of hospital personnel, the long archaic white coats—his people had given up on the wigs, why couldn't the docs let go of the white coats?—constantly drew his eyes up. There was a large bay window that overlooked the water behind him, and he could hear the noises of waves and birds allowed through the sound filters. Even with the hospital's closed system, he imagined he could smell the salt.

Nigmatullin was somewhere on the hall. She had lost a lot of blood, but would be fine. Her comrades had not fared as well, both dead by the time help arrived. Calvin tried not to think of what he had seen, but the face of Contreras as he took the shot kept appearing before his eyes. He would rather have remembered the proud, laughing face, but couldn't see it, just remember the feeling it had created, a feeling he had held so briefly.

Tri's door opened, and a pale, redheaded woman looked out.

"Calvin?" she asked. Her voice was high but had good tone. "Tri would like to see you."

Inside the room, he held out his hand to meet Tabby and Joshua Marlin. He felt vaguely guilty. It was not as if Tri had been in his charge, but Calvin had younger sibs and had known full well that his parents held him accountable for their safety.

Tri had several tubes running into him, and the small, transmitting monitor so ubiquitous in hospital rooms sent out signals intelligible to medical professionals. Tri opened dreamy eyes and smiled at Calvin. "I'm glad you came."

Calvin grunted. With Tri's parents standing behind him, he didn't get to light into the younger man like he needed. "You need to start being careful. You'll never make it off the planet at this rate."

Tri raised a scornful chin. "Just watch me."

Some of the tension finally left Calvin. He'd met Tri the previous year when the *Aeneid* first turned off its bubble drive and began its long journey in through the solar system at sub light speeds. The boy had stayed with him while protesting the interstellar policies of the U.S. Administration for Colonial Development. He might even have inspired or augmented Calvin's own contributions to commercial interstellar travel. Calvin liked Tri, and the thought of him dying or permanently disabled—not that that was likely if they got you soon enough—had given him a serious knot in his stomach. It was gone now.

He survived the encounter with Tri's parents. They made it worse by laying the blame for Calvin's danger at Tri's door, clearly aware that Tri had arranged the timing and logistics of his friends' attendance.

Back in the hall, he took one last look out the large window before turning to leave. He stopped. He saw a man he had not expected in that setting. Ryle Feder was stepping out of a patient's room.

Calvin watched the older man, who hadn't seen him yet. Although Ryle had decades on Calvin, he looked no more than thirty-five. His hair was still jet black, straight, and thick. His Roman nose and the hard panes of his face gave him the look of someone famous, but he was only a mid-level bureaucrat, a lawyer with the U.S.

Administration for Colonial Development, the agency that oversaw U.S. interests on the Moon and Mars—and now Elysia.

The two men had not parted on amicable terms when last they saw each other. Ryle had been scheming to keep the next visit, if any, to Elysia under the control of the government for the good of everyone. Calvin had publicly revealed the information necessary for a private corporation to demonstrate that the designs to the starship belonged to it. This had been embarrassing for Ryle Feder, but it did mean that MarsCorp was building a new starship for private persons to go to Elysia.

It wouldn't have been appropriate to wait to be noticed with a big grin on his face, so Calvin didn't, but he wanted to.

Ryle's own face showed grim satisfaction, as he pulled the door shut quietly behind him. He looked around as if he wanted to share that emotion with someone who could appreciate it.

His eyes met Calvin's.

Ryle recovered quickly, but not in enough time to hide his distaste. The Roman nose rose.

"Howdy, Ryle," Calvin said cheerfully. "What brings you down here?" He took the other man's hand and shook it firmly. He knew he shouldn't be enjoying himself, but he couldn't help it. He really couldn't.

Ryle must have noticed Calvin's lack of self-control, for he stiffened and let go of Calvin's hand as quickly as was decent. "Work," he said shortly.

"For USACD?" Calvin pronounced it U-sack-dee as was correct. "Are you trying to find Nigmatullin to charge her with something?"

Ryle froze. "Who told you that?"

"You're kidding," Calvin said. He'd been joking.

The casts contained continuous debates about whether the colony the *Aeneid* had left on Elysia was an illegal action, but it had been a constant source of puzzlement as to what law might have been violated and who could have been harmed. Science was a possible victim. Elysia's environment another. Calvin, with his firm conviction that it had been a brilliant idea, found the discussion ridiculous. With the assistance of much beer he and Sean, who worked at USACD and so needed to know, had researched the question one evening. No law or regulations prohibited the creation of interstellar colonies.

"Mr. Tondini," Ryle said, "you have no need to know my business here." He took Calvin's arm and walked him to the large window. Calvin allowed himself to be led. Birds wheeled overhead, and Calvin was certain that the smell of salt was no illusion. "I admit I'm curious as to yours."

Calvin's mouth quirked. "I came to see the starship's crew. You did, too, I guess?"

"Listen to me, you glory hound," Ryle said. "Just because you somehow manage to get yourself on all the casts doesn't mean you're protected."

Calvin was bewildered, if insincerely. "Protected? From what?" He lowered his voice and leaned conspiratorially toward the other man. "Or, should I say, from whom?"

"Your sense of security is misplaced. You are still in your first four years." New government personnel had a probation period of four years. At that point, an agency winnowed its entering class by a large percentage. The intention had been to avoid the creation of an aristocracy, but it just made those who were left feel even more lordly.

Calvin nodded sagely. "True. I am *still* in my job." He grinned to underscore the significance of his change of emphasis.

"You shouldn't be after what you did in September," Ryle said.

"I did nothing wrong," Calvin replied. He paused to watch the birds. He liked the birds. They didn't shoot at each other. Tri had looked so pale. Tri was going to be fine, but he might not have been. "I have a transcript that proves it." Calvin had unearthed the information relevant to MarsCorp's ability to build a starship at a public hearing. If a probationary lawyer was going to defy his boss, having a court reporter taking down one's every word while doing so could save your ass later. Calvin knew he was safe.

"I hope you're looking for another job. You'll need it when your four years are up."

Calvin smiled. The vast expanse of blue water filled him with peace, and he had very little desire to continue needling Ryle. "I don't think so. I have a very good win record." Maybe he regretted the win against Sara Seastrom. Maybe a loss would have made no difference to her refusing to see him. Maybe Calvin's interference in her case was why she had refused to go to dinner with him when he was finally free to ask her. So much for serenity.

"But I," Ryle said, "know your managers. And I do not like you."

It took Calvin a moment to return from the path on which his thoughts had taken him. It took him an even longer moment to realize that Ryle was threatening him. It was time to be winsome again. "And I am not worried," Calvin said. "I properly explored a related issue. And I have the transcript that shows it." After the lessons he had learned the previous year, he even had a paper copy, although he had no intention of sharing that information.

"Something you don't understand, Calvin," Ryle said, "is appearances. You must always avoid the appearance of impropriety, and the government can't afford to have glory hounds like you in its employ."

"That's the second time you've said that," Calvin observed. Asking if the older man had been practicing the phrase would have been juvenile, so Calvin controlled himself.

"You get yourself on the casts a lot. Makes me wonder what you're engineering."

Calvin pulled away, physically shocked. "Seriously? You think I arranged all that shooting so I could help Nigmatullin when all the police ran off? I'd say it's more likely that you know something about that than I do. You're the one who's so connected and powerful." He stopped—so much for controlling himself.

Ryle was smiling, as if pleased that his baiting had worked. "I didn't say any of that. You did, but I think we understand each other."

When Calvin returned to Tri's room the next morning the Marlins had not yet arrived. Tri's parents had been all that was appropriate in parents, but Calvin couldn't shake his feelings of guilt over their son's condition. The feeling was inconsistent with how he viewed

Tri's responsibility for Calvin's own bruises, but the blend worked for him.

"You're an idiot, you know," Calvin said to the invalid.

"That's what we like hearing," Tri replied dreamily. He sported a sleepy smile, and was obviously pleasantly altered. "Those of us who are brave and inspired and want to travel to other worlds. We like being told we're idiots. And you're one, too, Calvin, my friend. Just so you know."

Calvin perched himself on the visitor's divan. It grew out of the bed, and allowed for varying distances from the patient. He wasn't seated as close as Tri's mother had been. "I'm only an idiot for listening to you and coming down here to be shot at."

"You weren't hit," Tri said. "You did the whole thing better than I did." He tried to roll a little bit, as if he wanted to lean confidingly toward Calvin. He abruptly reconsidered the attempt. "I got hit, you know. I'll tell you something. You might not know it."

Calvin leaned forward warily.

"Getting shot hurts. A lot. I could have guessed it, but it's not the same as knowing it."

"First hand," Calvin said. "Like you do now."

"Exactly," Tri replied. "It's something I plan to take into account in the future."

"When you decide to run out into the gunfire?"

"You understand," Tri said, pleased. "Where are my friends?"

"The students? They want to see you, but the hospital is only allowing you a few visitors. I claimed seniority."

Tri made an attempt to nod. "That's good. Tell them I love them all. Especially Ned. He has a beautiful mind."

Calvin's palm told him he had a call. When he saw who it was, he asked Tri, "Do you want to talk to Sean? He had to go back to D.C."

Calvin had met Sean in law school, and they still played pick up ball in the evenings. Sean had the good fortune to work at USACD and so knew everything one could about the new planet, the plans for the *Aeneid*, and anything else anyone could possibly access, if only Sean had cared to. Calvin, who only worked at the Department of Energy, was more excited about Elysia than Sean was. Tri knew Sean from when he had spent the previous summer in DC as Calvin's houseguest.

"Of course, I do. He's probably worried about me." Tri's brown eyes were large and sorrowful.

"You are an empathetic soul," Calvin said and let Sean show in holo.

Sean, who was geographic and geological in his coloring, a mottled medley of blonde and black and brown, had been geneered to the specs of his parents, who had thought they were artists at the time of his conception. Sean stared down at Tri and frowned.

"You need to be more careful," Sean told the university student. "I almost had a heart attack watching you run out there like an idiot." He turned his attention to Calvin. "You, too. You are also an idiot, just luckier."

Calvin jerked his chin at the figure on the bed. "That's what he said, but he's all doped up so I forgive him." He hoped his implication was clear. "I was trying to protect Tri."

"Right, but no. You were running to the crazy woman. Both of you. You're equally moonstruck." He frowned. "That's close but not right. We need a word that means someone who's a groupie or a fanboy for a planet he'll never see and has sunk into complete sloppiness of thinking. Planetstruck is no good."

"Sunstruck?" That was Tri.

"Starstruck?" That was Calvin.

"Suns are stars," Sean agreed, "but Tri's is better because it sounds like the heat may have gotten to you." Sean was done with that game. "Are you going to live?" he asked Tri.

"Sure," Tri said. "Probably longer than you." He yawned. "You're old, you know."

Calvin snorted. Fortunately, the door opened, and Calvin looked over, expecting to see a nurse. Instead, a dark-haired man in his thirties, his skin unfashionably pale, stood framed by the door.

"Mr. Tondini?"

Calvin nodded.

"I'm sorry, I don't mean to interrupt, but my name is Zeke Salisbury, and I'd like to talk when you have a minute. No rush. Just didn't want to miss you if you left."

Calvin told him he'd be out soon, and Sean told them both to please keep their heads down. Tri's eyes closed in the middle of his attempt to agree, and Calvin let himself out when Sean hung up.

Curious, he checked the hall for the other man. Salisbury had been dressed in a uniform of the *Aeneid*'s crew.

Calvin found Salisbury at the window looking over the water. Two other similarly clad people were with him, but he extricated himself when he saw Calvin.

"Do you have a minute?" he asked as they shook hands. "I have someone I'd like you to meet."

Calvin agreed, and started in the direction of the crew at the window, but Salisbury re-directed him to a hospital door not far from Tri's. It was the one Ryle Feder had come through the day before. The other man scratched quietly and let himself in without waiting for a response.

"Captain?" Salisbury said. "I found him."

It shouldn't have surprised him but it did. Calvin found himself in the same room with Paolina Nigmatullin, recently of the *Aeneid*.

She lay propped up by pillows, her pale skin a little yellow, maybe even waxen. Her hair was thick and dark, and her bones stood out. She looked as if she had recently been shot and undergone surgery. "Calvin Tondini?" Her voice was mellow, stronger than the rest of her looked. "I wanted to thank you. And your friend. Is he all right?" She held out her hand.

Calvin took it carefully. She looked brittle. "He's going to be fine, ma'am. And you?"

Her smile was weak. "They tell me I'll recover. I'm not worried." She did not let go of his hand, but searched his face, scrutinizing him carefully. "You're a lawyer, I hear."

"I am," Calvin said, and carefully disengaged her fingers and set her hand on the bed sheet. He looked across the bed to find Salisbury standing at parade rest, watching him closely.

"One of those people who fights other people's battles for money," Nigmatullin said.

Calvin didn't know why he felt offended and tried not to. "I work for the government," he said somewhat stiffly, and worried about how it came across. These two had explored other worlds. They were from another time, over thirty years out of sync with the present. He should remember to ignore any oddness.

Her eyes closed. "That's too bad," she murmured. "I may need a mercenary."

CHAPTER 3

THE BEAR BLANC WAS CLOSE to George Washington University's basketball courts, the ones the school rented out to those in need. The university's students did not frequent the bar when their elders finished their games. The air was too rich, awash in phenol derivatives and other volatile organic compounds. The human wave that swamped the bar had most of them the decency to change their shirts after the game, but they were immune to each other and mostly didn't care.

Calvin's tunic, which reached to his thighs, was dry, and covered shorts, which reached his knees. Current fashion dictated gear that resembled Victorian swimwear of another era, but more baggy and more comfortable. His arms were bare and glowed in the yellow light.

"Tri is home safely and mending just fine," Calvin told Sean over his beer. They stood pressed near the bar. "I talked to him this morning."

"That's good," Sean said. "I feel like I should worry about that kid."

Calvin shrugged, although he, too, worried. Tri was on the mend and heading back to school soon. It was the right place for Tri, Calvin told himself. "So far, so good for him, although I'm always curious about what he's going to do next. Also, your boss found me." It had been several days since their trip to Florida and Calvin's exchange with Ryle Feder. Everyone at the office had been jealous that he had met the last surviving starship captain. His former classmate, on the other hand, was not impressed.

"I heard," Sean said. As usual, the multiple shadings of his face obscured any expression, but Calvin could tell by Sean's voice that

Sean was laughing at him. "After you upset him so much at that hearing, I've heard a lot about you. Ryle kind of can't stand you, if you want to know the truth."

"I kind of could tell," Calvin said. "He thinks he can make Tarkov keep me from getting tenure, but he's wrong about that."

"Maybe he'll get Tarkov to say you suborned the government's interests," Sean offered helpfully.

Calvin took a swallow of beer before speaking. He wanted to sound casual. "Did he say that?"

Sean received his beer from the counter. "Of course. I don't sit around thinking of ways to get you."

"What interests?" Calvin asked out of curiosity. He looked around, but the bar was crowded and there were no empty seats. His legs were shot, and he would have been happy to sit down.

"That's not clear," Sean admitted. "Ryle tries to say it's our interest in getting a starship, but we can build a starship even if MarsCorp is building them, too. Thanks to you."

Calvin had known the risks he was taking at SPInc's hearing, helping MarsCorp, an uninvolved third party, get information it desperately needed. He had not advanced the interests of the government. He had done it no harm, either, but that didn't mean that his boss was pleased. Or that his boss's fetid mentor hadn't gone around complaining high and low about Calvin's strategy. "And USACD is commissioning a starship, right?"

Sean grinned and the pigments of his face shifted. "You know we are." He lost the smile, and said, "Seriously, Calvin. You want to watch it. He says he saw you in Florida. He's irrational about you. Going by Ryle, you weren't helping someone who'd been shot. You were seeking the spotlight. Last fall, everyone at USACD was talking about what you did to Ryle because everyone who didn't see your hearing live watched it afterwards, and now everyone's talking about you again, and remembering the hearing. He's hating it."

Calvin felt his jaw tighten. "He can't do anything to me. He can't drive me out of the government, and I don't quit. Even if he gets Tarkov all spun up I have my record and it's a good one." Colleagues who had watched Calvin's hearing in pursuit of justice for a dog unduly warmed by the beams of a solar power satellite had congratulated him on the slick work he had done for MarsCorp. More had watched it later and slapped him on the back and told him he had real guts, and they thought that any review of the transcript would confirm he had committed no ethical violations, but what had possessed him? The ones who were equally enamored of the thought of a newly discovered planet with a small human colony left behind on it understood his motives, but they just gave him wry smiles, and one of the older fellows had thanked him on behalf of the human race with no irony. That last statement had given him a moment of unease.

"Maybe you could be more of a faceless bureaucrat," Sean suggested. "Invisible would be good. As a lifestyle choice."

There had been one interesting thing in what Sean said. "Do you know why he was at the port?"

Sean looked away, and his chest rose in what was likely a silent sigh.

Calvin's spidey sense started tingling. "You do know."

"I can guess. That's all. And I shouldn't." Sean took more of his beer so as to stop talking.

"He's up to no good. Am I right?" He remembered Nigmatullin saying she might need a mercenary, and now he wondered briefly if she could have meant him. That seemed very metaphorical and unlikely.

Sean's smile was wry. "From your perspective, most definitely."

It wasn't until Calvin turned on the casts the next morning that he learned the reason behind Ryle's visit to Paolina Nigmatullin. USACD had charged her with mutiny.

Calvin had trouble focusing on his latest matter. Once he reached the office that he called his at the Department of Energy, all he could think about was how Paolina Nigmatullin, the last surviving starship captain—and wasn't that convenient?—was going to get locked up for leaving a colony on Elysia. The other two captains were dead, and she was possibly one of the few who knew how to get back. Sure, there were computer records and navigators who knew how to read them, probably better than the commanders, but, still, she was one of the leaders of the original expedition and would have been a perfect choice to command the second if only she weren't rotting in jail. MarsCorp, which was building, if not a fleet, several new starships would not be able to hire her away from the government now.

In the depths of his darkest conspiracy theories, Calvin found it in himself to wonder if USACD had been behind the murders, and if the mutiny charges were just an afterthought. Maybe USACD had thought it would be too difficult to charge all three of the expedition leaders with mutiny. Two down, one to go.

He finally managed to cease his repeated checks of the news, his long moments of staring at the walls of ivy in which he was healthily and ergonomically ensconced, his creation of lists of suspects in the murders and alternative leaders for future expeditions, and turn his attention to his maintenance case. The regulations regarding maintenance record keeping for solar power satellites were strict, and, as an enforcement attorney, he had the privilege of representing the people of the United States against the operators of those satellites when they failed in their safety duties. It was a decent living, and he was glad of the job, but it didn't come close to the excitement of colonizing a new world.

He had achieved a good ten minutes of work when his palm tickled, and he saw that he had a call from Jasper Brughel. Calvin was endowed by nature, not by geneering, with a strong physique, good shoulders, and the ability to convince others that nothing ever troubled, much less frightened him. The sight of Jasper's name, however, raised his pulse to such an extent that he could hear the sound of his own blood in his ears.

This irritated him, so he quickly answered the call to make it stop.

He hadn't spoken to Jasper in months. His intersection with Jasper had been brief but intense. Jasper had been a ringleader for those who had come to Washington, DC the previous summer for a chance to get a ride on the next starship. A lottery line had formed within days of the *Aeneid*'s reappearance in the solar system, despite the lack of official announcement or encouragement. Jasper had been at the front of the line. He had quietly pushed at USACD, at Congress, and at Calvin himself; and had gone home only when MarsCorp was able to announce its plans to build the next starship after the hearing where Ryle Feder, who wanted only the government to build the next starship, had learned to hate Calvin Tondini.

Jasper, a large man with sober eyes, still looked like someone you wouldn't remember, but he still had the voice that you did. He was warmly friendly on the call, and inquired after all of Calvin's friends, if not his relatives, not having met any of them, and Calvin attempted to do the same, all the while wondering at the timing of the call.

Finally coming to it, Jasper said, "That's bad about Nigmatullin."

Calvin agreed, but controlled his desire to do so vehemently. Jasper was one of the people who could make Calvin nervous, and Calvin—at least at the beginning of any conversation—managed a measure of circumspection.

"I'm wondering if you'd like a new job, Calvin," Jasper said.

Calvin leaned back from the screen and put his hands on his desk. "You too? You're the third person to talk about my changing jobs in the past week."

Jasper's bland, mud colored eyes stared back at him. "Should I ask the context for the other offers?"

Calvin laughed. "They weren't offers. I'll tell you that much."

Jasper perked up. "Do you need to leave?"

"I do not," Calvin said shortly. "I do not quit."

The head in the screen nodded. Calvin didn't have him on holo, not feeling like having the other man check out his windowless office. "I know that. I know that very well. That's why I'm calling."

Calvin waited.

"I have," Jasper paused, "someone. Someone who needs a lawyer. And I thought of you."

Calvin wanted to be diplomatic. "That's very intriguing, sir. But I have a job, and I can take on a *pro bono* case, but only if it's not

25

against the government. I don't know if you want to tell me more, but I need to let you know at the outset that I'm not looking."

Jasper smiled indulgently. "That's very proper, and I consider myself warned. But for this client, you would have to leave the government to represent her."

Calvin's ears grew loud again. It was distracting. He had no reason whatsoever to believe it, but he was convinced he knew the identity of Jasper's mystery client. Still, he couldn't believe he said it aloud. "Who is it, Jasper? Paolina Nigmatullin?" Maybe Jasper would take it as a joke.

"Yes," Jasper said simply, without surprise. "Of course it is."

"How the hell do you know Paolina Nigmatullin?" It was almost a rhetorical question. Jasper Brughel knew everyone, and knew a lot more about the *Aeneid* than he had ever shared with Calvin. Calvin wasn't surprised, but maybe Jasper would actually tell him something for once.

Jasper's face was serious. "My sister's on Elysia. I knew some of the crew."

And that, Calvin knew with equal certainty, was all he would get from Jasper Brughel. Calvin tried anyway. "And how did you know Nigmatullin?"

"It's a long story. I'll tell you when I have more time. Are you interested?"

Calvin was very interested. Calvin had not gone to law school out of any great passion for the law. He had been a smart kid who liked to argue and who knew how to stick to his point without digressing. Several of his teachers had told him he should consider the law, if not with any great amount of love.

So he was a little surprised to discover the intensity with which he wanted to protect this stranger. He knew preserving her freedom coincided with his own interest—ok, obsession—with Elysia, but he suspected he was not the only one who found the charge of mutiny a little dubious.

Jasper let Calvin stare at him. Jasper had always been very good at keeping quiet when he needed to.

It would mean a loss of job security, leaving the government.

Calvin knew that. On the other hand, it only meant losing the chance at job security. Calvin was in the third year of his four-year probation. Ryle Feder's cranky threats notwithstanding, Calvin believed strongly he would be one of those allowed to make it. A probationary class was always twice the size of the class that achieved tenure and all the attendant property interests in civil service. He would be giving up a lot.

But he had trouble visualizing himself the next day, returning to this desk to continue pursuing a case about desultory recordkeeping, having said no to what Jasper was offering. "Of course, I am," Calvin said, and his smile was large.

They discussed Calvin's need for resources, the connections either Calvin or Jasper had with law firms in town, and kept coming back to Feintuch and Sommers. Feintuch and Sommers was a good firm. Calvin knew it well. Sara Seastrom worked there, and had represented SPInc in response to Energy's enforcement action. Sara's presence could be awkward. He had misread everything with her very badly. There were other firms, but he suspected he had a boost for this one. He figured it wouldn't hurt to interview there.

"I have already spoken with them," Jasper admitted. "I knew you wouldn't be able to do this solo. The hiring partner is hoping to hear from you."

Calvin didn't care whether he was easily read and manipulated, and it was a question he had no intention of exploring. He knew that when he had a moment to think he would be more than happy about this turn of events. He did have one question. "Does Nigmatullin know you're talking to me?"

Jasper looked surprised. "Of course. She asked for you by name."

CHAPTER 4

SARA SEASTROM WAS WORKING HARD. Feintuch and Sommers expected hard work from all its associates, especially its rising stars, and Sara's work on the MarsCorp matter had turned out very well in the end, notwithstanding a few bumps along the way. Even if, and she had to acknowledge the truth of this, she didn't deserve full credit, she was closely tied to the victory, and there were those who murmured that she had somehow manipulated the government lawyer into doing her work for her. She hadn't. She was sure of it, despite how hard she worked at not thinking about him.

Her MarsCorp issues were no longer all about patents. MarsCorp had taken the designs for the starship engine to the intellectual property lawyers who dealt with filings with the Patent and Trademark Office, and started re-tooling one of its facilities to manufacture bubble drives and starships for interstellar travel.

The killings of the *Aeneid*'s captains had been gut wrenching. To have made it through several solar systems on humanity's first interstellar starship only to die at the hands of mysterious killers on Earth made Sara too sad to allow herself to dwell on it very long. She focused, rather, on the building of the next starship. The thought of it thrilled her still, and she didn't mind that she had shifted from the glamor of litigation to working on supplier issues. She still had her powersat appeal, but she also had a lot of contract work, and was starting to get involved with MarsCorp's purchase of one of its bigger suppliers.

If not happy, she was content.

Her office was not large, but it had a window and a door. The door was open, and she was staring out it lost in thought when a familiar figure walked by. It was someone who had no business in her firm that she knew of. The decision in the SPInc matter had come down against her client ten days earlier, and she was working on the appeal. She had not contacted the government attorney, one Calvin Tondini, but there he was, walking by her door looking very formal in full legal armor, suit and tie and white shirt. He was walking with Judy Aleman.

Calvin either felt Sara's eyes on him or was looking in each of the offices he passed, for he saw her and gave her a big grin. She did not return it, although her mouth started to against her will. She put a quick stop to that.

He looked the same as when she had last seen him in person, the day of the hearing. The green eyes were warm, and his face was unplanned and exotic, a little barbarous with its large jaw. As for the rest of him.

She looked away quickly, but back again so quickly that he saw it and his smile grew bigger. She had made him happy.

Sara wasn't happy. She had made the terrible mistake of becoming attracted to opposing counsel. She had grown to like him, to the extent it was possible ever to like opposing counsel, and their interests in the starship had been something they shared. For him the starship was personal. For her, it was, at least, professional.

He had called her the day after the hearing. They had each departed the hearing room with their respective clients, Sara with two of hers, SPInc and MarsCorp. MarsCorp had been represented by a very happy general counsel who gushed about the bravery of that government lawyer, that Calvin Tondini, who had so cleverly managed to get that crabby old engineer, who happened to have worked on the design of the stardrive, to testify that MarsCorp had indeed created the drive.

And Sara had begun to understand how deft and brave that Calvin Tondini really was. And how generous. He had offered her the opportunity shortly before the hearing, and she should have taken it. MarsCorp was her client after all, but she had lacked either the courage or the imagination or both. He had not. She had more than once read the transcript of Calvin's cross-examination of Armothy

Brewer, and it had been a beautiful piece of lawyering. He had not crossed any lines in his marvelously irrelevant inquiry into Armothy Brewer's work background. He had recognized the hearing room for the opportunity it provided the older man to finally crack open all his bitter secrets. And Calvin had taken it.

Sara had not.

As the thrill of resolution had worn off the evening after the hearing, she had pondered all this long and hard. It had not made her happy with herself. It did not make her unhappy with Calvin, but it did make it difficult to face him.

She had known she was not alone in her attraction, and had not been surprised when he called. She had managed to sound grateful and congratulatory, which were both necessary and right, but she had not meant it. She had offered him no assistance when his grin went awry, and he'd said he'd called for another reason, too.

She knew.

"I was hoping," he said, "since we don't have the SPInc case anymore, that you might be free for dinner?"

"No," she told him, very clearly. "One of us will lose, and there could be an appeal." It was very proper, what she said, for one did not become involved with opposing counsel. Were one to do so, one recused oneself from the case. It was rather romantic, actually, that he had not waited for a decision to make sure he won, and she appreciated the gesture.

And then he had said what he'd said. "I would likely recuse myself at that point." Which was more than romantic. He had believed they understood each other. For a lawyer, as her overly dramatic friend Antonia had observed later in disbelief, it was the equivalent of laying his sword at her feet.

Her heart pounding hard, she heard herself mete out his punishment. "That won't be necessary. I'm not free." Which was when she knew that not only did she lack courage and imagination, but that she was a horrible person who couldn't accept a gift that she knew full well she should have taken care of herself. And, she was mad at the person who had won or stolen a victory she had not had the nerve to go for on her own. So.

And now there he was in her firm, looking clearly like he didn't have a broken heart.

It was going to drive her crazy: why was he talking to Judy, the partner in charge of the firm's relationship with MarsCorp?

The doorway was long empty, Calvin was no longer there to ask, and Sara stared at her hands for a good long while, wishing she'd gone to dinner with him in the fall.

Calvin received an offer of employment from Feintuch and Sommers not two days after his interviews with the firm. Feintuch and Sommers offered him a position as a fourth year associate, which meant he could be considered a year earlier for partnership than he otherwise might have, given his year of graduation from law school. They offered him a sum that boggled the mind of a junior government lawyer. When he checked with friends in firms they assured him he was being properly valued. One friend pointed out that Calvin would be overpaid compared to her, but not when you factored in the visibility that would accrue to Feintuch and Sommers for hiring the man who not only represented a starship captain but had rescued that same captain and hauled her to safety. And, by the way, if Calvin ever wanted to grab a bite to eat or catch a Wizards game, she'd be up for that.

That was the point at which Calvin realized he might be able to get other offers and, perhaps, even more money. But the offer had been a princely one, and Feintuch and Sommers represented MarsCorp, which was building starships for persons who did not work for the government. The presence of Sara Seastrom was the only drawback. On the one hand, all the warmth he had felt, and he knew he had not imagined it, when she was opposing counsel on the SPInc case was gone. He was not sure he understood why, but perhaps she had considered it inappropriate that he had asked her out when the matter was still going on, despite his offer of recusal. He had been careful to—eager to—call her before they heard the decision. He had not wanted his invitation construed as taking advantage if he won, or worse, looking pathetic if he lost. Timing was everything.

Clearly, timing had not been enough. Her expression when she'd seen him as he'd walked by her office had given him a glimmer of how she used to look at him, but that had vanished quickly. It might be unnecessary aggravation to be working in proximity to her. Or, it might be a great idea. He put her in the neutral column. He had analyzed the situation sufficiently. He was sure of it. She certainly wasn't the reason he was considering her firm.

He supposed someone like his boss could view Calvin moving to that particular firm as payback for doing the firm a good turn during the SPInc hearing for MarsCorp. That kind of thinking was so obviously wrong, and he had the transcript to prove it, that he didn't worry about it for long. On that front, he had no worries.

The firm had the resources in litigators, it had a good reputation throughout administrative law circles, and Calvin himself needed to start soon in his defense of Nigmatullin against the mutiny charge. If he paused to do something foolish like consult with older and wiser heads, like those of his parents on the other side of the world in a time zone directly opposite to his own, all those good things could stall.

It wasn't impatience that led him to make the call. It was decision. The firm was pleased, thrilled even, and very much looked forward to him starting at his earliest convenience. He was hoping that would be Monday, but first he had to deal with Tarkov.

Calvin's boss had a window office. Tarkov Davis looked up from a back-blackened screen. The black out was ostentatious, as if he had so many outside visitors that he needed to keep privileged information occluded at all times. Perhaps it made him feel important.

"What can I do for you, Calvin?" Tarkov asked. The two of them did not seek each other out. After a couple abortive attempts on Tarkov's part to impress upon Calvin the impropriety of his SPInc hearing, Tarkov gave Calvin the occasional assignment, but otherwise a wide berth.

Calvin took a seat. There were people at the Department of Energy with whom he enjoyed working. Tarkov was not one of them, and he had not dreaded this conversation. To the contrary. He crossed an ankle across a knee and clasped his hands around the other knee. "I've accepted a job offer," he said. "I am here to give you my notice."

Tarkov's eyes showed surprise, and a strange moment of panic, as if he had abandoned the notion of ever getting rid of Calvin and now didn't know his own next steps. "Where will you be heading?" he asked stiffly.

"Feintuch and Sommers," Calvin replied with some pride.

"SPInc's firm?" Tarkov asked quickly. There was something else now in his eyes, but Calvin couldn't read the expression. The malice in his next question, however, was unmistakable. "With Sara Seastrom?" Tarkov had once accused Calvin, however incorrectly, of a romantic involvement with her. It would have been grounds for dismissal if true.

Calvin had foreseen this question, and nodded as if Tarkov inquired merely of a colleague they shared. "Yes, the same."

"I am pleased for you." Tarkov's smile was genuine, but whether he wore it on Calvin's behalf or not was unclear. "You know who else will be happy for you? My friend Ryle Feder."

CHAPTER 5

SARA SEASTROM TOLD HERSELF SHE had to do it. She was the only one who had worked with Calvin Tondini. He was new to the firm. He was just down the hall. She mustn't hide or act like his presence was any kind of issue for her. She had to go say hello before he came to see her and make her the rude and awkward one for having failed to welcome him in any kind of timely way. It was very simple, but very hard.

She did it. She got up from her desk, walked along her corridor which paralleled 18th Street, and went to his office overlooking K Street. He wasn't in it. It was still fairly bare. He had his diplomas on the wall, but no pictures, and an ivy clipping in a cup of water. The firm didn't have the walls of plant life that were the latest in ergonomics, and she wondered if it was some kind of commentary to bring the ivy in. Probably.

There was no picture of a woman on the desk. He had not gotten married between September and January. Not that it mattered to her, she told herself harshly and falsely.

She was walking away when she saw the familiar figure approaching her. He was still just right. A little taller than her, but not too much. Even in the heavier winter suit he still looked to have a ball player's musculature. It was atavistic, this attraction thing. She kind of hated it.

As he approached, she saw that his smile was warm but his eyes were wary. How she could read that she didn't know, unless she was projecting her own state of mind. "Mr. Tondini," she said demurely, with lawyerly affectation. It came out as a joke between intimates. She didn't know if that was good or bad.

"Ms. Seastrom," he replied in kind.

"Welcome," Sara said. "Everyone is very excited about you joining the firm."

This got a laugh. "Me?" he said, and she remembered how deeply, happily frivolous he was. Or, just a big flirt. "Or my client?"

She resisted the urge to play with her hair. It lay long and golden down her back, and she made herself leave it there. "Maybe both." She was smiling. It was odd. She was speaking with the warmth she had felt inside when dealing with him but had never let herself show—she hoped—while they'd been on opposite sides of the powersat case. "Your client is amazing. No one understands how she hired you, or even had heard of you, especially while she was unconscious." That was stupid, she told herself. Of course Nigmatullin would have wanted to know who had carried her to safety.

He was watching her very carefully, and she wondered if he had actually listened to what she said. It was as if he were trying to translate foreign words coming from her mouth, or looking for a clue of some sort. Perhaps the latter, she admitted to herself. She must be confusing him. She was certainly confusing herself. "If you need any help, please let me know. I'm sure you'll get lots of offers, of course."

"Thanks," Calvin said. "I'll keep you in mind. I'm meeting her tomorrow. Her doctors said she's well enough, and I fly out tonight."

"Take good notes," Sara said. "Historians will want them years from now." She wanted to stay, which meant she had to leave. She backed away down the hall, smiling, "Well, welcome. It's good to have you here."

Florida had a hot sun for January. It shone far too brightly on the glass and plaster of the hospital entrance, but after a childhood in Bangkok Calvin found it mild and marvelous. Washington was too cold.

It had been a little unclear to him that his new client really needed to be in the hospital, but she had written that the alternative would have been a more obvious form of incarceration. Besides, she had a host of medical tests that she needed done. She'd been moved to the mainland. The bougainvillea, angel's trumpet and frangipani trees made it far more pleasant than one might have expected from a VA hospital.

This was to be his first meeting with Nigmatullin since he'd seen her in the port's hospital bed, and he attempted a *sang froid* he did not feel. Just because the entire planet had been projecting on to her a closeness manufactured by her fame didn't mean she would feel the same level of familiarity, even for her lawyer. Her lawyer, however, felt as if he knew her well, that they were the best of friends, and soon to be confidants. He couldn't wait to hear the inside story on everything that had happened on Elysia and whatever else she might have to share. He was almost giddy with it. It wasn't even that he had carried her off the causeway and away from her dying colleagues that created this false sense of intimacy. No, it was an intoxicating combination of her first announcement about the human settlement and the constant chatter that the planet had indulged about her ever since.

He knocked on the door, which read his palm and let him in.

Nigmatullin's room was pleasant. The blinds were open, and the tropical landscape visible through the window reminded Calvin of a happy childhood. The hospital bed had no one in it and was neatly made.

Captain Nigmatullin stood by the window. Nigmatullin herself was tall for a woman, and carried the posture of her military past. She had served in the early missions to Mars and back, before MarsCorp built its fleet of commercial liners, before the rocks spurred a somnolent nation to try for the stars. In person, she in no way reminded him of his mother. Had he not known better he would have thought that the *Aeneid* offered some form of cryogenic suspension. Her dark hair was pulled back in an austere horsetail poised high on her head. She remained loyal to fashions long gone, but it suited her long slanting eyes and large mouth. She was too frightening and far too old to be beautiful, even if part of that age had been earned through relativity. Chronologically, she was only forty-four, but if you'd seen almost a century pass, you were old.

Like Calvin himself, she had received no geneering. He knew this only because he had read two biographies and everything else he could find on her. The biographies had been written and published in the six months since the *Aeneid* came back into contact with Earth. There were biographies of everyone on the starship, including the two who were now dead.

He resisted the urge to bow or to sink to one knee like a courtier.

"You're my lawyer now?" she asked quizzically.

"Calvin Tondini, ma'am," he said. He couldn't help himself. "At your service."

The strong sunlight in the window shadowed her face, but he could tell she smiled. "Well, good. How long have you been practicing law, son?"

"I'm in my third year." It still made him nervous, wondering why she hadn't wanted someone more experienced.

"Have you ever handled a case like this before?" Maybe she was wondering the same thing.

Calvin was sure of it, but he had no intention of losing the client. He hoped she was making conversation and not interviewing him. It would be a little late for him now if she suddenly gained her senses and decided she wanted someone more seasoned. "Mutiny? No, but I've been on the government's side of a few enforcement cases."

The winged eyebrows rose, and the remnants of the smile vanished. "Just a few?"

He kept his hands still. They wanted to ball into fists. "I won them all." He knew that, Jasper's claims and intentions nothwithstanding, he was being interviewed.

"That's heartening," she said.

"I completely understand if you want someone with more experience." He did understand. It would be hard to explain losing his first client on first meeting, but he had an ethical obligation to do what was best even if he hated it.

"You'll do," she said. "I remember Jasper. Probably better than he remembers me." She was watching him.

"He has a defense fund for you," Calvin noted. "Were you expecting to need one?" Jasper's disclosure of the defense fund had thrilled his new firm. There had been some uncertainty about Nigmatullin's ability to pay given that Feintuch and Sommers did not typically defend mutiny cases and none of the partners knew if the starship captain's sizable back pay might not enter some sort of limbo.

"We had no idea," she said. "People can very intensely feel the need to protect themselves while a threat is recent. After it recedes, it requires a lot of fortitude to keep doing what you're supposed to, and most people forget. Some people know more history than others," she finished cryptically.

Calvin wondered what she thought she meant by that. That history showed there was always some disaster waiting around the corner? Or, that people like her and Jasper knew that other people forgot?

Her eyes were intense. "We were almost wiped out, Mr. Tondini. For me and the rest of us it wasn't that long ago. You might want to make that part of your defense. We want the human race to survive."

"A lot of us do," he said matter of factly. "I wish I could get you a jury trial. You're military?"

Her chin went up. "Yes, detailed to USACD."

Maybe he was past the first hurdle. He certainly felt on more comfortable ground. "USACD has its own judges and hearings, and it's USACD that's bringing the charges. Do you have any reason that you know of to prefer a military tribunal?"

She gave him the quizzical look again. "Do I? You're the lawyer."

"I'll be looking into it, but I wanted to check with you first," he said. They had been standing since he arrived. There were two visitor's chairs, and a very small table. She had not invited him to sit down.

Calvin had not come all this way to get nothing out of his visit, however, even if he might have to work harder than he'd hoped to get the information he needed. Indicating the closest chair, he asked permission only by looking quizzical himself.

She granted it with a nod. They seated themselves.

Everyone was amused.

"How is everything here?" he asked. The question did not

come out as he intended. He wanted to know if she was free to come and go, but had found himself tongue-tied over the issue of whether she was incarcerated. The rest of the crew was at liberty, the whole quarantine question being resolved by the families calling their members of Congress and demanding to get to their relatives. Everyone pointed to the long voyage and agreed it satisfied the Mars protocols and then some. Scientists throughout the planet had cringed, pointing out repeatedly that Mars had no life. Elysia did.

She might have been laughing at him. Her expression was just too sober. "Everything is fine."

His fingers started tapping the table. He made them stop. "Are you allowed to leave?"

"When I'm fully recovered," she said. She sat very straight and looked much improved from when he'd seen her in her hospital bed. "I'll be heading up to USACD's medical facilities in Bethesda. That's where the rest of the crew are right now."

That wasn't far from where Calvin lived. "Good. That will be convenient for us to work together. For planning your defense."

"Mr. Tondini—"

"—please, call me Calvin—"

"Calvin, my defense won't be very complicated. I did everything they said."

Calvin had read the charges. "And was it only you? The other two captains were senior to you."

She blew air through her nose. It sounded like a horse snorting. It wasn't elegant. "Having three captains was some crazy political gimmick USACD dreamed up in a utopian notion that since we were on a quest to find humanity a new home, we would all be nicer. So they screwed with the chain of command and tried to say that we were all three of us jointly in charge. Which is crap. Contreras was the captain. Orlova was second in command, and I was the third officer."

There were two interesting points in her comments. His client had left thinking she was charged with finding humanity a new home, a place, in other words, where people would go and stay. Of more immediate interest for the defense, she had likely not given the orders regarding settlement. Why had they picked her to prosecute? Other than the fact that she was the only one of the three still alive?

"So you weren't in charge," Calvin said as a statement of fact.

"Not exactly," Nigmatullin replied. "Just figure the senior ranks were messed up."

"So the other two 'captains' also approved of the settlement?"

"Look," she said. "I know where you're going with this. You need to know something. I did what I did, and I'm not planning to deny it. I'm proud of it actually. If that means I spend the rest of my life in jail, so be it. I've lived in smaller rooms." She looked a little rueful, as if aware how much envy she would create with her next statement. "And I've gotten to see what I've gotten to see."

"Another world," Calvin supplied immediately. "So what did you do?" He was well aware of how badly everyone wanted to know the answer to this question. He recalled a particularly awful vid he'd watched about how Nigmatullin forced a mob of sobbing people to stay behind, never to see Earth again. The show had been pretty wretched, but he'd been pretty mesmerized. Some things you just had to watch.

Nigmatullin looked at him, steepling her fingers in front of her mouth. "We let them stay. Apparently, a large number of people who came with us came with every intention of staying behind if we found the right sort of planet. Elysia was the Goldilocks of the places we stopped. There was no doubt in anyone's mind that we wouldn't find better. They wanted to stay. We let them."

"Did you have orders prohibiting that?"

"No," she said. "But I understand that when I'm operating under government orders I don't get to revise them to expand the scope of my mission."

"You have some latitude," Calvin said. He'd been researching all of this.

Her face became very cold. They weren't going to have quite the exchange of confidences Calvin had envisioned. "In how I carry them out. You're a lawyer. You should know that the IRS doesn't get to start inspecting the food supply for bacteria. In the government, if it's not ordered, it's forbidden. You private people get the 'If it's not forbidden it's allowed' mantra."

Calvin was only half listening to the starship captain lecture him on the law. Mostly, he was reflecting on how people should be allowed to quit their employment, when and where they wanted to. "Do you have records on how the settlement was formed?"

She nodded. "It's all on the ship."

"I'll check all this, but just for my own background, Captain, did you do anything official to recognize the settlement?"

She looked at him as if she knew exactly how much of the bad vid he'd been watching. She may have seen a fair bit of it herself while in the hospital. "Like raise the flag and claim the planet in the name of the United States? No. We did not."

"In the name of anyone else?" He had a mental checklist and was going through it.

"No," she laughed. "Nor in the name of planet Earth."

"What's the name of the settlement?" Calvin asked.

She shrugged. It was an odd gesture contrasted with the rigidity of her posture. "When I left they were calling it the town. I don't think they're unimaginative. I think they were just busy."

"And the other two captains didn't try to stop anyone from settling there?" He had asked the question before, in different words. But Nigmatullin hadn't answered it.

"You can probably leave them alone, Calvin," she said quietly. "Their families don't need any additional losses."

"And yours does?" He hadn't meant to argue. The question came out on its own. Nigmatullin fenced with him. He was on her side, but she was acting like he wasn't.

She leaned back in her chair, hands clasped behind her head. "Isn't it a matter of what I did?"

He controlled himself this time and didn't push it. He couldn't even assume he understood what her silence meant. Not yet. His clients in the government hadn't been reluctant. By the time they reached him, they were firmly persuaded of the justice of their position and the need for retribution. He hadn't expected this reluctance to talk or her apparent unwillingness to pursue her own defense. He chose his words carefully. "Captain, it is entirely possible that you did nothing wrong. What you did may have been perfectly legal."

"USACD doesn't think so," she pointed out.

He realized why he was starting to feel insulted. She didn't trust him. "I am required by the rules of ethics that I treat anything you tell me in confidence."

"There's a nice theoretical construct," she observed.

Borrowing a page from Jasper Brughel's book he said nothing and waited.

Finally, she relented. She folded her hands on the table and told him all about it. Sort of. The story she told seemed simple, but it contained little he would have minded her sharing with the world at large. She did not tell her attorney whether she had known about the plan, if, indeed, there was any such plan and not just a decision to do the obvious.

Maybe some of the crew had meant to stay all along, she hypothesized. When the *Aeneid* had reached Elysia and they had studied it for almost a year, first from orbit, then in small groups—following the Mars protocols, thank you—and then allowing anyone who wanted to visit to do so, they put up a few buildings. Someone had had the good sense to stow printers and other fabricators, and it was easier to stay in buildings than in tents. The settlement contingent had approached her first. They were persuasive.

What if they returned to Earth and it was gone?

Calvin stopped her. "The *Aeneid* left after the asteroids were averted." He hadn't been around, but Calvin was sure he had that right.

Nigmatullin waved a hand in dismissal. "Yes, but that's not the point. The point was wouldn't we feel like idiots for not trying to establish an outpost somewhere else, somewhere perfect like Elysia? Especially after we had been warned like we had by the asteroids?"

She'd told him she'd done it, but he still couldn't shake the feeling that she had more to tell, something that might have exonerated her perhaps. "That worked on you?"

"Not the part about feeling like idiots," Nigmatullin said,

"although sometimes that's enough. There was another part, about crimes against the human race for not having a Plan B somewhere else. That is why we went, after all."

That was the second time she had said they all knew the reason. Given her reluctance to implicate the dead, and her willingness to take the fall, he felt reluctant to press the point. He didn't want her to say something she felt locked into later, even if it was just her attorney to whom she'd said it. He was waiting on copies of everyone's orders, including hers.

He tapped his palm and stood. "This has been a very helpful start, Captain Nigmatullin." He didn't mean it. The meeting had not gone at all as he'd hoped it would. "I look forward to working with you. When will you be in Bethesda?"

"I move this weekend," she said. "And, please, call me Polly." She paused and contemplated the table, her long fingers spread wide on it in front of her. When she finally looked up, her voice was very quiet. "Do we know anything about who killed my friends?"

The breath stopped in Calvin's throat for an instant. Whatever she meant to keep from him, she hadn't kept this.

He returned to his seat, slowly and carefully. He'd been watching the casts just as much as she must have. There were plenty of stories about the shootings. For all he knew, she knew more than he did. "You know it was Senator Donohue in the vehicle ahead of you?"

Nigmatullin's expression hardened. She stood abruptly and headed toward the window where she stood with her back to him. Her voice was bitter. "That's who the cops protected."

Calvin didn't point out that the MPs with her vehicle had died defending her. She knew that. "They found the weapons off-shore. They were printed and untraceable."

She turned back to face him, her hands clenching her elbows. "And the recordings were all focused on the parade." That had been a scandal. With all the casters, all the private recordings, all the satellite imagery, none had been focused on the water where someone had surfaced in the Banana River and then disappeared like just another wave. Autonomous scanners should have seen the shooter, but one on the causeway and two on Merritt Island had suffered a need for repair the day before the crew was released back to their home planet. "They're looking into how three eyes were out all at the same time," Calvin said. "That has to mean something."

She looked back out the window, and Calvin had the sudden thought that perhaps she shouldn't stand so close. Maybe Nigmatullin had the same thought for she hit the dimmer and the window went dark. The room lights went up, eerie in what should have been a sunny afternoon. "Do you think they're trying?" she asked.

Calvin had wondered the same thing himself, whether the police were looking hard enough. "There are a lot of people who don't like what you did. They say you despoiled another planet."

"Some are clearly in the government," she noted.

With the uncanny perception that was their mark in trade, a small group of reporters surrounded Calvin as he left Nigmatullin's hospital. He wished he knew how they did it. He had seen none of them coming in. Now they were everywhere, eye and ear visible at their necks. Despite the miniaturization that would let the equipment work while mimicking a mole, the law required that eyes and ears, shaped like little gems or charms, be visible and worn on a chain around the neck. And the neck had to be attached to a living person. That question had been answered by the courts, because the legislatures had not had the foresight to address the eventuality of a neck without the rest of the person.

Calvin was soon surrounded. The reporters' questions jammed each other, and it was hard to make them all out. Was it true Captain Nigmatullin took over the starship? Was it true she forced people to stay on Elysia against their will? Was Elysia really a secret penal colony? Research had been done, finally, on those left behind, and some had records not worthy of interstellar explorers. There was the fellow with the securities fraud indictment, although he had been cleared, and several with juvenile records. How had they gotten on board?

The deluge helped give him time to remember that all he needed to say was "no comment." It first came out as a shocked whisper, but he gained his bearings and started walking. They followed him through the tropical garden. Evasive maneuvers were in order.

Fortunately, he saw a bench and headed for it. He got the trick of walking so that they broke in front of him. A moment's pause and he would be pinned in by a wall of them. He reached the bench and sat upon it, touched the bone beneath his ear, looked up, and said the words that every citizen of the United States of America knew: "Excuse me. This is a private call. I would like my three hours."

They backed off, convinced by this aggressive measure that, despite his youth, he could not be intimidated, and drifted away, muttering but resigned. None of them wanted the three weeks of jail time that came with violating a request for privacy. Originally, it had only been three days of incarceration, but too many counted that as nothing more than the cost of doing business. Three weeks could lose a diligent journalist valuable scoops.

The day following his interview of Nigmatullin, Calvin arrived at work early. He still kept government hours for his arrival, and it allowed him a couple of hours before he was called in to Bartholomew Locke's office. Technically, Feintuch and Sommers had appointed Bart as the partner in charge over Calvin's client, although granting Calvin full billing credit. As a mere associate, Calvin could not be left unattended with a firm's client, not with the firm's reputation on the line. Calvin had not minded, and everyone was happy, although Jasper Brughel had been adamant that Calvin was really the one in charge.

Today, however, after Calvin's dull but definite appearance on the vids as the starship captain's new lawyer who said what lawyers always said, the firm's search engines had alerted Bart to the potential for public, if not legal exposure. "You did nothing wrong, Calvin," Bart said kindly. "It's just that you are young, and we need to make sure you have a steadying influence. We know that the client doesn't want to pay for a senior partner's heavy involvement, but someone with a little more seasoning will make us all feel more comfortable.

This case is apparently going to get more exposure than we thought it would."

"Sir, no disrespect," Calvin said, "but are you planning to have us speak to casters?" If that were the case, he understood them wanting someone other than himself, but he couldn't see how it was a good idea. It certainly didn't fit the conservative approach he had seen this firm employ even before he joined it. "I don't think that would be appropriate, and I think I said 'no comment' just as well as it could be said by anyone."

"No, no," Bart said hastily. He was an older man. Calvin had heard Bart was pushing seventy, although, like everyone at his altitude he appeared to hover around forty. Bart handled white-collar criminal matters and was perpetually saddened that such good, hard-working people had made such sad mistakes in their lives. He did what he could to help. It turned out he could do a lot, usually. "Not at all. And you don't need anyone looking over your shoulder on the written work. Except me, of course, and that's just to keep the rest of the partners calm. Your youth, you know." Calvin found the youth issue a little wearing, but, like the rest of his cohort, which existed at the bottom of an inverted population pyramid, he accepted it as a fact of life, like purple eggs.

"No," Bart continued, "we just want someone to second chair you when you are handling interviews and depositions. Their time on the matter will be minimal."

"I understand," Calvin said. He wondered who it would be.

"We think Sara Seastrom would be appropriate. We know you've worked with her before, although on opposite sides, of course, but we think she'll be the right sort of influence."

"Sure," Calvin said. "Sounds good." He understood perfectly. Although she had two years out of law school on him, he knew for a fact that she had nowhere near his amount of hands-on trial experience. Large firms didn't let junior associates handle matters on their own right out of school. The first case she had handled on her own had been against him, when she had defended the operator of the powersat that fried the poor dog—although the dog was still fine, the owners remained remunerated but continuously concerned.

46

Nonetheless, Sara was steeped in the ethos of how the firm handled things, discreetly and soberly, and the evidence he had provided so far was that he was not.

"I look forward to working with her." Calvin wasn't actually sure about that. She had been perfectly pleasant two days earlier, but he wasn't sure they communicated too well. All the silent attraction he had been convinced they shared while on opposite sides of the SPInc case had apparently only been his. She must have been completely mystified at his offer of recusal for any appeal. That hadn't been too humiliating. He usually tried not to think about his grand gesture that had failed so thoroughly, but now he had to.

He excused himself once it was clear Bart was done with him. He headed down the hall, drew a deep breath, and let it out. He would do what so many thwarted lovers had done in the past. He would pretend it had never happened.

In the meantime, he had a starship captain to save, and he would need to interview other witnesses. Fortunately, they were all holed up in Bethesda, right near his own home. The convenience was just too delicious for one used to the foul distances of Washington, DC. There would be logs, personal and official, to request, there would be stories he would hear. He reached his office and stared out at K Street below.

It slowly dawned on him what kind of opportunity he had. He would be one of the few people on Earth with access to the whole story. How had the settlement formed? Who made the decisions? Who kept the secrets and how? He would know everything. And, he would be one half of the team who laid it bare to the world, opposing counsel being the other half. It would be the real story, not the ones made up for the vids. He swallowed hard. He had a lot of reading to do.

He wondered if USACD had assigned a lawyer yet. Although USACD had arrested Nigmatullin without documentation of the charges against her, the agency had caught up with itself now that she was recovered.

He had notified USACD that he was counsel of record for one Paolina Nigmatullin, USAF, formerly of the USS *Aeneid*. At least

USACD's lawyer wouldn't be Ryle Feder. He did procurement. Calvin hoped it wasn't Sean. Sean was new enough that no one thought of him as having a settled area of expertise. Calvin really hoped it wouldn't be Sean. Maybe he needed to give him a call.

CHAPTER 6

As Calvin read through orders and logs, regulations and directives, policies and minutiae, he began to detect a pattern. The historical documents contained much about finding the human race another place to live. It was the U.S. government that built and launched the ship, but all the rhetoric was very inclusive of the home planet as a whole. The *Aeneid*'s monumental voyage was conducted on behalf of all of humanity. Alas, for the lack of time to screen a crew from each country in the world. This first one would, in the interest of time, just be Americans. And two Australians, but that seemed to be random because of their specialties. The documents showed a real sense of urgency, still in place even several years after the extinction-causing event had been avoided. It took Calvin some time to puzzle out the meaning of ECE. It was not an acronym that had seen a continuing need for use.

He mulled the mentality that thought it reasonable to suggest that the possible loss of Earth could be a defense to charges of mutiny. The rocks in the sky were history for him. His parents had lived through the threat, but, as time passed, and everyone took for granted that the relocator tugs had done their job and could again, the fears seemed quaint and silly. People in the past were never as smart as people in the present, and they had clearly lacked the sophistication to understand that what had happened had to have happened—the technology came through in the end and saved them. Calvin, having had his own recent glimpse into how uncertain that had seemed at the time, no longer thought the fears the equivalent of the various millennial hysterias, but it was strange to contemplate the way in which it had shaped the lives of those who lived through it.

The documentation corroborated Nigmatullin's memory in large measure. The particular orders did not. The reason for the journey may have been so obvious to everyone at the time that no one saw a need to put it in writing. But that wasn't how the law worked. If you didn't write it down, you didn't mean it. The closest he got to what he had hoped to find was a directive to seek planets like Earth or that might otherwise be compatible with human life and to report back immediately upon finding one. Lacking the mythical ansible, that meant coming home.

He turned his chair to look out the window. It was early evening, and the silvery light over K Street was starting to change to darkness. Perhaps, he considered, he could fashion an argument about an implicit order. He started calling up speeches.

He would rather have been talking to the crew, but he had needed to get through their logs first. Witness interviews were only useful if one was prepared. The meeting with Nigmatullin had been different because she was his client, and he had hoped she might have been more forthcoming. He had certainly expected her to take a stronger interest in her own defense.

A knock on his door made him look up. Sara stood there, all glowing and golden and luscious. He looked quickly away, annoyed with himself, and had to turn back with a bland face. You couldn't scowl at people you were supposed to work with.

Her smile faded at whatever his face had shown. "I hear we will be working together," she said.

"I'm looking forward to it," Calvin said. If he kept saying it, he'd mean it. "I hope it doesn't overload you." He had seen the billable hours for all the associates tabulated by fiscal year, and Sara was on track for over 2200, a more than respectable figure. He was beginning to realize that that meant she was a real workhorse, because one's time could not all be allocated to a client.

"Not a problem. I have a strong back." It was her turn to look away. "I hope you don't mind. This wasn't my idea. I certainly don't think you need my oversight."

"I will be very happy for your company," Calvin said politely.

She blushed, which was interesting.

"Do you want to come to all the witness interviews?" he asked. "I'm worried that would use up our retainer pretty quickly." Brughel's defense fund for Nigmatullin was healthy, but as Calvin started to internalize the time he was spending and what it meant in costs, he was feeling a little frugal about unnecessary expenditures on his case. Also, it was becoming clear, working with Sara would be awkward and not necessarily fun.

She made a small motion with her hand. "No, no. Of course not. Bart said he just wanted…." She stopped, and her golden skin lost color quickly.

Calvin stifled the urge to get up and go take her hands. Instead, he found himself laughing. "A babysitter?"

As if relieved, Sara started to smile, too, and sat herself down in one of his chairs uninvited, which pleased and annoyed Calvin both at the same time. "It was worse than that," she confided. She clearly wanted to tell him.

"Go ahead," Calvin said.

"You are star-struck and impulsive, and God only knows what you'll get it into your head to do, and, although your proclivities for legal legerdemain worked out great for MarsCorp and us last time, you are Someone to be Watched." She pulled her long, wheat-colored hair back and twisted it. The subtle tigering stripes played across the collarbones that showed between the V of her open necked blouse. Her parents had controlled their artistic impulses to some degree, and none of the tiger stripes reached her face, which was a set of clean lines and purely golden skin.

"Bart said 'legal legerdemain'?" Calvin asked, focusing on the important things.

"No," she admitted. "That was me. But it's what he meant."

"And what you meant?"

She stopped playing with her hair, and her gaze became level. "It is what you did. It was masterful. Everyone said so. Lucy Gunko was thrilled. She wanted us to hire you right away. She wished she could have given you a bonus."

Calvin felt nothing but horror at the thought. All a payment from an outside entity would have needed would have been for Ryle Feder to learn of it. "That would have been very bad. Besides, I just wanted MarsCorp to be able to build starships for hire."

"That you did," Sara said, and her voice was dry.

Calvin replayed the last minute in his head. There was something about it that wasn't right.

"Right," Sara said briskly, and she was standing, back in the doorway. "Let me know when you are going to do something death-defying and interesting, and I'll come along and be the killjoy." She was gone.

Sara Seastrom shared Calvin's dim view of the arrangement. Now that everything was awkward, even after a moment's ease, she forced herself to focus on his failings again. She did not think he had planned it so that she would feel like fool. She had seen his enthusiasm for the thought of star travel—she had shared it, in fact. She had also seen his need to participate, his excitement over learning of Brewer's role in the design of the engine for the starship and his eagerness for the information to be put to use by a company willing to take passengers to the new planet. She had even accepted his help, and that made her feel a little guilty now, but it didn't change her opinion of the grandstanding or the public invasion of her case. She seldom pulled out the analysis of her own lack of courage or imagination, and she denied she had been humiliated.

Others were more helpful in that regard. "He humiliated you," Tony said that evening. They were seated in the sitting area between their apartments. Antonia Roche practiced an aggressive, no-holds-barred form of friendship. To make up for it, she was rarely around, but her manic energy lacked an outlet at the moment because the *Blue Surprise* was over and *My Last Duchess* had yet to start production. Her day job as an accountant meant her long hours had started, but she had come home, she said, because one needed a little warmth. "Of course you can't stand him."

Sara sighed. "I used to be able to stand him just fine."

Tony smirked. "I knew. Not that you did."

To Sara's great relief she did not feel the heat of a blush. "That's not what I meant," she said, although that had been exactly what she meant.

"I never heard you talk so much about opposing counsel," Tony said. "And he was so helpful. And he undid the logjam you all had. From one perspective, you are just an ungrateful wench."

"Thank you," Sara said. "I am aware of that. But others are taking care of being grateful for me." She took a swallow of tea and stared out the window. The leaves were long gone, and she could see the haze of bare branches against the sky. She, Tony, and one other person she seldom saw shared the top floor of the boarding house in Silver Spring. She had a sitting room in her apartment, but the larger space, subdivided into semi-private enclaves by large plants, gave just enough extra space to make the steep rent worthwhile. Heavy wicker and an endless rug of Aubusson, worn and thin, made the room right for any season, and she still had her privacy to retreat to when she needed it.

She reflected with bitterness on Lucy Gunko's enchantment with Calvin's antics. With her, Lucy had vacillated between peculiar and astringent. With Calvin, she fawned. She had, in fact, pestered the firm to offer him a job. And they had. "And now I am second chair on his matter." Whatever objectivity she had gained in her assessment of the situation now lay buried beneath—although she didn't want to admit it—professional jealousy and resentment that he had done what she'd not had the courage for.

"He does have two of the most famous clients on the planet," Tony pointed out helpfully. "That can't be so bad."

"They're not my clients," Sara said, knowing how it sounded and not caring. Tony was a good listener and didn't talk. She was better than a lot of lawyers Sara knew. That was because, Tony had once said, confidentiality about money was even more important than confidentiality about legal affairs. Unless they were about money, too. It was an unwritten code, but all accountants understood it in their bones.

"Sara," Tony said, all fed up, "this isn't like you."

"I'll be working for him," Sara exclaimed. "And he's two years my junior."

"Yes," Tony said. "I know. You set a great deal of store by that, but you aren't in school anymore and need to get over it. He's the one with the amazing Captain Nigmatullin for a client and you aren't. If he were a senior partner and offering you second chair or whatever you call this, you'd be all giddy and stupid, and this would be an entirely different conversation."

"It would be a parallel universe," Sara supplied helpfully. She leaned her head on the back of the chair so she could see the sky. It was too light out for stars.

"And have you been drinking?" Tony asked.

Sara could be definite on that one. "Absolutely not. It might have cheered me up."

Ray Hillman had to take a walk, and he needed to be near people. What the cast had shown him live as he'd watched the death of the starship captains still troubled him.

None of them reached out to each other for days after the Canaveral killings. Then, in that eerie way the universe dealt with such things, the three all contacted each other within the space of minutes.

Except for his eyes, he was a man of no special features. Born before the geneering of one's children became affordable and popular, he was of no special height or physique, and his eyes of sparkling blue were gifted him by nature alone. Despite the lack of technical assistance, people still gave him a second look from time to time as he wandered aimlessly through Reston Town Center to meet the other two.

What had happened at Canaveral Port left him sick. He hadn't thought it would be like this. He hadn't thought that after all these years it would mean so much to him. The *Aeneid*'s crew had barely set foot back on Earth, and now two of them were dead.

He shivered in the cold, and stopped in front of the old coffee shop. It surprised him that it was still here so many decades later.

He had lived long enough to see one set of chain stores sweep the country, become embedded in every location, and then disappear to be replaced by others equally ubiquitous, equally entrenched, only to vanish themselves.

It was the coffee shop where they used to meet when they didn't want to be recorded or overheard at the office.

He hadn't heard from either of them in thirty years, but after the killings at Canaveral Port, and the strange way they left each other almost simultaneous messages, it had seemed right to meet again and at their old place.

The building was a false Tudor, and what should have been white stucco was a roseate sunset hue in some blocks, and gold and orange in others. The owners were staying on top of the trends.

He didn't see them at first, and it wasn't that they had changed so much—gene therapy prevented that—but that they didn't look as blank as he felt inside. They should have.

It had been many years since Ray's sojourn at the Pentagon and the hours of wrangling over the *Aeneid's* mission, and many years since he had had strong opinions on the questions surrounding it. He and the two civilians had formed a pro-settlement league of their own, but their view had not prevailed in the public eye. No view had prevailed. The topic had been too contentious. The *Aeneid* went out with most anyone you asked saying it was looking for another place to for people to live, unless that person was an official of the U.S. government. There, it was impolitic to recognize any form of consensus.

Ray had spent a lot of time negotiating and conniving with Sam Heller and Tessa Donohue, but they had not extended their shared passion for the *Aeneid's* mission beyond work. They had never had dinner together, and never met each other's spouses. He had not told his wife he was going out to meet them. She thought he was off to be alone was all. He hadn't said that, but she had seen the effect of the killings on him.

They all had their coffees, and Sam said, "I tried to find both of you when the ship started casting last June." Sam was a rangy man, always getting his elbows in your space, a lefty next to whom no one wanted to be seated. Sam's time in government as the Deputy Administrator at USACD had lasted six years. He'd come out of the space transportation industry and went back to it afterwards. Now Sam worked at Baldur, a large government contractor.

Tessa clutched her mug and nodded. Her face looked as if it had not lost its tightness from the cold, despite the steamy warmth of the coffee shop. Freckles stood out on her olive skin, and her brown eyes were hard. He had remembered them as warm. Ray had kept track of Tessa's career. She had almost always stayed in the government, never tiring of service. He had started a second career in the private sector after he left the Pentagon. Tessa had gone from the White House to academia and back to two different Cabinet level jobs, before cycling through academia again, many times over, whenever her party wasn't in control. She was on the Hill now, the senator from Massachusetts. "It was such wonderful news," she said. "At first, anyways. I don't understand the hostility to the settlement, now that it's a done deal."

"We saw that before," Ray pointed out. It was why there had never been a public confirmation that settlement was one of the goals of the mission. "Lots of people are thrilled."

"Lots aren't," Tessa said. "I don't know why, but they're the ones who get all the air time."

"They're bitter over Mars," Ray said. "They're convinced we could have found alien life if we had gone more slowly."

Sam laughed very quietly. "There we had the advantage of fear of the rocks. Everyone has forgotten about that now. And that type is embarrassed by it."

"Do you think any of them lived?" Ray asked. The settlement had no support from Earth. Years had passed for those left behind. He worried about them, and the worry was shaded not just by concern for individuals but by the thought that they were humanity's back up drive. He checked a text feed, but nothing had changed from when he had checked ten minutes earlier.

"We can only hope," Sam said.

"We did what we had to," Tessa said. "Back then."

They asked each other awkward questions about their lives while they finished their coffees. Finally, Sam said, "Let's walk?"

The sidewalks were crowded with shoppers returning gifts from the holidays.

By unspoken consensus, the three left the crowds and headed toward the small park they used to visit. The park wasn't as secure as the highly jammed coffee shop in one respect, but there were fewer biological eardrums in the vicinity, especially in the sharp air.

Ray wondered if he should worry about being alone with them, or, even about being seen with them.

They reached a stand of fir. The swing set in front of it had a few toddlers climbing around, and a pair of mothers. They kept walking.

Finally, at a distance from the other people, Sam said, "Tessa and I were talking before you came in. We were thinking we shouldn't say anything. Even if anyone asks us."

They all stood in a little circle, gloved hands in their pockets. Ray thought back to the conviction they had all had so long ago. It had been long ago, and lives changed. Hearts changed. Whatever else happened, humanity had a settlement on another planet, and it was a lovely one from the looks of it, never mind his worries. He looked at the two faces across from him. He had considered them friends of his heart once. Maybe they still were, but thirty years was a long time. If he had gone for years without thinking of the *Aeneid* and its orders, they might have as well. It was a lifetime ago.

"I completely agree," Ray said.

They walked back in silence.

CHAPTER 7

PAOLINA NIGMATULLIN, LAST AND ONLY living captain of
the only starship in the solar system, surveyed her crew. They
were in an NIH cafeteria large enough to hold all of them.
There were still a hundred crewmembers topside on *Aeneid*, and
they all liked it that way. It had been strange to return to Earth
and find it so different. The geneering had taken off in a big way
in the States, and all the parti-colored people seemed garish and
peculiar. The albinos looked like lab rats, and everyone else had the
perfect tan. The poor souls with evil parents who gave them tails or
checkered skin she couldn't begin to think about. It was too bad that
geneering against poor judgment was illegal.

Her own crew was bland in comparison. The faces in white,
brown, and black were all just one color. She could handle that.

"I am told," she announced when they were all quiet, "that
you've all been cleared for release. I think that's great news. You're
medically sound." She wasn't speaking to them as their captain in
light of her mutiny charge, but she had been allowed to say good-
bye. They had all accepted her non-mandatory invitation to meet.

"They didn't find any creepy crawlies," Francisco Morgan called
out. He was not a scientist. "I told 'em I was worried. Oh, God."
He clutched his mid-section. "I feel it. I feel it coming! It's going
to burst." He doubled over. His neighbor shoved him in the upper
thigh and Francisco fell to the floor from the end of the bench.

"They found no creepy crawlies, Morgan," said Nigmatullin.
"Except in you. You have to stay for extra special study. They have
some eggs and want to see if they'll grow in your eyeballs."

The laughter they'd held back for Morgan's fall spilled out but quieted quickly.

The room held three hundred people. Not everyone was there. Aside from those still on the ship, almost three hundred souls had stayed behind on Elysia in the end. It seemed the smart thing to do at the time. Everyone back here seemed to think it redundant. And hostile. It was, but these people had no sense of urgency. She determined never to volunteer for time travel.

"We are being mustered out," she went on. "We have a lot of back pay coming. People will try to part us from it. Watch out for that. USACD has professed a concern for our Rip Van Winkle ways, and has doctors and clinical anthropologists available to help us adjust. The latter will give you better fashion advice."

Groans and chuckles greeted this recommendation. Nigmatullin had heard from many who wanted to stay in their uniforms, and one woman had pointed out that fashions were already mimicking the *Aeneid*'s outdated look.

They'd all been told to provide USACD their new addresses and to report any changes. USACD felt it had a legitimate interest in their whereabouts, even of those they mustered out.

"Do we have jobs if we want to keep them?" someone else asked.

She nodded. "I was getting to that. Technically, yes, but it sounds like it's just to make sure we don't go around saying we were thrown out on our butts. The science people should be in good shape, especially the xenobiologists. I'm sure you'll be needed. There's a big push underway to understand Elysia before USACD sends the next ship back. But you might find there are others besides USACD who want to hire you. Operations folk and engineers might not want to sign anything permanent too quick. I might be wrong, but I think there will be bidding wars on you. Start with Baldur and MarsCorp. MarsCorp has grown since we saw it last. Some of you may not even have heard of it."

One person put up a hand. "Salisbury?" she said.

The dark-haired man in his thirties stood. "What will you be doing, Captain?"

"I'll collect my back pay, spend it on legal bills, visit my family.

There's a big wide world folks. And it's not being blown apart by rocks from space. Go enjoy it."

Then she said the things you said to people with whom you have spent a decade of your life on the most important job any of them might be likely to have. They shared memories none of the rest of their race had experienced and mourned the ones they lost. It was a big, wide world out there, and it was alien to them, this place Earth. Maybe she should have stayed on Elysia, after all, especially since she didn't need to protect the freedom of Orlova and Contreras. She would have to make up her mind about protecting their reputations. Their arrangement had not addressed whether it extended beyond death, since that could have provided bad incentives. The other captains had driven a hard bargain when she'd held them at gunpoint, and the coin Nigmatullin had paid was a world swimming in the clearest air she had ever seen, where the fauna was more strange than any unicorn ever imagined, and life always smelled like breakfast. Every day.

Maybe she would cooperate with her attorney after all. Maybe she could go back.

It was the day after USACD announced the dispersal of the crew that Calvin felt ready to talk to them. He had cut it too close, and USACD informed him that it did not have their new addresses yet. He checked with his friend Molly Easton, a journalist with a legal publication in town, and she told him she had received the same information.

They stared at each other for a long moment while they each waited for the other to say who in particular they looked to talk to. Neither succumbed to the temptation, and Calvin ended the call.

As a result, he found himself on the fifth floor of USACD facing across a tall desk a human clerk who was giving him the same answers as the damned machines. There was a very small reception area, and it held one couch big enough for two people. There was no window. Not only did a clerk not get a view to the Mall, he didn't merit a peek at 20th Street either. It was too bad.

Sean had accidentally on purpose walked by when Calvin required admittance. Calvin missed his government ID and ping, and would not have minded a moment's return of the access he used to have. He had only needed it for lunch a few months ago, but, now, when it would have done him some real good, it was gone. It was a good thing the laws prohibited continuous tracking without probable cause, a national or local security emergency, or personal health crisis, or he would have already been thrown out.

The clerk was puzzling over how Calvin had gotten as far as he had. This was the fifth floor. People did not just wander there by chance, so he must be authorized. "But if you're supposed to have it, wouldn't we have sent it to you already?"

"I'm supposed to be able to have access to witnesses," Calvin said again. He pulled up the manual on courts civil. Nigmatullin had started out in the military, but because USACD was a civilian agency she was being tried under civilian rules peculiar to that agency. The rules weren't that different from those for a court martial. He pointed to the pertinent paragraph on his palm.

"Then why didn't we give it to you? People do have privacy protection," the clerk added. He was solid, an umber pillar of placid person, not likely to be rattled by someone waving code citations at him.

"Not from the justice system, they don't," Calvin said. "These people know what really happened on Elysia, why all those others got left behind, and who was responsible. I need to know that, too. Therefore, I need to talk to them. And now they've all left quarantine."

"I understand all of that," the clerk said, "but I'm still trying to figure out why we didn't give that to you."

"Let me give you the lawyer's name," Calvin said. "He should have sent me this information when they were released. I at least need their names."

"Fine, who is it?"

"Ryle Feder," Calvin said. "He's somewhere in this building." It was a calculated risk, providing Ryle's name. Ryle was involved in procurement matters, not employment; but it had been Ryle who had gone to see Nigmatullin, and Calvin suspected that Ryle had wormed his way into this case. It was of too high visibility for that particular career attorney to resist.

The clerk had turned back to his screen but made the mistake of looking up. "What are you doing?" he asked.

"Waiting for you to talk to the attorney on the Nigmatullin matter," Calvin said. He hoped this ploy worked, although he wasn't banking a great deal on the clerk's pull and influence.

"I wasn't going to call him right away," the clerk said.

"Why not?"

"I have other things to do."

"Like what?" Calvin had been in the government. He knew this phenomenon and had experienced it frequently. The likelihood of the clerk being this sort was so high that it warranted sitting down and waiting. "Are there other people ahead of me who need you to call a lawyer?"

"No, but…"

"Excellent." Calvin leaned enthusiastically across the barrier between them. "Thank you so much. I'll wait right here."

Defeated, the clerk turned to his screen. Moments later, he asked, "What was your name again?"

But it was all worth it, in a horrifying sort of way. Ryle Feder descended upon the fifth floor with his hair, his suit, and his expensive tie. He was so sorry he had not gotten back to Calvin earlier, and he was really sorry in light of the difficulties Calvin would have tracking these people down since, of course, they had no permanent addresses anymore.

Ryle turned to the clerk, his eyes shining. "Do, please, share with Mr. Tondini the list of names he has requested."

Calvin popped a dime and handed it over for insertion. Sometimes you shared your palm, sometimes you wanted a little distance.

CHAPTER 8

THE LIST OF CREW NAMES had only three addresses on it. Calvin would feel bad billing the visit to USACD for the list, he had gotten so little out of it. Sean had been more pleased than he was, meeting him in the street afterwards to describe Ryle's displeasure.

"He's acting all triumphant," Sean said, "but we can tell he's furious."

Although this was gratifying, Calvin had not been satisfied. "I swear he got all the crew released just to make it harder for me to talk to them."

"That's great," Sean said. "You're an instrument for freedom."

"But USACD doesn't have all their addresses. That's incredible. And until they start settling in I can't use my finder."

Sean looked embarrassed, and said, "I should get back inside. I probably don't need to be seen talking to you. You haven't been Ryle's favorite person for a while now." He laughed, the patterns on his face shifting mysteriously, and pounded Calvin on the back. "But you are mine."

Calvin wandered across Constitution Avenue, and looked around for a place to sit. It was cold but sunny, and his coat was warm and he didn't want to go back inside. The walk back to the firm should have qualified as outdoor time, but he hated to return so unsuccessfully. He found a bench by the water. It was on a little false isthmus protruding into an artificial pond, and no one sat out there.

He built a small holo bubble and started looking at the names. There were a lot of biologists. There were xenobiologists, too, which might have seemed like carrying a bunch of science fiction writers when they set out, but probably turned out to be useful.

The crewmembers were all famous. Someone should be hounding them. He left Molly a message, since she was professionally in the hounding business. All the casters would want Nigmatullin, which would be tricky given the charges against her. He would have to warn her against public appearances. If he read her right, she would ignore him, and he'd have a constant nightmare of public admissions to worry about.

He started scrolling, touching each name to start a search on the public disc, and so that he would be pinged any time any one of them was mentioned in the public world. His finder helped him out first. It found Ezekiel Salisbury now in Tenley Town. If he wasn't mistaken, this was the crewmember who'd introduced him to Nigmatullin.

He wanted to see Nigmatullin again, and left her a message.

Finally, he left his work area and ran a search on Jasper Brughel. The older man had not made any speeches lately. He was about to close his search on Jasper when a small item caught his eye. The IRS was conducting an inquiry of Jasper's company. That was interesting. Jasper was an accountant there. He would be responsible for any errors in the numbers. Calvin put the inquiry in a certain folder.

He only needed to start with one. He left Salisbury a message. He was geographically convenient.

Polly Nigmatullin's lawyer had told her she would be officially released the next day. In the meantime, she was allowed to roam the lawns of NIH, and, this far south, they were still green in the wintry sunlight. Where she grew up in North Dakota they would have been white by now, and she would have seen no sunshine.

She went by a gate, and, per usual, the youngsters pulled themselves stiffly to attention and saluted. She kept her face serious and the wry grin inside as she returned the gesture. They were cute, and it was this shift who had asked for autographs. She could have walked right out and strolled down Old Georgetown Road, and they would all have sworn they'd seen nothing and no one.

It wasn't like walking by some of the biologists or putting up with the people who took samples off her. The biologists who didn't pepper her with questions about everything she'd seen were disapproving, and some even sniffed to excess. Speaking of biologists, she thought, she needed to send for her things. She had many interesting things, and wanted to share them with the world.

The shock of her colleagues' deaths had kept her from realizing how much the fact that Contreras and Orlova no longer required protection had changed things for her. She no longer owed them her own martyrdom.

She thought about the dead some more, and she thought about those who had stayed behind and wished she were with them. Lastly, she thought about the small package she had received from Wisconsin. It was tucked in her coat pocket, and she hadn't unwrapped it yet.

She found a bench that circled an enormous umbrella tree. Its leaves were all gone, so the shade lay in patterns around it beneath the pewter sky. It offered shelter and privacy, although she did not need the former and could never be certain of the latter.

She sat, and with careful hands drew the box from her pocket. She was careful about the seal and the code, because these things had changed since she left, and she didn't want to break anything. Her lawyer had given it to her, saying it had been sent to him by her defense fund.

It was a little palm, which was a stupid name for something you fit to the back of your hand. It seemed to be keyed to her, and she played with it until she found the programmed numbers.

It appeared to work as advertised. She assumed he would recognize the number and take her call. She hadn't spoken to him in the longest of times and wasn't using video.

He picked up.

"Hello, Jasper?" Nigmatullin said. "It's Polly. Jammie sends her love."

"Polly," said the voice on the other end. That seemed to be all he could muster.

"Do you have a minute?" she asked. She knew he did.

"I do," he agreed quickly.

She talked into the air. "It's about my defense. I've changed my mind. I don't intend to go to jail." Ten years wasn't as long as thirty-some, but it was long enough to recover from what was in retrospect, only a mildly broken heart and certain rash promises made back then. To people who were far older than she was now. She wasn't sure why that mattered, but it did.

"Fine," he said. "I never meant you to." There was another long pause. "Polly, I do have a favor to ask. You are very popular, and you could use that. I would consider all debts paid if you'd use it. Your lawyer won't want you to, because he'll be worrying about your defense, but you have the greatest chance of helping."

She understood. Wanting to go free didn't mean she would throw away anything important. "Is there anything in particular you want?"

"I leave it in your hands," Jasper said.

The next day she looked up the agent she had left in charge of her affairs, a man who had been younger than her when she met him but was now older, and asked him to find her a house that might be convenient for a court martial. She wanted at least a small yard, and some roses, and it had to be well watered, even in the winter so she could smell it all the time. There had to be screens on the windows, and if they'd been retracted for the winter she wanted them back or reprogrammed or whatever was necessary. It wouldn't be Elysia, but it wouldn't be the inside of a starship either, and that was all to the good. She was done with space adventures, she told herself. Really. She wanted a little real estate, and she knew she could afford a lot. She just wanted it on another planet.

Zeke Salisbury agreed to meet with Calvin that very afternoon. He had nothing better to do. He wondered if Calvin would mind a walking meeting? He needed his land legs back.

They started with his background as they walked two blocks in a residential neighborhood of small brick houses. They were ancient and fiendishly expensive.

Salisbury had risen to the rank of major, replacing someone who had died or resigned on Elysia, it was not clear which, and Salisbury stayed vague on that point. Salisbury was willing to talk in broad terms, but he did not identify individuals, with few exceptions.

Calvin found it personally interesting to learn the role Brughel's sister had played. Brughel had made her famous when he'd announced on a jumbotron their plan to establish a colony if they found someplace good. Amanda Brughel was an engineer, and one of the builders. She'd had responsibility for constructing the temporary habitat on Elysia and establishing life support on the ship. Someone else had been in charge, but she had come up with the specifications, including for the radiation hardening, conducted the purchasing, handled the logistics, and ensured that the habitats were S qualified. They could withstand most things a mere environment could throw at them. "Someone told me she packed the parts by hand," Salisbury laughed. "But she was kind of little. We all learned eventually that it wasn't just her, but she was one of the first to talk about staying, kind of casually, just to start. She kept patting herself on the back for being paranoid, is what she called it."

The reached Wisconsin Avenue and turned north. Calvin had to force himself to walk more slowly.

Salisbury seemed happy to talk. "Then Conley and some others started talking about how it was too bad we couldn't leave a few people since we had such a good set-up. It was all really just sort of fantasizing at first. Bernovsky was the one who said it first, that we should have a bunch of people stay. What if Earth wasn't there when we got back? Wouldn't we feel like idiots for not having a safe haven, especially after what we went through with the rocks?"

"That's all it took?" Calvin marveled.

Salisbury shot him a look, but didn't slow his pace. "You have no idea what it was like when the rocks were coming. We really believed it was the end. Of all of us. Ask your parents sometime." He paused for emphasis. "Bernovsky wasn't one of the original conspirators, but it occurred to him. It probably occurred to all of us."

"This is kind of a delicate question," said Calvin, "but did you know?"

Salisbury gave him a sidelong glance, chin up. He was Calvin's height, or close enough. "I think you'll find that of those of us who came back, none of us knew. Everyone who knew stayed. And then some."

"So Captain Nigmatullin didn't know?" Calvin asked.

"I'm sure she told you that," Salisbury said.

That was helpful. He didn't know if it was a hint or if the other man was just being difficult. He was hard to read.

"So Janice Brughel had all the materials ready for a stay," Calvin prompted.

"Amanda," Salisbury said. "She preferred her middle name. And Trung had the animals."

Maybe it was that he already knew this story, but Calvin felt a child-like sense of wonder at hearing it from someone who had been there. He could ask for his favorite story again and again. There were hundreds of members of the crew left to reach. He would have to edit somehow.

"How did no one know about the animals?" Calvin asked.

Salisbury gave him a pitying look, like Calvin was supposed to understand all that Salisbury hadn't said. "Lots of people knew about the animals. All the storage operators stayed. Some of them had to have known that there were frozen pigs, lots of them, chickens, dogs and two horses. We were a friggin' ark."

"It was a laugh," Salisbury continued. "First, Trung's saying how isn't it a happy coincidence he'd thought to test the biology against other Earth species than humans. But he didn't bring anything you wouldn't see on a farm. Amanda thought it was great. At that point, we all did."

"No one questioned it?" Calvin asked. "Was this going on at the same time Amanda Brughel was getting happy?"

"No. We were there about six months before she was allowed to do more than set up for the xenos. The xenos were running tests all the time, and they had finally allowed shirt sleeves for twenty people. Every single one of them caught a cold, but that was it. It's really, really close to Earth, the way life developed there." Salisbury was walking faster, as if getting stronger as he walked. "Could have meant it was really easy for one little bug to wipe us out."

They could drink the water. The entire planet of Earth knew that, and Mars, too. You couldn't always drink the water on Earth. Calvin wanted to slow down to drag the conversation out, but he could see Friendship Heights. "Then what happened?"

"The rest of us were allowed down in batches. It was just one sad skeleton crew on the *Aeneid* by the end of it. Orlova never came down. She volunteered to be one of the ones who was never exposed. Just in case."

"Why?" Calvin asked.

"Someone had to report back to Earth. We sent you drones and radio transmissions, but the drones didn't have the drive. You'll get messages from us next century, one way or another."

"When did they tell you it had been planned?" Calvin asked.

"They didn't. They never did. We just had to keep guessing." Salisbury sounded nonchalant about it. "But we saw a lot of secret handshakes."

"These were your shipmates. Didn't it bother you?"

Salisbury shrugged. "We approved. Don't forget that."

Not that it was his lookout, but, "Did you look for intelligent life?"

They passed a strip of restaurants, and Salisbury slowed to check their menus on his palm. "Sure. We didn't want to land in it. But there was no radio, no video, no grid. Any fires we found were natural. There was no one with thumbs. The xenos took some trips in the ocean."

Calvin didn't have to puzzle over that one. "Looking for dolphins?"

"Yeah. Something like that. It's hard to say you've found intelligence when you don't even find tools of bone. There were a lot of animals, and the sky was full of feathered lizards."

"Birds?" Calvin asked, smiling. They were way off track, but it was his own doing. Salisbury wasn't being evasive, but it wasn't Salisbury's responsibility to keep Calvin on track.

"Right."

They had reached the Metro. "If you don't mind," said Calvin,

"I'd like to sit down with you and get a record." The air had turned chilly, and he had his hands in his pockets.

"I'll be in town for a little bit," said the star traveler, and turned back south.

CHAPTER 9

"**A**BOUT THE JURY TRIAL," NIGMATULLIN said. Calvin couldn't think of her as Polly. No one could. Like Jesus, she just had the one name.

She sat in his office across his desk from him. She had showed up unplanned and unannounced several days after his talk with Salisbury. Calvin wasn't the only one who had fallen under her sway, it would appear: she had successfully gotten past the receptionist without hindrance. She wore a long, dark wool dress, with the horsetail swinging high from the back of her head. He had a Cossack in his office.

Her eyes were dark and bright at the same time, and she had more vivacity to her expression than she had showed at their first meeting. "Would that be better for me?"

The change was puzzling but heartening. Also, mildly terrifying. Her attorney had never tried a case to a jury. Jury trials called for a different skill set than hearings in front of administrative law judges who were hearing the same sorts of cases all the time. "It could be," Calvin said cautiously, his mind working feverishly over what he knew of such things. He'd done a moot court in law school where the volunteer jurors consisted of other law students, but he hardly thought that compared to the real thing. "If you have a sympathetic case, some sort of emotional appeal, you may improve your chances of avoiding a guilty verdict."

"Do I have emotional appeal?"

Calvin surveyed the figure across from him judiciously. She was courageous, brave, and intrepid. She had gone places no human had gone before. She was an explorer, and she had enabled or, at least, permitted other brave people to take an incredibly brave step. But he had to be objective. He agreed with what she had done, her aims, and goals. He wasn't yet clear on her methods, and, if they were foul, that might color his thinking.

Calvin was being watched in turn. "You are taking an awfully long time to answer my question," Nigmatullin observed.

"I'm thinking," he replied. "To someone like me, yes, you have great and overwhelming emotional appeal. I say that with anthropological detachment," he assured her in response to a raised brow. "But I'm one of those who agree with what you did. There are people who view you and the settlers as spoilers. You have raped a virgin planet."

She laughed. "Do they know how big a planet is?"

"They know ours is crowded, full even, some might say."

Someone walked by the open door of Calvin's office.

Nigmatullin looked disgusted. "Do they know that even now the settlers might all be dead? Jamestown all over again?"

"Also," Calvin went on. "There have been rumors. Have you heard them?"

She waited.

"You forced people to stay." Calvin raised a finger. "You brought back diseases and the crew still on the ship are horribly disfigured mindless zombies. You are just waiting for the chance to release them on an unsuspecting populace." He raised another finger. "You found intelligent life, and there is a massive cover-up to conceal it from the rest of us." Another finger. "You found intelligent life, they took over your bodies, and you are now the forefront of an invasion force for the puppet masters."

She was laughing hard. "No one said that," she insisted.

A couple more people walked by, very slowly.

Calvin looked sheepish. "I may have made that one up."

"But they *are* saying you committed genocide to establish a human colony." He shrugged. "I wish I were making that one up."

Her laughter was gone. "Do people believe these things?"

He shrugged. "The ones who want to do. Even among the ones

who are pro-settlement there are those who like the idea of finding intelligent alien life and hope your findings were wrong."

Nigmatullin studied the ceiling. "We didn't even find systematized smoke from campfires or mud huts. We deployed satellites in polar orbits to sample every square foot of the globe, and explored caves and the oceans and the very top of the mountains. We had some really excited xenos hoping desperately to find intelligent alien life." He couldn't read her expression, as she said, "We found something stranger."

The hallway appeared very crowded. Calvin had never seen so many people stroll by in such large numbers at this hour of the morning. "Excuse me," he said, and walked around his desk to the door. He shut it. He looked down at the seated figure with her straight back and high cheekbones and ageless face. The eyes were laughing again. "We have paparazzi. My apologies."

Seated again, he asked, "You were saying?"

"We found that it is very much like Earth. The xenos and the bios had huge arguments about parallel evolution."

"What did you find? Sabre toothed tigers?"

"Not quite." She folded her hands in her lap, and, if it were possible, sat up even straighter. "Listen, let's go test the advisability of a jury. I have an interview on one of your shows in two hours up in Kensington. I'd like you to come and watch the audience and see if it sympathizes with me."

That was not acceptable. "Captain. Polly. You can't do that. Pending your hearing you should not be talking to the public or appearing on any casts."

The saturnine eyes were annoying. "Why not?" she asked cheerfully.

"Because anything you say about the mutiny can be used to impeach you," Calvin said. "It will be recorded, I won't have prepared you, and we don't know what the other witnesses are going to say yet."

"Where to start?" Nigmatullin asked the air. "First, I don't need you to prepare me. Second, I am being court martialed, not impeached. I would think you should know that. Finally, I don't see how what the other witnesses say should affect what I say."

"My apologies," Calvin said drily. She was going to be a handful. It might have been better when she was a little morose. "If I may take your concerns out of order. I was using legal jargon, I suppose. 'Impeach' here means to show either that you are lying or wrong."

"You could have said that."

"'Impeach' is quicker and more precise, but I will avoid it from here on out. Second, and this covers both your first and third points, you need to be consistent. Your story needs to be consistent with every one else's recollection of events so you look credible. People forget things, including you. If you go out in public and say one thing, then you later remember a little detail that we realize is important it will look sneaky to bring it up after it matters. Or like you're lying. Maybe another crewmember took something you said or saw in a way that we didn't expect but you are now contradicting yourself trying to answer what he said. Or, maybe you'll want to take back something that may have been true but confusing. Regardless, we will have a mess on our hands because the government will bring it up in court, whatever you said that you wished you hadn't. It'll be a big mess, and one that could make you lose. It is standard operating procedure for you not to speak to reporters or casters of any sort. And there are good reasons for it." He was pleased with fitting in 'standard operating procedure.' He might get through to her if he spoke her language.

She looked skeptical. "And if I'm willing to take that risk?"

"You will have increased your chances of losing exponentially." And, Calvin worried whether the firm would continue representing her. That sounded threatening, so he didn't say it out loud. Bart had stressed the great importance of reticence, emphasizing as well that Calvin not grant interviews or discuss the case. Many a lawyer had regretted statements made while the facts were still being uncovered. Most problematic, a lawyer's statements could be used as admissions against the client. Calvin had no intention of speaking to the casters ever.

She stood and walked to the window behind his desk. "What if I don't discuss the settlement? Notice how I didn't say mutiny."

Maybe he needed to bring Bart in. No, he told himself. He had to handle this. He certainly wasn't going to call on Sara. "It's very hard. If you start talking about one thing, you will get asked questions about the settlement. It's very hard not to answer those, particularly when they tell you that one of your crew said something you think is shockingly wrong. Then you are dragged down the rabbit hole and everyone thinks you held all those people at gunpoint."

She opened her mouth and closed it, leaving unsaid whatever she had been about to say.

"Did you?" Calvin asked.

"What?" Nigmatullin did not look at him.

"Hold anyone at gunpoint?"

There was a long silence. "I don't want to talk about it."

He couldn't sit there craning his neck to look at her. He left his chair and perched on his desk so that they were both staring out the window. "What was it like there?" Calvin said.

There was another long silence, but this one less fraught. "Like Earth, only more so." She turned, her skirt swirling around her calves. "I want to go. I told them I'd go, and I won't talk about the decision to settle. I promise you. I saw what you did a moment ago. I understand."

Except that she didn't, he knew.

Calvin felt little guilt about the waste of money caused by Nigmatullin dragging him out to the recording studio on Howard Avenue in Kensington, Maryland. There Heather Young held court in front of a live audience every weekday afternoon. People signed up months in advance to be in the audience, and today it was packed. Heather was very excited about her surprise guest, and whipped the audience into a frenzy of anticipation, striding across the stage in heels and a pantsuit, or leaning forward from her soft, comfy chair to reveal ample cleavage. She was all black and gold, her tiger striping visible wherever her skin showed, and her eyes glowed with a fire that was neither human nor natural. However good the geneering she'd received, it had to be contacts and the lights, Calvin figured.

He felt more guilt about the waste of his time. He needed to be arranging witness interviews. He had a paralegal helping to set them up as she found the crew, but if someone didn't want to talk, the paralegal turned the conversation over to Calvin, who tried harder to persuade them of the urgency of his need. He wasn't sleeping a lot. It was important to read through all their materials before interviewing them. You didn't want to find out later that you should have asked about something. On the other hand, it was equally vital to get them done quickly before the story the witnesses told USACD became set in stone or media pressure forced them into a particular position. No one liked to feel isolated.

Sure, he had a front row seat to Heather's show, but since he was neither a stay-at-home mom nor unemployed, she wasn't part of his life to such an extent that he experienced any special thrill. He did experience anxiety. The lights were almost audible in their violence, and he put on a pair of sunglasses. He assumed it made him look like a bodyguard, and then wondered why Nigmatullin didn't have one. As her lawyer, should he broach the topic with her?

Heather was on fire, metaphorically speaking, although between her coloring and the bright reddish gold of her hair, the agonizing lights and the vivid stamping about, interspersed with the more maternal seated posture, one might worry about latent incendiary qualities. She was very popular.

"I have today," Heather cooed from her lofty height on stage, "planet Earth's only living starship captain."

Calvin pulled back, but when he looked around, no one else seemed offended.

The music to an old science fiction vid played, and Polly Nigmatullin strolled onto the raised stage. It was made up like a living room, the host's theatrics notwithstanding. Nigmatullin suffered Heather's embrace, her enthusiasm, and her ministrations as she got Nigmatullin seated, fussing as if she were dealing with a very elderly woman.

Calvin watched with amusement as Nigmatullin's long eyes

narrowed. Calvin had sisters. He could see what was happening. He tried to set his anxieties aside and enjoy himself.

Heather began immediately with the mutiny. What had really happened? Did Captain Nigmatullin want to take advantage of this opportunity to tell the world the real story? This was a show that reached tens of millions of viewers, every day. How could the starship captain pass it up?

To Calvin's relief, Nigmatullin did just that, gracefully and, laudably, blaming her lawyer as so many had before her. There were rules about all of this, and Nigmatullin didn't pretend to understand them, but she knew Heather would. It was a relief to be talking to such a professional, and Nigmatullin was truly grateful for Heather's understanding. Nigmatullin failed to point out the presence of her pesky lawyer. Calvin had a moment of terror that Heather would turn on him next, but Heather Young knew when she'd been outflanked and didn't want to risk two failures in a row on live vid watched by tens of millions (every day).

The tiger's next tactic was to lull her prey, asking about the decision to leave Earth, and, really, wasn't everyone who went on that starship just so noble and brave? The audience clapped obligingly, some of the older ones with more feeling.

Nigmatullin replied modestly and noted how all the crew were just filled with an overwhelming sense of duty to the rest of the race, a sense of how important it was to find the world a back up. The terraforming of Mars hadn't been looking too successful back then, and, if one's palm needed a back up, and one's data needed a back up, and, honestly, she knew people who backed up their memories every night in a journal, didn't it make sense that the planet could use a back up? "So, yes," Nigmatullin concluded "we were scared of the unknown, scared of the new bubble drive, and sad about leaving our families, but we felt we had to." She looked out over the audience. "A lot of you people are mothers, parents, I'm sure. You know what you do to keep your children safe. It was that kind of feeling we had."

Calvin leaned back. The front row was not the best for

surveillance. He saw a lot of people nodding. Nigmatullin's faith in her own abilities might not have been misplaced.

"Like we were your children?" Heather breathed.

This took Nigmatullin aback, and she gave a short laugh. "Or, siblings, maybe?"

Heather laughed. "That's so sweet still. And the voyage? What about the other planets you found?"

Nigmatullin spoke of the boredom of the voyage, about the inhospitable nature of the first two planets. Of what a joy it was, after the acid air and earthquakes and heavy gravity of those two, to reach Elysia.

"And Elysia," Nigmatullin said, "is paradise." She looked straight into Heather's alarming eyes, and Heather leaned forward from her comfy chair, her chest rising and falling quickly.

"Tell us," Heather said.

Everyone around Calvin was leaning forward, too.

Calvin forced himself back in his seat.

"Tell us what it was like there," Heather repeated.

"It was wonderful," Nigmatullin said. "You could still see the stars at night, each and every one of them. Do you know how different that makes you feel, seeing the stars? We're in a little bubble of light here on Earth, and we think this is all there is. We can see the Moon. That's inside our bubble. But we don't see much of anything else, just a few pin pricks of light. It's a cliché, but it's true that the stars are thick out there. It makes you feel part of the whole universe to lie on your back in the grass on an alien planet and look up and see a field of stars. And you know that Earth is out there, too. It's kind of wonderful."

Heather had forgotten all about the mutiny. "Did you bring pictures?" She was in maternal mode now, a mother tiger.

"I did," Nigmatullin said. She raised a languid hand and looked back over her shoulder to the side of the stage. Heather waved, too. One of Heather's assistants brought out a box that was maybe knee high, and just as wide again.

"Heather," Nigmatullin said, "I chose your show because you reach tens of millions of viewers, many of whom wonder about the future for their children. I want to show all of you what that future could look like if you are as willing to take risks as we were. Your courage would be greater, because you would be leaving a very comfortable Earth behind. We went out of duty and fear. We had just lived through the long terror of believing we would become extinct. Happily, it's not as if our sun is going to go nova any time soon."

"That we know of," Heather said darkly, clearly needing to contribute to this soliloquy, even if, like the audience she channeled, somewhat mesmerized by it.

The projector was set up. Nigmatullin apologized for the old technology. Heather, no longer treating her as an old woman but as an explorer across time and space, would have none of it.

People had seen them before, the images of a new world, but the *Aeneid* had, for the most part, sent back long panoramic shots of landscapes under drone or close ups of foliage, green and purple and black. Nigmatullin's holos showed views of the new human settlement.

Calvin felt himself drawn forward in his seat along with the rest of the audience, as if a planet's gravitational pull had reached through space via the holo to capture them all. He struggled to lean back. No one else did.

The holo located its audience in front of a single story building situated on a sward of green and black lawn. Puffy clouds floated in a blue sky overhead, and a large tree shaped something like an umbrella cast shade over an outsized picnic table where two women and several children ate. Strangely, the fact that one of the women was scowling and growling at one of the kids, just like happened in real life on Earth, made the scene heartbreakingly real, and heartbreakingly lovely. It was so strange and so familiar all at the same time. Calvin felt his throat close up.

He looked around. He was supposed to be watching the audience, not the show, and he needed the distraction.

On the vid another group of children ran by, chased by a dog. How many children had gone on this expedition, Calvin wondered. This had to be important. You didn't send children on interstellar voyages, surely, if you weren't thinking of settlement, and the *Aeneid* was a government vessel.

The recorder panned to a line of small, low bungalows. They were tiny enough to be one-room buildings, for all Calvin could tell. Yet, still, they were someone's homes. Another row of bungalows, also running perpendicular to the largest building, flanked it on the other side. He was startled to see what looked to be a planted field beyond the bungalows to the left. He would have sworn he recognized corn and pumpkins. He wondered how much heavy equipment the settlers had brought with them.

As if she read his thoughts, Nigmatullin said, "We decided early on we might as well try some planting."

No one hollered about anyone defiling anything. It wasn't that kind of crowd.

Heather was also in the business of reading her audience. She swept a glance around the room and gave Nigmatullin a feral grin. "Did you eat any of it?"

"Some very young corn," Nigmatullin said. She changed the display. "I want to show you something the xenos are talking about with the universities and the government right now. I don't think it's been made public before."

Calvin repressed a grin. Nigmatullin was plenty savvy about the modern casters' desire to be first with a story.

"We can't wait," Heather said.

Aeneid's captain brought up two images of corn magnified to the size of the women on stage. They both had green husks, one segment peeled back, and kernels of yellow, white, and red. Nigmatullin leaned back in professorial indolence. "Which one is from Earth?" she asked.

Heather's eyes were wide. "You grew one of these on Elysia."

Nigmatullin sat up straight, as befitted her announcement. "We *found* one of these on Elysia. There are more."

Calvin closed his eyes, alone with himself at the implications. This was even better than everyone had hoped.

The audience keened.

Heather was, however, perhaps tired of being impressed. "How do we know that?" she asked.

"We brought some back," Nigmatullin said. Her tone was prosaic. She reached into the container and retrieved an oblong box, of the size one might use to store carving knives. She held it on her lap. "I'm not a scientist. But I'm very interested in it. I knew that all the scientists here would be studying everything very carefully. Very cautiously. I knew that it could be decades before anyone declared corn from Elysia, that looks to be almost identical to Earth corn according to *Aeneid's* xenos, fit for human consumption. So I ate some."

There were several cheers from the people in the room. Calvin had a hard time himself not laughing. The glee ended abruptly as he realized what the crazy woman had to be holding on her lap.

She would start a panic. What if everyone stampeded out of the room and people were hurt?

"But that's amazing," Heather said. "A whole ear?"

Nigmatullin laughed. "Not hardly. The first week, I ate one kernel. I did that for about two months." She grimaced wryly. "Ship life can be dull."

That got a laugh.

"Nothing happened. I didn't grow donkey ears. My stomach didn't ooze out of my nostrils. Then I ate a whole ear." She paused for dramatic effect. "Still nothing happened. I kept a journal."

"How could you do something so dangerous?" Heather asked.

"Heather, I got in a starship with a very untested bubble drive that might have landed me in the middle of a space rock. Eating corn didn't seem so scary."

Heather placed a hand on Nigmatullin's knee. Their comfy chairs were that close. "What's in the box?"

"What do you think?" Nigmatullin asked her.

"An ear of corn?"

"It's a gift for you," Nigmatullin said, and opened the box to display the corn, still in its husk. "I had a bushel freeze dried, and there's more."

"This is for me?"

Nigmatullin shrugged. "I've been watching your show since we entered the solar system. Yeah, it's for you."

Nigmatullin had done her work well. Heather was all on fire about her ear of corn. "I'm going to take this home and have it for dinner tonight," she announced.

"Don't," someone shouted from the audience. "It's not tested."

Heather looked out to her well-wisher. "But it has been."

"I'll be the first to tell you that I'm not a scientific sample," Nigmatullin said. "But I've been eating a little for over a year. So it's not poison."

"She's lying," someone else said.

Nigmatullin brought the holo back up. It showed her in ship's uniform, popping a kernel off a husk and placing it in her mouth.

Heather expertly peeled back some of the husk, shaking the sticky silk away when it clung to her wrist. She used a long talon-like nail to pop a kernel from the tip, held it up high and placed it in her mouth. She chewed and swallowed, her eyes closed. When she was done, she said, "I do prefer it cooked."

She looked around expectantly. Nothing happened. She did not keel over, turn any kind of color other than black and gold, or start bleeding from her nose. She stood, clutching her ear of corn to her breast. "Thank you, Polly. I am honored by your gift."

Calvin figured that if she did get sick as a dog later in the day she would count it worth it for the ratings. This whole scene was already going viral and Heather Young would be the most famous person on the planet after Paolina Nigmatullin in very short order.

Outside, after Heather turned to her next guest, and as Calvin and Nigmatullin headed to her vehicle, what had just happened began to sink in. The studio was located at the top of the hill, near Connecticut Avenue. They headed downhill, Nigmatullin walking swiftly, her face alight with victory.

Calvin was not as pleased. "What were you thinking?" he demanded.

She kept walking, and he grabbed her arm and turned her to face him. One did not generally manhandle one's clients, but one's clients did not generally expose a roomful of two hundred people to what had to be a quarantined item.

"Life is full of risk, Calvin. Nothing will happen to her."

"That's not what I'm talking about and you know it. All those people will have to get tested. Heather's going to be put under a microscope."

"I have a clean bill of health," Nigmatullin pointed out.

"You brought an alien plant into a room full of people," Calvin said. "Did you check the protocols? I know you've violated one of them."

"I am not going to ask my lawyer to research every move I make," Nigmatullin said.

Calvin heard a siren in the distance. "You were doing really well until you pulled out the plant. You should have stopped there."

"Maybe," she said, "but you and I don't need to stop here. Come along, Calvin. I have a little time left."

Sara caught Heather's whole show. So did a lot of other people in the firm. Judy showed up in her office first.

"Do you think he knew what she was going to do?" she asked Sara, as if Sara had special insight into the working of Calvin Tondini's brain.

"No," Sara said emphatically. "Even Calvin…" she stopped.

Judy smirked. "You are the third person I've talked to who started out with 'even Calvin.' It was all great when Calvin's, ah, way of being, worked in our favor."

Bart Locke showed up behind Judy. "Did you see? He was sitting in the audience. He was right there. He had to have known. I saw Captain Nigmatullin here earlier today. I was hoping to get to meet her," he concluded somewhat wistfully. "Sara, do you think he knew?"

Now Sara was the expert on Calvin. If only her colleagues knew how wrong they were. "I doubt it," Sara said, and, looking straight at Judy, "because even Calvin would have tried to stop her from releasing alien plant life and getting into more trouble."

"They're testing the air now," Bart said. "They're requesting blood samples from everyone in the building, and Heather Young has been airlifted to NIH for study."

Sara couldn't help it. She giggled. "A little overreaction?"

Bart shrugged. "USACD says it will have a statement tomorrow morning, but right now it's dealing with the emergency. I'm sure Heather's network isn't hating the publicity."

Judy moved out of the doorway, where Bart was apparently occupying too much space, and sat down in one of the chairs across from Sara. "I wonder," she said contemplatively, "whether Heather needs a lawyer. Bart, do you think we have a fourth amendment issue here?"

Bart brightened up. "Of course she does." He sat down, too. "I'll do a quick post. Give me your thoughts everyone. I can handle any medical invasion issues. Anything else?"

CHAPTER 10

PAOLINA NIGMATULLIN'S DRIVER KNEW HIS way around, and, Calvin suspected, had been watching Heather's show while he waited so that he understood their urgency. As an officer of the court, one did not encourage flight, but if one were gone before it became clear what the sirens were for, it didn't necessarily look like flight, regardless of what the actions might actually be. Or, so he told himself.

They drove smoothly along Beech Drive, Rock Creek to their side, its water low and icy. The starship captain and her lawyer had maintained their own icy silence at the start of the evasive maneuvers.

"I think you need to tell me what you're doing," Calvin said.

"I was sharing," Nigmatullin said. "Everyone seemed very interested."

"But your corn, it's alien plant life." Calvin was having trouble believing what she'd done. "I'm someone who wants to go to Elysia, and I don't think what you did was the smartest thing in the world."

"You and I disagree," Nigmatullin said.

He tried again. "Why did you do it?"

"People should understand about risk," Nigmatullin said. "Even you. Everything involves risk. You have to manage it, but you also have to manage perceptions of it. I was doing the latter."

He wanted to strangle her. "You weren't helping your case. In fact, you made it worse."

"I can't always worry about that," she said.

Calvin wondered if he could have his client put under house arrest. "That's why you shouldn't make public appearances."

She pursed her lips, staring straight ahead. He could tell she was watching him out of the corner of her eye. "You are my lawyer. Not my handler." She shifted in her seat, and her hand strayed to the barrier separating them from the driver, as if to check it was in place. "Calvin, there's more at stake here than my personal freedom. I want it, trust me. But I get death threats."

He sat up straighter, but she waved his reaction away. "The point about the death threats is that people think what we did was bad. It wasn't. It was wonderful, and we want the people who agree to feel safe doing so. We have to say why. We have to show it's appealing. And we have to laugh when the bugs from space don't hurt us."

"They don't know that yet," Calvin said.

"I do. I wasn't the only one running science experiments. All the xenos were growing it and eating it themselves to see what happened. Even on the way back."

"You didn't say that at Heather's."

She shrugged. "Not my information to share. I'm the most visible, so it's important for people to know."

The soundproofing of the vehicle was good, but piercing sounds like sirens made it through. The driver pulled smoothly to the side of the road. The woods left a verge with room enough for both vehicles.

The police officer who walked up to the car had to be older, judging by his girth. He was stouter than most. Calvin pushed the plate for the window to go down. "Yes, officer?"

"The Feds asked us to stop this car and bring you in," the Maryland trooper said. "You all willing to follow us to the station or would you like a ride?" He was peering into the interior, and Calvin saw the moment when he recognized Nigmatullin. The man's face went still, except for his eyes, which went wide. "Is that…? Are you….?" He came to a decision, stood back, and saluted.

"We'll follow you," Calvin said drily. He had once thought Jasper Brughel had charisma, but, in retrospect, he just had tactics. Nigmatullin had it, or she represented so well the new world for which people so longed that she had the functional equivalent. It didn't apply to those who hated her, because she represented the human race despoiling the universe. That got old. As for Nigmatullin, Calvin himself was beginning to feel inoculated against her spells.

"Feeling like the body guard to the queen mum, son?" she said, equally dry, as the vehicle rejoined the road.

He had to laugh. "It has its moments."

She placed a hand on a large box on the seat between them. "Would you mind bringing this in?"

"They'll impound it. I suppose it's got more corn?"

"Lots," she said.

The police station up Rockville Pike was a long, low building with one high tower at its end. The holding area was pleasant enough. Calvin had spent the remainder of the drive in contact with Bart, who was on his way out. Maryland had no law against the importation of alien materials. That was a federal issue, and imports from the Moon and Mars no longer presented the excitement they once had.

As they waited in the police station, he perused USACD's regulations. It was rather delicious. All the quarantines, mitigation measures, waiting periods and other inadequate or redundant features were specifically written for Mars, the Moon, and asteroids generally. Some lawyer had taken great care to force his or her successors to deal with Venus or any other planets later. He didn't see that USACD had any grounds for complaining whatsoever. He checked through the table of contents, the scope and applicability provisions again, looking for any general language which might be construed to apply to Elysia. There was no way they could claim Elysia was an asteroid. Working backwards, he turned to the statute. Congress, which had given USACD its authority in the first place, also spoke only of the Moon, Mars and the asteroids. That was good. There was no need to check case law for anything on point. He and everyone else would know if other planets had been the source of organic materials. It was moot—humanity had just barely reached Mars when the asteroids threatened Earth.

Before successfully settling Mars, scooping chemicals from the atmosphere of Venus, or otherwise thoroughly exploring its own backyard, the United States had left the solar system entirely in search of a planet to live on without terraforming. The asteroids dispensed with, and the incentive to throw people into the void gone, no one replicated the very expensive *Aeneid*. The financial case for Mars improved once MarsCorp's evacuation measures purchased the first foothold on the red planet, and the terraforming began.

No one had needed an Elysia they didn't know about.

The Maryland police told Calvin and his client that they were waiting for a USACD representative who wanted to ask Captain Nigmatullin some questions.

No one suggested putting Nigmatullin in a cell, and they were not in one of the interrogation rooms they showed on the vid. Instead, they sat comfortably in what appeared to be a visitor's lounge with people who appeared to be families, not felons.

The trooper who had escorted them in returned to their area. He carried two cups of coffee, which he offered and they accepted. "I'm at the end of my break," he said. "I watched you on Heather Young just now. What have you got in the box?" He gestured at the pandora's box Calvin had carried in for Nigmatullin.

Nigmatullin's smile was mischievous, and Calvin groaned inwardly.

"More corn?" the trooper asked.

"How did you know?" Nigmatullin said.

"Could I see it?" Shoving it back to make room, he sat down on the coffee table in front of their couch.

"It's not all Elysian," she replied. "I brought some corn from Iowa for comparison. But it didn't seem like Heather's was that kind of show when I got there."

"She didn't have any xenobiologists on the stage with you," Calvin noted.

Nigmatullin opened the box. She pulled out an ear.

"Who are you?" the trooper asked Calvin, but he was watching the corn.

"I'm her lawyer."

"So there's some USACD rules about alien corn?" the Marylander asked.

"Not that I could find," Calvin said. "I don't think they've had time to write them. There's not even an emergency order or direct final rule."

"Whatever that is," the other man said.

He didn't even know how right he was on that last point, Calvin reflected.

"Well, good," the Marylander said. "Even on my break I wouldn't want to violate a USACD rule. May I see the Elysian corn?" He held out a hand.

Nigmatullin handed him one. "And here's the one from Iowa." She held up what looked to be an identical ear.

Two officers entered the room, and Calvin felt a trifle *en flagrante*. But he'd had the feeling before. "Has USACD arrived?" he asked them.

"They were wondering if you could wait another hour?" the woman in the pair said. She was looking at the corn. "What's that?"

"Alien and American corn," said the original trooper. His nametag read McAfee. He was holding two ears.

"Which is which?" she asked.

McAfee looked up. "You tell me. Did you see the Heather Young show?"

The new pair gave each other guilty looks. Perhaps, Calvin figured, they had seen it, but not on their regularly scheduled break. The woman shrugged. "Maybe," she said.

"Do you give out souvenirs?" McAfee asked Nigmatullin.

"Obviously," she said. "That's why I brought this box. Here you go. Take two. I'd put them in the freezer, of course." She cocked an eyebrow at Calvin. "Any problems with that, counselor?"

"No," Calvin replied slowly. "But I'm only just starting to learn this area. I could be wrong."

"You most certainly are," said a voice from the doorway. Ryle Feder, senior attorney at USACD, stood there in all his glory. He was very handsome, and his hair was very thick, and he was very annoyed. It had not been an hour at all, just long enough to have lots of witnesses to the disbursal of alien corn.

Calvin hastily called back USACD's regulations. "Which rule is it, Ryle?"

"We don't have a regulation that covers this," Ryle said. "I have an emergency order, effective today, that bans the widespread distribution of Elysian plant life."

Calvin whispered to Nigmatullin.

She ostentatiously counted the contents of her box. She whispered in his ear, "Twelve, counting Heather's ear."

Calvin held out his palm. "May I see the order?"

Ryle shortcast his document to Calvin's palm, and Calvin expanded it in case others wanted to read it. A few more people entered the room, and the station chief, going by the nametag, began talking to Ryle about what he was doing at her station.

The two newcomers asked for a souvenir. Nigmatullin handed them each an ear from her box. The station chief allowed as how she would like one, too. McAfee explained that in his previous career he had been a biologist and had been reading some of the xenos' journals from the *Aeneid*. He was looking forward to eating one of his ears himself, and probably planting the rest.

Ryle's handsome countenance was stiff and wooden. "What is going on here?"

"It's the order," Calvin said diffidently. "It says it's effective today, but, well, we can all read." He waved his hand at the wall, where he had displayed USACD's rules, and a quote from a court case dated the previous year. The rules said that all orders took 30 days to take effect. The case of *Cardinal v Bierce* also addressed the issue, and the court there had said that if an order said it took effect that day, it could only apply to actions later than the day of signing. Emergency orders could be effective the same day, but only if they used the term "immediately," which the order at issue did not.

"You're not their lawyer," Ryle said to Calvin. "You can't give these people legal advice."

"He's not," McAfee said. "We're reading over his shoulder."

Ryle spun on the policeman. "You are an officer of the law. You should be ashamed."

"I don't arrest people for eating corn," McAfee said, blithely ignoring his earlier role as an escort.

One of the other officers was busy with his palm. He appeared to be sending a message, maybe taking a static of the words on the wall.

Calvin knew better, but he couldn't stop himself. "And the order doesn't apply to them. It forbids widespread distribution. It says nothing about receipt. Remember the OSHA case with the ladder." Calvin had found that one hilarious. The OSHA regs required that an employer provide a ladder. The employer received no penalty for an employee's injury when he stood on a chair because the rule didn't require the employee to *use* the ladder.

"As for the meaning of 'widespread,'" Calvin continued, "if you look at copyright cases, which is probably the best place to turn for this novel situation, sharing your work with a handful of people— say five or six—does not constitute publication. I'm not sure you'd get a court to agree with you here, especially when you may have issued an illegal rule with no opportunity for notice and comment. It seems to be of general applicability." Calvin admitted to himself that it was moderately entertaining, using the arguments private persons got to make against the government.

"Copyright principles have nothing to do with disease vectors," Ryle snapped.

"Then why did you let the crew off the ship? Either the protocols have been satisfied or they haven't."

A few more members of Maryland's finest had filtered into the room. They had all likely spent their fair share of time in a courtroom, even if only for matters so benign as mere traffic infractions. They listened to the nicer points of administrative law with educated ears.

McAfee, too, was having a good time. "Kind of got you there, counselor. Or should you be more worried than you are about being in the same room as the Captain here?" He dug a thumb into the ear of corn where he had peeled back the husk a little, and popped a kernel. He placed it in his mouth and crunched. "Kind of stale," he observed.

"You shouldn't do that," Ryle said.

"I'm offering myself up in the interest of science," McAfee said. "It's not very brave of me. I know the Captain here has been eating the stuff for months. Some of the xenos have, too, you know, going by their journals. A lot of them are public. You should check 'em out. Interesting stuff."

Nigmatullin stood, and Calvin picked up the box. "I take it we are free to go?" she asked Calvin.

"Unless you have further need of us?" Calvin asked Ryle. "My client is not a biologist, so if you have more questions along those lines, you might want to check with the xenos on the crew list."

"Or just read the journals," McAfee reminded the government lawyer helpfully.

Ryle left. He made no threats. He did not yell. He just left.

"Got any corn left, Captain Nigmatullin?" someone called out.

Nigmatullin reached into the box.

"You know, son," McAfee said to Calvin, "that was a whole lot of fun, but you've probably made an enemy there."

Calvin shook his head as the box emptied out. "You don't know the half of it, sir."

Nigmatullin went back to her hotel in Bethesda to, she told Calvin, continue house hunting. Roses didn't bloom in winter, did they? She wanted to be sure the place had good roses. He opined as how she should be able to afford to add all the roses she wanted to at any house she liked, and she told him that having the roses be the sole criterion had been a way to narrow her choices, thank you.

Calvin returned to the office. Sara was waiting for him. "Where's the rest of the corn?" she asked. She was leaning in his office doorway, and wore a suit of golden wool, which went well with her golden skin and the golden stripes that didn't quite reach her face. She could have been a very warm figurine.

"The Maryland police have it," Calvin said.

She tilted her head, puzzled. "Not USACD?"

"They were too late. You know who the lawyer for USACD is?" He sat down behind his desk, and she seated herself in one of his chairs. His work screen pinged, but he ignored it. He had a visitor.

"Should I guess?" she asked.

"Oh, yes," Calvin said. "But you only get one shot."

"Ryle Feder?" Her voice was sympathetic, and a balm on his nerves.

"In one. I think he's mad at me."

Sara's eyes lit up. "Still? Or again?"

"Both." Calvin laced his fingers behind his head. If he had been alone, he would have closed his eyes, but it was more interesting to watch Sara's. Had he not known better, he would have said she was checking him out.

"Why does Maryland have the corn?" Sara asked.

"Not Maryland. The police. Individual people who are police."

The admiring expression disappeared, and replaced by one that managed to combine puzzlement, concern, and a wee bit of frustration.

Calvin tried to explain what had happened with Heather and at the police station. It was complicated, but she got it eventually, and told him he liked to live on the edge.

"Going to Elysia would be living on the edge," he said. "Annoying USACD is not."

"You do have a live client to worry about now," Sara pointed out.

This was getting tiring. If this was what Sara thought of as oversight, he didn't need it. "My live client is the one who lives on the edge."

His work screen pinged for perhaps the third time. "Excuse me," he said. "I better see." It was certified mail. He opened it, and heard Sara get up, but his brain was frozen, and he knew that this was one hound that Ryle had unleashed. Or, if the hound wasn't Ryle's he'd given it to Calvin's former boss. He swore.

He heard Sara stop, and he swore again, this time at himself. He didn't feel like sharing right that moment.

"Did something happen?" she asked.

He hoped he wasn't pale. "Looks like it," he said. "Ryle looks to be playing hardball, and I'm going to have some administrative work to do."

She waited.

He took a breath. If he sounded calm, it would all be fine. "The state Ethics Board wants to investigate my conduct at the SPInc hearing, and why I'm now working for the firm I helped back then."

Sara turned pale for him. "Oh, no."

He really hoped it didn't show on his face, how his mind raced, and his heart pounded. Now that it had been pointed out to him with such immediacy, he realized it did look bad. But the transcript would show.... He had done it so well. If only he'd gone to any other firm but this one. That was the part he hadn't thought through, to be perfectly honest, in his need for new employment and his interest in being near work for MarsCorp. But he hadn't done anything wrong.

He looked at the golden woman standing worried before him. Maybe there had been another reason for coming here, but God only knew how pointless that reason had been. God and Sara herself.

He couldn't have been happy, but he told her his strange news very flatly. She could understand how he must be feeling. If it had happened to her she would feel the same. Nonetheless, the stolid expression and the monotone were not what she was used to, even after she had treated him as she had. He was acting as if an ethics violation were a matter of complete indifference. Maybe he had foreseen this. On reflection, it seemed odd that the firm had not foreseen it.

She took a deep breath. "Calvin, you may need a lawyer. I'd be glad to help."

"Thank you," he said. "I'll keep that in mind. You are kind."

"I don't know if it will make you feel any better," she began.

"I am fine," Calvin said.

She plowed on anyway. "—but Bart is very happy with you. Several people in the audience at Heather's show have asked for representation. People here were watching, so he knew to do a Fourth Amendment post right away."

"That's good," Calvin said absently. "Could you excuse me? I have some work to do."

Crushed, she left. She had her own work to do, and some of it involved kicking herself.

CHAPTER 11

CALVIN DECIDED THAT IF HE had thirty days to answer the ethics inquiry he would worry about it then. He did, however, get another copy of the transcript from the SPInc hearing. With it in hand he highlighted his own brilliant stratagem, and pondered how much he wanted to share with the Ethics Board that he had acted purely as a starship groupie, not someone angling for a job with the firm. He had done the right thing. He was still convinced of that. He had even known he had risked the wrath of Tarkov on behalf of USACD and, consequently, his cushy government job. Not that he had reached the cushy stage, but he had hoped to.

More importantly, he had to focus on Nigmatullin and her problems. She had distributed no more Elysian corn, and had assured him that her other souvenirs remained in orbit with the xenos. The *Aeneid* orbited under the command of a USACD employee who was not expected to capture the starship and go haring back to Elysia or anywhere else. The starship held only a skeleton crew, with very few of the original complement aboard, just enough that those familiar with it could train their replacements.

He had tracked down more of the crew and lined up interviews. He had started his research on mutinies, looking at actions brought against crew on the Mars run, of which there had been only a handful, the famous one on an early lunar base, and a handful of mutinies on the water, when they offered useful insights. The lunar one was interesting, and maybe offered some parallels, he was thinking when he got a call on his office line. That didn't happen a lot.

It was Zeke Salisbury, who wanted to come talk to him in

person, preferably at the firm so he didn't have to worry about being overheard. It was about Captain Nigmatullin. And some other things.

Calvin was happy to see him, and learned that the man was downstairs and available immediately. Could he come up?

Calvin offered coffee when Salisbury settled himself in, and Salisbury accepted. "I'm worried about the Captain," he said. "And some other things. Do I need to hire you to talk to you in confidence?"

"I am already representing your captain. If your interests are adverse," Calvin trailed off. It seemed harsh to say aloud, that he would have to choose one over the other.

"I'm not worried about a mutiny charge," Salisbury said. "They'd have done that by now if they were going to."

"Not necessarily," Calvin said. "They can always discover what an instigator you were and bring charges later. Paolina Nigmatullin was kind of easy and obvious. So were the other two. It's really hard to believe that anyone got left behind without the three of them condoning it."

Salisbury scowled at him. He was a compact and tidy man, with lots of muscle, but clean with it, not overly bulky. He looked like he could be fast, and Calvin wondered idly if he played ball. "I'm trying to help," Salisbury said. "I want to talk about Nigmatullin's attempts to get in trouble, and also some information I've gotten about the starship."

"She hasn't done anything wrong," Calvin said.

"I saw the show with the damned corn. Do you know how many people were using themselves as guinea pigs on the way back? All the xenos. One was eating berries. One was eating corn. One was having shark steak every week. They were kind of mad, some of them, that they hadn't gotten to stay, but Captain Contreras said it was more important that they come back and explain how closely Elysia resembled Earth."

This amused Calvin, but he refused to let himself be distracted by the shark. "Not everyone was allowed to quit, I gather?"

Salisbury snorted. "Absolutely not. Trust me, there was a lot of pressure, and it ran in all directions."

It wasn't a formal interview, but it was, Calvin decided, a great opportunity. "Were people forced to stay?"

"Not by the captains. Some by their families, and I'm not just talking about the little girl who wanted to go back and see her grandparents. Spouses were of two minds after the voyage, some of them." He said it with bitterness, and Calvin wondered if he had left someone on Elysia. He tried for an open and receptive face, knowing full well that a nosy one would get him nowhere.

The open and receptive faced failed. Salisbury did not take Calvin up on his unspoken offer to listen and just sat there scowling. Still, Calvin had often had trouble stopping himself, and said, "Did your spouse stay behind?"

Now Salisbury answered immediately. "Yes. But not on Elysia. On Earth. The kids visited me at NIH. She didn't."

"Sorry about that." That felt inadequate to the situation, but he didn't know what else to say.

"We had an agreement," Salisbury said. "We applied as a family, after we'd talked about it forever. We were going to take the kids. They accepted all of us." He shrugged, but his hands were clutching the chair arms. "She changed her mind, and she kept the kids here. I wanted them to come, even without her. We had a deal."

Calvin nodded. He had never been married. He had been involved with one girl through half of college and most of law school. He had dated a few other people, but they had never gotten serious, and, now, he had little interest in the topic. The man in front of him, however, was still unhappy even after ten years his time. And time back home had not stood still for the children, or even run at the same pace as Salisbury's.

Salisbury shook himself and let go of the chair arms. He stood and looked at one of the screens on the wall. It showed a view of Doi Intanan. Calvin had climbed it as a teen. It was more impressive than Doi Sutep. "Here's the thing," the other man said. "You need to keep her out of jail. She's the best one to make the case for the settlement."

"That's what she thinks she's doing," Calvin said, not that he wanted to divulge client confidences, but he didn't think that one was too hard to figure.

"She'll do stuff," her loyal crewman said. "You watch her."

"She reminded me that I'm not her handler," Calvin said. "It's true, and, frankly, I wasn't very good at the handling."

Salisbury turned from the view of the Thai mountain. "It wasn't your idea to hand out corn?"

"I didn't even know she planned to do it." There were times he wondered if the corn would come up in his ethics hearing.

Salisbury let out a large breath. "Good. I know lawyers are risk averse, so I was wondering."

"What else can I expect?" Calvin asked.

Salisbury sat back down. Standing, his bearing was upright and military. Seated, he slumped. "I've been hearing things. I'm not too good on the lay of the land around here, but there's talk of decommissioning the *Aeneid*."

Calvin hadn't heard such a thing. Usually, the least little rumor made it into all the casts and feeds. "I'm surprised."

"And worse," Salisbury went on. "Destroying all the records on how to get back."

"That seems unlikely," Calvin said. "Everyone knows where it is. The ship's records have all been downloaded and copied all over the world."

Salisbury looked at Calvin like the latter was not particularly smart. "You think everything was shared? With everyone?"

Calvin didn't try to answer that one. Perhaps he had been naïve. "May I ask how you are getting this information? It's not reaching the general public."

"I still have friends at USACD," Salisbury said.

"You may understand the lay of the land better than I do," Calvin said.

Salisbury watched him intently. "What was it like when we first started broadcasting in the system again? Was everyone happy?"

Calvin grinned. "I was. But you know how it is. There's always people with different views on things, from whether something's a good idea at all to whether it's being done right, even if it's what they say they want." He remembered well the utter jubilation at the discovery, the more mixed reaction to the announcement of a colony. "There was a line of people, literally, outside USACD, wanting to be on the next ship."

"I saw what you did for MarsCorp," Salisbury said, still watching him closely.

Calvin kept his voice steady. Salisbury might not know what risk looked like for an attorney. "That may not have been my best career move."

Salisbury laughed. "Yeah, but it's why I'm telling you what I've been hearing about the *Aeneid*."

"Did you tell your captain?"

"God, no," the other man said. "And don't you either. Who knows what the hell she'd do."

"You don't even know if it's true," Calvin said.

Salisbury stood and stretched, bouncing ever so slightly in the normal gravity. "We don't know that it isn't. Thanks for seeing me on such short notice, counselor."

Not a client.

Calvin spent a good amount of time watching vid of the crewmembers. He was talking to a lot of them once they started settling and having addresses. But it was sometimes more efficient to watch vid. Some crew were interviewed by professional casters. Others sold their stories on a pay-per-view basis. They were all intensely popular, judging by hits and rankings. He found several of particular interest, with one topping his list. All of them uniformly admitted they had been eating Elysian corn.

One of the *Aeneid's* xenobiologists told a caster how he had wanted to stay. For that one, Calvin got a fresh cup of coffee and settled in to watch. It was endlessly fascinating how many xenos the *Aeneid* had. Neither the Moon nor Mars had life, and yet here were all these people with degrees in the field. And it wasn't even most of them who had gone to Elysia. A lot of them kept studying Mars, even though it had no life. So, taking as a given that they were a strange bunch, Calvin expected a good show. He got one.

Samuel Tidy had been studying the animal life. He would have happily sent back complete reports of all his findings had he been allowed to stay. "I wanted to stay. The xenobots were able to bring back all sorts of samples, and I understand the reasons for not returning with more animal life, but I was someone who could have put an Earth education to use for the settlement. Coming back here to explain things to USACD wasn't a good idea when we were on Elysia, and it's turned out to be even more pointless now that I've met this lot. All they care about is the potential for danger. Danger is everywhere. We were almost wiped out by two giant rocks, and they were worried that *sus scrofa Elysia* might get loose and devour someone's garden."

"Or a national park," the caster interjected, not unreasonably.

Dr. Tidy was having none of it. "Now you're just looking for trouble."

The caster was less interested in the scientific drama, and more in the story of those left behind. "Who made you leave?"

Dr. Tidy sighed. "Captain Contreras. He said we would be needed back home to explain everything we learned so that good decisions could be made."

"Did any xenos get to stay?" the caster asked.

"One," the scientist admitted. "A woman with a family. I felt discriminated against, on the grounds that I might not reproduce. I think there was a little policy-making going on by Captain Contreras."

The caster wanted to move on from the dead. "How about Captain Nigmatullin? Was she involved?"

Tidy shifted. The holo backdrop showed images of Elysia, ever changing, but he wouldn't look at it. "Not that I saw, not about the xenos. I mean, there was the time they were all yelling at each other, but I don't know what that was about."

This got the caster's attention. "Who was yelling?"

"The three captains," Tidy said. "Someone who'd been on the ship told me about it."

"Do you know what it was about?"

The scientist looked at the caster with mild disbelief. "I told you I didn't know what that was about."

The caster leaned in. "Who told you about it?"

"One of the shuttle pilots? I think. I don't know. I just remember him saying there was yelling." He went back to talking about his alien piglets.

Calvin started trawling for other discontented xenos, and reached one at first try. That one was perfectly fine with returning to Earth, but more prone to gossip and happy to talk to Calvin. He'd heard that there was yelling between the captains, but it was Nigmatullin and Contreras, when the two were stationed on the ground. Orlova rarely came down, and never all three together. Contreras had looked smug, and Nigmatullin furious. He thought it was something about the construction equipment and the fabricators, and Nigmatullin had gone off to talk to Amanda Brughel right afterward, and then the printers started running and the cottages were put together. Then there was more yelling and Nigmatullin had had to go back to the ship. He hadn't personally heard any of it, but maybe Calvin wanted to talk to someone who had run the fabricators.

Calvin started looking for the fabricators and checking their journals. He was still collecting addresses, and maybe he could find one.

He also spoke with the managing partner about his ethics issue. After hearing Calvin's reasons, the managing partner said the firm would support him, but Calvin had to be very careful and avoid such risks going forward. It was not a pleasant conversation, and Calvin was glad when it ended.

He received two unexpected calls before the day was out. The call from Tri should have surprised Calvin, but it didn't. Tri had a way of inserting himself into things. Tri wanted to find a couple of people for Jasper, and Tri had learned that one of them had stayed in the Washington area. His name was Zeke Salisbury.

Calvin's curiosity was overwhelming his own anxieties. "Why does Jasper want him?"

"Do you know where he is? Have you talked to him?"

Calvin gave Tri's image on the screen a good non-committal stare. "I have professional obligations."

Tri was not fooled. "You're just nosy."

"That, too. So, come on. What does Jasper want with him? And why does he have you tracking people down? With his vast network he shouldn't need to bother someone who's supposed to be studying."

Tri grinned. He seemed all better, and you would never know he'd been shot and waxy looking. "Everyone thinks I want an internship. I am not alarming. Something like that."

Calvin nodded. "And you are easily beguiled."

Tri smiled. "That, too."

"Fine." Calvin handed over the contact information.

The next call was much worse. It was Sean. "Listen," Sean said, "I've got to tell you something. You're not going to like it."

Calvin had not heard this voice from Sean before. It was neither flippant nor annoyed, neither buoyant nor aggrieved. It was downright troubled. "Tell me. I don't need all this suspense."

"I'm second chair to Ryle on Nigmatullin's hearing."

"Ah, hell," Calvin said. He meant it, but went on. "How are we going to agree he sucks if you're on his side?"

"I'll continue to agree he sucks," Sean assured him. "You're just going to have to take pity on me from a distance."

"I'll do that all right," Calvin said. He thought of mentioning the ethics charge. He might have in the normal way of things. He didn't now.

Sara was working on testimony for the CEO of MarsCorp long after what should have been dinnertime when Calvin stuck his head in her door. He was looking a lot like she felt, overworked and worried, and was dressed for the outdoors with his coat on, but unbuttoned. "Sorry to bother you," he said. "I know anyone still here isn't looking to chat."

While that was generally true, she reflected that she could always make an exception. She did not share the thought aloud. "What's up?"

He was all the way through the door now, and sat down uninvited. "I thought you'd want to know, one of *Aeneid*'s crew came by this morning. He had nothing solid, or nothing solid that he was willing to share to substantiate his concern, but he said there's a rumor that something's going to happen to the starship. I thought, what with the firm representing MarsCorp, there might be some concern."

Sara stood up. "We have to tell Judy. Why didn't you tell us this earlier?" He had probably only just decided to share the information. What had stopped him?

Calvin had not moved. "It was very vague. Lots of hinting."

She didn't stop to think about it, although she knew full well what she was doing. She picked up his hand and tugged. "Seriously, we have to."

His hand closed over hers, and the muddy green eyes grew very warm. He stood easily, not using her tug for his own weight, and looked down at her. His grin was a little foolish. "Since you ask so nicely, I guess I have to come."

She let go of his hand and turned away quickly to hide the damned blushing. She had meant to be casual, spontaneous, but if there was blushing, it undercut the whole effort.

She did not hold his hand in the hallway.

Judy's office was bigger than both of the associates' offices combined, and was large enough for three area rugs, three old-fashioned floor lamps, one to either side of the couch, and one by a large reading chair with an ottoman. With an office like that, one needn't go home, and, indeed, Judy was still there.

With a large book of business Judy Aleman was one of the more important partners in the firm, particularly now, when her high profile client MarsCorp was battling every bureaucracy on the planet to build more starships. She was of medium height and build, and her figure reflected the fact that she had given birth more than once. There were no pictures of the children in her office, and it was not clear to Sara when, if ever, Judy saw her offspring.

Sara spoke quickly. "Hi, Judy. Calvin had an interesting visitor this morning, and I thought you'd want to know what he heard. It's all very vague, but the man came to see him in person to tell him, and everyone knows we have MarsCorp."

Judy tilted her head. Her eyes looked tired. "And what is this vaguely alarming information, Mr. Tondini?"

Calvin shot Sara the kind of look that suggested he was not grateful for being dragged down here. "It is vague," Calvin said. "And I wasn't making much of it, but Sara's points are well taken. Someone who was stationed on the starship told me he's heard talk out of USACD that the *Aeneid* was to be decommissioned. Also, he said that its records were to be destroyed. This seems very unlikely, but he did say it. He was not more forthcoming than that."

"Who was it?" Judy asked.

"I wouldn't want his identity shared with MarsCorp. We didn't reach any sort of agreement, but we talked about him hiring us."

Judy had not invited them to sit down. "That's worth knowing. I'll pass it along." She turned back to her screen. With her back turned, she said, "Next time, reach an agreement."

In the hall, Sara said, "She must like you."

Calvin raised an eyebrow. He was still in his coat, still ready to leave. "She's not very warm and cuddly."

Sara did not disagree. "If it had been me, she'd have had all sorts of questions. How did this Salisbury fellow know that? What do you mean he wasn't saying? Did you ask him? Why didn't you ask him? What do you mean it wasn't that kind of conversation? It's always a kind of conversation where you can ask nosy, probing questions that the other person clearly has no intention of answering."

Calvin was laughing. "I'd say she likes you more. She has higher expectations of you." He stopped and frowned at her. "Or, are you saying that these are questions you wish I had asked."

"All conversations are that kind of conversation," Sara said.

"I'll remember next time."

They had reached her office. "See that you do." She wondered if he might plan to invite her to dinner again. It would be ambiguous if he did, just two colleagues getting a bite to eat on a cold winter's night. It wouldn't be like when he was clearly asking her out after the hearing.

He smiled, and said "Good night, Sara."

When he left, she wondered if she should have suggested dinner.

CHAPTER 12

EVERAL OF THE FEEDS CARRIED the news. The bubble drive didn't so much have a pilot as a computer that calculated the availability of empty space and offered a range of solutions to its operator. Whether the *Aeneid* had pilots or navigators or—as one of the individuals in question vociferously preferred and had charmed the waiting public with his insistence on the term—astrogators, was not the latest concern. The concerns were worse. Someone had killed the world's first interstellar navigator.

It looked to be a robbery. A hacker had gotten through the defenses of the astrogator's house in Princeton, New Jersey, and stolen all his personal possessions, including his palm, his personal journals, and the house computer itself, thus precluding any possibility that he or she could be identified. The first one stopped looking like a robbery when the second one occurred.

The second killing took place in Georgetown in Washington, DC, where a navigator had purchased a small row house to facilitate becoming reacquainted with Earth and to have easy access to all the parties to which she expected to be invited. She was highly sought after, and, one evening, on her way home from a soiree not far from her own dwelling place, she was accosted, forced into her house, raped and killed; and her palm, journals, and house computer stolen. According to the neighbors, she had a rare looking plant, which they speculated was ET in its origins, in her windowsill. That was missing, too.

The police refused to speculate on the apparent connection. The casters suffered no such qualms. Many of a certain mindset considered it a plot to prevent a return to Elysia. The more professional casters, those who had access to USACD and wanted to keep it, scoffed at that kind of paranoid thinking and laid the blame squarely at the door of those who sought to colonize and despoil other planets. Obviously, these were revenge killings by pro-colonization forces angry at USACD for not creating a lottery for tickets to Elysia. The logic of that one was a little hard to follow, but its adherents were adamant, and there were a lot of them, so it became the prevailing view.

Polly Nigmatullin was sick with anger. The police refused to discuss their investigation with her, and USACD would not give her the locations of the other navigators. She called her lawyer.

"Calvin," she said, when she got him on her screen, "have you been able to track down witnesses in my case."

She must have sounded a little too eager, which was not in keeping with her usual cavalier attitude toward her own defense, for his reply was wary. "Why do you ask?"

She wasn't naïve. "Aren't you trying to corroborate my story?"

That was a mistake. His grin was a little wolfish. "Are you ready to tell me your story? Your whole story?"

"You've got it," she said.

"I've been hearing about you yelling at people," her attorney said blandly.

The conversation was not going as she had intended. "I don't yell at people. I rely on leadership and personal magnetism."

"Was someone yelling at you?" He was still bland.

"I'm not calling about that," Polly said.

"We will have to talk about all of it." She was sure he meant to look sympathetic, but it came across as gloating. "When you're ready, of course."

"I would have to come in to your offices," she pointed out. She was leery of the security of her communication system. In her previous life on Earth, anything could be hacked. She had no reason to think that had changed.

"Soon?" her lawyer asked.

"Yes, yes. Now, about the witnesses—"

"Today?"

"Not today. Tomorrow," she said, willing to say anything to get back to what she needed to know.

"Good. Tomorrow it is. Let's say 9:30?"

"Sure. Could I see who you are talking to?"

"Absolutely," Calvin said. "I'll show you the list in the morning."

She closed the line, and sat back. She could have pushed it further, but she suspected that she wouldn't get to see the list of witnesses for purposes unrelated to her own defense. She might be wrong about that, but she didn't want to risk it.

For the first time since they had all left NIH she called Zeke Salisbury.

Calvin's client showed up at 9:25 for her appointment. His calendar was accessible to others, and when he went to greet her in the reception area, it turned out that at least eight people had business that required them to cross through the entrance to the firm at a time convenient for an introduction. Calvin noted the presence of fresh flowers on the human receptionist's desk. The woman herself looked subtly different, as if she had changed something about her clothes or make-up. She told Captain Nigmatullin that she had greatly enjoyed the captain's appearance on Heather's show. Nigmatullin was sorry, but she had not brought any corn with her today. However, she had some static pictures of the picnic area around the settlement's main building, and wondered if Cecily might like one? Cecily most certainly would, and would the captain mind signing it? Nigmatullin signed several more for the staff and lawyers sufficiently enterprising to admire Cecily's prize. Several others also expressed their enjoyment of Heather's show, and Calvin finally rescued his client, who seemed unperturbed by all the attention, and escorted her to his office.

"Are you enjoying the glory?" Calvin asked.

"It's useful," she told him soberly, some of the ready charm gone from her face. "I'm in sales for Elysia, you have to understand."

He wished she were in sales for herself, but said nothing. Once in his office, she did not sit down but asked immediately for his list of the crew. He had annotated it, identifying those to whom he wished to speak, those who had made public statements, and those who were higher in the command structure who might know more about the decision making process.

She studied it closely, and took a few notes of her own. She turned to him, her smile one of purest sunlight, and said, "I've lost track of quite a few people. I'm glad to see you have addresses now. They're hard to find. Many have opted out of the public record, it seems."

The wattage of her smile tipped him off. "Who are you looking for?" he asked. And why, he wondered. She probably wanted to get to them before her lawyer so they could coordinate their stories.

"The navigators," she said. "They've probably figured out the danger they're in, but your news is very hard to follow for some. You have to figure out in advance what you want to pay attention to, and someone may possibly have paid no attention at all."

Calvin admitted that he should put himself in the second category. "The navigators who've been killed?"

"Yes, someone has killed two of the *Aeneid's* navigators," Polly said. "I want to make sure the others know about it."

And she wanted his list for their defense not her own. He shrugged mentally, but pointed at one of the chairs by his desk. Earlier he had programmed the desk to form itself to be more like a table. It was more convivial and collegial, both.

She looked as if she were about to leave. "You got what you came for," he said. "I would find my job much easier if you told me everything. The jammers are on, you are protected by attorney-client privilege, and I can counsel you best if I know what's coming."

She took a deep breath and sat down, placed her elbows on the desk-cum-table, and said, defiantly and unhappily, "Fine."

Calvin joined her. "Have you heard anything about the starship being decommissioned?" he asked her, to give her time.

"Yes," she said, "but probably from the same person you did. You've talked to Zeke?"

"He came by," Calvin admitted. "I don't want to put two and two together and get five, but these murders, and what he told me....?" He let the sentence trail off, waiting to see how much Zeke had shared with her. More, most likely, than Zeke had shared with Calvin himself, but one should be careful.

Nigmatullin eyed him quizzically, as if she, too, were attempting to estimate how much the other person knew. "I suppose that if I'm ready to tell you my deepest darkest, I should be willing to gossip with you about the rest. Will this conversation be privileged, too?"

"Ask me a legal question at the end of it, and sure," Calvin said.

She sat very straight. He was beginning to understand it was a sign of unhappiness. "Zeke told me that USACD is planning to wipe the records. Which is ridiculous. We all know what star it's at."

"But working the bubble drive so you don't wind up inside a rock is more complicated?" he asked.

Her elbows on the desk, she steepled her fingers. Her hands were long and fine, and the tilted eyes staring at him over her hands held a memory of fear. "Yes. It's like the riverboat captain who knew where the hidden sandbars were. We did a certain amount of holding our breath and counting on the whole vastness of space thing, before we just popped up in our next location."

It had been why the *Aeneid* took so long to return to Earth. There was no way anyone planned for it to just reappear in low Earth orbit, one of the more crowded orbital arcs around Earth. Even attempting to come in on Earth's orbital plane was a game of chance. So the ship had avoided running into a planet, an asteroid, or a comet, and taken months to arrive from when it first returned to the solar system well off the plane of the ecliptic.

"We have the record of safe routes," Nigmatullin said. "I'm sure there are other such routes, but these we know and charted, and surveyed, so the next traveller can figure the risks of what might come back around and be in the way when he gets there."

"Losing that would greatly increase the risks," Calvin observed.

Nigmatullin's voice was grim. "With two results. The first and more horrible is that a whole lot of people would die unnecessarily. The second, and the more likely reason this is happening—if it's happening—is because it will scare people away."

"I'm not sure people even know the risks you took," Calvin said.

Here eyes acknowledged the fear she had felt, but she did not address it aloud. "Zeke's source inside USACD is someone who knew Zeke's father. He won't tell Zeke why he thinks USACD is planning to do this, but we can all guess."

Calvin had something to offer. He pulled up an item on his screen. "USACD is on the Hill asking for authority to regulate passage to Elysia, to send a governor, and to review the manifests and passenger lists of those who go on private starships. I'm sure it would help them if they were the only ones who knew how to get there safely."

"But murder?" Nigmatullin said. "In my day, that was not something bureaucrats did. It was never necessary."

"They're saying," Calvin said, "that the murders are the pro-settlement forces trying to keep USACD from making everyone return."

"That doesn't even make sense," Nigmatullin protested. "It's all about who gets to go back."

Calvin noted her usage with interest. Was she, perhaps, interested in returning? "So, if it's not USACD, who is it?"

"There are lots of environmental groups, the Earth First folks, assorted loonies. Every age has them, doesn't it?" She leaned back in her chair, her hands gripping the table. "Let me write to the navigators. My story is a long one, and I want to know they are aware."

It was impossible not to be aware of the news, Calvin thought, but turned away, and let her write. It took her a few moments to compose and send her messages, but she was more serene when she was done.

Then she told him her story.

CHAPTER 13

CAPTAIN PAOLINA NIGMATULLIN SURVEYED THE pastoral scene that spread before her and Captain Aldo Contreras. It was something out of a dream, too perfect to be real. But real it was. Every day she stepped outside on Elysia, a part of her waited for the bad news, the horror, the disease that took out six children, or the horde of ravening jackrabbits that ate human ankles. And every day was like the one before, with lots of hard work, construction, scientific testing, planting, more testing, and school for the kids, who had discovered the joys of running, hiding, scaring their parents, and coming home only when they were hungry for dinner. There were no bogeymen.

There were places like this on Earth. There were also places that were foul, that erupted with violence, or housed disease. Whatever the flaws of Elysia, and there had to be some, Earth had them, too. Both planets were hospitable. Neither was without risk. But there were no guarantees of safety anywhere, and they all knew it. It was why they were here. Earth had been at risk from not one, but two asteroids, and could face something equally dire again.

The day itself was glorious, the day she and Contreras started negotiations. The sun was rising lower in the sky for fall, but the air was still balmy and perfect, probably the same temperature they kept the ship at, where no one was either warm or cold. Outside it was an entirely different feeling, even if the temperature was the same. The sun warmed your skin, and you were glad of the air, which moved in random currents and didn't just blow on your neck. She had let her hair grow out on the voyage from Earth. She wore it long, but pulled high on the crown of her head in a swinging horsetail, and she liked it when the wind tugged. There were smells, too, of plants and dirt and loam. One of the smells reminded her of roses, and she took it as a good sign for the place.

It was a far better place than the hells that were the two previous planets, the second of which would have been good only as a fictional penal colony. If it had been the best of the lot, she would have gone back to Earth recommending that the human race take its chances with the rocks in the system.

"Are you still thinking?" Contreras asked.

"I'm thinking I'd like to stay," Nigmatullin said quietly. They were near a group of medical personnel and geneticists who were laughing about something. They probably hadn't had enough to do since the Bad Cold afflicted everyone for thirty-six hours.

"That wasn't the deal," he said.

She couldn't disagree. She was to take the fall when they got back. There would have to be a scapegoat, and she had volunteered long ago in order to come at all. She wasn't a real captain. She was a third captain. The consensus had been that no one in the States would believe that anyone who came home hadn't somehow been involved.

And, no, they couldn't all stay. In the first place, they needed to let their countrymen know about Elysia's existence. Others had to be allowed to come, and the current settlement numbers were small enough to be wiped out by one bad disease or a long famine. Maybe paradise lacked essential nutrients. Tests said it didn't, but they were on an alien planet. Maybe this was where they would discover new things about the human body itself. In any event, not everyone wanted to stay.

Orlova herself had cold feet, and stayed in orbit on the ship as much as possible, as if afraid that it would leave without her. With time dilation, relativity, and complex math, the wrong people would never learn of the involvement of Contreras and Orlova in the settlement's creation.

Nigmatullin herself hadn't known how vast the conspiracy had been, or the details of what had been involved to provide for the earth-movers, the fabricators, the pigs, chickens, rabbits, seed, potatoes, rice, and cabbage. Much of the vegetables had been culled from the *Aeneid's* own hydroponics and atmospheric converters. People had learned to take plants with them to orbit, null-g, the Moon and Mars. Even with genetic modifications, they were the best converters for human health, if not for maximum efficiency. The machines came, too, it went without saying.

All she knew was that when back on Earth she had gone to Jammie Brughel during the crew selection for the *Aeneid*, and asked how to improve her chances, Jammie had put her in touch with her brother Jasper on the condition that Polly stop calling her Jammie and switch to her middle name. Jasper didn't call his sister Jammie anymore, but he was alone in calling her Janice, and Amanda allowed it only from him.

Jammie—Amanda—and Polly had gone to high school together, and Amanda had a berth on the *Aeneid* as an engineer and a biologist. She had explained the massive amounts of equipment to everyone as emergency measures. What if the crew had to hole up somewhere and needed to fortify themselves against the elements or hostiles? What if the ship needed repairs, and the crew had to wait planet-side for some reason? There were also provisions for sheltering on an airless orb. What if they needed food that could reproduce while they waited for circumstances to change? Everything that anyone might think was a plan for settlement could also be characterized as mere sound planning in case of untoward contingencies.

USACD's selection board had not been terribly interested in Nigmatullin at first. Her piloting skills were useful, of course, but the senior spot was taken, and they had a multitude of pilots to choose from who also had advanced degrees in useful fields such as biology or medicine. Everyone selected also had hobbies of a certain slant, one that might contribute to the well-being of a barely industrial civilization. So close on the heels of the rocks, the news picked it up and found it charming, the number of hobby gardeners, weavers, carpenters, and hackers amidst the engineers, biologists, geneticists, medics, and xenos.

Nigmatullin lacked any such useful hobbies. She just liked to read when she wasn't working. She hadn't planned ahead.

"Do you sew?" Amanda had asked her. Amanda always asked the hard questions.

"I don't even know what that looks like," Polly replied. "I can fix things."

Amanda gave her the fish eye. "Like what?"

Polly knew it was hopeless. "My console?"

"There are plenty of engineers." Amanda had not been optimistic, but a few days later she had called Polly and told her to get in touch with Jasper.

Polly had had to fly out to see Jasper, who wouldn't talk on the phone. He had moved again, like he always did, and was in Cleveland at the time. The lake effect kept the clouds low and grey on the fall day she'd visited him in his home. He was in one of the suburbs, in a large house from well over a century back. It was brick with a large front hall, and a living room too long for two people.

He assured her they had privacy. "And, it's more to protect me than you. Do you mind turning off your cuff?"

Amused, she complied. "This is all very conspiratorial, Jasper." He had been one of those older brothers who didn't let his kid sister in on anything. It looked like that had changed.

"Janice tells me you want to go on the *Aeneid*," Jasper said. "May I ask why?"

"I've always wanted to see more sky. This will be our shot. And, I don't want to wait for them to figure out if they'll pay for another. For all I know, they won't send the second until this one gets back." She had had personal reasons, too, which, from the vantage of Elysia, seemed both absurd and God-sent at the same time. She didn't want to be in the same solar system as Sam and his new bride. She had waited for Sam, but he hadn't waited for her. And Mars was just a lot of red rock, red sky, and failed terraforming.

"May I ask you something?" Polly said. "Are you on the selection board?"

Jasper smiled. He was very cocky for someone their age, as if he knew things about how the world worked that Polly would never figure out. He was a large man, with intelligent, sober eyes and a good brain. The teenage Polly had had a crush on him for a few months one summer. It had not survived his opacity. "I have some connections there."

"How?" The selection board was in Washington, DC. Jasper was in Cleveland.

"You may have noticed that the people we selected have their specialties, but they also have other skills. Useful skills."

Polly grimaced. "I've read a lot of books. And played a lot of games. I know. Even before Amanda harped on it, I'd noticed from the news. Everyone's noticed. It's clever and charming, as if everyone was going to stay. But three hundred people can't stay on an alien planet and survive on their own."

"They can if they have to," Jasper said.

Polly was shocked. "You're going to strand them?"

Jasper leaned forward in his armchair, his folded hands dangling between his knees. A large painting that looked like an Albert Bierstadt hung on the wall behind him. It showed the Rocky Mountains, with glistening sky above and a glistening mountain lake at their feet, virgin territory. Knowing Jasper, she wondered if it was an original. "Most of them don't view it as being stranded. If there's a good place to stay, it's what they want. But we need someone on the ship to help them."

They stared at each other.

She said nothing, and he went on. "We haven't been able to get it written into the mission statement. And we don't want written evidence that we failed, so that we can at least try to protect whoever helps us."

"How's that?" She didn't really care about the answer. Her mind was racing over what he said. She didn't think the mission statement was done, but she had heard nothing from the government itself about the voyage being to leave a settlement or even a base, not at those distances. A little base would mean certain death for its inhabitants.

"We don't want it being said later that settlement was considered and rejected," Jasper explained.

"Jasper," Polly finally said. She had gotten up and walked over to the piano. It was an upright, and there was a thin film of dust on it.

She wondered who played. Jasper was married with a couple of kids. Someone wasn't practicing. "Jasper, who's 'we'?"

He walked over to stand next to her. He folded up the sheet music without looking at it. "Does it really matter? I'm the one you know, and you've known me forever. We're people who were scared of the rocks. We're the people who pushed for the government to build this ship. It was very expensive, creating a whole infrastructure for one ship. We don't want it wasted. Science is good, but so is survival." He placed the music in a neat stack on top of the piano.

"You're not going," she observed.

"I would love to," Jasper said. "But I am just an accountant. My skill set isn't the best."

She smiled. "Surely, they need someone who can form clubs?"

He ignored that. "We need someone in the command structure who can ensure that if there's a good place to stay, as many as possible do."

"Who decides it's good enough?"

"Everyone. Everyone who goes." He turned to face her, one hand resting on the piano back. There was another painting that she didn't recognize over the piano. It showed a small lunar settlement. She had seen enough pictures to recognize it as the first one. More virgin territory. It was all very inspirational. "We can't plan everything, and I won't be there to help figure it out. It might be marginal, but people might want to give it a shot anyway. I don't know. The people who stay back here can't make those decisions."

She didn't give him an answer that day. Instead, she went home and read about the *Mayflower*, Plymouth, Jamestown, and other European settlements in the Americas. The first Jamestown was alarming, and there wasn't much on those who crossed the Bering Straits, but there was plenty to read on those who settled what became the United States. People had. She flew back out a week later, and told him she was interested. What did she have to do?

"You would have to come back," Jasper said.

"What if I wanted to stay?" Her imagination was filled with thoughts of founding a new world, a new nation. Her rational mind was convinced they would find more red rocks and gas giants, or die navigating the voyage, but the systems selected each looked to have something the size of Earth and not be inconsistent with the presence of water. More than that was hard to determine.

"You couldn't." They were in the kitchen this visit, and Jasper was pushing buttons for grinding the coffee.

She hovered as he worked. "Why not?"

The machine gave a smooth purr, and the transparent machine showed a fine grind shooting through a tube. "We need someone to take the blame. The selection board doesn't always see things our way, and we don't think the two in charge on the *Aeneid* will see things completely our way. They won't stand in the way, but neither wants to stay and they want their reputations clean when they come back."

"You didn't mention this before," she said.

"I wasn't completely certain it was this bad." The smell of coffee filled the kitchen. He pushed more buttons and milk shot through another clear tube and landed in its glass bowl with the hiss of steam. It started to foam. "You will have been gone long enough that your problems will have disappeared."

"I don't have any problems," Polly said automatically, but she was staring out the window thinking just that. She wanted to see new worlds. She wanted to see what Albert Bierstadt saw. She wouldn't get even that if she didn't agree to his terms.

She stared out the window for a long time, and Jasper filled two large mugs with coffee and steamed milk. When he handed her her mug, she gave him a small toast. Her back was very straight, and she looked him in the eyes. "I'll do it. Get me in."

Nigmatullin watched Contreras, and Contreras watched the little settlement from the window of a new building. It was another lab. The people outside wore heavy outerwear, but the hoods were no longer pulled close around their faces. "They seem pretty happy here," he said. "The xenos love it, but Davis is upset about the rabbits. He really can't believe we brought rabbits."

"Sure," Nigmatullin said. "Even I am appalled, and I don't care at all."

"So, rabbit stew for dinner again?" Contreras liked being on Elysia. He had led many expeditions into the bush, once they established that the larger predators that looked like tigers could indeed be tranquilized. He enjoyed the live capture and release that the xenos preferred. Nigmatullin took her turns at aerial surveillance, and they had the surrounding area well mapped.

"So I hear," she replied. The local spring approached, and they had resolved the problems with the power generators. They were on a river plain in a valley bordered by mountains to the north and west. An ocean lay several hundred kilometers to the south. No bears had appeared to devour them all. Whenever a possible food source satisfied all the lab tests, it was given to the rabbits. The rabbits were thriving, and none had escaped. The children understood that if any one of them gave a rabbit its freedom that child would be flung into the sun on departure. Some of the smaller ones had had nightmares at this threat, and Contreras had taken it upon himself to explain it was a joke, but no rabbits had gained their freedom, despite their very subtle blandishments.

"It will be time to leave soon," Contreras said.

Nigmatullin did not respond. She had her own plans. She had been talking to the navigators about how close to Elysia they were willing to leave from. It was coming back into normal space that was the problem, not leaving it. The shuttle's range should allow her to make it, with the *Aeneid* long gone.

Nigmatullin planned to plead sickness the day before the bubble drive went on, steal a shuttle, and return to the settlement as the drive took the *Aeneid* out of the system. Obviously, she made no mention of this plan to Contreras.

Contreras planned to return to Earth. They had found Elysia. They didn't need to keep looking at any more planets. For all they knew, USACD had built more ships, and found even more planets. It would be interesting to know what had happened while they were gone, he told Nigmatullin regularly, and, if the agency hadn't built more ships, it needed to know there was one good place available on which to back up humanity.

"I've been thinking," he said. "About our orders." They were alone in the front room of the lab. It was like an airlock against the cold, although bigger than any ship's airlock. Still, he looked around briefly, as if to ensure their privacy.

She didn't want to hear it, so said nothing.

Contreras continued without prompting. "I am very uncomfortable ignoring them."

This she couldn't ignore. "You were paid plenty to be comfortable. For a really long time." There, she'd said it. She had never let him know she knew about his bribe. She knew he knew about hers. He was counting on it, after all.

"I think the back pay will cover my discomfort on that front. I have to think about our duty here. The orders say nothing about leaving anyone behind."

"That's why they are volunteers," Nigmatullin said. "And the orders don't say they can't stay. Captain," she said very earnestly, "the entire population of the country thinks we are here to find new places to live. That's why the *Aeneid* was invented and built. We all know that."

"It's not in the orders. We are a scientific mission." He started putting on his outerwear.

"With families and children," she pointed out. "And seed crop."

"I don't believe that a lot of the cargo was on USACD's manifest." He spoke with sincere asperity, as if he had not known all about most of it. Not the rabbits, of course. No one knew about the rabbits, except the crazy soul who had brought the original pair. Maybe Jasper knew.

The *Aeneid* had become very expensive. Measured against the budgets for entitlements and defense, it was very little, but, as cost overruns set in and problems with the contractor began appearing in the news, and people—some of them—forgot about the rocks, the *Aeneid* had become a symbol of wasteful government spending. It had become hot, and the heat made its proponents nervous about a public dialogue on certain issues. Like settlement. But that, Nigmatullin reflected, sounded like Jasper. He always played his hand very close to the vest.

Nigmatullin made her own voice bracing, even as she struggled with her outerwear. "We have a plan. They stay. We go. That's it."

He was sealed in to his garments. "We'll see."

They went outside, and it was warm and balmy in comparison to what they had expected. They both immediately took their coats off.

They had the same conversation two more times. One session took place, unfortunately, when they were on the ship, and two crewmen came to see if anything was wrong, the commanders grew so heated.

Contreras and Orlova were inclined to forget their commitments. Faced with the prospect of returning home, they were no doubt having imaginary conversations with their superiors in their minds and not picturing those little talks going so well. Orlova had taken to pretending she didn't know anything about what the other two discussed, and would leave the room.

Nigmatullin had to bank on the settlers refusing to go if Contreras tried to make them. She had to ensure it. Part of her suspected that this was what Contreras had intended all along. Nigmatullin wasn't along just for the blame afterwards. She was along to conduct any real mutiny that took place.

So be it, she decided.

There was no place on the ship to gather everyone together physically in the same room at the same time. The largest building groundside did not hold the whole crew, but it would hold everyone in the settlement if they stood and held their breath and got too close to their neighbors.

Instead, Contreras called an all-hands for the outdoors area in front of the central lodge, as they were all starting to call the building in the middle of the settled area. It lay between two parallel lines of bungalows facing each other, its front door perpendicular to the small houses, with the three lines forming a tall H.

Night would have been too cold for the gathering. As it was, the afternoon sunshine was weak and did little to warm the crowd of people standing outside. Some of the families huddled close together. A small knot of children had reached adolescence on the voyage, and they stood together off to one side, alternately hugging and shoving each other for no discernible reason. No one with teens had been so foolish as to volunteer.

Contreras had called all-hands meetings a few times since the *Aeneid* started sending people groundside. The first one had been frightening and ecstatic all at once. They had reached a new world. They had reached a second Earth. They could breathe the air and walk the land, and they had found it and the human race need never face extinction again. For days afterwards, few had been able to speak for the nursing of their throats.

Other gatherings had been more prosaic, status reports on the lab work, updates on what local delicacies were fit for human consumption, and reminders on proper behavior and respect for others.

Contreras had not told the other two captains what he meant to discuss this time. At least, he had not told Nigmatullin. The *Aeneid* was ready for departure. It had been checked, repaired, recycled, and declared ready three times over in the last two months. The holds were full of biostuffs from Elysia and two other planets, although hardly anyone thought of, much less spoke of, the first two. The biostuffs took the place of some of the large machinery being left behind.

Contreras, Orlova and Nigmatullin stood on the platform that would have been a porch had it been roofed at the front of the lodge. Nigmatullin adopted a casual parade rest, because she never knew what to do with her hands otherwise. Orlova stood with arms folded, and Contreras just stood with his usual easy-going grace.

Contreras started with the tremendous work everyone had done and how much it was appreciated. He knew that everyone back on Earth would appreciate it. And, he wanted to talk about that. It was time to go home. He understood that there were a few people who wanted to stay, that there had been talk of leaving a settlement, but they all had to understand it wasn't in their orders.

There was a murmuring in the crowd. It consisted mainly of people who considered themselves groundsiders again. They tended not to use the term crew. If you were crew, it meant you were up on the *Aeneid*.

Saul Klein was one of the fabricating engineers. He had his family with him. "There's nothing in the orders that says we can't."

"You did sign up for the duration of the voyage," Contreras said.

Saul's voice carried well, even without the aid of the sound system. "If I don't get back on the *Aeneid* my voyage is over. That doesn't seem too confusing to me."

There was laughter from the crowd, and a few whoops from the knot of teenagers.

"The *Aeneid*'s voyage," Contreras said. "And that voyage is not over. Everyone needs to start planning what they're going to ship, what data needs to return with us, and what you want to bring back. We'll be leaving in two weeks from today. You'll find that's enough time. Pay attention to your weight allowance."

Nigmatullin sighed inwardly. He was going to force her into her role. She'd be damned if she made it too obvious. She didn't want to be locked up. Never mind the boredom, discomfort, and disgrace, being locked up would ruin her own plans. And, Contreras shouldn't want it, if she read him right.

"I'm sure folks have questions," she said. Her voice carried, too, but with the assistance of the sound system.

Contreras scowled at her. "Like what?"

Perhaps she had misread him. Perhaps he simply meant it. She would definitely get locked up if that were the case. The crowd was quiet, watching her. "Like whether their employment contract prevents them from quitting. Not everyone here is military."

"Military personnel can't quit," Contreras said, which he had pointed out more than once in their private conversations.

There was another deathly silence, as everyone pondered the

corollary. "I'm not military," Saul Klein said. "I might be handing in my termination papers."

"Me, too," someone else called out.

"I won't even ask for my back pay," hollered another voice from the center of the crowd.

The laughter broke the tension. Contreras didn't laugh, but stayed watchful. "This discussion is ended," he said, and folded his arms across his chest. "Dismissed."

The last was his mistake. Most of them weren't military. They all turned to each other and started talking. Only the children wandered off. One of the people who served as a biology teacher rounded them up, and herded them to the other side of the lodge.

Contreras stood watching as no one else left, and finally, apparently deciding that discretion was the better part of valor, dismissed himself by walking into the lodge.

Two weeks passed without incident, but without visible signs of preparation for departure. Messages started appearing on the boards. "Interstellar travel is not slavery" got a lot of votes, but casual criticism as well, as people observed that it wasn't very catchy. "Take this job and shove it," met counters from *Aeneid*'s crew, pointedly asking whether the groundsiders would be returning all the government's supplies when they quit? Signing his name, Saul Klein pointed out that the materials the fabricators used were Elysian, so they thought they'd keep the buildings, thanks, but the crew could take the inside wiring only if they didn't disturb anything on their way to it.

And, still, no one packed.

Nigmatullin stayed groundside. Why Contreras let her have charge of the security personnel, she didn't know, unless her first suspicions were correct. She took advantage of it anyway. She played with the rotations, and kept Zeke Salisbury and his unit on the ground even though they were slated to go topside a week from the deadline. She moved other people around.

Before she had left Earth, Jasper had shown her a list of names. He had made her memorize them so that there would be no record.

She had rolled her eyes at his theatrics at the time but was glad of them now. She supposed that Jasper and his ilk had not had to turn any of the military personnel so much as learn where their sympathies lay. They had all been alive for the threat from the rocks.

Two days before the deadline she was plotting routes across the plains to the mountains when she received a contingent of xenos, all of whom were furious. "Contreras has told us we can't stay," said their spokesman. He was a tall, bushy haired man with dark skin. He was almost shaking, he was so angry.

"He's said no one can stay," Nigmatullin said.

"But we have to leave now," he said. "We're really leaving."

"Really leaving?" she asked.

"He's not doing this to anyone else."

She considered this. They were in the smaller admin building across from the central lodge, and they all sat around a table of lab equipment. There were nine xenos. "When did he say you had to be ready?"

"Tomorrow. Before anyone else. We think he's going to let the rest of them stay. He said our knowledge was crucial back on Earth. He said if there was anything about Elysia that we needed to worry about, we need to be there to be part of the analysis. All of us? If anywhere needs redundancy in our specialty, it's here. We're willing to draw straws."

"Which isn't very scientific," one of his colleagues observed drily. "But we don't care at this point."

"How about the geneticists?" she asked. The geneticists were the ones who created counters to harmful virus and bacteria. They had heroically cured the Bad Cold.

The one who cared about science spoke up again. "About half of them got the same message. We think Contreras is going to let everyone else stay."

Or, thought Nigmatullin cynically, *these are the ones he values the most. If there's a fight, he doesn't want to lose the science.* These were the ones who had to leave safely and without being shot if it came to it. It made sense. She wasn't sure she disagreed with the reasoning, however much she might hate their loss of choice. They were all civilians.

The leader's name was Bill Cannon, she remembered finally. She hadn't dealt with him much. He was glaring at her, and then he uttered the words she had been dreading, the words that triggered all the obligations she had so foolishly shouldered back on Earth. "We want your protection," he said. "We were told that if it ever came to this, you were the one. We are a free people. We are Americans. We don't have to get back on that ship."

She rose to her feet. "Understood," she said. "I will help you." She held out her hand, and he rose, too. He held her eyes as they shook, and she knew deep in her bones that she had just taken on more than she ever intended. But, she told herself sternly, she would never have been able to come in the first place if she hadn't.

She put them on two of the runabouts, and sent them off with two pilots into the bush with arms and provisions and sensible shoes. They would walk back in two days. If there was a predator out there that they couldn't deal with, it was part of the risk of their profession. They all took it willingly.

The shuttle that called in for a landing the next day was full of security personnel. The landing site for the shuttle was a runway three miles from the settlement, and two miles long. It had been the first fabrication project, followed by the road of rock and gravel that led to the town. The names of this new batch of personnel weren't on the list Jasper had given her to memorize.

She called for Zeke Salisbury and the commander of the shuttle groundside. They reported in at the central lodge, both looking grim. She had not confided in Zeke, never divulging the terms of her engagement on the *Aeneid*, or her own plans inside Jasper's plans. Jasper, despite being the expert schemer that he was, hadn't realized how much easier it would be to lay the blame at her door if she didn't come back. Obviously, she would have to have been the ringleader of the mutiny if she stayed behind. Jasper would figure it out. He could make it all work without her.

She had to start her lies now. The truth of it was she liked Zeke. She didn't need him to share her fall, and she didn't want anyone beside herself to have to lie. The shuttle pilot, Hana Stamp, had started the mission young, and she had no family or children with her, but she had become involved with one of the civilians, and she was on Nigmatullin's list. Nigmatullin hoped that list was right, but she recognized that people changed over time.

"You have your cuffs?" she asked them, and when they nodded, Nigmatullin chose her next words carefully. "We have a situation. I'll call it a strange situation."

Nigmatullin had been told that the people on her list knew that one of the captains would be able to ensure settlement. She knew now they had been told it was her. She drew a breath. "I have orders from the Pentagon. They state that I must ensure that whoever wants to stay on a suitable planet must be allowed to do so. I can hardly think of a more suitable planet than this one."

Stamp nodded.

Salisbury spoke up. "If I may ask, why doesn't Contreras have these orders?" The subtext to his question was clear. Why didn't the real captain have the secret orders?

Her mouth felt dry and her limbs all hollow. If she didn't convince these people, she would fail. "I was told," Nigmatullin said with complete truthfulness, "that the politics of our selection and the decision led to it being me. That's all I can say."

"But he isn't going to agree with you," Salisbury pointed out. "Why don't you show him the orders?"

"Salisbury," Stamp snapped, "I'm sure there are reasons."

Salisbury's pale face flushed, and he scowled at Stamp. "I want to be prepared. I'm just trying to figure how this will play out."

"How it plays out for me," Nigmatullin said slowly and carefully, "is that I have to follow my orders. I am hoping to persuade Captain Contreras that he should follow them as well."

"May I see them?" the pilot asked before Salisbury could come up with any more irritating questions.

Grateful, Nigmatullin tuned her cuff, and the orders from the Undersecretary for Planetary Defense displayed on the table. She wished they were real. Jasper had told her they weren't. Salisbury scanned them, and then held out his wrist.

It was all right and proper, and Nigmatullin touched her cuff to his, and then to Stamp's.

Stamp's eyebrows climbed up her forehead, and she smiled. "These are real," she said as if surprised.

Nigmatullin felt a little of the tension ebb away, and her bones became solid once more. She had at least one ally.

Salisbury looked more skeptical. "You've got all the codes," he observed. "At least, none that anyone can question."

Nigmatullin pursed her lips but said nothing.

When the shuttle radioed its entry, Nigmatullin called Salisbury and his unit to the lodge.

The settlement was very quiet when the ground car rolled into town. It was more of a truck, but with no roof or sides, and uncomfortably cold when it picked up any real speed.

The unit's lieutenant greeted her with a salute. "We have come to escort the xenos and geneers to *Aeneid*, sir."

Nigmatullin returned the salute from where she waited on the porch of the central lodge. "Give Captain Contreras my regards, but I regret to report they are unavailable. They are working on a project and cannot come away."

The younger woman looked uncomfortable. "Captain, we have orders."

"And these are mine," she said.

"Permission to speak with the ship?" the lieutenant asked. She was Sonja Bering, and had red hair and blue eyes. Nigmatullin knew her, and Bering knew Nigmatullin. It was all very uncomfortable.

"Granted," Nigmatullin said, and opened the door so she could use the transmission system directly. "Your unit may wait outside."

Soon the lying would begin again.

Nigmatullin stayed outside on the patio. The more permanent residents of the settlement had vanished, but the open area around the lodge was full of people whose usual duties were on the ship. They had been coming down over the last twenty-four hours in shuttles that could carry fifty people at a time. Her security held the *Aeneid*'s shuttle bay. Nigmatullin imagined that the bungalows were crowded, and it was easier to be outside on this warm spring day.

Bering returned from inside the lodge, her blue eyes confused. "Captain Contreras will be joining us, he advises." Contreras was back on the *Aeneid*. It would be a wait. Nigmatullin was ready for this. Contreras had steadfastly maintained his position that everyone should return. He would not be perjuring himself. She just had to hope he didn't really mean it.

She turned to the assembled crowd. The Brughels had really packed the *Aeneid*, and she had not guessed the extent to which they had succeeded. She saw one family she knew had never left the ship before this. They were here on a lot of faith. Everyone was armed.

"I don't know that you all need to stay here," she said. She caught the eyes of the parents with children. "There's risk with all of this."

Saul stood with his three kids near the front. Saul's wife had died in a pressure accident on the previous planet, the one they had nicknamed Hell. "There's risk with everything, Captain."

As an hour passed, some people did leave, likely out of boredom. Nigmatullin desperately wished more people would take their children away, or at least to the other side of the lodge.

You swore an oath, she told herself. *You might want to think a little more next time you do that.* Maybe she could have gotten the post without the Brughels' intervention. Not from where she was on the wait list, she knew when she was being honest.

Nigmatullin's units were in place before Stamp reported that Contreras had arrived. Nigmatullin's shuttles weren't all lined up on the tarmac like sitting ducks. She had hers in the air. The personnel understood that the Pentagon might have a different policy view on the need for a human presence outside the solar system that was humanity's home. Most of them understood the importance of an industrial base and redundant capabilities. It all made sense and she'd shown them her orders.

Jasper had assured her that the very best of hackery had been involved and that the orders would authenticate. Maybe they'd authenticate because they *were* real.

She heard the ground car, and squinted against the sun as she watched it grow larger. One of Salisbury's men was driving, and

Salisbury was in the back seat next to Contreras. This was working, she thought grimly.

Contreras marched up to the patio where two weeks earlier he had told a smaller crowd that they would all be leaving. He appeared indifferent to the fact that he was surrounded.

They failed to exchange salutes. They seemed to be in tacit agreement that there would have been something too mendacious to the formality. "Commander, it is time to end this. The window for our departure won't tolerate this kind of grandstanding."

"We are not leaving," she said.

He swept a hand across the swollen crowd. If anyone had left earlier, they appeared to have returned, and Nigmatullin was sickened to see that the people she had suggested go on picnics for the day had come back. With their families.

"I was hoping it would not come to this," she said. She had the sound system running so that everyone could hear everything with utter clarity. "And I was asked not to resort to this unless it was absolutely necessary. Now that you have interpreted the silence in your orders—the deliberate silence, I would say—as meaning everyone must return, even against their will and in violation of their freedom to make their own life choices, I must reveal my own military orders."

She threw the projection up behind her for all to read. "I am on a USACD mission," she acknowledged, "but I am seconded from the Aerospace Force. I answer to the country's military, and I have separate orders."

Contreras was turning red. Maybe she had misread his intentions. Maybe theirs was not an elaborate game designed to ensure he was never on the hook for allowing the settlement. Maybe he had really meant to bring them all back. "The military," he said sternly, "is not in charge. The President is the Commander-in-chief."

"Of course he is," Nigmatullin agreed. "I have no reason to think he was unaware of these orders. Do you? Feel free to check their authenticity."

Contreras gave Bering the nod, and she uplinked with the ship in orbit. It took about ten seconds.

"They are authenticated, sir," Bering reported.

"The hell they are," he said. "You're in with them, too." He rounded on Nigmatullin. "You think you've got all the security people in your pocket, don't you?"

"They are following orders, sir," she said. It was important to maintain the fiction of her orders. She had told them all they were real. No one but she knew they came from Jasper Brughel and a hacker back on Earth. She was the only one who should bear the disgrace if she had the bad luck to be taken back home. Most of the military personnel were going back. She planned to look the other way if any weren't.

"Some of them are following mine," he said. "The xenos and geneers are back aboard *Aeneid*. We picked them up shortly after you dropped them off."

She thought of the group that had come to her for help, their faces both angry and hopeful. "You should let them go," she said.

"I am ordering all of you to get back on those shuttles," Contreras said.

The crowd murmured, and it was unpleasant.

Contreras faced her head on. "And you will come back and stand trial, and we will find out how real those orders of yours are."

Not very real at all, she thought. Aloud she said, "I have been ordered to facilitate a permanent settlement. You saw that. The ship authenticated it. You will be the one standing trial, not me, if you stop it."

Contreras looked out over the sea of faces. The crew was over ninety percent American, but that meant that all the colors of humanity were represented. He saw builders, engineers and scientists, dedicated people who had risked not only their own lives, but the lives of their families as well. Perhaps he thought of the agreements he had made back home. Perhaps he remembered how he felt when the rocks were heading toward Earth and the madness of the arks, the constant harping on the dinosaurs, the certain knowledge that the lunar enclaves would not survive the fiery hell that could have befallen their planet, the real source of necessary resources. Perhaps he made his own decision about the need for the human race to have a back up drive. Perhaps he thought he had put on a sufficient show.

"They can stay," he said gruffly.

A cheer rose, and Nigmatullin heard a sob from someone nearby. Sonja's eyes were red, but the young woman's face was like stone.

Contreras raised a hand. "They can stay," he repeated, "but you must come with me."

Not everyone in the crowd heard this. Some shouted against Contreras, while others were still being happy.

"If you do not," Contreras continued. "I will blast this settlement from orbit."

Nigmatullin knew her face was impassive. She was working hard to keep it that way. She hadn't thought it would be easy to stay. That was why she had prepared back-up plans of her own. And she would need those plans to finish her mission. She needed to get almost twenty people back here. She hoped that at least one of the xenos wanted to go home. It did seem like a good idea for Earth to have access to someone who had been on Elysia, not just get raw data dumped before preparing the next ship.

"You are not a monster, Captain," she said quietly, but her voice reached every person in the settlement. "Only a monster would do such a thing."

"And only you can stop it," he said. "All those deaths will be on your conscience."

"Don't do it, Polly," Amanda Brughel called out from somewhere. "He'd never do it."

Amanda was Jasper's sister. They had never discussed it, but Nigmatullin was sure she knew of Nigmatullin's deal with her brother. Perhaps this was her way of reminding Nigmatullin that she had given her word. Part of the deal with Contreras and Orlova was that Nigmatullin would take the fall, but those two weren't exactly living up to their end of it. And if they were, Contreras had done a very good job of acting as if he were against it. He would be fine without her. What the hell was all that talk of destroying the settlement?

Nigmatullin shook her head. "I can't risk it, Jammie," she said, using the old childhood name.

She turned to Contreras. "I'm coming with you. But I'll be on your tail until we're out of orbit. You won't be doing any 'blasting.'"

Contreras had had enough. Even if this was all an act, she had seen plenty of people get genuinely angry in role playing. He was there now. "You won't be on any one's tail, much less mine. You will be confined to your quarters."

"We'll talk," she said. "Right now, you are under my escort."

The whole crowd understood what was happening by now. People were hollering advice, most of it that she didn't need to go, that she should kill the bastard before he hurt someone, or that Contreras wouldn't carry out his threat. Someone even called out to her to take a shuttle back, and she groaned inwardly. The need to be helpful was a terrible, mindless impulse sometimes.

She held out her hand to Contreras. "Your weapon and your communicator, please."

He stared at her, disbelieving, but he had overplayed or revealed too much. Either way, she couldn't ignore it.

"You have just threatened to murder the people you have had under your protection for the last seven years. Hand them over. Sir."

She gestured to Salisbury, who came up and stood next to Contreras. The three of them walked back to the ground car.

The shuttles lifted in ten-minute intervals, and Nigmatullin rode to orbit aboard one of them.

Back on the *Aeneid*, Orlova was waiting, of course, and ensured that Nigmatullin was disarmed and confined to her quarters. Contreras was returned to his former dignity, and his affability suggested that perhaps it had all been a show, one that he felt strongly about, because he had had a live audience and didn't want to look a fool, but now that it was over, he showed all the signs of magnanimity. He even immediately started discussing how someone could be deceived by what were obviously false orders.

None of the returning security personnel were charged in light of their belief in the fraudulent orders with which Nigmatullin had deceived them and, perhaps, even been deceived herself. Contreras was not a sore winner.

Still, Nigmatullin whiled away her time accessing the security protocols for her door, which were—reasonably enough—denied to her, locating the quarters and labs of each of the xenobiologists in case she figured out how to escape her confinement, and otherwise engaged in focused but futile daydreaming that felt like planning. Her communications were all blocked. She packed a small "go bag," mostly with underclothes and toiletries. The *Aeneid* itself had been all but emptied of anything more useful to settlers than to the crew of a starship. There would be no more stops on the way back to Earth.

So it was that Nigmatullin lay in her quarters reading, with the book on the ceiling, wishing she was on the planet below with the wind blowing the scent of almost-roses toward her, when Contreras showed up.

She sat up and put her feet on the ground. It had been two days since her confinement, and her only visitor had been Zeke Salisbury who had stopped in to see if she needed any creature comforts.

Contreras's eyes were a little sad in his handsome face.

"We are out of range now, Polly," he said, after settling into the single chair available for a visitor. "I would like to let you out. We need you on the bridge to run your shift, but I need you to keep silent about the plan."

"I have already given my word," she pointed out. "I have no intention of making problems for you. I got to come, and that's enough for me."

The strong, mobile mouth curved, and she knew that he understood that she didn't mean that leaving now would ever be enough for her. "I hope that you may come back," he said. "If things are good on Earth, our knowledge will be very valuable."

"You truly don't believe they will be good on Earth," she said.

His face closed, as if he were looking inward to divine conditions on Earth. "No. Everyone was already forgetting about the rocks. There were points where the *Aeneid*'s mission was almost scrubbed.

So, no. All I know is that we don't know, and you agreed to be the contingency plan."

She took a deep breath. "It's true. I wouldn't have minded being let out of my agreement, but I did make it. Such is life." And she had contingency plans of her own. There was one shuttle and she had seen to its mods long ago.

Contreras said, "Your watch is in an hour."

This meant she had no time, and she had to round up the people to whom she had given her word immediately and in person. Electronic communications could be monitored, but she would start with Bill Cannon. If he was not the leader of the little group of xenobiologists, he was the most vocal and he was the one toward whom she felt the most guilt.

First, she checked their trajectory. Contreras had not lied. They were out of range for anyone wanting to get back to the *Aeneid*. However, even without the modifications, the shuttle could make it to the planet with reserves. She wondered if the *Aeneid* had left the settlers any shuttles.

The ship was an ungainly structure. Built in orbit, the bubble drive forcing the design, the *Aeneid* was neither aerodynamic nor streamlined, more of a football with lumps. The three uniform lumps contained the shuttle bays, and Bill's quarters were the farthest of the nine from the bay with the shuttle she wanted.

The artificial gravity allowed her a brisk stride that might have been a jog in a smaller woman, and she reached Bill's quarters in six minutes. He did not answer her knock, and she dared not palm his door for a mandatory response to a ship's senior officer. Her use of the system might alert the other captains—the real captains—to her intentions. His lab wasn't far, but she dithered over whether to head straight to it, or to stay and keep knocking. Bill had been angry, and might just be refusing her admittance on the supposition that she had come to try to beg forgiveness. The rooms did not contain private baths, so that could not be the cause of the delay.

She knocked again against the cold composite, swearing through tightly gritted teeth. She resisted the urge to set her forehead on the cool surface, which was just as well as the door finally slid open.

Bill stood there, his dark, kinked hair a black halo around his black face, his eyes still furious at her. "I'm the one who should be swearing at you."

She had no time for his emotions. "Do you want to get back to Elysia? We have a shot, and we can get the others."

"Aren't we too far?" he asked, but he was already putting on planetside boots, not the soft slippers they all wore aboard.

"Not yet, but it's getting close." She didn't want him thinking he had time to pause and think. Or tell her to go to hell. "Can you get the Stallyers? I'll get the others. We need to meet in the B Bay. Don't use your phone or any other ship communications."

Bill lifted a small rucksack from the floor. It was a samples bag, and stuffed full, the top folded over and sealed. "I'm ready. We're all ready."

She felt suddenly hollow. The xenos had shown more faith in her than she had felt so far. She could do this. She could get them all out, and they could all, herself included, get to stay and live on Elysia. Her eyes swam with water and she looked away. "Come on," she whispered, her voice too gruff.

He put a hand on her back and gave her a friendly push as she turned away and he let the door close behind him.

They shared a corridor for a minute before they split away from each other.

Because Nigmatullin needed to start the shuttle, she had assigned herself the married couple. Melissa and Robert were not in their quarters, but she found them in the small lab, and was unsurprised when they shouldered rucksacks that looked like Bill's. Two other xenos worked there as well, and had rucksacks of their own. They were optimistically wearing their boots, and their faith and their hope filled her with nothing but nervous dread.

There would be crew in the shuttle bay. She planned to offer to take any who wanted to come, but likely there would be a fight. She had no weapons, and no interest in using one.

She sent Melissa and Robert by a separate route to B Bay. There was no need for all of them to march along the corridors in a unit, particularly in the company of the failed and disgraced mutineer, "Captain" Nigmatullin.

She knew that bay like the back of her hand. She knew the alarm system, the hydraulics, and the fueling processes. She knew where all the cuts and corners were, and she knew how to work the doors. That was the most important part. That, and the fact that there was no time for pressure suits.

Shepherding her remaining charges, she managed to avoid the more travelled corridors. The ship had been the victim of out-of-the-box thinking when built, designed to avoid the unnecessary lines and horizons that the human mind had evolved under on Earth. If humanity was to become spacefaring, then so should its brains. That theory coupled with the fact that the ship did not need to resemble an oceangoing vessel meant that unmarked corridors twisted through three-dimensional honeycombs, whose only landmarks came from idiosyncratically painted doors and a good memory for numbers. It had made finding a planet an imperative for all aboard.

It also made reaching the B Bay a challenge, but one that would face any others trying to stop Nigmatullin and her party.

There were airlocks into the bay, and when Nigmatullin saw Bill Cannon and his small party stop at one of the doors, she gave him the nod, and he took his group in. The airlocks responded to anyone. Bay crew would greet both sets of visitors on the other sides of the doors.

Stepping into the airlock nearest her with her own group, her cuff told her that the pressurization for the bay was normal. It was what she wanted.

They cycled through with no more wait than was necessary for the interior doors to close, the tight seal thus demonstrating on a regular basis the doors' ability to withstand hard vacuum. The other doors slid open to a haughty woman on the other side. She was Tade Sides, and was usually indignant about something, not the best person to run into.

"Two groups?" she asked with a marked air of condescension.

She gave Nigmatullin the once over. "No offense, ma'am, but last I heard you were confined to quarters. For a reason."

Everyone knew what that reason was. "And now I'm not. Captain Contreras himself let me out, if you'd like to check." That had been almost forty minutes ago. If the woman didn't call, she would still have twenty minutes to get away.

The ship wasn't armed against aliens. It was armed against human marauders, since they had shown up once or twice in the new environment of the solar system. It was well armored against debris, micrometeoroids, and dust. They didn't have to worry about man made debris, but the human race had developed a keen sense of the perils posed by space rocks, and built accordingly. These people could shoot them down if they really wanted to. If military personnel were aboard, they might want to.

"Bill thinks he left something in *Merma*, Tade," Nigmatullin said casually, and tilted her head to the other little group. Miraculously, they weren't all holding their go bags front and center. Some must have had them strapped to their backs, for the rucksacks were invisible.

The woman looked at the two groups, and started to frown. She raised her cuff to her face as if she were about to make a call, and Nigmatullin grabbed her elbow and pulled her away. Nigmatullin was relieved to see Bill's group start moving toward *Merma*.

"Listen, Tade," she said, "I've got a problem here. Bill's really mad at me, about, you know, what happened down below. I'm trying to make it up to him by showing him around and letting his friends come, too."

"They're all carrying knapsacks," Tade said, as if Nigmatullin lacked the intelligence available to the nearest flatworm. "You don't think he's going to hit you upside the head and take off in one of those shuttles?"

This startled Nigmatullin, for it raised a question she had not considered. "Bill can fly one of those?"

Tade looked down her nose at the taller woman. "Or they're going to take you hostage and make you fly it." Tade also started strolling toward the *Merma*. She seemed casual, accepting of Nigmatullin's explanation, but as they passed the control room, she wheeled on the other woman and almost snarled at her. "Do you think I'm an idiot? You're planning to take the lot of them back to Elysia." Tade waved wildly at two crewmembers behind the glass wall. They got to their feet.

Nigmatullin sighed and waited for the other two, who were both large men. The taser she carried had two charges, but she doubted that anyone would hold still after she made her first shot. This was a very poorly executed escape attempt.

"We'll bring you with us," she said, loudly enough for the others to hear. This brought both Bill Cannon, who she wanted alerted, and the two men trotting over.

One of them, a man she didn't know well and who wasn't on her list, said, "I'll come." So she shot the other one first, and he fell in a spasm of twitching limbs and grunting noises.

Tade launched herself at Nigmatullin, and they both went down. Bill was telling everyone not to move or he'd shoot. "My weapon is real," he added.

This had no effect on Tade, who, taking advantage of the fact that Bill wouldn't want to shoot his pilot, rolled on top of Nigmatullin. Tade failed to get her arm bar, but settled for putting both hands on her senior officer's throat. With no compunction, Nigmatullin slammed the taser into the other woman's ribs and fired. Tade convulsed, and the charge didn't reach Nigmatullin, which it shouldn't have, but one could flinch legitimately when pulling that kind of stunt.

Nigmatullin threw Tade off and rolled to her feet.

The other member of the bay crew stood with his hands away from his side, fingers spread extra wide as if to show nothing between them. "I meant it," he said. "I want to come with you."

Nigmatullin stared at him for a long moment. His name was Ed Hempstead, and he had no family aboard. He was military, and he, like she, would be charged with desertion if caught, which would explain why he hadn't stayed behind in the first place.

"Let's not stick around here, Captain," Bill said, employing her false honorific for the first time.

She gestured Hempstead forward with her free hand. "We're

taking *Merma*," she said, pointing across the bay at the shuttle of choice. "Hempstead, grab Smitty. I'll take Sides." She couldn't leave them to be sucked into the vacuum when the lock opened, but neither was she going to leave them in the safety of the control room where they might waken and screw up her plans. "Let's move."

They crossed the distance at something that approximated a run, the scientists, although fit, were not all athletically inclined, and one or two stumbled on the perfectly smooth and even surface. Nigmatullin and Hempstead carried their burdens in the classic fireman's carry, and moved more slowly.

Robert opened *Merma*'s hatch, and started up the ladder, Melissa close on his heels.

Half the xenos were through the hatch by the time she and the crewman caught up with the others. They passed the unconscious bay personnel up ahead, so they could be strapped in while the others boarded.

Later, she realized she should have gone ahead, had someone else carry Sides, and started the checklist on the shuttle, run through the routines and prep the airlock commands. Most importantly, had she been first, she could have locked down the goddamn interior doors to the bay itself, which was the first and most critical part of the procedure. Seal the ship. You couldn't do anything else until you sealed the starship.

Bill was on the ladder just ahead of her and had tossed his rucksack through the hatch when she heard the tone that accompanied the opening of the interior door. That was when she first realized how badly she had gone wrong in just the simple matter of who should have been first into the shuttle.

Orlova's voice, the voice of the second captain, she who had visited Elysia only once in their time in orbit, sounded over the public address system and through Nigmatullin's cuff. "Stand down, Captain Nigmatullin. You and your friends will not be leaving this ship. The bay will not open."

Nigmatullin watched Bill Cannon's back freeze up. The sweat stains on the thin silky fabric where his rucksack had lain showed, and the sweat on his neck below the hairline was slick. His neck was fleshy, she realized. It was a strange thing to focus on.

She had several moments to do so, and to realize that she was frozen, as well, before he turned and looked down at her. Anger would have been better than what she saw in his eyes. She had raised hope in him and the others, and the death of that hope showed clearly in his face.

She had failed him, not once, but twice, and, in the end, been no good to any of them.

That was when Hempstead grabbed her in a chokehold from behind and dragged her back down, away from the hatch, away from the shuttle, and away from any chance of returning to Elysia. He was squeezing too hard, she thought. It didn't matter whether his desire to leave had been an act or this last minute sabotage was only to save himself a court martial, she didn't care. She did care that he didn't need to squeeze so hard. She kept thinking that as she struggled to tell him, and she kept thinking it as she blacked out.

CHAPTER 14

C ALVIN STARED AT HIS CLIENT. It had been very vivid, her story, despite the pauses and moments where she debated what she would tell him, how she would tell him, and whether she would tell him something or anything. Nigmatullin's face was very still, very calm. Even after each pause in her recounting of the tale, she had chosen to be free with her information and thoughts, and he wondered whether he was the first person with whom she had shared so much. It had a very unsatisfactory ending. He wished she had gotten the xenos and herself away, but then he would not have met her.

"Why are you not charged with attempted desertion? Or kidnapping?" he asked. He was her lawyer. He had to ask.

She gave him a look through hooded eyes, and the long horsetail swung like a cobra. "Contreras never entered it in the ship's records. No one said anything about Hempstead. The xenos are all civilians, and I think Contreras thought the mutiny charge was enough. Orlova didn't care, and she wasn't in charge any more than I was."

He wondered if there should be more. The tale he had just heard was so much more interesting than her first bland depiction of events around another star. He supposed he didn't need to know more if USACD didn't even know. "Will anyone else bring it up?" He was remembering the cast with Samuel Tidy, the xeno who had felt discriminated against.

"Not that I know of," she replied.

He let it be. He'd seen at least one man lie for her. "Do you think they're happy there? On Elysia?"

Nigmatullin stood. "Could I have some coffee? Or tea?"

Calvin shook himself. "Of course. I'm sorry. Which do you prefer?"

She picked tea, and he went to the dispenser down the hall for some Darjeeling. He returned with milk and sugar, and she spent a great deal of time fussing with everything. "I have always imagined they are."

He had almost forgotten his question, but he understood.

"I want to go back," she said. "I want you to win this thing for me."

He had started to guess as much, but it took a great weight off him. Having an indifferent client would not have been easy. "You have a very good chance," he said. He weighed his next words carefully. He thought of a question he wanted to ask, backed away from it, and took another tack. "Did you and Jasper write anything down?"

"About our agreement?" she asked.

"Yes," he said.

She took a sip of tea. "Certainly not."

"Do you remember it word for word?" He had to tread very carefully. It was important to do that when boxing in a teammate.

"No," she said, and she was wary now. She kept the tea cup raised to her mouth as if hiding behind it.

"What, generally, then, did you agree to?" he asked.

"That I would return. That I would never say Contreras or Orlova sanctioned the settlement. That I would not mention his involvement."

"Or anyone else's?"

"We didn't talk about that. I didn't know who else was involved. Why?" Nigmatullin put the cup down.

"You mentioned the perfection of the fake orders," Calvin said. "I'm sure you've thought about how they got so perfect."

"There seemed to be a number of options," she agreed, without actually sharing any of her thoughts on the matter.

"One of them is that they weren't fake," Calvin said.

She sighed, but the look she gave him was one of reluctance. "I was kind of hoping you wouldn't think of that. It seems to me that would violate my agreement to say nothing of Jasper's involvement."

"We don't know that right now," Calvin said. He realized he was leaning too far forward, perhaps too eagerly. At least his back was straight so he didn't look too much like a vulture circling. He settled back in his chair, casual and at ease. "For instance, you said Jasper gave them to you, but were they also programmed into the ship accessible only to you?"

This time, her look was one of distaste. "Are you suggesting that I lie?"

"No," he said, exasperated. "I am asking you a question. Were the orders also resident in the ship's system?"

She thought about it and answered slowly, the teacup forgotten in front of her. "Not that I know of."

"Could the ship have authenticated them because they were there, officially, from your military command?" Calvin felt it was a reasonable question.

"I never looked," Nigmatullin said. "I relied on the dime. Why would he have given them to me separately if they were there officially? What I've always thought more likely was that someone inside the military created them using all the proper coding. We weren't exactly updating our passwords once we turned the drive on. It wasn't as if we could communicate with Earth real-time, or even at all, after we left the system."

Calvin forced himself to relax back into his chair again. He just wasn't nonchalant enough sometimes. "And that person could have been commander of the joint chiefs or a petty officer with computer access and connections to Jasper and his kind. It would be nice," he mused, "to discover that they were real orders."

She picked up the teacup from his desk. "They weren't real orders, Calvin, and I knew it. Jasper Brughel was not in my chain of command."

She was likely correct, but he had started taking notes. He wanted all the options in front of him so that he could start checking them off. Fake, real from military hacker, real from rogue high command, real from high command with deniability, real secret orders that could protect his client, and what else? It really would be good to pursue the question of whether people couldn't quit USACD. He needed to research that in the Mars context. It was unlikely anyone had wanted to leave his source of air, for one thing, but it was more likely on Mars than the Moon. He looked up. Nigmatullin may have been talking, but he hadn't been listening.

"Tell me," he said, "do you feel that Jasper kept his end of the deal?"

"Sure," Nigmatullin said. "I got to go on the *Aeneid*."

"What if I told you that you had been selected but he got you put on the wait list so he could manipulate you?" Calvin asked idly.

That was a mistake. Nigmatullin was on her feet, her face stiff and her eyes filled with fury. "How do you know that?"

"I don't," Calvin said. He stood, too, so she wouldn't feel awkward. "I'm just thinking through the angles."

"You have a strange brain," she said, sitting back down.

Calvin sat, too, and said, "You read a lot of books. You should understand."

She gave him a guarded look from the corner of her eye, her face turned away. "Did I tell you that?"

"You told me a lot," Calvin said. "And it's all safe with me. Don't worry. I'm on your side."

"And you'd have me turn on Jasper." Her voice was disbelieving.

Calvin didn't care. Nigmatullin was his client. She was the one he owed zealous advocacy. "Only if you feel it doesn't violate your agreement. I wouldn't suggest that you do that if you had to break your word."

"Would that make me unsympathetic?" she said with deep sarcasm.

"It would make you human," Calvin said. "But I don't think you'd do it, so it's moot. I was just trying to see if Jasper had already broken the agreement. You might not think that mattered, but there I'd be happy to argue with you. You operated outside your orders once, so I could probably persuade you."

It was too much, and her face turned ashen. "There was nothing in the orders against it," she insisted. She stared at him for a long moment. Maybe she was realizing how much she cared, how much she had believed that what she'd done was right. She covered her face with her hands, wiping them across her cheeks and brows, and said, "I'm tired. Is this enough for today?"

"This has helped tremendously," Calvin said. "I have a lot of people to talk to, and I've been wanting to hear your version. Most of us tell our own stories best."

Sara knew that Calvin Tondini had never tried a complicated business case, or even one where there was more than one lawyer on his side. She watched as he marshaled two first year associates to start the interviews, and set another one to researching legal issues. It was nice, of course, that his client had all the money in the world, but he also showed no signs of seeking the assistance of Sara Seastrom.

She tried not to let it bother her. It was difficult, because she was having trouble remembering how annoyed she was about the SPInc hearing, and she was getting tired of waiting for him to come ask what was bothering her so that she could tell him. She certainly couldn't march into his office and explain how he terrible it was that he had used her witness to help her with her unrelated case and stolen the credit she didn't have the guts to go for herself. It would sound ridiculous. And, that, she told herself, was because it was ridiculous.

Partly this had all been brought home to her by the injustice of the ethics action against him. She had pulled the transcript of the SPInc hearing, and no one who didn't know what Calvin had been after would have thought he was doing anything untoward. He may have wasted a small amount of the court's time, but, fortunately, that wasn't an ethical obligation or lots of lawyers would be moldering in purgatory. There was a good defense, she thought wryly: the reasonable ignoramus. She smiled. If she ever used that line of reasoning, it might be better to speak of clean slates.

There was a knock at her door, and Calvin stood there with his very famous client, Paolina Nigmatullin, late of the U.S. Starship *Aeneid*.

This wasn't too terrible. She stood, and tried not to blush or stammer as introductions were made, and confined herself to being deeply honored, which was true. Nigmatullin herself was regal and slightly tragic. Nigmatullin did not blush.

Calvin explained that Sara had been working on a patent question to allow the real inventor of the bubble drive to build more ships, so they wouldn't all have to wait another lifetime before more settlers headed to Elysia.

This brought a sparkle to Nigmatullin's eyes, and Nigmatullin asked Sara to put in a good word for her with MarsCorp, because she wanted to be on the first ship back, as passenger or crew, she didn't care which.

Pleased, Sara assured her that she would. Then, Nigmatullin turned to Calvin and asked if Sara was working on her case.

Sara's breath stopped as she waited for the answer. She was sure Calvin had not intended to be placed in this position, and she was even more certain he was regretting his friendly impulse.

Nigmatullin was a good height for a woman, but Calvin was still half a head taller and intent on looking inscrutable. Sara realized with a start that their eyes were very similar, long and barbaric, although Nigmatullin's sported an upward tilt that Calvin's lacked.

Sara recognized that she didn't like the way he was looking at Nigmatullin. Just as she was about to open her mouth and take everyone off the hook, Calvin spoke up. "I've been hoping some of her time would free up. Sara would be a tremendous asset to the team." Calvin gave Sara one of the smiles he had given her before the hearing, the same smile as when he had called after the hearing to suggest dinner, but she couldn't tell if it was real.

"It would be an honor," she said to both of them.

Calvin stared at the phone for a long time. He didn't like he what he was about to do, but he'd sworn to himself after the SPInc hearing never to put himself again into a situation where he had reason to regret a lack of courage. So he wouldn't do it now, even if it had been Jasper who had taught him this lesson the hard way. If there was a small part of him that thought it wouldn't be the worst thing in the world for Jasper to suffer the results of his effort he told that part to be quiet.

He reached for his screen and then realized he needed coffee.

He went and got one from down the hall, put plenty of milk in it, poured it out because it was too cold, and made himself another that was more acceptable. He returned to his office.

He called Jasper Brughel and hoped very much that he wasn't available even while at the same time praying that he was there so he could get this over with.

Jasper's assistant answered, and asked Mr. Tondini if he could wait five minutes and Mr. Brughel would call him right back? The assistant knew how much Mr. Brughel wanted to be available for Mr. Tondini, but Mr. Brughel was tied up right now.

Calvin waited five minutes. He waited ten. His coffee cooled as he forgot he needed it, and he spent the time writing to various members of *Aeneid*'s crew to request interviews. He worried about the incident with the xenos. How would USACD not find out about that? All it would take was a little complaining, one comment too many, and USACD would know to add attempted desertion and kidnapping to the mutiny charge. Nigmatullin wasn't a civilian, and she was far too insouciant about the quagmire waiting for her on that front.

His mouth felt dry, and he wrote to Bill Cannon. He'd start with him.

Calvin no longer felt nervous about talking to Jasper, but found himself growing more and more stricken about all the things that Nigmatullin had done and described in such reasonable tones. Sure, they had all seemed to her like the right thing to do, hiding personnel, attempted theft of a shuttle, unauthorized modifications, attempted desertion, attempted kidnapping, aiding and abetting the desertion of others. The list went on.

He was sitting there, shocked and appalled, when Jasper finally came on. Jasper's office showed a window with a cloudy sky. His broad face smiled, and his eyes searched Calvin's face like they always did, as if he could read in advance what Calvin was about to say. Calvin didn't think Jasper could this time, not and look as interested and cheerful as he did.

Even Jasper's greeting was warm. "Good afternoon, Calvin. I hope things are going well."

This just made Calvin feel worse, and the more immediate effort caused his stomach to tighten. He could worry about his client's many offenses later. He'd planned his words carefully, but when he finally opened his mouth as Jasper's face took on a worried look, all he said was, "I need to talk to you."

"Of course." Jasper was on guard now, and his eyes kept up their searching.

This wasn't going to go smoothly, no matter what. Calvin ignored the eyes and, sitting straight, although not as straight as Nigmatullin, said, "My client is hampered by promises she made you long ago. It is making her defense difficult."

Brughel gave Calvin the look that said he was older and wiser than the lawyer and that Calvin didn't really need to worry about all of this. "I don't see why. The main thing is that it should be clear that the other two didn't condone the settlement."

Calvin felt a moment's irritation. The other two were dead. "She will never ask to be released from her promise to you." It struck him as odd that Nigmatullin set such great store by the one promise but not as much by whatever loyalty she felt to her service oath. Then he remembered her look of shock when he'd suggested that she'd operated outside of her orders. She hadn't thought of it that way. She'd thought it a matter of interpretation. And, despite her words to the contrary, maybe she shared Calvin's view that the orders could have been real, not faked.

Jasper Brughel looked thoughtful, but not as if he was reconsidering anything. "No." It was a simple word. "We had a deal. We still do."

"Across time and space both?" Calvin tone was dry.

Jasper smiled. "Indeed. It's not just me she protects."

"The other two are dead," Calvin said harshly.

The smile went away, and Jasper's screen went dark for an instant. When it came back, he was shaking his head. Calvin felt a pang. Had Jasper known the other two captains as well? "I'm sorry." He even meant it.

"They understood that their memories would be protected as well," Jasper said.

Jasper wasn't making it easy for him. Calvin had hoped that he wouldn't have to push too hard against this man he admired, but he had no choice. This wasn't even a matter of courage. It was his duty to his client. "Jasper, you know what I'm talking about."

Jasper was quiet.

Maybe he didn't want to give away one iota more than he had to, and if Calvin didn't know something he wasn't going to give it to him for free. Calvin, of course, had client confidences to protect and had no intention of sharing what happened on Elysia or in any shuttle bays with anyone else unless compelled to do so by force of law.

"I'm talking," Calvin said, "about the person who prepared her orders."

"What orders?" Jasper asked blandly.

"The ones you got her," Calvin said. "The ones she relied on to ensure the *Aeneid* left a settlement if they found someplace good."

"Calvin," Jasper said with some asperity, "I'm quite sure Polly wouldn't want you coming to me like this."

Calvin was getting mad. He knew he shouldn't, but the older man was trying to weasel out of this, and he didn't mean to let him. "My duty is to defend her. I want to know where the orders came from."

"I've made promises, too," Jasper said. He hunched his shoulders forward and got too close to his screen. Calvin could see the lines around his eyes clearly. He didn't look old. None of the older people looked old.

Calvin kept his voice level. "I don't want to send you a subpoena, Jasper. I respect you a lot and admire many things you did, but my client needs this information."

"Aren't I your client, too?" Jasper asked in such a way that Calvin knew he knew the answer and was just trying to see what he could get away with.

Calvin had just one client, and he knew who it was. "No. You are not." Struck by inspiration he continued. "I know you care about such things, Jasper, and Polly is doing a great job with making Elysia attractive to the public. It will do your cause good for her actions to be legal."

Jasper raised a brow. "And if they're not?"

Then things were more grim. "We'll need to know that, too. So we can bargain with full information."

Whether it was the thought of Nigmatullin in her role as Elysia's spokesperson or because he didn't want to receive a subpoena, Jasper let out a sigh. If Jasper weren't so studiously inscrutable, Calvin might have said Jasper looked angry. "There's someone I know who maybe can help you. His name is Ray Hillman."

Polly stared into the wood fire in her fireplace. The wood was a profligate gesture, but it reminded her of Elysia, and she was clearly determined to wax melodramatic about her loss. The flames showed mostly red and orange, and those were highly adequate colors and more than sufficed. Occasionally, something on the wood caused a streak of green or blue, iridescent like a molten opal, to shoot through the flame.

The wine she drank was red, and it glinted more secretively. She sat alone in a club chair in her new house.

She had not enjoyed being taken back to her final days on Elysia by one so much her junior. And a brutal junior at that. She still did not see the point to his observation about her split loyalties.

She tried very hard to remember what Jasper told her when he gave her the dime with the manufactured orders. Had he hinted in any way as to their origins? Had he stressed their authenticity with a wink and a nod? Had he let slip a name that she had let slip from her own mind in her joy at the message that she had been selected? It had been ten years, and it was so very hard to say. For the people on Earth it had been more than three times that amount of time. The math of it was beyond her.

She looked around the living room of her new home. A picture window framed cold darkness outside. Inside, there was room enough for two oversized couches and a rug with a grid pattern like the phased array of a solar panel. End tables made setting a drink down easy, and she marveled at not only the comfort but the happiness of it all looking so pretty, with the stripes and the glazes on the cloth. Her salary had accumulated, and her parents had husbanded it well. She was a rich woman with a house of her own.

And she could lose it all here on Earth, never mind whether she would ever return to Elysia.

They said trials were slow. She could ask Calvin to file a lot of motions to delay things. Lawyers did that. She was sure of it. Perhaps she could escape on the next ship out. Might Mars take her while she waited for another interstellar berth? Two in one lifetime? That seemed greedy.

Her lawyer had a lot of people to talk to. Maybe he would leave her alone for a while.

She sat upright suddenly. Carefully, she set the wine down. Had she told him to leave Jasper alone? You didn't make a deal with someone and then sic your lawyer on them. She was sure that getting Jasper to testify violated her own agreement with the man. And, it would do her no good.

She reached for her little palm, and tried to figure who to contact first, Jasper or Calvin. She could warn Jasper. She could instruct Calvin. There was something about lawyers having a duty of zealous advocacy. She really needed to contain that.

Calvin was probably at home, but she didn't care. Lawyers were on call at odd hours. She had read that somewhere, too. She reached Calvin on voice-only, and asked about Jasper.

On learning the subject of her call, Calvin assured her she need not worry. He had already talked to Jasper.

Nigmatullin stared out into the dark. She hadn't meant that to happen. "What did he say?" she whispered.

"He wouldn't tell me much of anything," Calvin said. "He seldom does."

"That's Jasper." It was strangely disquieting and comforting both that Calvin knew Jasper. There were connections between her old life and her new one. Her lawyer knew her childhood friend. It also made her nervous, but the worst had happened already, and she was selfishly glad of it.

She ended the call. She received another within minutes and took it with voice and vision when she saw who it was. She needed to face the music.

Greetings took place, but Jasper got to the point immediately. "Your lawyer threatened to subpoena my records from over thirty years ago."

Polly felt cold. She should have thought of instructing Calvin sooner. "I'm sorry, Jasper. I didn't mean him to."

"We each protect another person in the chain," Jasper said.

She felt terrible. "I'm sorry. I didn't think about it until he'd already done it."

Jasper's image looked stern. "I had to give him a name."

"You did?" Her eyebrows rose. So much for protecting the next person in the chain. "Who?"

When he didn't answer she gave him her best piercing, command look. She'd never used it on Jasper, but if Calvin could know then so could she.

Jasper understood her look. If it had been anyone but Jasper he would have frowned, but she knew he was irritated.

Jasper took a breath. "The man's name is Ray Hillman. I want you to instruct Calvin not to talk to him. You're his client and he will listen to you."

She felt a moment's excitement. Did this mean that Hillman was someone who could save her? Or was he the one who prepared the clever fake? If the latter, she didn't want Calvin to find him, but that would be wrong. A sense of fatalism crept over her. Let the chips fall where they may, she decided. She wanted to know all the answers, and she wanted to keep her freedom if she could. Her choice of a lawyer with limited experience had been her attempt to keep her promise, but he was proving more dogged than she'd expected. Perhaps that was a good sign.

Jasper couldn't see her raise her hands, so she raised her shoulders instead. "I'll think about it, Jasper. Good night." She thought about it briefly, and did not contact her lawyer.

Calvin was in early the next morning. He liked the solitude. Sometimes he saw Sara Seastrom sharing his hours, but he made sure to give her no cause for concern that he was pursuing her. The last thing anyone needed was someone in whom one had no interest blatantly pining at the office. When he let himself think about it, it was awkward, and he hoped she hadn't minded Nigmatullin's suggestion that she work on the matter with him. She was officially assigned to it, but he had tried not to bother her.

Before he got to the more interesting matter, he reviewed the subpoena he had drafted the day before. He needed the *Aeneid*'s records because he wanted to see if the starship's records contained official orders for Nigmatullin's eyes only. Different factions within the Pentagon had displayed different levels of nerve. Calvin knew the request might highlight that the orders didn't exist, but that wasn't going to pass Ryle by and it was what everyone thought anyway.

He hadn't wanted to get Nigmatullin too optimistic, so he thought he would check out what Jasper had told him first. Maybe from her perspective she had committed mutiny and lied to a whole lot of people in the course of it. The military personnel who obeyed her orders had believed they were real, and they would not suffer for their role. But Nigmatullin would.

He reached Ray Hillman, who was not shy about chatting by vid with a stranger. Ray was burnished by lots of sunshine, as if he had come back from an island vacation, and had startling blue eyes and jet black hair. He was no longer with the military, and, from what Calvin had gleaned, well into a second career in the produce sector. He had risen high in the military and looked to have done the same in the private sector. He was some sort of vice president for distribution.

That gentleman was unwilling to meet with him once he understood that Calvin represented Paolina Nigmatullin. He had the sense, at least, not to complain about Jasper outing him. Maybe they would have words later.

"Sir," Calvin said, "I can obtain records that will show all your contacts with Jasper Brughel in great detail. Don't you think it would be better if you told me your version of events than let me tell others what I gather from old records?"

"We didn't converse by phone," Ray said.

Calvin kept quiet, and allowed the other man to hear what he had admitted to.

Ray understood. "Come by. Come by this afternoon. I may or may not tell you anything. I may have called my lawyer. I may not. We'll see." With this ambiguous response, he closed the line.

Calvin felt a little predatory. It was not unpleasant. His first thought was that, perversely, for this individual, Hillman would have been better off if he had been some secret conniver in one of Jasper's plots. Calvin would have then had no interest in Hillman testifying at Nigmatullin's hearing. If, however, Mr. Hillman had been acting under orders, and handing Jasper the dime had been to protect someone higher up, it might turn out that Nigmatullin was carrying out perfectly legitimate policy that had not been shared with the general public.

"What are you so pleased about?" Sara said from his open door.

He had been grinning, but he let it fade. She was still entirely appropriate for the office, especially in winter clothes, which included a wool jacket that went up to her neck and sleeves all the way down to her wrists. Not a single stripe showed, and the only skin that was bare was on her hands and face. But the jacket and the pants hugged her very close, and her golden eyes were strangely luminous.

He might have to quit, he thought. He didn't know if a starship captain facing a court martial constituted portable business, but he might just have to quit, and then he wouldn't have to look at this woman every day.

"Polly talked a lot yesterday," he said, finally able to speak again himself. "I have something interesting to follow up on."

Sara looked down at her hands and laced her fingers together. "I know the Captain put you on the spot yesterday," she said, and looked back up. "But I really would love to help you on this case. As more than just the babysitter. I would like to work with you. On Nigmatullin's defense." She looked back down at her hands and extricated them from each other.

She had a good brain. He knew that. She had good follow-through. She was a good lawyer. But he might start pining.

Some of this must have been reflected on his face, for she mashed her fingers back together and said, "Of course, if you have enough help I perfectly understand. I was just hoping… That is, it seems very interesting."

What he wanted to do was ask her if she wouldn't find it awkward as hell, and what was she thinking, and, most importantly, had she changed her mind about dinner? But if he did any of that, it would be awkward as hell, and then she might never change her mind, and there would certainly be no dinner. So, instead, he said, "Great. I think we're going to find out more about Jasper Brughel's plots. And, you probably have some background that might help."

She sat down quickly, as if afraid he would change his mind.

He couldn't tell her Nigmatullin's entire story, and he knew he couldn't tell it as well, so he confined himself to the purported orders, and how he had wondered how it was they had been authenticated. Popular fiction notwithstanding, military security was actually very good. "But what I am wondering," Calvin went on, "was why, if this fellow Hillman was high up in the Pentagon, it wasn't a perfectly legitimate set of orders."

"But then why hand it off to Jasper Brughel?" Sara wondered.

"Yes," Calvin said, "but it is odd, and I have to look into it. The *Aeneid* went out several years after the asteroid scare was over. Maybe everyone was feeling less desperate, and there were questions about whether this was for science or for settlement."

"Was the mission statement unclear?" Sara asked. She crossed her legs. They were covered in wool. They were not interesting.

He kept his eyes fixed on her face. "Yes. Exactly. The work was underway. The public interest in it waned, but there was a lot of money being spent, and we know Baldur had a lot of influence at the time—"

"—still does—" Sara interjected.

"—and would have wanted to avoid controversy. So, if there was anyone against settlement plans, someone might have had no interest in billing the mission as one with that kind of goal."

"And the same would go for USACD," Sara said.

"Exactly," said Calvin. "But, I don't understand why anyone would be against settlement."

"People are," Sara said. She put her hands flat on his desk. "Even now. And, knowing there's someplace good to go seems to make them more adamant. They worry about Elysia being contaminated by us. They worry about Earth being contaminated, too. Look at how upset some people got about the corn."

"And the internationalists are still embarrassed there are so many Americans on Mars," Calvin said. "Which is ridiculous, because Mars is plenty big, and anyone else can go, too. The Chinese are doing just fine, in fact."

He might almost have called the look she gave him one of liking. "Calvin," she laughed, "you and I are not the ones to figure this out. We both think it's the best thing ever, and cannot fathom that mindset. I think we just have to take it as a given."

"Fair enough," he said. "So, maybe there was someone in the government who gave the orders, and used Jasper for deniability, and Nigmatullin did what she was supposed to."

"Or," she said, "Jasper got someone to do something he wants, because he's good at that." For some reason, she stopped and stared at him significantly, but then went on. "And this poor Hillman used his codes to create orders because he could, but he shouldn't've."

"There's that," Calvin said. "But that's not the optimistic scenario. You should come with me this afternoon."

CHAPTER 15

RAY HILLMAN'S HOUSE WAS IN Ashburn, Virginia, a long, flat ride away from the District. The house was set well back from the residential street, and appeared to command at least two acres. It was a mansion from another age, and it made Calvin wonder whether the man would have any incentive to risk all that he had achieved for a decision made decades ago, if not in his youth, at least in a different frame of mind.

The drive was lined with oak trees, and there looked to be stables in the back. Calvin was glad Sara had come along, purely so that his own presence in the face of this display would seem larger by sheer numbers.

Ray Hillman, U.S. Air Force (ret.), had been a two-star general officer. The Pentagon was apparently full of such people, so Calvin worked at not being too impressed. The former military officer greeted them at the door, his eyes no less startling in the afternoon sunshine than they had been on screen. He did not have a lawyer present.

They withdrew to a small sunroom that looked out over a paddock with two horses clad in blankets. The animals were grazing, but stopped as a woman with a couple of halters tucked under one arm walked out to them. "That's my daughter," their host said. "She comes out to ride from time to time."

Sara took a seat by the window, and the two men took the couch, which was situated so the house's owner had a full view of the paddock across from it.

Calvin turned his attention to Ray Hillman. He could not

imagine amassing such wealth himself. The house and its environs were not so far out of town that it wasn't exceptional.

"Thank you for seeing us, Ray," Calvin said, having been granted permission to use first names. "I'm hoping you can shed some light on certain orders Captain Paolina Nigmatullin received regarding facilitating a settlement on an acceptable planet."

Ray's answer came wearily, as if it had been a lot of work to dig it out and find it. "Those were not real orders. I had them prepared, and they had my name on them with all the right codes, but I did them on my own."

That was not what Calvin had hoped to hear.

"Did you have the authority to do that?" Sara asked. "You had a lot of authority in your former position." She said it as a statement of fact, but there was enough admiring subtext that Ray might have preened just a little.

"I don't know that anyone had the authority to do that," Ray said. "There were a lot of people saying no one had the authority to do that. The Outer Space Treaty forbade national appropriation. This was a government mission."

Calvin had to control his desire to argue the Outer Space Treaty. This man's legal opinion or lack thereof was not why the lawyers were seeing him. So he didn't ask about the settlements on the Moon and Mars and what the Outer Space Treaty said about them.

"Were you present at discussions about settlement?" Calvin asked. He didn't want to get to questions about Jasper at the outset. It was sometimes better to get all the innocuous facts straight first. They seemed less threatening, less in need of being spun, but capable of boxing someone in nonetheless.

The answer came slowly. "Yes," Ray said. "But they never resolved anything. No one made any decisions."

"What were your own views?" Sara asked.

"I favored it," Ray said. "I was not alone."

Calvin couldn't help stealing a look at Sara, and she shared it. Ray snorted at the two of them. "Don't get all excited. The debates were endless. We couldn't decide what to recommend."

"What did the military want to do?" Calvin asked.

Ray turned from watching his daughter. "We wanted a base," he said, as if that were an answer anyone should expect, as if it were entirely reasonable for the military to want a presence so impossibly far from home that it would serve no useful military purpose. "A base, not a settlement."

"If you say so," Calvin said, and the other man smiled.

"Do you remember the names of others who were at the meetings?"

"Sure," said Ray. "I can get you those." He rattled off four names right away, none of which Calvin recognized, but it wasn't as if Calvin had gone through school immersed in asteroid history. To the contrary, he would have liked it better if his parents had not attempted to impress upon him the horror of the time, the long years of waiting convinced that doom was headed their way, the sense of utter hopelessness. It was not interesting when the parents talked about it. It was interesting now only because of Elysia.

"Were there civilians at these meetings?" Calvin asked.

Ray looked back out at the paddock.

"Can you get me those names, too?" Calvin asked. It might be time to weaponize the Freedom of Information Act, but he wondered whether that would alert USACD to his line of inquiry. It might not pan out as he wished.

Ray nodded, his eyes on the paddock. It was empty now.

"How did Jasper know to reach out to you?" Calvin asked.

"I don't know," Ray said. "Everyone knew what everyone else thought. It wasn't surprising that he knew about me. That he had the nerve to do it was what was surprising."

"He seems to know how to get what he wants," Sara said from her perch to one side of the window. "How did he persuade you?"

Calvin wasn't sure she hadn't rushed this part of the questioning, but it came out very naturally, he had to grant her that.

Ray's smile was rueful. "It wasn't hard to persuade me back then. The military wanted a base, but I knew I wanted settlement. You have to understand, it all seemed very unlikely. We knew there were planets with water out there, but we really didn't think there would be anything that was easily habitable, so those of us who wanted settlement felt a little like that was a fairy tale. We didn't feel like we were asking for the paradise we got. We felt like we were asking for something difficult, the Sahara or the Arctic or Arizona. Elysia, Elysia is an embarrassment of riches. In retrospect, I feel greedy for having wanted settlement. What I, and other people like me wanted, was a toehold somewhere else. And Mars was two fingernails sliding down a wall back then, not what it is now. And the Moon?" He shrugged. "The Moon still needs Earth."

"And Jasper?" Calvin prompted.

"Jasper talked to me a lot," Ray said. "I don't know how he got past the gatekeepers. He had nothing to do with the military and was a young man. I would have no reason to speak to him in the ordinary course of things. But he got on my schedule. When I first heard him out, I said no. We were in my office, and when you're sitting there listening to someone ask you to do something so wrong, it's just automatic to say no.

"But I started thinking about it," Ray continued. "I felt guilty of cowardice. I had these strong views, and I knew the government would never pronounce settlement as a mission objective. It was too hard. It would unsettle our friends. The lawyers would scream about the treaties. If I thought the people who couldn't stand up to that were cowards, what did that make me?"

Sara sat with a very straight back, her lower lip compressed. Calvin couldn't figure why she looked upset.

"I drafted settlement orders," Ray said. "I thought I was being clever. I took them to meetings, and argued for them. I can't tell you how much the civilian side of the government leaks. It's a sieve. People write things that shouldn't leave their building, but if they give it to one other person, it's gone. You'd see stuff on the casts, on the Hill, in the hands of lobbyists. We weren't as bad. There's more discipline in the military. But it happened with us, too, sometimes. I would say later I had no idea how it got out and used this way."

"Why are you telling us now?" Calvin asked. It had been a clever plan. Ray appeared to be tossing it aside to no advantage now.

"My daughter has three children," Ray said. "They all have children. One of the great-granddaughters is nineteen, and she wants to go to Elysia."

They stared at him. Ray was one of Jasper's people, Calvin thought. He wondered how many general officers had ignored Jasper before he found this man. Or, whether Jasper had found this one early in his process.

Still, Calvin couldn't allow himself to be led off track. "I have been told there were real orders," he said.

Ray shook his head with a slight smile. "That is a question you will have to ask someone else. I cannot help you there."

Sara stirred, and looked oblivious to this bit of bad news, focusing instead on what Ray had been able to share. "But are you saying…?"

The older man gave her a nod. "You may use my name. I would be very proud." He smiled and stood, the interview over. "Those orders have my name on them. You can argue they were real. You can call me as a witness. I will say I made the call."

Sara and Calvin stood, too. "That might not work, sir. I don't want to give you legal advice, but you would be the one on the hook instead of Captain Nigmatullin."

"I am not a famous man," Ray said, "but I have always had a good reputation. I am happy to help lend my name in support now. Causes need allies."

Calvin put his vehicle on auto. "Let's see if he really has a nineteen year old great-granddaughter," he said.

Sara felt her jaw drop. "I believed him," she said.

"I want to," Calvin said. "I liked him even. But what if he was the one who ordered the shootings when the captains came down? What if Nigmatullin was the target, and the killers missed?"

Sarah felt a little silly. "I fell for him completely," she said. "How did you know he was lying?"

"I don't," Calvin said. The road had taken the vehicle off his hands, and he had a full screen in front of him. His search terms revolved around Ray Hillman of Ashburn, Virginia, and his family. "I do want to check him."

She turned from the screen so she could stare out the window at the chilly landscape. It had been very comforting to think they had found an ally, a respectable person who was on their side and wanted to help Nigmatullin. She had been impressed by his courage. She was more impressed by courage now than she used to be. Courage sometimes had consequences. Nigmatullin was on trial. She suspected that Calvin had been told he wouldn't get tenure. She more than suspected she should feel bad about her reaction to what Calvin had done at the hearing, saving her firm's patent case at the risk of his own career. She knew he knew what he was risking, and, now, the ethics charges brought home how very much it had been. She wondered why he hadn't had the wits to go to a different firm. Maybe he had had no other options, and no Lucy Gunko pulling for him elsewhere. One didn't get a panorama of choices for every decision in life.

"Will you look at that," Calvin exclaimed. "He does have a nineteen year old great-granddaughter. She's not too bad, either." He peered intently at the very attractive young woman with olive skin, a cascade of black hair, and bright blue eyes.

She must have moved or made a sound, for she saw him smother a grin, and give her a look, his own eyes bright and laughing. "I was thinking we could introduce her to Tri." He wrinkled his nose. "She's a little young for me."

"I'm glad," Sara said, and then quickly, "that Ray wasn't lying to us." In acknowledgement of her need to learn a little more cynicism, she added, "At least not about the great-granddaughter."

"You're catching on," Calvin said.

She let her head fall back against the head rest, and said drily, "Oh, I'm learning lots of things. In one sense, that man's courage may not have been so brave at the time. But now, decades later, he's willing to honor something he might wish to forget. And, he could easily have told us it was all a mistake. Like he planned."

Calvin snorted. "Not all mitigation measures work. He's making the best of it."

Sarah wasn't done. She continued relentlessly, resolved not to spare herself. "Some people try to mitigate, and it backfires. Someone else might look at what another person did and see how it affected her and ignore the fact that the first person was being brave."

He looked at her quizzically at first, as if unsure what she was talking about. "Every now and then I appreciate the benefits of my legal education," Calvin said. "Although I did follow what you just said I didn't understand you."

"I was very upset with you," she blurted out, "for fixing my problem with Brewer in the SPInc hearing. He would eventually have had to talk, and I felt like you took all that away from me. But, with the legislation pending and MarsCorp rushing its announcement, the timing was good. You did the right thing."

Calvin was very still, and the low hum of the vehicle was very audible. "You were mad at me? About the hearing?"

"Yes," she said. "That's what I'm trying to say." She was wishing she hadn't, but she was all in now.

"I'm not very smart," he said. His voice had a strange tone to it, almost a tightness. "I didn't get that."

"I didn't get what you did," she replied. "I didn't get what it cost you."

"I wasn't worrying about that," Calvin said.

"But you knew," Sara said. "And you did it anyway."

Calvin laughed. "It would have been better if I'd done it sooner, at the deposition when it wasn't so public. It took me a while to work up the nerve."

"I'm sorry," Sara said.

"It's okay," Calvin said. "I should have figured."

"But you would have done it anyway," she pointed out.

"Yes," he said. "I would have."

That was daunting. As least she knew it wasn't a bad sign about the past. She wondered if he might ask her out again. She wondered if she should ask him. She started to feel lighter. It was good to have these things out in the open. It was as if a tightness she hadn't even known was there had left her.

"It's too bad we didn't get this all cleared up sooner," Calvin said. "It's kind of too late now." The strain in his voice was perfectly clear now, as if he struggled to control some other emotion, maybe annoyance, maybe real anger.

She sat upright, the safety restraints cutting into her. The tightness was back, located specifically in her chest. "Why is that?"

The usual hidden smile was missing from his eyes. "We work together now. What if we were to get involved and it turned out I have other foibles? This has all been very awkward. Think of how excruciating it would get if I annoyed you again."

"Calvin," Sara said, "you are just saying that to punish me." She was glad her voice came out even and low, but the sinking sensation in her stomach told her she was faking it.

"Is it working?" he asked. His voice was very low, too, and he was looking straight at her. She supposed he didn't have any more certainty about her than she did him. She told herself that she had committed to this approach. He wasn't the only one with a modicum of courage.

"Yes," she said. "It is."

"Good." They reached the end of the highway, and Calvin took the car back. Neither said much after that, and neither said anything about what Sara's information meant.

Ray waited until the two attorneys left. He wandered over to the picture window and stared out at the empty paddock.

He had not spoken with Jasper Brughel in years, decades to be precise. He worried that he wanted to reach out now only because he needed a safety valve on all the old feelings that had come rushing back with the *Aeneid*'s return, the deaths of the two commanders, and his great-granddaughter's ardent longing for a new world. It was a mix, and the conflicts battling inside him left him highly unsettled.

When he had left the Pentagon he had left behind everything associated with that time. Unlike many of his colleagues he had not entered the aerospace or weapons manufacturing sectors. He enjoyed his role as a greengrocer, worrying about produce and perishability and profit.

Talking to Jasper could make that all change. He didn't want to talk to the other two. That one meeting with Sam and Tessa had been enough, and he had walked away from it feeling strangely flat, missing the sense of camaraderie. Tessa and Sam had been so helpful those decades back. Their shared goals had tied them together so tightly, but thirty years and more changed people. They grew into new passions and loyalties, new concerns.

He thought of his granddaughter again, and called Jasper Brughel. Jasper didn't change. Events since last June had made that obvious.

Jasper had time to talk. At the close of the call, Ray said, "My great-granddaughter wants to go to Elysia. What I'm about to do, I'm doing for her."

Jasper was watching him closely. "Am I understanding you correctly?"

"Oh, yes," Ray said. "You are. I'm sorry if there are repercussions for you."

Jasper's shoulders were large and well padded. They looked like they could carry a lot. He gave his placid grin. "Not something for you to worry about. You were one of the ones I was supposed to protect."

This struck Ray as strange in light of the fact that Jasper had given Ray's name to Nigmatullin's defense attorney. Ray smiled. "You haven't changed, Jasper. One other thing—she is my confidante."

Jasper searched Ray's face, as if trying to understand the significance of what the other man had just said. "Be careful, Ray. You're putting yourself out there, and we've done a terrible job of protecting our own."

Ray understood. There were four dead, two starship commanders and two navigators. He had no intention of adding his own life to the count, but nor did he mean to waste it.

CHAPTER 16

I T WAS ALL VERY WELL to have a cause, Calvin reflected, while watching the latest interview with Nigmatullin that evening over his solitary dinner, but people could have more consideration for their attorney.

USACD had declared the corn a fraud, which, the agency pointed out, should occasion great relief amongst those who ate it. To the contrary, those who had eaten it had promptly put up their own personal casts and declared that it had been delicious but not of Earth origins. The subtle difference was hard to capture in words, but several people who worked at a police station in Maryland announced that they were planning a crop and would share with those gourmands who had contacted them directly and offered large sums of money for a dozen ears from the first harvest.

USACD had countered that such harvests were forbidden, in case the agency was wrong. This led to prompt increases in the price of a dozen ears of Elysian corn—which had yet to be planted, it being January, much less harvested.

The talk show host started with the corn. Nigmatullin had not gone back to Heather's show, but had found someone else along the Kensington corridor, a person who went by the cast name of Vail Stone. Vail Stone was a large individual, maybe two and a half meters tall, and his voice suited the large tuba that was his body.

He, too, believed in comfortable chairs, but his were a lot larger. Nigmatullin, who was no hobbit herself, looked vaguely diminutive in hers.

"Captain Nigmatullin," Vail said, "now that you've just heard the dramatic reading of the press release from USACD, do you have a response?"

The show's lighting gave Nigmatullin's eyes an extra devil tilt, but her laughter was clear like a bell. "It kind of makes the safety case, doesn't it? If it's alien but identical there's no need to worry."

"So you're sticking to your version of events?" Vail boomed.

"I was there," Nigmatullin said. "I know what I saw, and I know what I ate. Unless we secretly hauled a huge load of corn with us, somebody planted it on Elysia, and told us all of it was native,...." She trailed off and looked thoughtful. "Could have happened."

But she wasn't done. "Don't forget the xenobiologists at MIT. They don't agree with USACD that we brought back Earth corn. The expressed genes are the same, but the junk DNA isn't. Who are you going to believe? The xenos at MIT or scientists taking money from a government with an agenda?"

The large personality across from her produced a smile wide enough to swallow her whole. "'A government with an agenda?' Those are fighting words, Captain."

She looked disdainful. "It's very obvious that one part of the government doesn't want more people to go, that it wants to have tight control of the process. Saying the food there isn't safe—despite all evidence to the contrary—is as good a way as any for stopping people."

"But why?" Vail asked plaintively. "Why would our government want to stop us?"

Nigmatullin shrugged expressively. "I don't understand it myself." Then she turned to Vail, setting one arm on the chair arm and crossing one leg over the other in that way guests on a cast had done since time immemorial. "It's pressure, Vail. Lots of people view humanity as a blight. Others want us to spend money on Earth."

Vail was breathless. "And what do you say to them?"

She looked out seriously at the audience and straight at the camera. "I'm no blight. And I don't think any of you are either." The studio audience cheered. Calvin heard at least two boos. "As for spending the money on Earth, I have two answers. First, that's where it gets spent when you build starships, and, second, if it's private money they get to do what they want with it. I don't go telling people they can't spend their money on a trip to Canada."

Finally, the moment her lawyer had been dreading arrived, and she was asked about the mutiny. Demurely casting her eyes down, she told her large interlocutor that she had a very bossy lawyer and really couldn't talk about that. Vail understood. He had encountered the phenomenon before.

Next Vail asked her about the man she had left behind, the one who reputedly broke her heart. She laughed that off and said that story, apocryphal though it was, should be a lesson to everyone not to make life decisions in the throes of a break up. Really.

Next, Vail's guest from Earth First appeared. Although the courts had once again thrown out the most recent iteration of the fairness doctrine, which required all stations to present countering points of view unless one of the myriad of exceptions applied, Vail's producers liked the controversy and a very sober Aaron Ryder, president of Earth First, a 501(c)(3) not-for-profit organization dedicated to tending to Earth's problems before expanding outside the solar system, arrived to explain the drawbacks of humanity going interstellar on a scale to support settlement. Science would be lost, the environments of Elysia changed and damaged, and the United States would lose its chance to live a more frugal and ascetic existence.

"But," pressed the show's host, extending one large but impeccably tailored arm, "is there anything in particular that bothers you about what the *Aeneid* did?"

As a matter of fact there was, and Ryder, a sober alabaster with golden hair, blue eyes to die for, and the look of someone who'd stepped off a sarcophagus and would start to glow immediately if not sooner, nodded. "The rabbits."

There was a titter from the crowd.

Calvin wanted to turn the show off, but stared entranced. The rabbits came up frequently. Half of Oz found them hilarious. The other half did not.

"I'm guessing you thought that was a mistake?" Stone asked.

This managed to rile Ryder. He turned the face of an avenging angel straight toward the camera. "It was worse than mistake. It was a crime against science and against all of us."

Stone turned to Nigmatullin. "Did you know about the rabbits, Captain?"

Nigmatullin looked bored, and allowed the overly large chair arm to prop her up. "Not really, Vail. I knew there were animals aboard, but the rabbits were news to me." She perked up. "They were awfully cute."

Ryder didn't let her get away with that. "You should have had them taken off planet. We all know what happened in Australia. They overran a continent, destroyed ecosystems. But, Vail," he went on earnestly. "It's more than just the rabbits. The rabbits are only a symptom of how slipshod the *Aeneid*'s approach was. It destroyed the chance to study an absolutely pure alien environment. Just look at the history of our own planet. As soon as humans show up, we change the environment."

A small smile played on Nigmatullin's lips. "Life changes things. It always has and always will. We went out to find a world we could live on. We didn't want all our eggs in one basket."

Science wasn't why the *Aeneid* had gone, Calvin thought. Why couldn't she say just that?

Irritated at both of them, Calvin turned off the show and turned his attention to his dinner, but that just resulted in thinking about Sarah, and he decided to close that train of thought off, too. He had meant merely to needle her earlier, when he had commented on her foibles. But in retrospect there was a lot of truth to what he'd said. He needed to keep that in mind.

In the morning, he got the news about Ray Hillman. Sara messaged him, and sent him to a channel with Ashburn coverage. The man was dead, shot in his house.

Calvin swore. The man certainly seemed credible now, and Calvin wondered if he could find out with whom Ray had spoken after he and Sara had visited.

The Ashburn police told him they were in the middle of an investigation and unable to help him.

"I represent Captain Paolina Nigmatullin, and the victim was helping us with her case," he told the officer.

"I don't care," the woman said, "who you represent. I am not handing out that information to anyone. Did you say you saw him yesterday?"

"Yes, my colleague and I asked him some questions."

"We'll need to talk to both of you," the officer said. "Could you stop by this morning?"

This was not a result Calvin had intended when he made the phone call, but it was reasonably foreseeable, and he didn't see how he could say no. Attorney-client privilege wouldn't apply to everything he'd seen while he was there. "I can come in. I'll check with my colleague."

He stared at the blank screen a moment before writing Sara back and explaining what had happened. There was no point in going into the office and then leaving immediately for Ashburn, so he arranged to pick her up on the Metro's Silver Line.

In the meantime, the police's lack of interest in sharing raised a delicate question for Calvin. He had always despised the ghoulish casters who descended on a family after a tragedy, but, aside from the opportunity to plaster their grief all over the public disc, they were the first and best source of information. He started looking up their addresses. He had banked a lot of information the day before, when looking for the great-granddaughter.

It was cold but sunny by the time he and Sara reached the police station. They had no more apologies, discussions, or episodes of needling in the car. Mostly, they agreed on the need for scrupulously sticking to the facts, not disclosing privileged information obtained from Nigmatullin, and not speculating. Sara brought up the issue that had occurred to both of them: would they be considered suspects?

Calvin planned to record his session. He hoped to gain information as much as to share it. Sara agreed she would do the same.

The police separated them and took their statements. Calvin's officer was perfunctory, and mostly asked leading questions from what was obviously a script.

Sara faced her inquisitor across a small table. There were no windows, and the space was utilitarian to the point of excess. There were not only no windows, but no pictures, lamps or shelves. It did not put her at ease.

"What were you doing there?" the officer asked.

"We were there on behalf of a client to ask some questions," Sara said.

"About what?" Officer Delaney was smaller and brindled. His parents had spent their money wrong, she thought irrelevantly, as one who was also the recipient of designed skin. It had really been a horrible fad, she always thought, the patterning of one's children.

"The topic is protected by attorney-client privilege," she said.

"This is a murder investigation." Delaney kept his elbows on the table and his hands folded. He had no nervous tics, and he kept his eyes on her face the whole time. Perhaps he practiced his technique in front of a mirror.

"And I am happy to answer factual questions," she said. It was different being on the other side of the questions.

So she got some factual questions about whom she was with, who she saw, and whether the deceased had discussed his plans for later that day.

Then he tried again. "Was the topic of your conversation something that could have upset him?"

Sara had to think about that one. "It didn't seem to," she finally said.

"Well, that's helpful," the police officer said.

"Maybe you should ask your questions in a different way," she snapped.

He pulled back, and his eyes narrowed. He looked as if he were about to get angry, but then, to the extent she could read him through his brindling, he grew thoughtful. "What did he talk about?"

She replied promptly. She owed him that much. "He talked about his work at the Pentagon, his daughter, and his great-granddaughter."

"The daughter who was at the stables?" the man asked. When

she nodded, "And tell me what he told you about his work at the Pentagon."

"He said he had been in favor of the *Aeneid* leaving a settlement behind if the starship found a good planet. He said he drafted orders to that effect, and that he signed them." Perhaps the police would find something that she and Calvin needed to know.

"Did he mention a Tessa Donohue or Samuel Heller?" He was watching her closely now, she could tell that much.

Sara ran through the people Ray had rattled off the day before. She didn't want to check the notes she had jotted down after the meeting for fear of them being appropriated. "Both of them," she said, realizing they were people from Ray's meetings.

"What did he say about them?"

"Why do you want to know?" she asked, knowing full well he shouldn't tell her, but deciding it was worth a shot.

"I'm asking the questions," the policeman said. "Not you."

She tried a grin. That sort of thing seemed to work for Calvin. "I need information, too." She had so much information, as it was. Ray must have called these two people after she and Calvin left.

To her surprise, he looked flustered, and then annoyed. "Don't try that stuff on me. Now, what did he say about them?"

"They were in meetings with him on the settlement question." She was careful not to try another smile. She didn't want to set him off again.

"Anything else about either of them?"

"No," Sara said.

The officer stood. "Thank you for coming in. If you think of anything else, please contact me." He touched his palm, and passed her his card on a shortcast. "Or, if you—" He stopped and scowled again. "Thanks."

Sara was careful not to dance to Calvin's vehicle.

Her glee was short-lived. "You told him all of that?" Calvin said. "Do you always crack under pressure?" His left hand gripped the top of the steering wheel, and his right flexed against the auto-control bar, as if he wished it were her neck.

"He wasn't our client," she said curtly. "Aren't you paying

attention? I'm sure we now know who he contacted after we left. It was probably both of those people. Let's get back to the office. I'll look them up on the way."

Calvin wasn't sure but that he preferred it when Sara was abashed and apologetic. He could see the sweater unraveling before his eyes because she had told the police about the meeting. He knew that Jasper Brughel could look after himself and had been doing so for a very long time. If Jasper didn't have some sort of back-up plan to avoid being implicated in anything affirmatively illegal, Calvin would have been very surprised. Jasper had, after all, given Calvin Ray Hillman's name and contact information. He might have done so under threat of a subpoena, but the former Pentagon official had been immediately helpful. Ray Hillman had not been a wild goose chase.

On reflection, and after perusal of the ethical rules of the Great State of Virginia and the District of Columbia, he had to admit that she hadn't committed any breach. Calvin might have done the same had his interrogator been less wedded to routine questions. As it was, regardless of who made it public, Ray Hillman's story was likely to see daylight. Calvin wrote to Tessa Donohue and Samuel Heller, asking for an interview with each of them. They had probably already retained counsel if they were suspects in a murder investigation. But, if they were innocent and had alibis and the police had no further interest in them, perhaps they would talk.

Bart Locke, who was apparently not posting about the Fourth Amendment at the moment, found Calvin when they were both getting coffee in the break room. "I hear you saw the police today," he said.

"Yes, we had just interviewed the man who was killed," Calvin said.

"Sara told me about it. We like to know that sort of thing around here," he said pointedly, slipping a packet of raspberry hazelnut espresso in the machine.

"Sure," Calvin agreed. He had his cup. He was ready to get back to his desk. "Makes sense. I'm glad Sara told you."

"We like to know in advance," Bart said. "I might have come with you." The espresso appeared, redolent of raspberry. Bart added sugar.

"Sure," Calvin said again. "I will plan on that next time." He escaped back to his desk.

Tessa Donohue could meet with him the following afternoon. Samuel Heller had not yet replied. Tessa Donohue, Calvin was pleased to see, had been an aide in the White House when the *Aeneid* was commissioned. Now she was a senator. He walked down to Sara's office. She was working on something for MarsCorp it looked like.

"I think I've got something interesting. It may be a link to the orders' legitimacy. Tessa Donohue was in the White House. Maybe she was the one who told Ray to sneak the orders to Nigmatullin somehow." He sat down, uninvited. "And, maybe, he was protecting her from us and called her after we left to warn her, and she killed him to stop him from coming forward."

"Because," Sara continued, "no matter how much you don't plan to reveal someone else's role in something, once the facts start coming out, it all unravels."

He didn't think he was too excited. "The only problem with this great theory is that she's willing to talk to us, so she probably has a great alibi for yesterday."

"Or," Sara said, "the police haven't contacted her yet, and she's trying to act innocent by talking to us, and the police will be very, very angry that we are using their information."

"That could happen," he agreed. They grinned at each other.

"You outed me to Bart," he said.

"Don't worry," Sara said. "It's procedure. I took care of it."

CHAPTER 17

I T OCCURRED TO CALVIN THAT there might be safety issues. Someone had arranged for the deaths of two, perhaps three, people at Canaveral Port, and two navigators. Someone had arranged for Ray Hillman's death. It might be the same person. That person might not like what Calvin had found out. He wondered why this had not occurred to him sooner, before he contacted Tessa Donohue. If their speculation was correct, she was one of two people Ray Hillman had contacted after they left.

He decided not to bring Sara with him to meet with her.

When he walked down to her office and mentioned all this, Sara was annoyed. "I do not need to be protected."

His brain, he decided, was not working properly. He should have seen the possible dangers before contacting the politician. He should have foreseen Sara's reaction before providing his reasons. He could have come up with something truthful as an alternative explanation. "I understand," he said, and resorted to what had to be a trump card. "This is, however, my case, and I don't plan to bring you. Or mention you."

"She's probably not the one," Sara said. "If there is one. She's probably willing to talk to you because the police aren't interested in her because she has an alibi. It stands to reason." She wore a pale burgundy suit. The wine color matched her mouth.

Fortunately, his palm told him he had a call from Sean. "I have to take this," Calvin said, exiting her office as gracefully as he could. "It's opposing counsel."

Sara had been opposing counsel once. It had almost been easier. Then the rules were very clear.

"Sean," Calvin said happily. "What can I do for you?" He reached the safety of his own office and shut the door.

Calvin was coming off the basketball court when he saw Zeke Salisbury on the sidelines, clearly waiting for him. It wasn't strange, given that he allowed his locator to talk to people he met through work. It was a little strange, however, in that people he met through work didn't usually hunt him down in a gym at ten o'clock at night.

Calvin and Sean had a regular pick-up game, and Sean had specifically called to make sure Calvin was playing that evening so that they could talk afterwards about something. In light of Sean's new role as the right hand of Satan, Calvin wasn't sure he wanted Sean or Zeke seeing each other or even being aware of each other's existence.

"Howdy," Calvin said, going for affability.

Zeke grinned, amused. "Howdy back at you. I live up Wisconsin Avenue and saw you were nearby in what's supposed to be a church. I thought we could talk."

Calvin waved a hand around the large room, with its uncomfortable bleachers and disappearing ceiling that was something like a cathedral, although not really. It certainly didn't smell of incense and myrrh. "This is a holy place in my book, but I can see how others might look at it differently. I'm supposed to be talking to another person tonight, but I'm happy to talk to you, too." He picked up his towel and wiped his forehead, hairline and the back of his neck.

"Got a date?" Zeke asked.

"No," Calvin said. He was soaked, and took off his shirt, looked for and found the dry one in his bag and put it on. "Unfortunately, no. Friend from school. We have business together."

Sean strolled over, and Calvin made the introductions. Sean also changed his shirt.

Zeke had his coat off and tucked under an elbow, his hands in his pocket. "Where do you work?" Zeke asked Sean.

"I'm at USACD," Sean said.

Zeke looked from Sean to Calvin and back again. "Washington's a small town?"

Calvin sighed. "Sean and I have known each other for years. He's now opposite me on Captain Nigmatullin's trial."

"First time you've come up against each other?" Zeke asked.

"Since law school," Sean said. "And that was just moot court."

"You guys have rules about this?" Zeke said, more as a hopeful statement than a question.

"Absolutely," Calvin said. "We don't share client confidences. Also, we both need desperately to beat each other, so the incentives are about what you'd expect."

Satisfied, Zeke nodded.

Sean was eyeing him suspiciously. "Where do you work?"

"Nowhere right now," Zeke said. "I just spend my very large accumulated pay. I was on Elysia, but I thought I'd look around before making any commitments."

"I'd think you could go anywhere," Sean said.

"Makes it very hard to choose," Zeke replied. He stepped back, surveyed the ceiling, the floor, the baskets, the collection of men coming off the court. "How often do you all play? Ever take new folk?"

It was clear Zeke wouldn't be sticking around to chat in front of Sean. "Check with Loi over there," Calvin said. "He runs the game."

"Beer?" he said to Sean when Zeke had left.

The bar was crowded and sulfurous. It was popular with those who indulged in games after work, and few put on make-up or worked very hard to look good. It was a younger crowd and mostly male, but that made it easy.

Tonight Calvin noticed what looked to be a woman's team. They were all tall enough to have played in college, maybe, and he had just started an elaborate mental explanation of why they were all there, when he had never seen them before, when Sean came back to their table with a pitcher.

Calvin put aside musings over women basketball players and

poured the ale. "Who was that guy?" Sean asked. "How do you know him?"

Calvin shrugged. "We met at work. " He wasn't inclined to elaborate. When he and Sean had both worked for the government, even if at different agencies, they had discussed work, with some measure of caution, but had at least felt free to get into the internal politics of their agencies and their relationships with colleagues, especially if there was any complaining to be done. That was no longer either appropriate or a good idea.

Sean did not pursue the matter of Zeke further. Instead, he said, "This has nothing to do with your starship captain, but I wanted to give you a word of warning. Ryle's behind the ethics charge."

"I'm not surprised," Calvin said. "He wasn't happy with me after the hearing. I do hold it against him that I did nothing wrong and he knows it."

The table was on the small side, and a little low. They had to huddle, and it added to the general atmosphere of collusion. Sean kept his voice low. "He's going around telling everyone that it stands to reason that you did what you did because you had an interest in the firm you're at now, the firm that benefited from what you got Brewer to say. As your friend, I assure everyone you're just mildly crazy."

"As your friend, I thank you," Calvin said, toasting the other man. They drank.

"What else?" Calvin asked. Everything Sean had just said was in the formal complaint.

"He says he has proof," Sean said. "I don't know what, but it's what he's saying."

"Well, that's a lie," Calvin said.

"I know," Sean assured him, "but the ethics board won't. You need to work on this. I just wanted you to know that. You can't just go in there and be charming."

Swearing, Calvin sat back. Old sweat fell out of his hair and down his neck. He did not throw the stein at the wall. "He needs to get a life. Maybe a different one. He can't spend the second half of this one validating every stupid call he made in the first half."

They both stared at the pitcher, Calvin brooding and Sean obviously worrying.

After a long moment of this, Sean abandoned the worrying and went for evil. "How's the golden girl?"

"Don't ask," Calvin said. "Just don't ask."

Calvin usually drove to work, but a walk to the Bethesda Metro from his house took him by a grill where you could go in and quickly be served a couple of eggs, maybe some bacon, and always some very good coffee. He went in once or twice a week, and with it being three blocks from his destination, and him wondering why the hell he had chosen to walk in such an artic hell, he stopped in the morning after his game.

He wanted something hot, and ordered oatmeal because they told him it was ready. He was pouring maple syrup over it and was on his second cup of coffee when someone sat down across from him. It was Zeke Salisbury again.

"This is very flattering," said Calvin, "but a little unnerving, too. If I'd known about your stalking habits, I might have changed your access."

Zeke was freshly shaved, and casually but impeccably dressed. Maybe he had hired someone to bring him up to speed on current tastes. "Is that any way to speak to a prospective client? And a rich one?"

"You aren't coming in to the office," Calvin pointed out. The oatmeal was really hot, and he covered his mouth to breathe out. He wondered if he had burned his tongue. "It doesn't make you seem like unto a client."

"Speaking of clients," Zeke said, "I'm concerned about the Captain." He ordered something from the table without waiting for a human. "Are you aware there are now five dead people?"

Calvin crossed his arms. He didn't care if it was a defensive posture. "I am aware," he said. "Why and how are you? And, who do you count as the fifth death?"

"Until I get a real job, I'll continue with my old one," Zeke said.

"Which is protecting the Captain. I know some people. Orlova and Contreras are the first deaths, there are two dead navigators, one of whom was my friend, and the fifth is Ray Hillman."

Calvin had to admit he was impressed. He didn't want to, but he had to, although not necessarily out loud. "I'm sorry about your friend. Why do you count Ray Hillman with the others?"

Zeke's coffee arrived and he added milk. The coffee turned very pale. "Because you do."

Was Zeke's thirty-year-old mil-tech somehow eavesdropping on everything Calvin did? That was guaranteed illegal. "Go on," he said. Maybe the guy would confess and Calvin could get a restraining order. Maybe he'd just rat Zeke out to Nigmatullin. That was the ticket. "I'm sure your old captain would be impressed by your tactics."

"I'm not sure she'd like to hear you called her old."

"Former," Calvin corrected himself. "Former captain is what I meant."

"Fine. I haven't been spying on you," Zeke said, blithely ignoring two recent interceptions at the gym and grill to the contrary. "I got this from the Maryland police. They're big fans of the Captain. They know I'm like a bodyguard. I've visited them a couple of times. The one who used to be a biologist, McAfee, is now a corn expert. He says biology was never very interesting to him, not his real passion. He preferred the human brain, but now, well, alien corn."

"Sure," said Calvin. "What's a human brain in comparison to an ear of corn? So what did he tell you?"

"He called me late yesterday. Apparently, you and some other person were among the last to see Ray Hillman alive."

"Who was the other?" Calvin asked. Maryland and Virginia did speak to each other, he noted idly.

"The murderer, of course," Zeke said.

"You've been tracking me to tell me this?" Calvin inquired mildly. He had to remind himself that this man had stepped foot on another planet, breathed alien air, was brave beyond all imagining, and deserved his respect. "What do you want from me?"

"I think we need to team up," Zeke said. "Hillman called two people, the senator, Tess Donohue, and a guy named Sam Heller."

Calvin wondered if he should be feeling a warning sign. A shiver or a shudder might have sufficed. He felt nothing. "You want to join my pick-up game?"

Zeke frowned. "Sometimes you need to be serious, man."

"I am working very hard at not feeling stalked. That's taking up most of my energy. What have you got?"

Zeke's very pale, almost white skin, reddened. "Do you understand the danger your client is in? Someone is killing the people who know how to get back to Elysia."

Calvin understood that better now, but he said, "Isn't it all in the ship's computers?"

"Sure, but how many people understand what it means? There are, I don't know, they call them 'shoals,' that the one fellow kept us out of. We almost learned the hard way what some of the signals meant. The ship's autonomous to some degree, but it still needs human intelligence. Human decisions. Know what I mean?"

Calvin did not. That was why he was a lawyer.

"And, the Captain," Zeke continued, "the Captain understood a lot of it, my friend said."

"That's not something you should tell people, it sounds like." Calvin paid the table and stood. "I'm taking the Metro today. It's just a few blocks away. You've got that far to share your proposal."

The outside air reached all the parts of Calvin that he had foolishly left exposed.

CHAPTER 18

SOMETIMES IT WAS THE BREATH. Regardless of the geneering, the rejuvenation and the diet, there were tells. Sometimes it was the eyes, but always there was something that provided the sign of great age. None of the old called it that, but people of Calvin's generation called it great age.

Tessa Donohue was one of the rare exceptions. Had he not already known that the senator from Massachusetts had lived through the diversion of the asteroids, he would have taken her for a contemporary. Her hair was thick and strong as wire, her olive skin soft, not burnished, and all her parts were pleasing to the eye and, doubtless, to the touch. He was more amazed by her evident youth than by the fact that he was meeting with a U.S. Senator for the first time in his life. He knew well enough that it was knowing the identity of his client that had persuaded her staff to grant him thirty minutes, and not his own persona, limited as it was.

She took his hand, and, sure enough, hers was warm and sweet. He felt all beguiled, and wondered if she practiced black magic. It was all very well for the old to look perfectly young on video. It was something else to convey it in person.

Her office was smaller than his own. From his passage through the rabbit warren that was her staff's quarters he surmised that walls had been moved to make room for her personnel. Staffing was clearly more important than space.

Seated across from each other over her desk, they measured each other. Calvin told himself to pay attention. Sara had wanted to come, and, perhaps, he should have let her. She would not have been so distracted by the neckline.

"I am sorry for your loss," Calvin said. "I understand Ray Hillman was an old friend."

The senator bit her lip. "We went back a long way. I was very sad at the news about him."

He wanted to ask her when she saw him last, but he wasn't the police and he had other information he needed more. Perhaps at the end he would have time to indulge his curiosity on that front. And, although he and Sara had both been given the information by separate sources, he was quite sure no one should have shared it. He needed to let her know that he knew of the linkage between her and Hillman without alluding to the dead man's call.

He took a deep breath and began. "I represent Captain Paolina Nigmatullin."

"In USACD's action against her?"

He nodded. "Yes, and it is our view that she operated under orders." He could leave it at that. It might be true. He hoped to prove it, even without Ray Hillman's testimony. "It is our understanding that you participated in much of the decision making at the time of the *Aeneid's* departure."

"Who told you that?" Her very full lower lip had the smallest of pouts in it.

He almost blurted out an answer. Instead, despite the lack of pout in his own lower lip, he tilted his head and said, "I'm afraid that information is privileged."

Tessa leaned forward. "Who is we?"

Calvin blinked. "My firm. It's a figure of speech." Surely, she had heard it before.

She leaned forward even farther, and Calvin pulled his eyes up to her face. "Are you working this case solo? It seems like a very important matter for just one person."

"Senator," Calvin said manfully, "I don't want to bore you with my own affairs. I gather you were an aide in the White House at the time?"

She gave up and leaned back, and the blouse returned to more sober folds. "I was. I had quite a large portfolio, and the *Aeneid* was one of the things I was supposed to keep up with." She was better at this than Calvin, and left unspoken the implication that she hadn't devoted herself to the *Aeneid*.

He did not let himself be sidetracked into what it was she spent more time on. "Were you in meetings about it?"

Her eyes did not narrow even imperceptibly. "I was."

"Do you remember any discussions of the *Aeneid* leaving a settlement behind?"

Her fresh, open face lit up. "You can't imagine. It was constant. Should we or shouldn't we? What about the science lost? What about the future of the human race? What about having a back up? What about the fact that we didn't need a back up anymore with the asteroids so infrequent and so controllable?"

"Do you remember who was at these meetings?" Calvin could not pin point why he felt uneasy. She was being entirely forthcoming.

"Everyone," Tessa Donohue assured him. "Ray Hillman and I were there, but there were always about twenty people, at the very least."

"Was the president ever there?"

She smiled benignly at him. "It doesn't work that way. It wasn't at his level, this question. We couldn't even agree on how to frame it up for him, and I think the people who wanted a settlement didn't want to be told not to do it by someone they'd have to listen to."

"Who told you that?"

"It was so long ago, Calvin, I really couldn't say. One comes away with impressions. It was well over thirty years ago. I'm pleased I remember that much."

Calvin set his jaw. "Did you ever discuss it outside of White House meetings?"

She dimpled. "Counselor, I think that would be telling."

"I'm here to listen."

She interlaced her fingers and set her chin in them. "I've been thinking," she said. "I think I would like to meet your client. A close associate of mine is having a fundraiser for me this Saturday, and I would like to invite the two of you to attend."

With a wave of her finger she conjured a holo of what looked to be a list of names. "May I count you in?"

"Will you be able to answer my questions?" Calvin responded. He knew he didn't need to mention serving her with a subpoena. Someone in her eighties or nineties should know of such things. He was getting angry. A man this woman had known—long ago, true, but she had known him—was dead, and she was acting cute. Two of the expedition's senior leaders were also dead, and there was still no news as to who was to blame for such a publicly staged event. If the authorities couldn't find who had killed Contreras and Orlova, how likely were they find the killers of the dead navigators? He needed to make sure that one of the people who knew these "shoals" on the route back to Elysia was free to go. And, this woman was acting as if Nigmatullin was a performing bear to be trotted out at the senator's pleasure. But, because the senator was a senator, Calvin kept his mouth shut, and had to be content with the one question he had allowed himself.

"I'll be able to tell you that after I speak to the Captain," she said. "I'm so looking forward to meeting her again. We met at the spaceport, you must know."

Her subpoena needed to be ready right after her party, Calvin told himself.

CHAPTER 19

SARA WASN'T SURE HOW SHE had been invited to a fundraiser for Senator Donohue. She had asked Calvin if he knew, and he had scowled and said something under his breath about people being clever but creepy. There may also have been something about people not knowing when to stay out of the way, but she figured he couldn't have meant her, and ignored it.

So it was that she stood on the top floor of a building overlooking the Potomac River and Virginia across the way. Had the Whitehurst Freeway not intervened just outside the window, the view would have been stunning. As it was, the wide expanse of windows across from the foyer just barely skimmed a guardrail above a low wall designed to keep the traffic safely moving on the freeway. Her own offices being farther east, she didn't see Georgetown's commuter traffic on weekdays, but on a Saturday, most headed into town along the riverside of the freeway, away from the building. Given the building's location at the bottom of Georgetown on K Street, Sara knew it for an expensive piece of real estate. The condominium itself looked over the freeway, not under it, after all.

The owner of the condominium was someone named Spike, a man well known in Washington for his ability to bundle donations for politicians, who were then all over grateful to him for his perspicacity and knowledge of the officially permissible forms of bribery. Having a middleman made the First Amendment work better, Sara told herself sardonically. He appeared to own the whole floor of the building.

The firm had been happy that she and Calvin had both been invited, and made clear, without ever saying so, that, of course, they had to go, and, of course the firm could not reimburse them the price of admission. She did come away from the conversation, however, with the distinct impression, although, again, no one said it, that any bonus she got for this calendar year would at least be as much as what it cost to attend Spike's soiree.

She had not asked Calvin if he wished to go with her, and he had issued no similar invitation to her.

She looked around the room. Unlike the events her roommate sometimes persuaded her to attend, the music was not loud. One likely needed the ability to connive and strategize.

Several of the women wore fur, possibly faux, but likely not.

She wished she had insisted that Calvin tell her more about his meeting with Tessa Donohue than that it was unsuccessful but likely pointless to worry about that woman. Sara had tried for more information, but he had withdrawn into a reserve she was reluctant initially to assail. When she had tried to trap him in his office later, he had claimed he needed to make a call, and she had given up. He had recommended that she decline the invitation, but she had felt that she had to go. In Washington, there were people one did not snub.

Looking around, she regretted her failure with Calvin.

Finally catching sight of him, she regretted it more. He was talking to a woman who could only be described as stunning. She wore a business suit so well tailored it looked like evening wear, despite the herringbone. Calvin leaned in to listen to what she had to say, and then looked to be introducing the woman to Paolina Nigmatullin. Sara checked her palm quickly, and, after it synced to the house, it told her that the woman was Senator Donohue. Calvin's smile was very big, and he looked tremendously pleased, as if having this woman preen at him delighted him no end.

He was worth being preened at. He looked to be wearing a new suit himself, and it was tailored to fit. She looked away from the big shoulders, the tapering waist and long legs, and found herself meeting the eyes of a dark haired man. He was pale and his eyes glittered. She looked quickly away, unsure, but with the feeling that she had seen him before.

Another man walked toward her more deliberately. He was blond, sun-kissed, and tall, with long, loose limbs and an easy gait. He introduced himself as Sam Heller, and she felt a moment's pang. He was one of the people Ray Hillman had called before someone had killed him. Why had he approached her?

"I hear," Sam said, "that you were one of the last people to see my old friend Ray. That was terrible news."

"I'm sorry for your loss," Sara said automatically. She looked at him inquiringly.

"The police came to talk to me," he said.

"They told you about me?" she asked, and immediately regretted it. He might have fabricated something more interesting if only she'd kept her mouth shut. He didn't look like a murderer, but she had to admit that she didn't know any murderers to have a clue as to what they looked like. They either had to be evil, and their madness shone from their eyes, or so clever and cold that they could act their way through any situation, defeat any polygraph, and otherwise fool people such as Sara, whose natural tendency was to believe everyone was good. She was learning, on an intellectual level, to get over that.

He nodded absently, his eyes more intent on searching her face. "May I ask what you spoke about?"

Now she swallowed. She no longer worried about him as a matter of simple logic. Her hind brain was trying to give her a big kick. She couldn't imagine why he would care what she and Calvin had discussed with Ray Hillman, but what if he did, and Ray had called this man and the senator to tell them of it? If she lied he would know. If he cared, and didn't know, and Ray had called him for an unrelated reason, she might cause this man to take an unhealthy interest in herself.

"I'm sorry," Sara said, "but may I ask your relationship to Ray?"

"I told you," Sam said, and his face was closed, and his eyes stopped searching hers, "we are old friends. We were colleagues once."

"Where do you work now?" she asked.

"I'm at Baldur," Sam said. "But I was with the government when Ray and I knew each other. Ms. Seastrom, my friend was murdered."

"I know," she said flatly, and stared at him.

She felt a presence at her elbow, and turned to see the dark-haired man who had been staring at her earlier. "Zeke Salisbury," he said, and stuck out a hand to shake. "Of the *Aeneid*. I'm here with Captain Nigmatullin." That probably got him far in most circumstances. Introductions, which Sara suspected were redundant, were made, and she learned that Zeke knew Calvin. She was grateful he had shown up. Sam Heller unnerved her.

"It sounds like you're all talking about the same thing everyone else is," Zeke said.

Sam started. "Everyone else is? Why?"

Zeke smiled, and it was not a nice smile. "Why does that upset you?"

Sam looked disgusted. "He was a friend." He walked away.

Sara breathed out. "Thank you," she said. "I don't know why, but he was making me uncomfortable." She shot a glance over to Calvin, who was still looking pleased with his companions and surroundings.

She turned to Zeke and hoped that her face showed none of what she had just felt.

He was saying that he and Calvin had a common interest.

"What is that?" she asked.

"We are both trying to protect the Captain," Zeke said.

She shifted her position just a little, and was able to watch Calvin and the two women talking. Their figures were bright and clear against the evening sky outside the large windows. There might have been some pretense that the fundraiser was a social affair, but it was early enough that one could meet with one's real friends after the event. She could see lights across the river.

"From what?" she said absently, and made the mistake of turning her attention back to Zeke.

He was grinning, and she felt herself grow hot. The blush would show on her golden skin. It always did.

She scowled at him. "Calvin hasn't told me about this joint protection."

"Would he?"

"I'm working with him on Captain Nigmatullin's case," Sara said.

He lost the grin and looked serious again. "As I told your

colleague, I am worried about her physical safety. I think there are opportunities to share information."

She sipped her drink. "I think you'll have to get that from our client. Our communications with her are protected by a privilege."

"But not your communications with others," Zeke said. "I speak to the Captain already. I am interested, for example, in what you learned from Ray Hillman."

Polly had met many politicians, but it was long ago, before the *Aeneid* set out on its journey, and she had been the most junior in the command structure, always part of a crowd, and never the focus of just one individual politician.

Senator Donohue was a charmer, and Polly enjoyed the woman's sincere admiration and constant questions about Elysia. Her enthusiasm was clearly genuine, and Polly found herself relaxing for the first time at one of these events. She was not so foolish as to disdain them, although she would have been much happier alone at home with a book, but she knew that support and goodwill never hurt someone up on charges. She had seen that more than once.

Her lawyer seemed relaxed, almost boyish, as if he were able to enjoy himself and not always be on guard, ready at a moment's notice to save her from handing out ears of corn.

"You know, Polly," the senator said, laying a hand on Polly's arm. "This settlement sounds so wonderful, but I would love to hear how you left. I've watched many interviews with you, and you never seem to talk about that. Everyone is dying to hear more."

Polly wanted to tell her. Instead, she tilted her chin toward Calvin. "Ask him. That's one thing he won't let me talk about. He doesn't want me pruning myself."

"Impeaching," Calvin said automatically. It worked every time, but then she always used a different fruit.

"Seriously," Polly went on. "I would love to, but I'm not supposed to have all sorts of random statements out in public with which USACD can make it seem like I'm contradicting myself." She raised her brows at Calvin, and he nodded approvingly. She could pay attention, if not always listen.

"I'm not the public," the senator said.

"Well," Calvin began, in the way that meant he was about to make a legal point no one cared about.

"I know," Polly said hastily, before Calvin could explain how Donohue was the public, "but someone might want to depose you to see what I told you."

Calvin looked hurt.

Tessa Donohue, who was draped in the most stylish of herringbone suits, all nipped waists and mandarin collar, looked dreamy. "I have an idea about you, Captain," she said confidingly.

Polly Nigmatullin, who sometimes felt awkward around more petite women and was only wearing a tunic and slim pants and short boots, suddenly felt just as elegant as the darker woman. No wonder the woman got elected and re-elected so many times. Were politicians really just a sub-species of the super charming? "What is your idea?" she asked.

"I want to grant you immunity," Tessa Donohue said. "I want you to testify to my committee and tell your story to the world. It's an important one, and I was around when the *Aeneid* left. I know you weren't forbidden to leave a colony."

"That's not—" Polly began, but Calvin bumped into her and her drink slopped in her hand. She had forgotten he was there, so mesmerized had she been by the other woman's offer. She understood her attorney's reluctance to let her talk, but she felt safe saying, "What does that involve?"

"I'm not sure," Tessa said. "I just got the idea, and I would have to check with my counsel as to how it would work. I just think you should be able to tell your story wholly and truthfully without fear of suffering for it. The world needs to know, and you know how lawyers make you watch everything you say."

She turned to Calvin. "No offense."

Polly's lawyer inclined his handsome head. He lacked the perfect features she saw in so many of his cohort, but in another age he could have looked good on the side of a coin. "None taken."

Donohue laid soft fingers on Polly's arm. "Let's talk to our lawyers, shall we? I'll be in touch." And she slid smoothly away.

Calvin was used to people trying to get Nigmatullin to talk about the circumstances of the *Aeneid's* departure. It was normal to be curious. An offer of immunity from prosecution was a different matter, and it coming from Congress was not something he knew much about. In the general way of things, it was not in the public interest to have Congress indulge in circus shows at the expense of the wheels of justice, however slowly they might grind.

His client had no such reservations. "Calvin, let's do it. I can make the case. I can make Congress want to fund another ship. I got through the settlement, I can handle a few politicians."

"And the media?"

"Sure," she said scornfully. "I've got them eating out of the palm of my hand."

"Eating corn, anyway," he said.

"See?"

He wanted time to look into this, but all he said was, "Donohue just had the idea." He wasn't sure as to the truth of that statement, but he would take the senator at her word for the moment. "We have to hear the real offer. I need to look up what's been done before. It isn't a common thing. I would have to negotiate terms."

"You can handle it," she said bracingly. "I have every confidence."

His mind raced. "We could really push the fact that it's more of a political question. There are lots of policy issues. Congress has to start planning now."

Nigmatullin beamed. "There you go."

"On the other hand," he began, and his client groaned.

"I hate it when you say that," she said.

"On the other hand," Calvin went on, as if he had not been interrupted, "what if she's just using you for an hour in the limelight? It's not only reporters who want the scoop. USACD thinks you've violated its regulations."

"You don't," she pointed out.

"No, but as to the principle of whether it's appropriate for Congress to offer you immunity, I think we have to look at the competing interests of the different branches of government. It is appropriate for the executive branch to pursue you in its prosecutorial capacity." He stopped.

Nigmatullin's eyes were wide. He thought it a bit of an overreaction to what was only mildly pedagogical, and offered to someone who should, at least theoretically, have a strong interest in what he had to say on the topic.

Then he realized that she wasn't looking at him. He had his back to the large window, but Nigmatullin faced it, and something had more than caught her attention. He turned and beheld an astonishing sight.

A single figure stood balanced atop the concrete barrier at the edge of the Whitehurst Freeway. In what felt like an eternity, but was the clarity of an instant aided by abject terror, Calvin saw that the figure silhouetted against the sky was dressed in a drab gray that rendered his outline indistinct against the road, the water, the lights of Virginia, and the darkening sky. He was masked. The most important detail, however, was the fact that the figure held a powered weapon to his shoulder.

He pointed it straight at the former junior captain of the starship *Aeneid* before he raised it and fired twice, once at either corner of the picture window. The safety glass shattered, splintering into a thousand shards of crystalline black light.

CHAPTER 20

CALVIN MOVED EVEN BEFORE THE assailant finished his first two shots. He dove at Paolina Nigmatullin, she who knew the way through the shoals to Elysia, caught her and rolled so that he landed on his back to cushion her fall.

People were screaming. He couldn't see Sara.

He heard shots from within the party, and rolled again, covering the woman with his body. A quick glance showed the shooter to be Zeke Salisbury, and he was aiming out the window. Calvin and Polly were too far from the window and thus visible through it. He didn't want to drag her closer and into the broken glass, but the alternative left her in the open. He pointed toward the freeway, but at a western angle so they could be out of the shooter's line of sight.

Captain Nigmatullin might have had her own views on combat, but she started crawling in the direction Calvin indicated. He had spotted a door. If it led elsewhere, it might provide a means of escape. If it led to a closet, maybe he could stick her in it.

He took a quick look at the window. No one stormed its shattered perimeter, and Zeke crouched behind a chair, siting his weapon at any assailant who might await them outside.

Vehicles sounded, and two distinct noises filled the night, noises that only meant vehicles were colliding outside. Someone was hollering on the freeway, reminding anyone who was shooting back that there were innocents outside. Calvin could see only a sliver of the night through the picture window, and he saw two drab figures run along the freeway's barrier before disappearing from sight. In a bloodthirsty sort of way that he attributed to being shot at, he hoped that Zeke had gotten one of them.

He still couldn't see Sara, but he could see that lamps lay shattered on the floor, wood splinters were everywhere, and several had pierced a couch. One man held a bleeding knee and another male figure lay supine on the floor for no visible reason. Calvin still couldn't see Sara.

Calvin and his client reached the door to the side of the window and were free to stand. The door was locked. Lacking a weapon with which to shoot the lock out, he kicked the door. Much to his surprise the tactic worked, and he went through the entryway.

It was not, as he had feared, a closet, but led fifteen feet off to the right, paralleling the interior of the room, to a corner that turned right, back away from the freeway toward Georgetown. It might, he figured, be wise to get out of the party, where apparently someone had known Nigmatullin was going to be.

A few quick steps allowed him to check around the corner. He saw another hall but no people before he went back to the doorway where Nigmatullin waited, comfortable with the notion that someone else was going to risk getting shot before she would be risked. He pulled her through, shut the door and dithered.

"Calvin," she said, a hint of amusement in her eyes. "We're just standing here. I don't think that's wise."

"I have to get Sara," he admitted, and the door opened, and he pushed her back again, hoping she would get her ass around the corner.

It was Zeke, and he was not smiling. "I've got Sara," he said, and, indeed, Sara stood at his shoulder, with what looked like far too much blood on her blonde head. "You should be moving."

Calvin forgot his client and her safety and started forward.

"Move, damn it," Zeke snarled. "What the hell is wrong with you?"

"I'm fine," Sara said. "I think it's just a cut. Glass maybe."

"Enough," Zeke said. "I'm going first." And he pushed past Calvin and Nigmatullin, and they all ran, Calvin in the rear and the women between them. The end of the hall took them to a flight of stairs which, Calvin saw by looking over the railing, wound tightly down many stories to the ground. It was bare and utilitarian, a function of the architect's decision not to have any windows on the side with a neighbor, thus leaving room for all the stuff usually stored in a building's core. The stairs ran around a large pipe-like tube, which likely served to provide water and air, or to remove sewage.

A scream sounded back of them. "There they are," the voice shrieked. "Now let me go." There was a lot of moaning.

Calvin caught a glimpse of red satin in the direction from which they had come, but a dark figure quickly shoved the satin's wearer in back of him. If he wasn't the same person who had shot up the cocktail party, it meant that more than one drab-clad figure in grey was terrorizing the building at the bottom of Georgetown.

"Go," Zeke hissed to Calvin. The four of them had stopped at the top of the stairs when the screaming started. "Take them."

"You go," Calvin said. "You can protect them better than I can."

Zeke's eyes went wide in what looked like outrage. "Are you arguing with me? Now?"

"Come, Sara," Nigmatullin said grimly. "Move." Their feet hit the metal stairs, which clanged like a series of bells. It was an old building.

The woman with the masked man was still screaming, this time inveighing the figure not to shoot. She was clinging to one of his arms. The man turned casually but with a swiftness that was deliberate and efficient, and clocked her on the side of the head with an elbow.

Calvin, who had no military training and was keenly aware of that lack in this instance, knew, because he had seen and read enough fiction, that he was violating all sorts of efficiency and command protocols. Calvin, however, was not in the military and didn't need to follow those protocols. "She's my client. You're arguing with me. They'll do better with you. Go."

Out of the corner of his eye, Calvin saw that the woman in red had gone down, but now she clung to the attacker's leg.

Zeke's outrage changed to something that might have looked like hysterical laughter had one had the time to notice such things, but Zeke handed him what looked like an old projectile weapon.

"It's loaded. I have two more. You've got nine bullets, and, for the love of God, use the finder." He turned and flew down the stairs.

A small red light danced across Calvin's chest as he turned, and he dropped flat to the ground faster than he ever had in his life. His feet, his knees, his hips found the edge of the stairwell and hid in it while the rest of him wished it could do the same.

The woman was sobbing now, and the attacker, perhaps contemptuous of the ineptitude at the head of the stairs, took the time to shoot her in the leg. She rolled away screaming. Calvin used the laser pointer, because he was not completely inept, to aim at the man's stomach, and pulled the trigger.

He missed, which surprised him, and allowed the figure to come at him running, as if unconcerned that Calvin had any chance of hitting him.

Calvin's second shot hit him in the chest, and the assailant went down. There was no blood.

Calvin swore. No blood meant the other man was armored. He might have been knocked out, but he might only have been winded hard. Again, Calvin was relying on fiction for his martial information, but it was all he had to go on. Between pauses in the woman's screaming he could hear the steps of his friends sounding far away, remote and hollow.

He contemplated fleetingly throwing himself down the stairs after them, but a vision of his assailant rising again like always happened in *Resurrection of the Machines* stopped him.

Zeke's pistol held in two hands, Calvin rose out of the stairwell and approached the fallen figure. The weapon belonging to the supine figure lay on the ground out of the man's reach. Calvin would have liked to kick it toward the stairwell, but he didn't want to set it off.

The woman was still screaming, and he wondered why no one had come to help her. It occurred to him that perhaps there were other masked figures waiting in the room with the view, the shattered glass, and all the fresh evening air.

He picked up the dropped weapon and paused, assessing his choices.

He looked at the figure. With the mask on, the fallen figure showed no signs of consciousness. It was all very unnerving, and Calvin found himself wishing he'd shot the man in the face. Perhaps he should shoot him in the leg, and then the attacker wouldn't be able to follow. If he used the weapon in his hands for that, it would be very unclear whether the hit happened during the firefight.

He couldn't do it. He should do it: the man had tried to murder Nigmatullin, and that was wrong in so many ways.

He set the assailant's weapon down, well beyond the figure's feet; and, being right handed, approached from the left. He dropped to one knee and placed the muzzle of Zeke's pistol against the man's neck, and with his other hand pulled the mask off.

The yellow of their assailant's hair was like straw drawn in crayon, and his skin a reddish, umber brown. His eyes were closed and his mouth ajar to show perfect teeth gleaming white in the industrial lighting. Calvin was fairly certain the man was unconscious, and took his picture with his palm.

Picture taking could have been a silent affair, but the law mandated a soft popping sound to indicate the theft of another's soul, which was too bad in this instance despite the usual virtues of, in a general way, requiring consent, because the man's eyes flew open to show clear green, like spring. Calvin was crouched close enough to see the specks of violet in the irises. His assailant did not hie from a poor background, going by the money that had been spent on his very vivid hues.

"Don't move," Calvin said.

The man managed to keep his lips almost immobile as he said, "Erase that picture and I won't kill you."

"I've sent it already," Calvin said, which wasn't true, but he hoped the lie would protect against the threat. "Now, here's what I want. I don't want you to move at all. I will shoot you if you do." This was entirely true. He suspected that he had made a mistake placing himself this close, and, from what he could see, he could remedy that error only by pulling the trigger. Calvin needed to back off, but he didn't want green-eyes grabbing the gun.

"Hands up," a voice called.

Calvin turned his head very slowly toward the turn in the hall. The wounded woman was gone, although he thought he could still hear her. In her place stood another masked figure, and this one was also armed, his weapon pointed very distinctly at Calvin.

"Put it down," the new one said, and Calvin very carefully placed the pistol on the ground while pivoting his heels. He saw no need to place it within easy reach of the man he had hit.

"Where are the others?" the new man asked. His voice came clearly through the mask, and it, too, sounded educated and not-poor. Calvin had a couple of thugs with whom to contend, but they were educated thugs.

"Long gone," Calvin said and hoped.

"He took my picture," the man on the ground said as he stood, keeping clear of his partner's line of fire. "He says he sent it, but he's lying."

"Then check his palm," said the other.

Green-eyes stooped and picked up Zeke's pistol.

Calvin felt his heart speed up as if his body understood the implications of the green-eyed man's concerns before the rest of him caught on. If he hadn't sent it, he'd be dead. He was the only one who had seen one of their faces.

He fell back on his hands, and crab walked away. "No. I have confidential information in it. I can't let you see it. I'm a lawyer."

This got the intended derisory snort from the second masked figure. "For the love of G—." He checked himself, and said, very deliberately, "God."

Greenie was a little wobbly from the force of the impact that his vest had not absorbed, but steady enough. "Give me your hand."

It was wildly stupid. If he hadn't been convinced they would kill him anyway, he would not have taken the risk. He sullenly held out his left hand for inspection, and, when the other man leaned over and took it Calvin grabbed hold and surged to his feet, grasping the gun hand in an iron grip. Calvin's parents had geneered him no special beauty, but he was a strong man. He felt the flight of the shot that should have hit him, but he got green-eyes' arm behind his back and the pistol in his throat, Calvin's very own human shield.

"Damn," said his captive calmly.

Again, Calvin was struck with the realization that he didn't know what to do with the situation now that he had it. He wanted to tell the other one to get back in the cocktail room, but he didn't want him acquiring any human shields of his own. It had been established that a laser pointer did not give one perfect aim.

The same thoughts may have taken place behind the mask, for the man turned and went back toward the party room.

"Walk," Calvin said grimly, and marched green-eyes back down the corridor, through the door and into the wrecked room. The second masked man was gone.

Faces stared open-mouthed at Calvin and his captive. "Somebody please take his picture," Calvin said. "He just hates it."

"Perhaps someone should take yours," an acerbic voice said over the sounds of the wounded woman's sobs. Ryle Feder was in the room, a presence which had somehow earlier escaped Calvin's attention. "The ethics board might be interested in a picture of you holding someone at gunpoint."

"Good to see you helping the wounded, Ryle," Calvin said. It was unclear to Calvin how it was that he had acquired the pain in Sean's ass. Ryle was Sean's problem, not his, originally, but that had changed, and now his hostage was trying to take advantage of his distraction. Calvin could feel the man tensing as several people obligingly took his picture.

"Also," Calvin continued, "calling the police would be good."

"We did think of that, Calvin," Ryle said.

Calvin murmured in his captive's ear, his breath stirring the man's hair, "How did you know she was here?"

"I don't have to talk to you," the other said.

"But you want to?" Calvin murmured.

"Shut up."

"Do you have friends who told you about this party?" The slight tremor in the body he so closely held gave him his answer. "What if I accidentally shoot you unless you tell me?" He was sure the pressure of Zeke's pistol had not escaped the thug's attention.

"Earth first, asshole," the man said.

"Calvin," Ryle said, having apparently stopped feigning concern for the wounded woman, "I'm not sure you are an appropriate person to handle this man." He walked up to them, his brow glistening enough to match the shine of his too black hair. He held out a hand as if offering to take the gun.

"Are you crazy?" Calvin said. "Get the hell back."

Sirens sounded. They were distant.

"See," Ryle said, "we need someone more appropriate to handle this. I am with the government, and you no longer are. Give me the gun."

Calvin refused to release his grip. "Ryle," Calvin grated. "Get away. This man is dangerous. I have got him. You are old and not strong enough."

That might not have been a good thing to say. Ryle's face turned red enough that Calvin could almost feel the heat of it himself. More unfortunately, Ryle put his hand over Calvin's gun hand, and Calvin moved his finger off the trigger. He couldn't risk shooting Ryle, however much he might want to.

Whether he read the situation right or just took the risk, Calvin's captive seized his chance. He shot a hand up and dislodged Ryle's hand from Calvin's, struck Ryle across the eyes and put an elbow in Calvin's sternum. Calvin was able to ignore that, and tried to bring the gun barrel down on the other's head but only grazed him, and a back fist caught him in the temple. He hadn't wanted to shoot in the crowded room, but quickly had reason to regret that call, as green-eyes leapt for the window.

He balanced on the ledge as a vehicle went by on the Whitehurst, its light catching the yellow hair against the black night. Again, Calvin didn't shoot.

"Shoot him," Ryle screamed.

But the intruder leapt cat-like to the barricade and ran several paces before dropping back over the edge to the street below the freeway.

Calvin felt sick and furious. He hoped Zeke had gotten the women well away. He rounded on Ryle. "You're the one I should shoot. Do you know what you just did?" He grabbed Ryle by the throat. "You helped him get away. Are you in on this, too?"

He paid no heed to the people watching. All the campaign donors and their recipients stood hushed. Eyes gleamed on necks all around the room as people recorded the event. This kind of ridiculousness called for full recording, not just the static shots of a palm.

But Calvin paid them no heed at all as he grabbed Ryle by the throat with his left hand, the weapon held rigid in his right hand by his side. "You want her dead, don't you?" Calvin demanded. "That's why you helped him get away."

Ryle was smiling. "I'm not the one who let him get away. You did that. You should have shot him."

CHAPTER 21

THE FACT THAT CALVIN AGREED with Ryle on this rare occasion didn't make it more palatable. He should have shot the man. He opted for squeezing Ryle's throat harder instead.

A woman placed her hand on his arm. "Let him go, Calvin," Tessa Donohue said. She was hard to ignore, and Calvin realized he needed to calm down. He had used up his powers of reason on the decisions not to shoot, and he didn't need to abandon them now. With great effort, he let go his grip.

"You can see," Ryle said savagely and hoarsely, "why this man is facing ethics charges. He just attacked opposing counsel."

Several catcalls greeted this observation.

Then the District police came.

It was, Calvin realized, his third police jurisdiction.

The police finished with Calvin and Zeke long before they finished with Nigmatullin or Sara. Neither of the men were willing to leave without the women.

"Do you think," Calvin said, leaning his head back against the wall from his perch on a tall stool in the police station, "that all these people would look so tired if the party were still going on?" The police had asked all the guests to come down to the station while the experts came in to go over the crime scene. It wasn't late, and Spike had kept the bar open until the police asked him to please stop serving so they could get folks to go where they were needed, but the guests in their finery had shocked eyes and numb faces. A few strange souls were quite animated, and kept talking long after the police finished with them and they could have gone home.

Zeke also leaned against the wall, but he stood watching Sara responding to questions from one of the cops. His arms were folded across his chest. "I have a different question." His voice was flat. "Do you think you're in charge?"

Calvin also watched Sara. "I do."

"If that ever happens again, do what I say. Right away."

"See," Calvin said indolently, "I don't think you're in charge. If there'd been someone else around, you're better at the fighting, so it made sense to keep you with Polly. She has to live."

Zeke radiated hostility. "You're not paying attention. I have the training to make those calls. You don't."

"She's paying me."

Zeke puffed a snort. "That doesn't make you a mercenary. That's my job."

"That's why you had to go with her."

"You're her lawyer. You don't get to make tactical decisions."

Calvin laughed. "I do it all the time."

Zeke's voice lost some of its rage. "And, man, you have to stay alive, too. We need Polly alive and out of jail."

Paolina Nigmatullin had bought herself a sunny house, and the grass in front was green despite the cold. Calvin could see velvety sward from the large bay window where he sat in warm comfort with Zeke Salisbury, Sara and Nigmatullin.

His client had insisted that they get together, and, since it was Sunday, suggested her house, which was far more comfortable than the firm's deserted offices.

Everyone looked tired, and Nigmatullin had served them all coffee. He and Sara had turned down her offer of scrambled eggs and bacon, but Zeke had taken her up on it, explaining that real food, which was limited on shipboard, was not something he could pass up.

When the smell of the frying bacon reached him, Calvin changed his mind, and Sara immediately followed suit. Nigmatullin smirked from where she lounged with her cup on the couch. "You all need to get your act together. Once you smell bacon you have to have it, and you should have figured that out in advance."

"You're right," Calvin said. "It speaks poorly of both our judgment."

"Nope," Sara said. "I just changed my mind in an erratic fashion. My judgment is fine."

Zeke laughed, and Sara looked pleased.

Nigmatullin stood, and said, "I need to crack more eggs. Why don't you all just come into the kitchen?"

They followed her there, and Sara poured everyone more coffee while Nigmatullin tended the breakfast. Everyone but the starship captain seated themselves at the kitchen table. "I wanted everyone together," Nigmatullin said, "because Zeke told me about your conversation, Calvin, and I want you to treat him like you would me. What I've told you, he can know, and if you think I need to know something tell him, too."

"I'll need some signatures," Calvin said. "It's your right to say anything you like to your friends. Even though I wish you wouldn't." He wished Zeke worked for her, but Zeke had not liked that suggestion when he'd made it at the grill the other morning.

Sara opened her palm and pulled up a keyboard at half-visibility to the rest of them. Her fingers flew as if she practiced magic, and she said, "I'll fix some agency acknowledgements."

"Good," Nigmatullin said briskly. "Now, what did everyone learn last night?"

Zeke gave Calvin a considering look, but said nothing.

"You were supposed to be killed in Florida," Sara said absently, intent on her editing.

This time Zeke's look was not approving. "What makes you say that?" he asked harshly.

Sara looked up, a little startled by his tone. "Because someone tried to kill her again last night? In the same showy way as in Florida?"

Zeke lifted a hand in acknowledgement. "Fine. It seemed like you knew something."

"Sorry," Sara said. "I was just trying to list the obvious stuff."

"What else is obvious?" Calvin asked.

"Anyone who can help in a return trip is being killed," Zeke said, repeating the point he had made at the grill the other morning.

"Could Orlova or Contreras navigate?" Calvin asked Nigmatullin.

She nodded. "We all did our best to understand the navigation. It was harder than anyone had anticipated it would be, and we ran all the back up checks and watched the monitors coming out of the drive. I can't say I understand why we didn't all die in an explosion when we travelled through some interstellar dust, but they showed me what to look for when we dropped back into real space. If we didn't have the bridge, we'd work back up."

"And killing them was very shocking," Sara pointed out. "It made quite a statement they way they did it."

"But no one took credit," Calvin mused. "It's a lot of trouble and risk to go to and not get credit."

"Unless it wasn't a lot of risk," Zeke said.

"Which doesn't seem to have been a bad call," Calvin said. "There hasn't been a hint of finding who did it, and it happened in broad daylight in a place filled with cameras."

"Official and personal," Zeke said.

Calvin figured it might be time to drop his little bomb. The police had asked him not to share it so that they could follow up on the lead. "I have something that isn't obvious that could fit here. The guy shooting at us, he said, 'Earth first.'"

Eyebrows went up all around the kitchen.

"Damn," Nigmatullin said. "I knew it."

"Which means he's either with them or wanted you to think that," Sara said.

Calvin lightly tapped the wooden surface of the kitchen table. "The guy was a little stressed. I am inferring that from how stressed I was, and I was the one holding the gun. He might have meant it."

"And," Nigmatullin said slowly, "if the killings are political, and there are sympathizers in the police or the government, that would explain why there has been no progress on any arrests."

"Or," Zeke said, "they are just really sneaky."

Calvin gave him a nod. "See, for example, the masks."

"Good job, getting that off him, by the way," Zeke said. It was the most Zeke had said since he had attempted to bring Calvin in line at the police station. That little made Calvin uncomfortable and he looked away. He was sure Zeke would not have let the man escape, even with Ryle's officious meddling.

Sara said, "Do we think Ryle wanted him to get away?" She had watched several videos of the interaction. They were in all the casts, and she had been frowning at a re-play when Calvin arrived at Nigmatullin's house earlier.

"Ryle is an idiot," Calvin noted with measured objectivity. "So, it wouldn't be inconsistent with that that he thought I'd screw up."

Zeke put both hands on the edge of the kitchen table and pushed himself away, as if he couldn't bear thinking of the scene. He, too, had watched the re-plays. "He's an amazing idiot if that's the case." He got the coffee carafe and inspected the bacon over Nigmatullin's shoulder. She was still cracking eggs.

Calvin swallowed. "He told the police that it was my fault. I should have shot the man as he was escaping." He looked away from Zeke's eyes. Zeke would undoubtedly have had the nerve and the accuracy to have fired, hit the man in the leg, hit no one else, and saved the day.

Zeke choked on his coffee. "Jesus. He is an idiot. There were people everywhere, I assume? You could have hurt someone else."

Calvin sighed, and tapped his fork against his mug. "Sure, but Ryle might not have thought that through. He really doesn't like me."

"At all," Sara chimed in.

Calvin put the fork down. It was probably annoying. "Combine idiocy with hate, and he might have thought he had a chance to screw me over."

"Or he wanted the man to get away," Nigmatullin said, sweeping the eggshells off the stone counter with the back of her wrist. "Tell me about Ray Hillman."

Calvin had not yet filled her in on that conversation. He gave Sara a nod. She had gotten the most out of the police.

She blinked, and he thought he detected moisture in her eyes.

He wondered if she had ever known anyone who had been killed, or even died. It was rare.

Sara summarized what they had learned from Ray about his meetings with Sam Heller (who she hadn't liked) and Tessa Donohue (about whom she looked grim but said nothing negative). "And," she concluded, fixing Nigmatullin with her golden gaze, "he told us that he would testify to the validity of the orders he signed. Jasper told you the orders weren't real, but that was to protect Ray. Ray, told us, however, that he would testify that he signed those orders and, given who he was, they were valid. He was planning to stand behind them before he was—before his death."

Sara took a deep breath. When she continued, her voice was steady. "The police interviewed Calvin and me later, since we were the last to see him. In my interview I learned that after we left he contacted Sam Heller and Tessa Donohue. Both of them were at that party. You met Senator Donohue. Calvin talked to her earlier, too."

"Ah," Nigmatullin said, her eyebrows climbing high. "I've been curious how that went."

Calvin frowned. "She very definitely didn't answer my question about who she met with outside of official meetings, but it can't be a coincidence that she was involved in the settlement discussions and that Ray called her and Sam the day he died." He didn't want to mention that the senator had agreed to answer his questions if he and Nigmatullin showed up at her party. He didn't want to mention it because she hadn't answered any of his questions. Instead, he said, "Polly, who invited you to that party?"

"I received an invitation from that Spike person. I wasn't going to go, but then I received a note from Tessa Donohue that she would like it so very much if I would attend." She grimaced. "I have my dancing bear duties, and I know it. So I went."

"And that's when she offered Polly immunity in exchange for her testimony to her committee," Calvin told the others.

Nigmatullin was grinning at the scrambled eggs, and Zeke slammed his mug down. "Are you serious, man?" Zeke asked. "That's incredible news."

Sara was frowning. "Has USACD agreed to this?"

"She had the idea last night," Calvin said. "It just occurred to her completely out of the blue."

"Why are you so skeptical?" Nigmatullin asked him, carrying the frying pan to the table. "She's a senator."

"She's in the legislative branch," he said. "USACD is part of the executive branch, and it's the one with the ability to prosecute people."

"But it's been done before," Nigmatullin said in that way people had who thought that precedent was the only legal principle one need ever employ. There'd been clients like that at Calvin's old job, and he always wondered why they thought it took three years of law school to learn just that one thing.

"It's not without merit," Sara said gravely. "The whole settlement question is so political, and the case against her so shaky—"

"—according to us—" Calvin interjected quickly.

"—that it would make sense to turn it over to Congress. The people who write the laws need the information for policy decisions," she explained to the two who had not attended law school.

Calvin's news feed gave its soft automatic burr, and he spared it a glance. He had just added Tessa Donohue to his list of interesting persons he wanted to hear about, and there she was, holding a press conference. "We may want to watch this," he said.

Nigmatullin threw open the kitchen screen on one wall, and Tessa Donohue's attractive features filled the wall from the waist up. "Every now and then," she was saying, "members of Congress have to remember that we are here to represent the people. And the people have a right to know all the details before important decisions are made." Calvin noticed that she left it unclear who was making those decisions, but it might have been the people themselves. Might not have, too.

"I am mindful," the senator went on, "that the Executive Branch has its interest in prosecuting any violations of its regulations, or even any possible misconduct of its employees, but we all know— especially those of us who were there—how very confusing everything was. It is entirely possible that at the end of this inquiry, no one will find that the *Aeneid* or its commanders did anything wrong."

"Ryle Feder might be bursting a blood vessel right about now,"

Calvin muttered, and Sara choked. She shot him a look, but it was impish. He took it as a good sign. Their conversations had been strictly professional since she had disclosed the reason she turned him down. He had been successful in not dwelling on what he might have said differently, but it was still good to receive a friendly smile. "We'll play these statements at your hearing, Polly."

"Shush," Nigmatullin said. Her eyes were fixed on the house screen, and she looked pale.

Watching her, Calvin realized that she had returned to the present, and had left whatever bubble of unreality had surrounded her since her the deaths of her colleagues and her own return from another world. She didn't want to face prison.

His own mouth went dry at the thought of it. He wanted her free for so many reasons that had nothing to do with her, but watching the woman, the person, look so hopeful and so worried, all in a single fleeting expression, filled him with dread at the responsibility he had taken on. She should have hired someone with more experience. Maybe they could discuss that later when the other two weren't around.

Tessa Donohue was still talking and her chin went up defiantly. "I am prepared to consult with my attorneys to look into a grant of immunity to the *Aeneid's* Paolina Nigmatullin so that she may testify to the Senate free of concern of prosecution. I know that immunity is usually only offered to small fish to catch a big fish. I know that Captain Nigmatullin is one of the big fish, but this is a different kind of question, a political question. The people have a right to know what happened and why, and we don't need her pleading the Fifth Amendment."

"Excuse me," Calvin said, looking to Nigmatullin, "client of mine, but were you planning to take the Fifth?"

"No, of course not. You would be the first to know. Now, be quiet." She kept her eyes fixed on the screen.

Calvin would not be quiet. "This is called making things up," he said. "Before you get too excited, please, note that she has given herself an out in case the White House calls. She claims she hasn't yet talked to her lawyers. It's very clever, lets her get her limelight, and drop you if she has to." The president and the senator were of the same political party, but it looked obvious to Calvin she hadn't coordinated with the White House.

"Shut up, would you?" Zeke said. "Please?"

They missed the end of the senator's bold statement to man, God, and the portion of the populace that actually watched such things. She had managed to get newscasters present in the flesh, and pointed at one agitated young woman who desperately wanted to ask a question.

"Will you," the woman said, "be announcing a new initiative? Will you be proposing to fund another starship?" It was a logical question. Why else would Donohue be making all this fuss?

Donohue blinked owlishly, as if surprised to be caught playing the role of an investigative caster. "I will, Ms. Prinz, but what it will look like depends on what we learn from the starship captain."

"Now that," Nigmatullin interjected, "she just made up. How could whether I broke any rules have anything to do with what we should do next?"

"Well," said Sara, who apparently did not know when a question was rhetorical, "she might want to know which USACD regulations you violated so that she can undo them legislatively."

"I'm not going to tell her that," Nigmatullin said.

Sara scowled, caught out in her rote response. "Sorry. I was thinking out loud."

Donohue continued to fend off questions about her imaginary initiative.

Sara chose her words more carefully this time. "It would make more sense, of course, to learn your violations from your hearing. Then she would know what USACD thought you violated and be able to require revisions of those regulations."

"So she wants to grandstand," Zeke observed.

Calvin folded his arms across his chest. He knew it was a defensive posture, but he didn't care. "Polly, don't go thinking this is necessarily a good idea. This senator thinks she's got an opportunity to grab the spotlight, and she may or may not offer you a proper grant of immunity. USACD may still go after you, and it will have any admissions you make on a very public record. One thing Donohue was right about is that you are the big fish."

Nigmatullin watched the screen. "That's your job, isn't it? You need to make sure I can get out from USACD's thumb."

"I'm telling you I'm not sure you can," Calvin said.

She looked up, and there was no pale longing for freedom in her face this time. Instead, she wore the face of a military officer used to being obeyed, or the face of a very difficult client, cold and demanding. "Have you looked it up yet?"

"No," Calvin said.

"Then don't start out all pessimistic," Nigmatullin replied and went back to watching Donohue discuss the importance of understanding the ecology, the environment, the compatibility with man, a whole host of issues, none of which required inquiry into the facts underlying USACD's charges of mutiny.

"Are you listening to this?" Calvin asked. "She's not making sense. All this stuff she wants to learn about can be found talking to your crew."

"I'm more glamorous," Nigmatullin said smugly.

Calvin clenched his fists. "I know that, she knows that, and you know that. And it is not the point."

"I think you need to get to work," his demanding client said.

The view from Sara's apartment in Silver Spring was not as good in winter as at other times of year. Now she looked out, not at leafy branches on ancient trees, but into other people's windows through branches that were bare except for the light fall of snow they collected.

Staring, quiet, no longer answering questions from the police like she had the night before, no longer needing to meet with the client like she had that morning, no longer needing to do anything at all like she was doing now, she thought about how very cold it was outside, and inside, too, come to think of it. Her flesh shivered, but her bones shuddered.

She knew what was happening, and asked the room for more

warmth but got a blanket from her bedroom while she waited for the heat to catch up to the tremors of cold coursing through her body.

She didn't like it. She didn't like it at all. She would very much have liked someone to put his arms around her and tell her that nothing like the previous night would ever happen again.

She had been safe. Zeke had protected them and gotten them to safety, but the other one, the man who had stayed behind, she hadn't known what had happened to him for the longest time. She hadn't like that either. Not at all.

She wondered what had motivated him, to risk himself like that. She wished she knew the answer and that it was the answer she wanted, but she had her suspicions.

She wasn't crying. She was just cold. Her eyes were wet and overflowing, but she felt no sobs, just the giant shivers that ran through her like open fault lines. It was aftershock, or something medical. She wasn't used to shooters. No one was, of course.

It was stupid, after what she had seen the night before, to focus on such things, but her mind kept running back to the fact that he had not wanted to stay with her after the horrible night or even after the meeting that morning.

She had come up with no pretext to stay with Calvin, and had no one but herself to blame for that. He had made it very clear that he would not seek her out.

It was all a matter of courage. There were so many different kinds, and she wasn't sure that she had any. Or, maybe she did. Maybe there was something she could do about all of this.

She waited awhile before the room got very hot, and her eyes dried. She asked her palm to make a call on voice.

He picked up on the third ring. "Hello?" The man's voice sounded puzzled, fading into pleased.

"Zeke? Mr. Salisbury? This is Sara Seastrom."

Calvin worked that Sunday afternoon. He had resolved not to let the exchange with Nigmatullin bother him, but the rest of the visit had been strained. Zeke grinning and Sara looking embarrassed had not helped.

Zeke had stayed behind when Calvin and Sara left, and Sara had looked as if she wanted to talk, but he didn't feel like hearing her explain what else he had done wrong, so walked her to her vehicle and waved her off.

He had not been wrong, but the legal situation was worse than he'd realized. Calvin suspected Nigmatullin thought that "immunity" meant immunity from any prosecution by USACD at all. That was wrong. Congress could force Nigmatullin to testify even if she invoked her privilege against self-incrimination under the Fifth Amendment to the Constitution. Congress could then ask a district court to grant immunity to varying degrees. Many types had been tried over the centuries. Early grants of transactional immunity resulted in wrongdoers getting a friendly member of Congress to compel a person's testimony so he could confess all his sins and obtain an "immunity bath." In addition to the self-evident drawbacks to that approach, it offended the Constitution's separation of powers between the legislative and executive branches. Congress could gum up a prosecution just to show it was "doing something." This had happened more than once.

"Use immunity" also proved a failure, because it permitted, for all intents and purposes, self-incrimination despite the fact that the compelled testimony itself could not be admitted into evidence. A prosecutor was still free to read the compelled testimony and use what he learned to obtain admissible evidence in a criminal proceeding. Once the Supreme Court pointed out that the doctrine failed miserably to protect the accused against self-incrimination, congressional committees stopped granting use immunity. The drawback there was that "use immunity" was the best way around the separation of powers problems created by the legislative branch horning in on prosecutions pursued by the executive branch.

Derivative use immunity had once offered an effective out, but had proved problematic because it, too, effectively suborned the Constitution's separation of powers between the legislative and executive branches of the government. A prosecutor could neither introduce compelled testimony into evidence nor use it to find other evidence, but he could find the evidence through other channels.

In a very recent case, the Ninth Circuit spoke approvingly of the saga of an adventurer from the 20th century, which case made clear why someone could think that an offer of Congressional immunity was a get out of jail free card. The individual had been accused of trading guns for people, and created a scandal that led to the President's office. Congress demanded information and held hearings. Even though the prosecutors in the case developed their evidence in advance of the Congressional hearing and even though they cloistered themselves like nuns from the ensuing hysteria over the hearings, the court held that their witnesses were tainted by the coverage of the man's compelled testimony. This made a successful prosecution practically unattainable, as the dissent put it.

Coming back to the twenty-second century and the more recent past, the Ninth Circuit found similar taint in a case before it, and threw out most of the charges against someone who had been forced to testify to the California legislature. Calvin found himself beginning to warm to the senator from Massachusetts and her offer, as well as to his pig-headed client for insisting on pursuing this path.

But the Supreme Court had granted certiorari when the government appealed. The Court had agreed to hear the Ninth Circuit case. Why would it do that? The Ninth Circuit's holding represented almost two centuries of settled law. Calvin sighed. He must have read or heard of something that gave him pause when Senator Donohue broached her brilliant notion. He wished his instincts had been wrong, but sure enough, the grant of cert. showed the reason. There was a split in the circuit courts of appeals. The D.C. Circuit, from whom so much law regarding the operations of the government flowed, had taken a bold step.

In a little noticed Congressional hearing over three years earlier—little noticed by Calvin, at least—Congress had compelled the testimony of a commissioner of the Securities and Exchange Commission to obtain information about the partisan nature of certain prosecutions. The SEC had spent several years only investigating securities fraud claims against persons who donated to a certain political party. This certainly appeared a political question suitably investigated by Congress, particularly when it appeared that the executive branch's own prosecutors were asleep at the switch and the Commission was staffed by persons belonging to the President's party, and it wasn't his party's donors who the SEC had investigated. Nonetheless, in *Volokh v SEC*, the D.C. Circuit held that a Congressional "offer" of immunity constituted an unconstitutional trespass against the separation of powers doctrine on the grounds that the Constitution only granted Congress legislative powers. For Congress to properly pass new legislation, both houses, the House and the Senate, had to pass the law. Then the President had to sign it. For a single committee of a single house to compel testimony without following the process dictated by the Constitution was not only, the court held, flawed legislation but impinged on the fundamental executive decision of whether to grant immunity in the course of a prosecution.

Calvin leaned back from his screen. He was quite surprised. Had the witness Congress attempted to drag before the Committee in the SEC case been a private person accused of something mundane like embezzlement, he would have happily nodded along with the D.C. Circuit's opinion. As it was, he was starting to recall the outrage at the time, an outrage he might have felt more strongly himself had he not been in the midst of studying for the bar exam. The government of the United States of America was not supposed to be used for partisan witch hunts.

The merits of Congress pursuing a political question notwithstanding, he felt a little smug. Some part of him had remembered all this and had warned him of the perils through the mechanism of instinct. One had to know the law, but it also helped to internalize the thought processes and develop instincts. Perhaps he could get good at this.

He had to warn Nigmatullin.

When he reached her by phone, however, she assured him that the D.C. Circuit gave her no cause for concern.

"Do you even know what that circuit is?" he asked in astonishment.

"It's the one in D.C.," she said cagily.

"You don't know," Calvin said. He wasn't sure she even knew that a circuit court was the one that heard appeals for a geographic region's trial courts.

His client sparkled at him through the screen. "No, but I am sure you will tell me."

"It's the circuit that hears the most cases about the government, the agencies, Congress, the President, whatever, and it has real depth. The high court pays it a lot of attention on these kinds of issues. Like the Second Circuit and finance."

"That makes sense," she replied with a look of understanding that was entirely faked, "they have Wall Street."

"How did you know that?" Calvin demanded.

"I guessed on the basis of your finance reference. See, I'm good at this. I think you need to trust my legal instincts here and let me testify to Congress."

Calvin tried hard not to scowl at his very famous client, his only client. It was difficult. "Ryle Feder—who is Satan—will use everything you say in front of Congress against you in your hearing. Even if Congress says it is offering you immunity."

"Only if the Supreme Court agrees with the D.C. Circuit."

"Which they are likely to do," he said with asperity. "It's the D.C. Circuit."

"They might not," Nigmatullin said. "As you pointed out, the whole SEC scandal was very political and likely should have been investigated by Congress."

Here, Calvin could parrot the D.C. Circuit. "And it should have, but with legislation properly passed by both Houses, not just a committee of one house. Getting the process right is more important than the outcome."

Nigmatullin looked skeptical. "Even if someone goes to jail?"

"Precisely, and that could happen to you. Also, and no offense to the senator, but your testimony about what happened on Elysia has nothing to do with whether the U.S. should fund another starship, and everything to do with whether you committed mutiny. Which means you are a less likely candidate for immunity even than that SEC commissioner who turned on his fellows."

Nigmatullin wore a look of great patience, likely the same look she wore before keelhauling errant spacemen. "Calvin," she said in a kindly way, "let's talk about this tomorrow when you are rested. You have had quite a time of it in the last 24 hours, and I am sure that if you think about all of this some more you will figure out a way for me to get immunity without my having to worry about the District of Columbia."

"The D.C. Circuit," he mumbled in defeat, but determined to get something right in the exchange.

"Yes, them." Nigmatullin signed off.

It was several days before Senator Donohue's staff granted him an audience to discuss the terms of Captain Nigmatullin's immunity. The lawyer from the Judiciary Committee and Donohue's staff director had excellent poker faces. At no point did they give him a grin, sheepish or wolfish, intimating that they knew full well that they might as well have been the staff of Heather Young setting up a particularly juicy interview. Instead, they acted as if the starship captain's testimony would help shape great policy decisions about whether to allow people to emigrate to Elysia.

"Will you be having any of the xenobiologists, then?" Calvin asked innocently. It seemed to him they were more relevant to questions of emigration than whether his client had committed mutiny.

"No," said the lawyer, a blonde woman with black hair, at the same time as the staff director, a rumpled man with red hair, said, "That's a great idea."

Calvin let his hands fall open modestly on the table. "I just assumed, what with the goals of the hearing, that you would want testimony from scientists."

They sat in a very small room with a very large table that probably violated a fire code somewhere else. The august body that was the Senate had packed the venerable and ancient Dirksen building with its salaried attendants. Calvin and Sara had wended their way through the maze of small offices partitioned by bookcases and flimsy walls, as if a college dorm had become inhabited by persons wearing suits. One bed sheet hanging from a ceiling would have sealed the image.

Now, the four of them squeezed themselves between the table

and the walls. "We do," the staff director said quickly. "We just haven't settled on our witness list." He glared at his lawyer.

Calvin nodded and refolded his hands. He was glad he had dissuaded Nigmatullin from accompanying him. "I understand. That's very helpful for us, of course."

The lawyer eyed him warily, but it was the staff director who asked. "Why is that?"

Calvin made sure they were both looking at him before he spoke. The staff director had a tendency to take notes. "So we can ensure that Captain Nigmatullin receives no questions about the events surrounding the *Aeneid*'s departure from Elysia."

The attorney folded her arms across her chest and sat back, as if she had known this was coming all along.

"I don't see why," the director said. "The Senator—the Committee, that is—is very interested in exactly that."

Exactly why? Calvin did not say aloud. "Mr. Sheffield, Captain Nigmatullin is facing very serious charges surrounding those events. USACD has leveled a charge of mutiny against her, and if the Committee were to question her about the departure, that testimony could be used against her."

"Is she planning to plead the Fifth Amendment?" the lawyer asked. Her name was Fiona, Fiona what, he couldn't recall.

"Not so far," Sara said quickly. Calvin had begun to understand that Sara didn't like options closed off. She served as a useful check on his own tendency to be all too clear. He wondered briefly if she had other options on other fronts. He had seen Zeke Salisbury's face on her screen several times in the past week. "I'm sure she'll be just as truthful to the Committee as she will be in her court martial."

Calvin waited. He wasn't going to broach the topic of immunity. He had tried with quiet desperation to talk Nigmatullin out of accepting the invitation. She had insisted on relying on the senator's offer of immunity so that she could make her impassioned plea for emigration and human settlement of the stars to a very public forum. He had talked her into watching some Senate hearings in the hopes that the exercise would cure her of the notion that she would be allowed any grandstanding. Most of the senators' questions were speeches of their own, only thinly veiled as questions. Most of them used up their allotted time on their own questions. Very little might be available for any witnesses. So far, Nigmatullin remained unpersuaded by either legal arguments or observations as to whose platform for showmanship the Senate was.

Calvin waited. He didn't want to ask for immunity. He wanted to make demands when they offered it.

"If she's not planning to plead the Fifth," the lawyer said, "it's not as if we need to offer immunity."

"That decision has not been made." Sara was very firm about it.

"I would like," Calvin said doggedly, since it was becoming clear that the immunity offer was going to be used to bargain for something, "to understand the relevance of the last days on Elysia to your policy goals."

The Committee lawyer managed to look menacing without moving a muscle. "If," she said, "your client doesn't plead the Fifth, we can compel her testimony without offering her immunity."

The staff director looked uncomfortable. "Fiona, please. We aren't trying to scare these folks away."

Or bully them, Calvin thought. He wondered if Donohue knew how her attorney was carrying out her task.

Fiona looked bored. "I have to be mindful of the D.C. Circuit opinion. I don't want us accused of overstepping our bounds or interfering in the prosecutions of the executive branch." Either she didn't think she could get both houses of Congress to grant immunity, or she hadn't tried. Calvin doubted that the House would go along with it. They might be wishing they'd thought of calling Nigmatullin themselves.

Sheffield's face started to morph toward his hair color. "I think we both have to be mindful of what Senator Donohue wants, Fiona."

Fiona gave Calvin a look. "I would think you would be just as worried. It's ultimately the courts that decide immunity, regardless of what we offer."

Calvin was well aware of that finer point of law. "I want my client's testimony limited to what is relevant, to issues of emigration and settlement."

Fiona just wanted to toy with him, he could tell. Her eyelids drooped sleepily, in counterpoint to the waspish sound of her voice. "You don't think a settlement of criminals is germane to whether the thin veneer of civilization will be ripped away once people think they can get away with that kind of behavior? That probably needs to be explored in depth."

There was a point Calvin had not considered. He would have to think very carefully before he sprang that on Nigmatullin. He could only imagine her reaction.

"Mr. Sheffield, I take it your attorney is assisting you in this?" He wished he could remember the woman's last name.

Sheffield's lips pursed. "If she won't, I will. We would like to offer your client immunity for her full testimony on all items of interest to Senator Donohue. And the committee."

Calvin nodded his head once gravely. It wasn't what he wanted, but Nigmatullin would be happy, however foolishly.

"Have you raised this with the attorney for USACD?" he asked.

"We thought you should do that," Fiona said, and her evident enjoyment began to grate on Calvin. "I talked to Ryle Feder, about the possibility of this offer, and he said he'd be happy to discuss it with you. He also said he has everything he needs so far."

That was just so much trash talk, Calvin figured. If the other attorney had not so clearly wanted to be asked, or had been remotely civil, he might have casually inquired whether Ryle was upset. The way she told him about the USACD lawyer's response suggested Ryle wasn't upset at all. He had no doubt that the two government lawyers had had the nicest of chats about him.

The traffic was too dense to make getting a cab worth it, and the afternoon too grey and cold for the long walk back, so Calvin and Sara took the shorter walk behind the Capitol to get to the Metro at Capitol South.

Even through the tight weave of her winter wrap, Sara felt the wind reach into her bones. It made her slightly resentful. The store had advertised the wrap as containing the latest in anti-winter technology, beloved by arctic explorers and residents of Cleveland alike. She wasn't so sure about all of that now.

The rest of the discussions on the Hill had gone pretty much as they hoped. She knew Calvin was worried sick about the D.C. Circuit opinion. *Volokh* was up on cert., and she was worried, too. But they had the immunity offer, and now they just needed to talk to Ryle Feder. "Calvin, have you explained to Polly about *Volokh*, that she might lose her immunity if the Court agrees with the D.C. Circuit?"

His jaw set, and she suspected that if she'd been walking closer to him she would have heard his teeth grinding. His voice, however, was light when he answered. "More than once. I have even explained that *Volokh* is a much stronger case for granting immunity so that Congress can explore something political than hers is, and she doesn't care. She's very confusing."

The wind picked up, and the bits of Sarah's hair that her cap didn't contain spread across her eyes. Calvin tossed his head like some kind of horse. "She's lost that martyr complex she had coming in, but she insists on putting her cause first. I don't think she understands. It's not like the vids up there. She's not the one who gets to speechify. The Court will decide *Volokh* by late spring, her USACD hearing is set for July 2, and she'll be screwed."

"Maybe she won't say anything incriminating," Sara said.

"That's the best case," Calvin said. A snowdrop hit his cheek. Sara saw no others. "Even if she rides through it totally clean, it will still give Feder a big advantage. He'll know exactly what to take apart."

"He has to ignore it," Sara said. "He won't be allowed to watch."

Calvin looked at her at last, his green eyes unfriendly and harsh. "That guy? He'll put on a disguise and go watch it in a bar where we can't subpoena his viewing habits."

When they reached the firm, Calvin found the government lawyer waiting for him in the reception area. It was late afternoon, and a thrill of cold air followed Calvin and Sara into the foyer. He should have been surprised by the unannounced visitor, but he wasn't.

He was more surprised by Ryle's companion. Sean Han stood behind the older lawyer, his face a stoic mask. Only the set of his shoulders revealed his misery, and only if one knew him. Calvin knew his friend well.

"Mr. Feder," he said affably, extending a hand. "Mr. Han." He grinned and shook Sean's hand as well.

Sean did not return the grin, and Calvin tried not to feel slighted. Ryle had doubtless brought Sean merely to torture both of them, or, at least, Calvin.

Calvin asked the receptionist for an empty conference room, and escorted his uninvited visitors up two stories to a room with no view of the outside. It would suffice.

"I received a call," Ryle said, "from the Senate committee calling your client to testify. They told me you would be coordinating with me, since it is my case that is being put in jeopardy. Sean and I were in the area, and thought we'd save you the trouble. And, I was curious as to where you landed." He looked around the small conference room in which they were seated as if he were unimpressed with the results.

"I would have been happy to come by your offices," Calvin said. He waited, expectant. He saw no good coming of this visit and felt no impulse to be helpful.

Ryle required no assistance. It was his turn to smile. "I shouldn't be telling you this, since it is not my lookout to help the other side, but you are new to the practice of law."

Again, Calvin looked within himself and found no desire to play straight man. He waited.

Nonplussed that Calvin had not risen to his bait, Ryle pushed on. "I have to assume from your pursuit of the immunity offer, that you are unaware of the portion of the *Volokh* matter that reached the Supreme Court. That you don't understand the danger your client faces. She may testify, and, if the Supreme Court decides *Volokh* correctly, USACD will be able to use her testimony in her mutiny hearing."

"We are aware," Calvin said. "We are not concerned."

Ryle sniffed.

The sniff was too much for Calvin, and he abandoned his plan to stay silent. "If ever," he said quietly, "there was a case that was appropriate for Congress to ensure received the light of public scrutiny, it was a government agency's deliberate targeting of people and companies based on their political contributions. I am confident that the Supreme Court won't disturb Congress' ability to grant immunity in that case."

Ryle pounced on the last words. "In this case. But what about yours? Donohue can call it a political question all she wants, but mutiny isn't politics."

"Immunity covers what it covers," Calvin said. He tried to sound smug, but wasn't sure that he succeeded.

Ryle leaned back in his chair, and put his hands behind his well-coiffed head of black hair. He was better at sounding smug. "I'm glad you know about the *Volokh* case. From what I hear, you should be thinking twice about letting your client testify."

Calvin did not point out that he had insufficient control of his client. Calvin spared a glance for Sean, who sat slumped in his chair staring at the table.

"That you aren't," Ryle continued, "makes me perfectly happy." He looked happy. His eyes were warm and kindly, and his handsome face was relaxed.

"You shouldn't be hearing anything," Sara said. "The Supreme Court's deliberations are confidential."

"You are correct, my dear," Ryle said. "But one hears what one hears." He twinkled. "Did you know that one of the law clerks on the Court was once an intern at USACD? We still keep in touch."

Leaving Sara gaping, he turned his attention back to Calvin. "Fiona wanted to make sure I knew what the Senate was doing with Nigmatullin. I told her I couldn't be more happy."

Perhaps the man was playing a subtle game, trying to spook them off of taking the immunity offer.

Sean couldn't talk to him about this, Calvin thought regretfully, but a beer after basketball might be a good idea. Maybe Sean could be vaguely helpful, or helpfully vague, or something.

If Ryle wasn't sincerely happy, he was, at the very least, enjoying himself. "Now that we have my conscience clear on your immunity decision, and I've told you of my happy acquiescence, may I ask one more question?"

"Of course," Calvin said. How would he have stopped him?

"How is your ethics case going?" Ryle asked.

"That is well in hand," Sara said. "As you know full well, we have no cause for concern."

Ryle nodded, his lips pursed, as if he were actually listening. He leaned over and slapped Sean on the shoulder, as if the younger man also appreciated the delicious victory they faced together. "You know what Sean and I think?" Ryle did not wait for an answer. "We think that a mutineer and an unethical lawyer don't make the best poster children for allowing emigration."

"It's not forbidden," Calvin snapped.

"Not yet," Ryle said. "What do you think the hearing is about?"

CHAPTER 22

WITH RYLE GONE, AND SEAN moping along after him, as if embarrassed to be associated with the man, Calvin and Sara were left to get back to work or leave. It had been a grueling day, and Sara rather wished that Calvin would suggest they leave and get dinner, collegially, of course. Maybe they could talk about what had happened the previous Saturday. He didn't.

"We have a lot to do," he said.

Sara took a deep breath and got her second wind. They walked by several empty offices. Other people had left for the evening. "We do. I'm glad to hear you sounding more optimistic on *Volokh*." *Volokh* really was a political question, in every sense of the word.

"I'm not," Calvin said. "I'm not optimistic at all. We have to find the great-granddaughter." They reached Calvin's office and she followed him in but when he didn't sit down she remained standing. She was getting used to the view out his window. She recognized the pattern of lights in the building across K Street. It was always the same people who stayed on to work in the dark.

"The granddaughter?" She said it slowly, to cover the fact that she didn't know why he was bringing up granddaughters.

"Ray Hillman's great-granddaughter. Remember? He was all doting about her and her wish to move to Elysia." He sounded scornful, as if wishing to move to Elysia was nothing but a young's girl's fancy and foolish to boot. The girl would pack her things in a Barbie suitcase.

She remembered now. "Maybe they talked, you're thinking?"

Calvin passed his hand over his screen as if checking his messages. "Maybe they talked."

"I'll take care of that," Sara said. She had to volunteer sometimes, as if he were more conscious of her seniority with the firm than the fact that he represented the only living starship captain on the planet.

He moved away from his desk and stood in the middle of the room as if dithering. He was much closer than he usually was.

"Thanks," Calvin said. He reached behind his office door and pulled his coat out. It was clearly new, and more expensive than the one he had been wearing when he arrived at the firm. "See you in the morning."

Polly and her bodyguard, as she thought of Zeke Salisbury, entered the quiet restaurant. It was done up as an early 19th century barn, complete with rafters and uneven planks on the floor.

It was situated on F Street near the White House. If she had to explain to one more person that the reason she figured she hadn't been invited to dinner in the President's residence was because of the pending mutiny charges, she might have to strike someone. She had been invited decades ago, when the *Aeneid* was sent to save humanity, not to despoil the universe. F Street was close enough.

They were meeting other crewmembers. Robert had news about the shark.

It was a very expensive restaurant, she saw, with lots of human interaction. She didn't care. She had all the money in the world. The maître d'hotel, dignified in streamlined clothes of black and white, recognized her. "Captain," he said, "it is an honor to see you here."

She thanked him, and answered his questions about what a sunrise on Elysia looked like as he led them to their table. Zeke sighed, but he regularly received much the same treatment. Many people set their palms to inform them of crew in the vicinity, and most of the crew had been all over the casts in their own hometowns if not always the nation's capital.

Bill Cannon was at the table, with Melissa and Robert. Polly had gotten to know the xenos in the long horrible trip back, after the failed attempt to get them off the ship, after some of them had forgiven her and after others had not. She had never been able to tell with Bill, but at least he suffered her. He had raged at her when they didn't make it off the ship. He had held her responsible, relied on her, trusted her, and she had failed. But whenever she saw him after that day, he had been unstintingly civil, although not warm. She was surprised he was in the dinner party.

"It's landed," Robert said. "It's in one of the big cargo containers."

"Is it still alive?" Polly asked.

"The monitors say so," Robert replied. "I haven't tried to access it, but that's just because I don't want to make a big deal of it." He sniffed. "We're not all the queen of corn."

"Robert," Bill said, "is the shark king." He ran his hands through the thick curls of his hair. He gave Polly a serious look. "We're here to offer you any help you need, Captain."

She blinked. She had not been expecting this. "You are kind. I think my lawyer has things well in hand. I will be testifying to Congress." She looked around the table at the collection of minds and courage seated with her. "Has the Senate contacted any of you?"

Robert barked a short laugh. "You're the face of all of us, Captain. You're the only one they'll call, I'm betting."

It was strange to be called Captain. They hadn't done it on shipboard. "You all know a hell of a lot more about Elysia than I do," she said.

"And some of us could even provide the drama they want from you," Bill said.

"Not without admitting to attempted desertion," Melissa said quietly. She was the only xeno who had been a member of the military.

"Not me," Bill said. "I was just trying to quit my job."

The sommelier appeared, also clad in streamlined black and white. He was an older man, in the sense of the word that Polly understood. His hair was grey, and there were lines around his eyes and across his brow. His eyes were brown, and the whites very clear. "The wine list, Captain?"

She was used to it, the entire population of the planet knowing who she was, but she smiled and thanked him. He handed her an ornate sheet of stiff parchment. It was lovely. When she took it, she felt something small drop into her palm. She almost shook it away, suspecting a bug, but something made her open her hand.

It was a kernel of dried corn, and might have come from a bag of popping corn. She looked up quizzically at the sommelier, a small smile tugging at her lips.

He answered with an equally small smile of his own.

"Thank you," she said.

"You are most welcome. I will be back after you have ordered your food to advise on the wines."

After he had left, she laid her hand on the table and opened it. "Look at this," she said to the others. "What does it mean?"

Melissa peered at it closely. "I have no idea."

Bill gave it a casual glance. "It means he likes you and supports you, Captain. I have received about half a dozen myself."

"It's because you are so vocal, Bill," Robert said.

With the drinks, each of the others received a kernel of dried corn. Bill received two.

The xenos were working in USACD labs near Quantico in Virginia, but had come into headquarters about the shark. It was Robert's shark, but the others had come along for the discussion. At the end of dinner, after they had finished sharing information on where everyone lived, and wasn't it nice to have lots of money with which to actually choose a decent place, Polly asked Robert about the shark again. Once the settlers off-loaded their supplies, livestock, and machinery, the *Aeneid* had been left with large, empty spaces. Robert had used part of it for a shark.

"The quarantine procedures are really strict," Robert said.

"And redundant," Melissa noted. "We've been through them. We've been around the shark and everything else on Elysia." Melissa had swum in the ocean first of them all. She was a quiet woman, had told no one she was going to do it, but there, Robert had told Polly later, she was. In the water, in what turned out to be shark-infested water. "A lot. Now they've found something else to quarantine."

"Isn't this part of your training?" Polly asked. "All this quarantining?"

"Sure," Robert said, "but we didn't go down in bubbles, and we weren't supposed to. Life is messy. Anything you study on Earth or Mars is 'contaminated' by other life, including us."

"We didn't find anything on Mars," Polly said.

"We might have," Melissa said, continuing Robert's point, "and we'd never have known if it didn't come from us or our early robots."

"There were strict decontamination procedures," Polly said.

"And microbes can survive in a vacuum," Robert said.

Polly shook her head. "So the science is never pure."

Bill laughed. "Not ever. Not in any sense. What was so great about Elysia was that we were there for the low-hanging fruit. We could make gross observations and it was all new. We got to establish the big categories, see the parallels to Earth. We were first."

"Find the shark," Polly said, trying to circle back to the original topic.

"About the shark," Robert said. "USACD doesn't want the public knowing about it right now."

Polly's eyebrows went up. She could think of a number of reasons for that, none of them to USACD's credit. "The people who like the corn are going to go wild for the shark," she said.

Robert and Melissa nodded, and Robert said, "But we're following your lead."

Polly felt the grin start to form. "You're going to take it to the Heather Young show? She'll want to have your children."

"We thought of that," Bill said. "But it's too hard to remove it from the labs."

"Which is kind of too bad," Robert said, "because we'd like to bring it to your hearing."

Polly gulped a laugh and covered her mouth with her hand. "You would upstage Senator Donohue so very badly if you did that. What will you do with it?"

"We had to settle for a press conference," Bill said.

Noticing Bill's use of the past tense, she said, "When was it?" She was sure she would have noticed a press conference about the shark.

"Tonight, after dinner," Melissa said. "We want you to come."

Calvin would kill her. Polly was quite sure of that. Sometimes, Calvin took things too seriously. "Sure. How are you getting the press into the labs?"

"Captain," Zeke said. "You can't. That is classified information, and you are in enough trouble."

She was about to respond, but she felt a presence hovering over the table, and looked up into the face of a woman standing to the other side of Zeke. Polly thought she recognized her as having been seated a couple of tables over, but the restaurant was lit mostly by candles, and barns were dark and cavernous, so she wasn't sure. If she hadn't come from another table, she had appeared out of nowhere, like a ghost.

The woman's beautiful face was stern and stark white, her brow high and her hair red. She looked like Elizabeth I, and wore a pale blue sari that flowed gently around her body. "You have destroyed a world," she said to Polly. Her voice was beautiful, too, the voice an angel would have.

Polly pushed back in her chair, sliding it at an angle away from the table and the woman. She was free to stand if she had to. She wondered if her antagonist was armed, and if she knew the man who had shot his way into the party the previous week. She hoped not.

Zeke very slowly and carefully stood, placing himself between the two. "I'm going to ask you to leave us," he said softly. A lone man two tables over covered his face with his hand, as if embarrassed. As if he couldn't bear to watch.

The stranger stepped back, so she could stare Polly in the face. "I am not Earth First," she said. "But I do think what you have done is wrong. We will never be able to study this world in its purest form. You may have ruined an alien ecology because you were pursuing your own selfish path."

"Instead we should pursue yours?" Polly asked. "You have no claim on Elysia."

"I am a biologist," the woman said.

"So are we," Bill informed her. "Elysia is a fascinating place. I would have preferred to stay and have a claim there myself." He looked over at Polly automatically. He couldn't help it, apparently. She returned his glance gravely. She still owed him that much.

"You have disrupted any hope of good science," the woman persisted.

"We were just talking about that," Bill said. "I am a scientist, too, and I can recognize that science, like life, is messy."

Polly stood. This was just an obnoxious middle-aged woman who thought the world should go as she and her friends and colleagues, all right-thinking people, no doubt, would have it. "I am sorry," Polly said. "We had different imperatives. Humanity should never have all its eggs in one solar system again. I think you've forgotten that."

The calm angelic face grew irritated. She could see Polly well, with Zeke only partially blocking them. "You mutinied," she said, her voice stiff.

"I carried out my mission," Polly said.

The woman stared at Polly, and then, with no preface, no working of her mouth, no warning, spat in Polly's face. Just as suddenly, Zeke had the woman on the ground in an arm bar, the back of his knee across her throat, and everyone was standing and shouting, and the embarrassed man from the other table came running over, yelling at Zeke to leave his wife alone. Polly wiped away the drop of spittle that had reached her cheek.

Zeke flipped the woman over onto her stomach and frisked her while she struggled unsuccessfully to squirm against the search. The sari lost some of its structure, but Zeke did not let himself be deterred from being thorough.

"I'll sue you," the woman said from the floor in her lovely voice.

"I have lots of lawyers," Zeke replied. He finished his search and helped her to her feet. "You have to understand. I believed you to be assaulting my captain. There have been two attempts on her life, and our crewmembers are being killed. It's not going to happen in front of me."

Robert signaled to his colleagues. "We have to go," he said. "We can't get caught up in this."

Zeke rounded on Polly. "And you are not going with them." His face was set. He wasn't angry, but he was adamant.

The maître d' appeared and turned to Polly. "I saw the whole thing. Would you like to press charges?"

"I should press charges," the woman said, her face the countenance of an avenging Elizabethan angel.

Her husband laid a hand on her arm. "Milla. No. You started it."

"It was a biological attack," Zeke said. "We're going to want your saliva analyzed, your blood drawn, a urine analysis, your medical history, your family history, any history of mental illness. Or you can leave now."

Zeke may not have been angry. It was hard to say. But he was effective. "We are leaving," Milla's husband said.

The xenos had already left, fading away when she wasn't noticing. Dessert lay uneaten, and Polly looked longingly at her lemon meringue.

She sighed. "We better get moving if we're going to catch the xenos."

"You're not going," Zeke said.

"I am."

Zeke shook his head. "You have obligations."

Calvin woke to excited casting. He wasn't expecting it. His alarm woke him gently, not with the urgency it would have employed had "Nigmatullin" and "arrest" been used in the same sentence anywhere. The cold, wintry sunlight filtered through the mullions, hitting him just below the eyes, and he stared at the ceiling for several minutes while the news and weather washed over him unheard. His brain didn't reboot at great speeds, and the ceiling was about what he could handle at first. The anxiety that grew within him on a daily basis sometimes brought him wide awake too quickly. Other days, it provided his brain an incentive to remain in shut-down mode. Nigmatullin's Senate hearing was only a week away. All the interviews he had been able to conduct corroborated her story, but her story didn't exactly get her off the hook. Sara had not found Ray Hillman's granddaughter. She had vanished, and her parents were concerned. Calvin worried that she had shared the fate of her grandfather. The FBI was proving remarkably inept at finding the persons who had shot the starship captains, and the local police were apparently equally clumsy in their search for the killers of the navigators. Calvin had made sure to allow several people to hear him repeat his own assailant's claim to an affiliation with Earth First so that it wouldn't be a secret he could be killed for. Nonetheless, he had also sucked it up and paid the house extra for enhanced security of his own. Each morning he ran through reports of fallen twigs, scampering squirrels on the roof and airstrikes from birds who thought that March was soon enough to return to the nation's capital.

The volume on his alarm increased to the point where his brain had to listen. After reporting on issues with package drones—his new security settings meant his house accepted such deliveries only in his absence and scanned appropriately—his house let the announcer share that several xenobiologists from the *Aeneid* had held a press conference at 1 a.m. to report the return of a shark from Elysia. USACD had ordered them all arrested earlier in the morning for revealing classified information, and pictures of the alien shark were available if only he would turn over and power that up. He did.

"Here he is," said a man whose tag identified him as Dr. Robert Jones, a member of the *Aeneid*'s crew and possessed of a doctorate in xenobiology. This was likely one of the people Nigmatullin had failed on Elysia. Calvin kept the image flat, as it was too early to have a host of people and a shark tank in his bedroom with him. His bedroom wall showed him what looked to be a cross between a lab and a warehouse, with a large tank the size of a swimming pool housing a creature from either the distant past or an alien planet. It was definitely a shark, six feet maybe in length, with teeth both rapacious and frightening. The size of the tank gave him a sudden realization as to the size of the *Aeneid*. The starship was huge. Maybe the tank had taken the place in the hold of a tractor or two. No wonder the United States had built only one. He hoped MarsCorp was building more and planning to reap economies of scale.

The scrolling text at the bottom of the screen gave him a recap of Jones' speech. The shark was in Virginia. Maybe Earth would tilt as everyone rushed there to see it. Maybe there would be more long lines.

Jones was attempting to discourse on parallel evolution, while responding scornfully to questions from the press about panspermia.

Elysia's was a very, very distant solar system—farther than the Moon. His sarcasm did not endear him to the casters.

Calvin finished reading about the biology of the shark. It was not exactly like an Earth shark. Like the corn, the DNA were not entirely identical, but the teeth and the capacious maw looked from the pictures just as terrifying, regardless of its planetary origins.

He finished the readings, opted not to continue watching the repartee between the xenos and the reporters, some of whom were xenos themselves, and switched over to arrest reports. For those, he sat up. It was hard to filter through the humor. USACD Fears Alien Shark Attack! read one headline, which was alluring but not informative. Even that report made clear that USACD had classified the existence of the shark as secret information for reasons of national security. The xenos who invited the casters into the lab had been arrested, their security clearances suspended, and the scientists were now being questioned.

Calvin's first thought was that they would need someone to defend them. His second thought was that others would realize this as well. He checked his palm, which he had been ignoring. There were several messages from the firm's Bart Locke, who was also an early riser, it appeared, and one from the Senate Committee on Planetary Space and Extraterritorial Jurisdiction.

He checked the Senate's message first. The Committee had either invited or commanded—it was hard to tell—the presence of one Captain Paolina Nigmatullin, formerly of the U.S.S *Aeneid*, to testify regarding the events surrounding the departure of the starship from the planet Elysia. It was now official. Her Senate hearing was next week. Calvin swore, and all thoughts of the problems of the xenos and their shark left his mind as he headed for the shower.

He received another message after his shower. His own hearing date, for his ethics charge, was scheduled two days after Nigmatullin's.

CHAPTER 23

IT WAS MONDAY MORNING, AND the Senate Committee hearing was scheduled for that Wednesday. Calvin, his co-counsel, his client, and her bodyguard had sequestered themselves in a conference room. Again. For days now, they had been mooting Nigmatullin to prepare her testimony and responses to any questions, friendly or not, that might come her way. For days now, Calvin had been encountering Sara and Zeke conversing quietly in person or by call. For days now, he had been putting it out of his mind, but as the hearing approached, their assignations, as he had taken to referring to them, bothered him more and more, and he noted the aura of camaraderie that emanated from them now.

His palm buzzed him, and he would have ignored it, but it insisted on his attention. It wasn't exactly an electric shock, but the sensation was unpleasant. He only had one news item at that setting, so he leaned away from the table for a quick look.

His jaw set, and he bit back an expletive. Then he swore anyway. The Court had decided early, releasing its opinion in the *Volokh* matter long before the Court's usual June releases of its opinions. The early release suggested two contradictory reasons for the decision: the Court wanted to give any potential Congressional witnesses, such as a starship captain, for example, time to reconsider testifying so as to avoid that testimony being used when confronting mutiny charges, or, someone had rushed the Court to avoid any starship captain persuading a Senate oversight committee of the merits of interplanetary settlement. Calvin wondered if anyone had the power or the pull necessary to rush the Court.

The others looked at him, surprised. "What is it?" Nigmatullin asked.

"The Supreme Court upheld the D.C. Circuit in the *Volokh* matter. Suddenly—when they know damn well this isn't right—they discover the Constitution." He studied Nigmatullin. She looked tired, and he knew her well enough now to read the stress in her eyes. Her hair was pulled back too tightly, and it hardened her face and made her eyes look too big. She would not have been out of place in prison fatigues—which thought he quickly banished.

"What does that mean?" she asked, as if his reaction hadn't already told her.

"It means you can't testify," Calvin said.

It was Zeke's turn to swear, and Sara covered her mouth with clenched fists. Her eyes were too big, too.

"The hell I can't," Nigmatullin said. "I have accepted the invitation."

"You can plead the Fifth," Calvin said. "If you testify, everything you say can and will be held against you. I recommend that you take the Fifth. You are not required to incriminate yourself. If they can get both Houses to vote on compelling you, then fine, you can testify. But they won't."

"That's what would happen in my mutiny trial," Nigmatullin said. "Here, I have a chance to change a few minds."

Calvin found he had placed his own hands on top of his head, a posture of pure frustration from childhood. He thought about bringing them down, but left them there. This situation called for extreme gestures. "Polly, you are very eloquent. You have brought the hair on the back of my neck upright and filled me with elation and a sense of the boundlessness of the universe. I've laughed. I've cried. In the Senate, all the speeches will come from the senators. Not you."

Nigmatullin pursed her lips. "This isn't *Captain Nigmatullin Goes to Washington?*"

"Not even the first version," Calvin said.

"Polly," Zeke said, "you have to listen to him. That's what you are paying him for."

Calvin tried again, but brought his hands down. "Remember, you agreed to this because you thought it would benefit your desire for freedom. The testimony is a public good, sure, but it was also going to affirmatively protect you. Now, without any chance for someone on your side—namely, me—to ask you follow up questions, you can be used, abused, and discarded. This does you and your cause no good. That protection is gone."

Nigmatullin stared at the conference table. She laid her hands on it flat, and spread her fingers wide. "You are my lawyer, so you have to think about protecting me. That was an advantage you saw. I saw others."

Calvin could see where this was going, and it was nowhere good. "Polly, your mutiny hearing will be cast far and wide."

"But then you'll be telling me to take the Fifth," she pointed out.

Calvin groaned out loud. "Maybe not. If you testify at your mutiny hearing you'll have a lot more chances to talk. Look, you asked me to represent you, to keep you out of jail. You want your freedom." He took a quick glance at the other two. His next statement felt very personal, even though he would couch it in terms of protecting Nigmatullin's interests. "You want to be able to return to Elysia when MarsCorp builds its ships, don't you?" Maybe that was what Calvin wanted for her. "If you go before Congress, you can't answer just some of their questions. And, that Donohue wants to ask you about the exact same things that USACD is charging you with: mutiny. It's what everyone wants to know, and she wants to take full advantage of it."

Nigmatullin gazed at him calmly. She looked better now than she had before the bad news came in, as if hope had riddled her with anxiety. Now that she'd lost that chance, she had less to worry about, but only if she ignored her lawyer's advice.

"Captain," Zeke pleaded, as if he read the same things in Nigmatullin's face. "He's telling you you've lost your get-out-of-jail-free card. Literally."

"I understand that," Nigmatullin said. "But I've spent the past month working on what to say, how to persuade them to allow emigration, how to convince them of the wonders of another Earth.

I want to show them all the parallels to our planet, that it really is a place we can live. I can't give up that opportunity."

If Calvin read Donohue right, and, really, he had nothing to go on except a feeling and Ryle Feder's unreliable comment about the true purpose of Donohue's hearing, this was the senator's opportunity—although for what, he didn't know—not the starship captain's. It was a politician's forum, not the bridge of a ship or even a basement courtroom in the executive branch. Nigmatullin was wandering into a political environment with which she was unfamiliar. One thing he had learned in the past week's prep was that she still found the threat of asteroids or some other form of extinction profoundly persuasive on an emotional level. As a native of the current decade, Calvin knew how wrong that was. He had shared that perspective with her, but she had not believed him, not in her bones where it counted.

"It's your decision," he said.

"Besides," Nigmatullin said, and her smile was an evil one, "I have a great lawyer. You'll be able to get me off."

Back at his desk, Calvin began more research. He needed answers to questions he had only just acquired, and he needed them before he heard from the Senate's lawyer. He wanted to limit the scope of Nigmatullin's testimony, but he suspected that would not work for any number of reasons, Polly herself being the main one.

He was distracted by seeing Zeke and Sara walk past his door on the way, presumably, to her office. It was almost an hour before Zeke left. He waved cheerily at Calvin, and gave him a big grin. Sara appeared in Calvin's doorway not long after. She was all aglow.

"What are you so happy about?" He hadn't meant to sound so waspish, but it was a legitimate question.

She ignored him. "Have you given any thought to your own hearing?"

"No. I don't have to. Ryle just sicced the ethics board on me out of spite. There's nothing for me to worry about, and you and I both know it. So does Ryle."

She smiled at him dotingly. "Calvin, there's always something that can go wrong. But, you should be glad to know I'm taking care of everything, and the board has not even noticed you for a deposition or anything like that."

"That's because they have nothing to ask me," he said. "Although, come to think of it, that's a little complacent of them."

"I've reviewed the transcript from your hearing. Your questions of the witness were entirely legitimate."

Her good cheer started to make him nervous. "That's all good. Where are you going with this?"

"I think they are just out to get you." She smiled beatifically, as if this was good news. "You did absolutely nothing wrong. So there is something else going on."

"You do know I think Ryle is just doing this to rattle me?" He felt he had made this point clear. Hers was not a new insight.

She sat down. "Yes, but when people do things like that a little sunshine is the best remedy."

"All right, Mary Sunshine, but could you take your rays of hope elsewhere? I have work I'm doing."

She didn't look at all dejected as she rose and walked off down the hall. She looked happy, like a woman in love.

He received a call sooner than he wanted. Fiona Franklin was calling to inquire whether his client still planned to testify in light of *Volokh*?

Despite the premature nature of the call, Calvin was relieved. If he'd made the call, he would have had to immediately disclose that the mad woman he represented wanted to testify without the immunizing effect.

"We are looking at that," Calvin told the Senate attorney.

She gazed back at him stone faced and indifferent. "I've tried to explain to the Senator that Captain Nigmatullin should no longer wish to appear—except maybe to plead the Fifth."

"Which would be poor theater," Calvin noted.

"Agreed. She insisted, however, that I call."

Calvin could tell that Fiona didn't appreciate being forced into the call. She knew perfectly well that the starship captain should have lost all interest in testifying. "Do you have something to offer us?" Calvin asked blandly. It was a bluff, but maybe he could get something out of this conversation. "You just need both Houses to vote on an immunity grant."

Fiona didn't quite scowl. "You know we won't get that." She paused, as if what she had to say next pained her. "We can offer to limit the scope of the questions."

They hadn't even tried to see if a vote was possible, Calvin figured. "From all of the senators?"

Fiona sighed. "Donohue says she will limit her questions. We will only ask about Elysia, its environment, the state of the colony."

"And the other senators? Have they agreed to these limits?" He wondered why Donohue was so anxious still. This could be a dull hearing, with no startling drama about the last days on Elysia.

Fiona sighed again. "I'll have to check on that."

"Could you?"

Monday afternoon was upsetting. Calvin had called off any more preparation, saying he had to look at a few things, and that he was looking to bound the scope of her testimony. If he had his way, Polly wouldn't talk about the departure. She was fine with that. She wanted to talk about going back.

She and Zeke sat on a cold bench near the Lincoln Memorial. They had wandered quite a ways in the frigid air from her overheated lawyers on K Street. It was bracing. The walk had unnerved Zeke, who was convinced that someone was going to shoot at her again, but that could happen regardless of where she walked. The thought that someone knew she was scheduled to attend the party on the Whitehurst and had likely shared that information didn't seem to make him feel better.

He had scanners, and she suspected he had hired other people she couldn't see to keep an eye out. He continued to refuse her offers of pay or reimbursement for his self-appointed bodyguard duties.

"Captain," Zeke began. It was what he'd already said several times on the walk. "You mustn't do this."

"I won't talk about the last days. Or the trip back. Calvin's negotiating all that. This will work."

Why, he had already asked several times, couldn't she just wait until her mutiny trial? Partly, she knew she could sway public opinion. She wanted to sway public opinion. She wanted the senators to see that happening. She wanted to sway them, too. It had been so nice and tidy before the Supreme Court ruled. She would have gotten to eat her cake and have it, too.

Now, her lawyer was sweating bullets, and she should be, too. But all the reasons that made the decision good before still held. She was the only one who might suffer going forward. Strangely, the part of her that felt she had gotten her spot on the *Aeneid* by cheating felt that this was appropriate and just. She was supposed to suffer. Besides, she might not. She just had to refuse to answer any of the wrong questions. That would end her testimony, of course, but she would get out what she wanted right away.

"Zeke, if I wait until my mutiny trial, if I back down now, I'll look frightened. I'm not. And, if I wait until the trial, it will all be about whether I'm an evil mutineer. The Senate hearing will be about what we should do about Elysia. It's very tidy. Everything will be fine."

His gaze was level, and his look one of great unease.

She hadn't meant to pry, but found herself saying, "What's going on with you and Sara?"

He looked away, scanning the people walking along the other side of the oblong stretch of water in front of them. "I'm helping her with Calvin," he said. He seemed inclined to say no more than that, and Polly didn't press the matter.

She hunched her shoulders against the cold. The sky was grey, and it suited her mood. She had planned on feeling elation about sallying forth to do battle and all of that, but apparently her plan had counted on that gesture providing a guarantee of freedom, a guarantee she had just lost.

Sara had stopped worrying about Calvin. She recognized the nature of his current indifference to her. His previous indifference still worried her, but now that he just looked at her as another warm lawyer to throw in front of the harm heading toward his client, she was unconcerned. She had felt that way herself in the past, with far less personal interest in the outcome of the results. One hated to lose. One wanted to win. Regardless of how one looked at it, the uncertainty was harrowing. He would not be suggesting dinner anytime soon.

When Nigmatullin was safe, Sara would be there. She had figured it all out. She had spurned him. She had to reach out. She had foolishly waited for him to try again, and only a crazy person would try that in the workplace with someone who had given every indication of disinterest. She just needed to remedy that. When he was free to look up from this case, she had a plan.

She worried more about Calvin's ethics charge. Calvin's ethics hearing was only two business days after the Senate hearing, and Sara needed to be prepared. Sara really needed to be prepared because Calvin himself was ignoring it. Was he planning to wing it? Review his transcript the night before? He displayed a complete indifference to the future of his career, and a couple of the partners had checked in with her to make sure the firm's reputation wasn't about to suffer.

She was ready, so Calvin would be fine. She had a good plan.

She looked up from her desk, smiling. Someone was standing there.

"Would you like to get something to eat?" Calvin Tondini stood in her doorway, looking handsome and male, if not a little like someone scheduled to fight a duel at dawn, and she smiled with true happiness.

The night was dark, and the cloud cover blotted out whatever stars might have shown through the streetlights. Their reflections rippled in puddles of melted snow. It had warmed up that day, and rills of icy water ran into the drains.

The restaurant wasn't fancy, and Sara had passed it many times without entering. Being only two doors down, it was just too close to the office to hold any appeal. Spangled chiffon curtains and stars and moons from a decade ago decorated the place, which was odd, when it would have been so easy to reprogram the walls. Booths offered privacy between the tables, and the two of them sank into theirs like a pair of oysters in a silk-lined shell.

"I've not eaten here before," she said.

Calvin was reviewing the menu and nodded absently.

How awkward was this going to be, she wondered. She ordered a glass of wine, and took several quick swallows when it arrived. The warmth hit her stomach and she took a deep breath. "Are you ready?" she asked.

Calvin leaned back in his seat, and she noticed how tightly his hands gripped the edge of the table. "I hope so. Have you ever fired a client?"

Sara's own hands grabbed her side of the table. "You can't do that," she hissed.

"I know," Calvin said. "But I want to. She's driving me crazy. She is crazy, and I don't know how to make her see reason."

"If you fired her," Sara said, "things would go even worse for her. And, anyway, you can't."

"I'm not going to. But I want to. Although I would never." He stopped and gave her a wry look, as if he realized he was babbling. "She needs to live so she can help MarsCorp." Nonetheless, he circled back around to his original complaint. "And, she doesn't need me at the Senate hearing. I won't be able to object or rehabilitate her or anything." Polly wouldn't have counsel at the witness table. This wasn't a trial, merely an inquiry on matters of public interest. The committee had just tried, a little late, to add one of the xenobiologists to the panel, but he was unavailable, according to his lawyer. The committee had issued no subpoenas for the man's presence.

Aaron Ryder, who was also scheduled to testify, served as the president of the environmental organization Earth First. The casts were all atwitter about whether he had ties to the violent subculture that had appropriated Earth First's name, but a thorough background check had shown no ties. This was not heartening in light of the failure to find any of the attackers. With the attack on Polly at the party, everyone now assumed that an Earth First death squad had murdered the *Aeneid's* senior commanders and maybe the navigators, too. Earth First disavowed possessing a death squad, because that wasn't done, but did think it had useful views to offer on whether additional ships should be permitted to go to Elysia. Earth First was against it.

"I'm worried for her safety," Sara said.

As if reading her thoughts, Calvin said, "The Earth Firster will be searched. Everyone gets searched going on the Hill. Do you think he's going to turn and try to strangle her?" His eyes held some spark of amusement, she was glad to see.

"I was more thinking about right now," Sara said. "People are always recognizing her."

"And giving her corn," Calvin said.

They both grinned.

"You know," he confided, "someone gave me some corn once—just two kernels."

"Were you with Polly?" she asked.

He looked very pleased. "No, that was the good part. I was just walking back from lunch."

"You have groupies," she said, laughing. "What did you do with it?"

"Gave one kernel to Polly. Kept the other. I'm going to take it to Elysia."

Her breath caught. He had said it so lightly, as if he were joking. "You're leaving Earth?" Her voice came out small and strangled. She hated men, or, if not all of them, at least this one.

CHAPTER 24

THE SENATE'S DIRKSEN BUILDING, ALTHOUGH renovated and expanded several times since its original construction two centuries earlier, was still large and white, and filled a city block in back of and to the north of the Capitol. The sun shone brightly on the stark, white stone.

Paolina Nigmatullin and her entourage endured the security check. They submitted to x-rays, backscatter, and other assorted radiation emitted by suns long dead to ensure that neither their clothing nor any of their body cavities contained energy or projectile weapons. Her status as a witness did not allow them to escape the invasive radiation, but she had experienced far more in space, and suffered it all stoically. There was even a physical pat-down. The one thing she didn't have to worry about today, she figured, was a shooter.

She felt mildly guilty that they were taken to a separate line from the general public. A snake of people wound down First Street, and her lawyer muttered something about being glad to see that Tri had stayed in school, given his proclivity for standing in line. She remembered Tri. He had been one of her rescuers that terrible afternoon in Florida when Contreras and Orlova were killed.

She needed to pull her mind away from death. She felt as if she faced the gallows. She was well armed with polite phrases intended to turn away questions unrelated to the arrival of the *Aeneid* at Elysia, the logistics of getting there, and what a great place it was. Calvin thought that she was not an obvious witness for the questions of whether it was appropriate to settle Elysia or whether it was indeed a good place to settle, and Polly didn't disagree. She didn't, however, go so far as her attorney in concluding that this was all just a chance for the committee to attack her on the mutiny. Even senators and their committees had to take their publicity where they could find it.

The people in the foyer included some who had to be attending her hearing. Several carried stalks of corn. She wondered where they had found them in March.

Someone recognized her. "Captain," came the call, and others picked it up.

"Hello, Earth," she called back from the other side of the foyer, grinning foolishly at them all.

The ones who liked her started cheering. It was very loud and echoed, and she felt a strange shiver of excitement, like maybe this could work.

She blew them a kiss, and the cheering got louder. A guard scowled at her. "Ma'am, could you not encourage them?"

His voice found itself alone in a pause in the shouting, and everyone heard him. There was another stunned pause, and the people in the other line started laughing. Young women who had removed their coats to show bare arms, older men whose age showed only in their eyes, young men and middle-aged women grew giddy and silly. One of the girls started bouncing as if she were a child. She blew a kiss back to Nigmatullin.

Nigmatullin received many more before she got out of the foyer.

Ebullient herself, she turned to Zeke. "Did you see that? They want Elysia, too."

Zeke did not stop his scanning. Zeke had been nervous the whole drive over, and had not let her take the Metro or a cab, but insisted on driving her himself. The air was warm enough to make it unnecessary, but he had had her keep her hood up for the block they walked.

"Not all of them do," Zeke said. He pointed back to the crowd leaving the security point. One man was staring after them, his eyes serious, and his arms crossed across his chest. "He doesn't want Elysia."

"You don't know that," she said, determined that if she could shed her gloom he could shed his paranoia. Today was her day.

She glanced at Calvin. He had lost the grin. She couldn't say he looked haunted, but his face was set. "You need to show more confidence in your client," she whispered. She still felt ebullient.

His look was very serious. "I have every confidence in you." He clearly meant it.

"The last rehearsal didn't go so well," she said. He called it mooting, but she thought of it as a dry run, and there had been a lot them. Lovely young Sara, who apparently had an evil side, has asked her during the dress rehearsal whether it was true Polly had forced some of the colonists to stay behind against their will. When Polly had answered no in outrage, they had all yelled at her. She had been supposed to say questions about the departure from Elysia were outside the scope of the hearing.

She wasn't the only one who was tense.

Calvin finally smiled. "It means you are so ready that you stopped paying attention. I suspect you'll be paying attention this morning."

She certainly would. The last rehearsal really had been a debacle, but she had spent the previous evening reviewing her notes, checking the responses to trick questions, and was ready to say she had never had a wife, just in case anyone inquired whether she had stopped beating her.

The large halls leading into the atrium were two stories high, and she supposed it to be an attempt at either grandeur or intimidation. She had faced larger spaces.

As if reading her mind, Sara said, "I suppose this doesn't bother you at all, after the *Aeneid's* voyage."

Polly smiled at her. "Been thinking about space travel, have you?"

To her surprise, Sara blushed and said, "No, no, I haven't. I was thinking how nervous I would be if I were you, and then I figured this wasn't the most nerve-wracking thing you've ever done."

A large knot of people brushed by them, walking fast. They all looked very governmental, in suits and ties and clacking shoes. They also looked like they knew that other people looked at them and wondered who they were.

Calvin led them to the hearing room several stories up. It was one of the few with stadium seating and occupied the southwestern corner of the building. Two banks of windows stretched well beyond eye level. Skylights let in even more light, and she saw Zeke frowning up at them. The walls had wood paneling in pale blonde, and the room could hold several hundred people.

The single witness table faced an elevated podium, so that the senators could look down on the persons they had called to testify. That, Polly thought, was unattractive of them. In a democracy someone should have stopped the architect.

The audience was boisterous, a sea of purple containing islands of green. There were people dressed in less political colors. She hoped that the people she had seen at the security check had found seats. A man caught her eye and waved an ear of corn at her. She grinned and nodded back. She saw her USACD prosecutor, Ryle Feder, in the audience.

One side held several rows of seats for casters and other reporters of events. A child sat in one of them, and Calvin waved. Polly had heard about his friend Molly. Molly waved back. The seats back of the witness table were reserved and mostly empty, and Calvin, Sara, and Zeke moved to the three behind her place.

Bill Cannon, apparently out on bail after participating in the stunt with the shark's press conference, was already settled in, and Polly saw the blond man she recognized from Earth First standing chatting with a small group of people. A young woman with long brown hair pulled into a bun hurried over to them.

"Captain Nigmatullin," she said, taking her hand and shaking it with vigor, "we are so pleased you could make it. Everyone has been looking forward to this so much."

"My pleasure," she murmured. She greeted Bill, shook hands with Aaron Ryder from Earth First, and settled at the table between the two men.

It wasn't a courtroom. When the senators entered, the audience and witnesses did not stand, even though the senators got to sit at the elevated bench. Not every senator on the Committee was attending the hearing, and there were several empty seats. Calvin had warned her that if a bell rang, the senators would leave for a vote and the rest of them would have to sit there twiddling their thumbs.

She kept her focus while the senators greeted each other, thanked each other, and commended each other on their presence at the hearing that they had arranged. Tessa Donohue looked sleek, almost sleepy, and something about her gaze reminded Polly that the woman had been married seven times. True, at her ripe old age she was not alone in having been married more than once, but seven times seemed like a lot to someone who had never married even once.

Polly reviewed her lawyer's marching orders. She even planned to follow some of them. There would be plenty of questions unrelated to the last days on Elysia. Calvin had negotiated that, but she was now well rehearsed in avoiding any clever traps.

No, Captain Nigmatullin had better things to talk about. She would remind them all of the asteroid threat, and remind Donohue, who had lived through it, of the terror of extinction. She would describe the glories of Elysia, and say that even if it had been a desert just barely capable of supporting life, it was still good to settle it. Humanity had to have a presence elsewhere, and this was the first place besides Earth that had air. Real air. That you could breathe. It was not the Moon or Mars. She almost giggled: also, it had corn.

She understood her risks. Calvin had told her over and over again how the questions would skirt around the mutiny, attempt to terrify and distract her enough that she might admit to the charges against her. The sneaky questions would undermine her endorsement of settlement, rattle her, make her lose her train of thought, and, worst of all, lead her into admissions that could lose her her freedom. She knew this because of all those damn rehearsals, but she was sure she had gotten the hang of it. Aglow with her own intentions, she resolved to take those risks and let Calvin argue about it later. That was what she paid him for.

As the Chairman of the Committee, Donohue was allowed the first question. It was for Polly. "Captain Nigmatullin," she said, "did the U.S. government cover the costs of your interplanetary journey?"

"It did," Polly replied soberly. Perhaps the senator was thinking the government should spend that kind of money again.

"And Elysia was the third solar system you visited?"

"It was." Polly's lawyers had asked better questions than this.

"And you liked Elysia?"

"I did." Polly smiled. "Everyone did."

Tessa Donohue's smile was equally warm, her eyes limpid and large, even at the distance between. "Is that why you chose that planet for your act of mutiny?"

Polly drew in a breath, slowly and softly. This was how it was going to be, was it? She could handle that. Her attorneys had not rehearsed this part of her testimony, but she had. They had no intention of her responding to these questions. Calvin had obtained assurances they would not be asked. So much for the word of a politician, but she had always known better.

There was a long beat, and the room was completely still, waiting to see what she would do. Had she really come all this way for nothing? Calvin had warned her that this could happen. Who would have thought that such a young man could be so right in such a cynical prediction? Thinking of Calvin reminded her of another point he had made. It was one she had ignored, but, now, in the heat of the battle, she recognized it for the weapon it was, and she was no longer blinded by her own strong desire to make the case for settling Elysia. If she answered this question, all the rest of them would be about the mutiny, and they would all be in this "yes" or "no" format against which she had so strongly been warned. She would not make her case and she would lose her freedom—for nothing.

Calvin had assured her that pleading her rights under the Fifth Amendment of the Constitution did not allow an inference of guilt. One could refuse to testify out of mistrust for the government's ability to twist the facts, out of concern for a political vendetta, out of worry that she didn't know what the hell was going on.

Carefully, telling herself not to be an idiot, Paolina Nigmatullin set aside her vision of oratory and powerful persuasion. She set aside her image of herself as nobly self-sacrificing, accepted that she had failed again, and did what she had to do to protect herself.

She let the breath out. "I decline to answer, in an exercise of my rights under the Fifth Amendment."

Calvin Tondini watched the starship captain's back. He could have watched her face on one of the many screens in the room, but it was more merciful to keep his eyes fixed on her back. He knew what it had cost her. The length of time she had taken to respond told the whole room what it had cost her.

The room didn't care. Isolated cries of "No," mingled with a minor descant of "no, no, no."

The back remained rigid. It hadn't moved, but what had looked like confident pride earlier changed to nothing more than a determination not to collapse.

Calvin was in the front row, directly back of his client. He debated turning. The overhead screens didn't show much of the crowd, just the witnesses, and his need to look these people in the face was overwhelming. Most were wearing purple. Did people turn that quickly? If so, it was really too bad.

He turned and looked. Those in green were smirking, it was true. Not everyone in purple was booing Nigmatullin. Others raised their voices at Senator Donohue, whose lovely face showed both her serenity and indifference. It was a different member of the panel who banged her gavel for order, and the room finally quieted.

"Dr. Cannon," Donohue said, "you have published a number of monographs since your return from Elysia. Please tell us about the edibility of the plant life."

Calvin listened to the xeno's answer with only half an ear. He watched Nigmatullin's back, and felt as if he were experiencing the first instance of lawyer-client telepathy. She was humiliated. She had been invited as a stunt, a dancing bear to be put in her place, an advocate to be shown that, despite her popularity, the government made the decisions, thank you, and Captain Paolina Nigmatullin, late of the starship *Aeneid*, could sit there and be quiet. She was nothing but a straw man over whom Donohue had poured a bucket of warm water. She was certainly not on fire.

Bill Cannon might have been passionate about his desire to stay on Elysia. He might, as Nigmatullin had told Calvin, have hated her with a deep and abiding hatred for her failure to get him back there, but his discussion of alien flora left a lot to be desired. Calvin started making bets with himself as to how long the audience would last. He knew full well which scene would make the casts, and it would not be this discussion of plant life that grew really, really far away. It wasn't like the man had the brains to talk about the corn.

Calvin couldn't be too obvious about his perusal of the crowd, since, whenever the camera did an occasional pan to Nigmatullin's stony face it showed the people sitting behind her, but he couldn't fall asleep either. That would be worse than fidgeting.

The occasional pan to Ryder showed that he, too, was entirely serene, if not a trifle smug. His straight back emanated a satisfied happiness that Calvin found obnoxious.

While experimenting, Calvin found that if he crossed a leg, put an elbow across the back of his chair, and loosely clasped his hands, he was able to convince himself that he looked as if he was listening attentively, not unlike an elderly deaf man turned to put an ear to his listener. The pose allowed him to look back into the crowd.

A young girl, a university student perhaps, held an ear of corn in her lap. She wore a long purple scarf tangled in her auburn hair. She had skin of the deepest midnight. The blonde with her had hair the same color, and carried a whole stalk. They both looked sad, but as if they were trying to pay attention to Dr. Cannon.

Calvin knew he should pay attention, and he knew he would listen more closely to this testimony later, but right now, he experienced a displeasing combination of sadness and relief himself. He was so very glad she had claimed her right to remain silent. He had been so very worried that she wouldn't.

There was a woman just beyond the pair of girls. Her shirt was lilac, and she was a big woman. Her green eyes looked familiar. He saw that her neighbor also had eyes of the same vivid green, a strong contrast to his umber skin. Lots of people had eyes that color. It was very popular, and one saw it still in small children.

Calvin's mouth felt dry, and he found it difficult to look away. This was the man who had tried to kill him. He was sure of it. He'd looked at that picture often enough. His face had been everywhere after the Georgetown invasion. How had the man gotten in? The only attempt at disguise was a change in the color and styling of his hair, which he now wore buzzed to his scalp.

Any doubt Calvin might have felt vanished when those eyes met his. The male owner of the green eyes was the thug from the cocktail party, and he had the same dark lashes and dark brows, the same light of insanity that he had showed Calvin before, so up close and personal.

Calvin's heart felt as if it beat very slowly and very loudly in his ears. He had already made a spectacle of himself once in a hearing room, and it was possible this was not the same man. He was having visions of testifying to a criminal court that, yes, your honor, I leapt over nine people and lunged at this poor schoolteacher because I thought he had crazy eyes. Yes, I appreciate the irony of me thinking someone else was crazy. Yes, your honor.

Also, he had his client to think about. She had taken enough of a body blow to her public image in this room without her lawyer doing something foolish.

The man had not looked away. Calvin suspected that the thoughts running through the mind of a trained assassin did not rise to the level of frivolity of those of a paralyzed attorney. Was being frozen in fear worse than being frozen in indecision? If he waited too long to do what he should, he would be sorry later. That had happened to him before.

He took a deep breath, not quite a sigh, and let his hands unclasp. At least he wouldn't have to face his ethics hearing in two days.

The man with the green eyes smiled, and Calvin would have sworn his teeth were sharp. It was not an attractive look.

Time stretched for Calvin. Despite the tunnel vision, a small part of him noticed a face he recognized in the back of the room. Jasper Brughel walked with a young woman, her youth evident in her elven slenderness, as if she were still fourteen. Calvin had been looking for that girl with the olive skin and bright blue eyes. She was Ray Hillman's great-granddaughter.

At the same time, the assassin turned to check what had caught Calvin's attention, and spotted the pair making their way down the aisle. The green eyed man rose smoothly, carefully, gracefully to his feet. He was a natural athlete who could swing across highways and literally crash parties to carry out his goals. He carried and raised a small crossbow at the girl.

Calvin did not see what happened, for he was standing, too, shouting, "No," as a slender, feathered missile from somewhere else whispered across the back of his neck. If it had been intended for him, it missed, but when Calvin turned he saw it had found a far worse target in Polly. He could do nothing for the girl, desperately though he wanted to, for he suspected the screams he heard were hers.

There was no time for feeling, but the part of him that didn't believe it, that had thought the worse that could happen today was a loss of face or a case, cried out against the loss of life and possibly a world. Scanning the crowd behind him with all the focus he had ever deployed, his heart clanging like an anvil in his ears, he searched for the other bowman. He was high in the back of the auditorium.

There was no meeting of the eyes with this one. There was only a raised bow aimed at the last surviving starship captain. Nigmatullin might have already been dead, slumping forward across the table as she was, a bolt sticking out from her back. A dark red pool spread beneath her. Without meaning to, without thinking about it, without any sense at all, Calvin moved ever so slightly to his right.

Time slowed again, and he was privileged to watch the physics of the thing. He saw the crossbow. He saw the release. He saw the bolt launch. He watched it grow, and it was as if the speed at which it travelled showed itself sedate, deliberate, agonizingly slow, with plenty of time for him to listen to the part of his brain screaming at him to move. But he couldn't. Polly needed a shield, and he was it.

He was astonished at the force of the thing. It took his breath away, and possibly more, and he staggered, turning. His left arm hung limp, and there was a pain that he had never felt emanating from it.

Fortunately, Zeke, who was a good fellow, and more prepared than Calvin, stood with a pistol in his hands facing up into the crowd. There was a lot of screaming now, and the portion of the audience that wasn't on its feet trying to run huddled under the seats.

Calvin hoped he wasn't screaming. That would be embarrassing.

His arm felt as if it had been cut through with a butcher's blade, and the wet sensation on his forearm failed to compete with the pain in his upper arm.

Donohue stood at the dais. The other senators had vanished, whether to huddle beneath the dais or to be whisked away by staff, Calvin had not seen.

Donohue's beautiful face was fearless, the only person in the room with no concern for her own life. Even the assassins did not bother to spare her a glance, despite the rich target she offered, both physically and politically.

Calvin, suffering from pain and blood loss of unknown quantity, the still form of Nigmatullin collapsed in front of him, abandoned all the caution he had so carefully cultivated over the past months. "It was you, Senator," he called out. "You let them in."

Donohue rounded on him. "Be quiet, you idiot."

It wasn't necessary to say anything else. The implications were clear—now the bowmen might shoot her to ensure her silence.

There was a cry, and Calvin turned. The security officer's former concerns for bystanders notwithstanding, Zeke apparently had sufficient confidence in his aim to pick off one of the shooters, the one high up in the seating area.

Green-eyes, who was only a couple of rows back, lunged through the few people still in front of him. As he headed toward the senators' dais, he spared a glance for Nigmatullin, as if to make sure she was dead. It was the glance that drove Calvin.

His left arm wasn't working and maybe he felt a little lightheaded from the pain, but he was damned if he was going to let this man escape again to do more harm. "Zeke," he said. "Get him."

Zeke was, as far as Calvin knew, the only other armed person in the room. To Calvin's horror the other man raised the bow as Zeke started to turn.

Calvin didn't really have a lot to offer the situation other than his head and right shoulder, which he used, going in low and ramming the shooter in the midsection. They both went down, and a bolt flew high. The man had, in addition to his crossbow and a set of bolts, a knife. Calvin shoved it free with the heel of his hand, and it sped across the floor. How the attacker had gotten through security was, Calvin didn't think, any kind of mystery, and he wished very much that he was grappling with the petite Senator Donohue instead of the man beneath him.

It was all a muddled mess of arms, legs, agony, and rage. Someone was pounding, and his right fist was cracked and numb. It was wet, too, and hurt like hell.

"Stop it," someone said, and Calvin felt a hand on his shoulder. He wondered what he was supposed to stop, and realized he was slugging an unconscious man repeatedly. Green-eyes must have hit his head when he went down, but it was his jaw that was swollen and bleeding, and his eyes that were starting to puff.

Calvin knew he should have been horrified. He should have recoiled at what he had been doing, but he only felt a grim satisfaction that his autonomous systems knew how to wreak justice. Now, however, that the immediate threats were gone, the pains he felt ratcheted up. He wanted to clutch his left arm, but his other hand hurt too much.

Calvin looked up at Bill Cannon. Past him he saw Donohue turning away. "Watch her," he said to the xeno. He looked over at Ryder. "Him, too."

Zeke had an arrow in his stomach.

"Is there a doctor?" Calvin cried, and a fresh wash of adrenaline hit him again. "We need you down here." He didn't wait to see if there was any response, but ran the short distance to the bench, and, with a convenient chair for a stepping stone, scaled it.

Tessa Donohue tried to run, but he caught her before she reached the private exit. His left hand was stronger than his right at this point, despite the blood all over it. He resolved to call the slice of flesh missing from his left arm a mere scratch.

"Let go of me," she hissed. "I will have you arrested." He did not let go, but brought her round the bench to the space between it and the witness table, and saw that the Capitol police had finally made it through the frantic crowds exiting the room. "Help me," she called out to them.

"Don't even try it," Calvin said to her.

It took the police very little time, despite the state of the crowd, to reach the floor of the stadium-seating arena. Calvin waited, his large hand gripping Tessa's arm.

When she opened her mouth, he spoke first. "You have to arrest her. Check the video and check her visitors. She let those shooters in here armed. They may have killed three people."

The Capitol police were not inclined to believe Calvin, and the squad leader, armored to her eyeballs, said, "Who the hell are you?"

"I am Captain Nigmatullin's lawyer. Do you have a medic? She is hurt, so is her bodyguard, and a young woman in the audience." Had he been asked, he could not for the life of him said who he hoped more was still alive. They all needed to be.

The squad leader spoke into her voice.

"There are two men with crossbows," Calvin began.

"Crossbows? How the hell did they get in here?" The woman was not happy and Calvin assumed the question to be rhetorical. She turned and started issuing instructions.

There was a commotion at the witness table. Aaron Ryder was trying to get past Bill Cannon to the fallen man. "And him," Calvin pointed at Ryder. "Don't let him near that guy. They're probably all working together."

He thrust Donohue's arm in the general vicinity of the police. However old and however cunning Tessa Donohue was, she wasn't cunning enough. She broke and ran.

Calvin looked at what he could see of the squad leader's eyes and raised a brow. She sighed. "Go get the Senator," she told one of her unit.

Most of the casters had remained in the room, their need to record everything—and comment on it—keeping them from joining the throngs attempting to exit. The stampede had slowed, if not stopped. Calvin inspected his arm. Despite the throbbing pain and the slick of blood covering his jacket, it probably was just a scratch. He saw his friend Molly, and called out to her, "Follow Donohue. She's a suspect." Molly wasn't the only one who raced after Donohue.

He watched Bill Cannon keep Ryder at bay as he walked back to the table. He couldn't bear the next part. He really couldn't.

Nigmatullin represented too much for Calvin. She represented another world and the way back to it. It wasn't all lost, he knew, if she were dead, but he really didn't want her to be dead. She had her own value, independent of that other world.

Sara was there, crouched by Nigmatullin. She had a lot of blood on her hands. He couldn't look at Polly. He kept his eyes on Sara, instead. She looked strange, her own eyes swimming with tears, but her mouth quivered upwards as if there were reason to smile, if only she could. "She's alive, Calvin," Sara said.

Polly was right in front of him, but he hadn't seen with a medic in the way. Polly was leaning back, her face deeply cut, and the table in front of her was covered in shattered glass. No arrow protruded from her chest. He looked from her to Zeke and back again. Zeke was grinning at him. He and Polly were both armored beneath their clothes, Polly up to her neck behind the stiff collar.

The glass that had held her drinking water lay a shattered mess on the table. The medic picked pieces of it from Polly's face. The force of the blow must have sent her forward into the glass and the table and knocked her unconscious.

He sank to his knees next to her and took her hand in his left. "Don't ever do that again," he said.

"Hush," she said, and the medic told her not to talk. Polly had a cut on her lip, but the real source of all the blood was a long, jagged wound just beneath her hairline that the medic now worked on.

Calvin sat back on his heels, and felt the relief as a physical force. The crash of adrenaline ebbed away, leaving him light and stupid. A medic pulled his jacket off before Calvin realized what was happening. "That's going to need stiches," the woman said.

He caught her eyes. "Can you just cover it up? I've got work right now."

Her lips quirked. "I'll just leave it for now, but don't wait too long. I'll stay."

He finally looked around the room. Not everyone was gone, but the Capitol police were trying hard to get them out. He remembered the surprise presence of Jasper Brughel and looked for him and his charge. Miraculously, the girl appeared unscathed, just trembling and pale, her hair shimmering with her shivers.

Calvin looked to where the casters had regained their seats and found his friend. Molly was his age, but the geneers had done something badly wrong with her, and she looked prepubescent. He caught her eye, and she strolled over. He tilted his head ever so slightly toward Jasper, and Molly started wending her way through the seating.

"Be right back," Calvin said to Sara, Polly, and the medic.

Taking the steps up the wall aisle two at a time, he reached the pair moments before Molly. Jasper had seated his charge, and her long slim hands clung to the arms of her chair. She had very fine dark hair, and it trembled, floating with each movement of her head.

"Calvin, Molly," Jasper said, "this is Barbra Hillman, Ray Hillman's granddaughter."

"Call me Babs," she whispered automatically. She blinked, swallowed, and took a deep breath. "Babs, I mean," she said in a more normal voice.

"Are you okay?" Calvin asked, settling on the arm of the seat in front of hers.

"I'm fine." She looked embarrassed. "My throat's a little sore."

"Why did you come?" Calvin asked.

"May I record this?" Molly interjected. She shared her credentials with Babs' palm.

Babs stared at them blankly for a moment, as if not understanding their meaning. "You're a reporter?"

Molly smiled softly. "I am. May I record you?"

Babs looked to Jasper. "Will this make it easier for people to find me?"

"I've been hiding her," Jasper explained. "Her grandfather asked me to protect her. I was bringing her here so she could share what she knows and not be threatened anymore." He shook his head ruefully, as if the idea had been obviously ridiculous, even if only in hindsight. "I think it would be good if you were recorded," he said to the girl.

Babs nodded assent to Molly, and Calvin, stifling the urge to interrogate the witness before allowing the press access, said, "What is it that you want to share with us?"

"My grandfather told me what he did," she said. "About Elysia, and Captain Nigmatullin's orders. He issued orders for the *Aeneid* to leave a settlement if it found a habitable planet."

Molly looked serenely happy, but Calvin felt all the adrenaline come flooding back in a hot wave through his body. He had none to spare, and felt so hopeful and filled with dread all at once that he wondered if he might not just be sick. Also, his arm and hand hurt.

"What's going on up there?" The voice was deep and filled with authority. Calvin turned to look for more police. No one had tried to usher his little group out yet. It was one of the senators, one who looked old, returned to brave the hearing room. His hair and beard were white, and he was more portly than most politicians. He was Senator Randall Alcott of Arizona. Calvin had found nothing in that senator's record about his views on Elysia one way or the other.

Calvin stood. "I'm talking to a witness for Captain Nigmatullin's mutiny hearing," he called back down.

The old eyes surveyed the scene. The senator pondered a moment. "Why don't you bring her down? Put her at the witness table?"

It was one of the more ridiculous suggestions anyone had made to trial counsel. Despite her absolutely wonderful news, Calvin had no intention of having her share it without proper back up, verification, and preparation. It could be a disaster. It was bad enough that in a fit of post-adrenaline friendliness he had brought Molly over. "That won't be necessary, sir," he replied.

He felt Jasper's eyes on him, and remembered all too vividly the last time Jasper had given him that look. It was after Calvin had failed to show either guts or imagination in deposing Armothy Brewster about the creation of a certain bubble drive. Calvin's chest rose and fell in a heavy sigh.

As if reading Calvin's thoughts, Jasper started smiling.

Calvin turned back to the senator. The older man was of an age that predated good geneering, and yet here he still was, surviving a political process which usually threw out people such as him. "We'll be right there," Calvin said.

The casters hadn't left. Some were a little dusty still from their hiding places under the chairs, but they were all smiles at the sight of yet another person at the witness table, and a young and attractive girl at that.

Calvin fussed over whether she was seated too close to the Earth First witness, even if he was wearing a suit and had no crossbow. Calvin made sure to pitch his voice so that it could be picked up by any casters in the vicinity, which made Molly make bug eyes at him so that he wouldn't think he was pulling one over on her.

Sara took the Earth First president to the end of the table, and placed Zeke right behind him, but only after first fussing over his physical condition. Calvin looked away.

The white haired senator banged his gavel. "This committee is back in session after a brief interruption," he announced. He looked pleased with himself. Some people had a work ethic. "We have called a new witness, one Barbra Hillman, granddaughter of Ray Hillman, once employed by the United States Department of Defense."

The muffled policewoman had been standing with arms folded. This new development was too much for her. She removed the mask from the lower half of her face and said, "Excuse me, Senator, this is now a crime scene."

The old man gave her a long, slow look. He waved an airy hand at those who had returned to their seats. "You all heard the officer. Don't disturb anything. I would also like the record to reflect that a number of people are looking quite a bit the worse for wear."

"Sir," the officer exclaimed.

"And you," continued Senator Alcott, looking back to the officer, "don't let the bad guys get away." He peered at the fallen assassins. "In fact, the Committee would take it as a favor if you would keep them here where we can all keep an eye on them. I'm interested in whether they have any testimony to offer."

Green-eyes hung handcuffed between two officers, on his feet but swaying, his face swollen and his eyes baleful. He said nothing.

"I think he'll be taking the Fifth, too," Polly said. There was laughter from the small crowd. Something flew threw the air, and guns were drawn. The missile was a kernel of corn, and bounced from Nigmatullin's shoulder to the witness table.

"No more throwing things," the senator said. He was the only one on the bench. It made him look like a judge. "It makes everyone twitchy."

Calvin surveyed the strange scene. The highly theatrical hearing room with its stadium seating and oversized flags was a shambles. It held only a single senator, and presumably, aside from the one taken away under arrest, the others had been scuttled to safety or were preoccupied with palpitations. Two people in the seats held long cornstalks, and the parti-colored girls with the matching auburn hair still held their places. They eyed him expectantly.

His cautious side, his constant concern for getting the law right, struggled hard against what he was going to do. "I would like Ms. Hillman sworn in," Calvin said.

Alcott nodded. "Fair enough."

Calvin's looked for and found the man he sought, but not before registering Sara's wide, shocked eyes, Nigmatullin's wary expression, and Jasper's encouragement. Ryle Feder was stone faced, shut off from any prying, and Calvin just nodded at him. "I would also like to offer USACD the opportunity for cross-examination." If he was in, Calvin figured, he was all in. Besides, he wanted to offer before Ryle demanded it.

Ryle's lips thinned, and he managed to look haughty and condescending all at once. He was trapped and knew it, but all he said was "USACD is not prepared. I doubt counsel for Captain Nigmatullin is prepared, but so long as we reserve the right for further questioning, I will handle the cross-examination."

There was a noise at the top of the room. The sound of a hollering crowd could be heard through the closed doors, and a single member of the Capitol Police force stood, face muffled with his arms folded in front of it. Alcott lifted his white and hairy head and called up to the officer, "If they promise to be good, let them in. I think we've got the shooters taken care of."

This prompted another exclamation from the officer in charge, but a look from the senator quelled her, and she turned and headed up the stairs to help her colleague. Her face was grim and unhappy, but no one else seemed to mind.

The crowd, boisterous and happy, having caught the latest developments in the hearing room on their palms, returned with great good cheer and settled back into their seats. They needed a song, Calvin thought idly, momentarily distracted from the questions he was scribbling with some discomfort into his palm. He wished the medic had offered him an analgesic spray.

"I would like a Bible," Babs said. "If I am to be sworn in."

The senator raised his bushy brows, as if unaccustomed to the request. He nodded to the woman with the bun, and she rummaged behind the bench and produced the book. Not a lot of people asked for Bibles in Calvin's own experience at the administrative hearing level.

Senator Alcott swore the young woman to the truth, the whole truth, and nothing but the truth, and she added, "So help me God," on her own.

Calvin stood to the side, waiting for Alcott to start his questions.

"Counselor?" Alcott said to Calvin. "You may proceed."

Calvin had expected this, but it still gave him pause. The fate of Babs Hillman's testimony was back in his hands. Calvin walked slowly to stand between the bench and the witness table. He had to make do with the configuration he had. It unnerved him that Babs sat where the counsel table was usually located, but he told himself not to focus on the shallow stuff. He knew full well that he was far more concerned about what Ryle might get her to say, hell, what she might tell Calvin. For all he knew she was about to tell them that Hillman's orders were in direct violation of a Presidential command.

Calvin took care to establish the relationship between Babs and her great-grandfather, and asked if anyone had told her what to say today.

"I talked with Jasper Brughel, but he only told me to tell everyone what Granda' told me."

It was a fine answer. Calvin considered the presence of the casters and their avid eye and voice. For the USACD hearing, he only needed certain answers. For public opinion, for the goals of Nigmatullin, his client, he might need a little more.

Nigmatullin, bandaged and alert, watched him. She was trusting him not to screw this up, and he swallowed, his throat dry all of a sudden.

He looked again to Babs. "When you talked to your great-grandfather, did you know that the U.S. Administration for Colonial Development had charged Captain Paolina Nigmatullin, who is sitting right next to you, with mutiny for leaving a settlement of people on Elysia?"

"I did," she said.

Calvin nodded approvingly. The girl looked nervous. "Do you know what job your great-grandfather held when the *Aeneid* left Earth?"

"Yes," she said. "He was the Undersecretary for Planetary Defense at the Pentagon."

"Was he a civilian?" Calvin knew the answer to that one, at least.

She wrinkled her nose a little as if perplexed, then her face cleared. "Yes, he told me that once."

"Did he ever tell you that he was involved in decisions about the plans for the starship?" There was only one starship. Calvin felt safe with his question.

"Yes, he did, and my mother used to tell me he talked about it all the time," the girl said.

"When did you last talk to your great-grandfather, Ms. Hillman?"

"The day before he died," she said, and her tremble made her hair shimmer in the light streaming through the high windows and skylights.

"Did he ever talk to you about Captain Nigmatullin?" Calvin asked.

"He did," she said, and waited obediently. Jasper had done a good job of prepping her. She had only answered the question Calvin had asked.

"Why was that?" It was a risky question, but one didn't cross-examine one's own witness.

"I told him I wanted to travel to Elysia," she said. She dimpled a little. "I was very excited when the starship came back. I went to the marches on the Mall. He knew all that, and he kept hinting things about the *Aeneid*. When the Captain," – she paused and looked over at Nigmatullin – "was charged with mutiny, he told me his big secret. I think he wanted to brag."

Calvin clasped his hands behind his back and walked thoughtfully in the direction of the casters' seating area. He turned and faced her again, just to the left of his friend Molly and the eye at her neck. "What was your grandfather's big secret, Ms. Hillman?"

"He told me he issued orders for a settlement to be left behind on any planet that was habitable," she replied. "He said they had to be secret because of the politics of the time. Everyone was already forgetting we were almost wiped out. It wasn't fashionable to talk about settling another planet. Lots of people had become upset about the terraforming of Mars and were complaining about all the science lost, and Granda' and his friends didn't want someone to say no to their plan. It was better to ask forgiveness than permission, he told me."

"Did you believe him?" Calvin asked.

"I did."

"Why?"

The young girl's face was very earnest, still tinged with sadness over her grandfather's death. "Because when I asked him why he didn't come forward and help Captain Nigmatullin he was ashamed. He said he would if he had to, but I'm not sure he meant it."

"That sounds like a good reason not to believe him," Calvin said. He saw Ryle mouth "objection," as if the other lawyer understood fully the futility of pointing out that Calvin wasn't the one testifying.

He hated asking the question. He hated not knowing her answers in advance. He hated how much he hated all of it. He hoped he looked more dispassionate than he felt. "So why did you? Believe him."

She reached into her pocket and pulled something out. She laid her slim arm flat on the table, looking at Calvin and all the people behind him. Her young face was reflected in the large screens to either side of the room, and it was a serene and beautiful face. Her hair continued to shimmer, and thin strands of it floated into the air as if she were just a little electrified. She opened her hand, and a wafer thin dime lay in her palm. "He showed them to me, and he said they still have all the military encryption. And they are countersigned by the President."

Calvin felt as if that little dime of information was all he'd ever wanted in life and now he had it. All eyes in the room were on Babs's hand, but he felt a different presence and looked to his client. She was staring at him, and her tilted devil eyes were strangely huge with the water in them. They overflowed and her mouth formed a single word. "Thank you."

The room got loud.

Calvin felt very quiet of a sudden, but he mouthed back, "You're welcome." His cheeks hurt he was smiling so hard.

Sara leapt to her feet and hugged everyone. Polly struggled to her feet and warmly shook Babs Hillman's hand. Ryle Feder stared at his feet, and then looked up, resignation stolid on his face, as if, really, what could one do about secret idiocy propelled by post-asteroid stress?

Calvin, who was already on his own two feet, continued grinning like an idiot.

He couldn't tell if the hug Sara gave him was as long as the one she dealt Zeke, but Calvin lifted her one-armed in the air, squeezed her ribs too hard, and said, "You're beautiful." He discovered his own ribs hurt, his hand throbbed, and his left arm was just a feeling he'd compartmentalized.

Her golden skin turned red, and he resisted the urge to kiss her hard. He set her gently down, and told her she was beautiful one more time, just to be sure she knew. He figured that if it bothered her, he would plead blood loss and the heat of the moment. She was beautiful. Also, he felt drunk and not a little giddy.

He did not consider the joy premature. Ray Hillman had not struck him as a man who would lie to his granddaughter as he gave her the orders he had provided the *Aeneid*. The president's involvement also explained why Ray had hidden his role for so long. Even a president hadn't wanted to take a controversial stand.

The chain of people protecting other people was a long and bewildering one, and he wondered if he would ever know why the president at the time had signed the orders in secret rather than the full light of day. Perhaps even back then there were those who found the need for control—no matter how great the distance—greater than the need to ensure the species' survival.

CHAPTER 25

I N THE DAYS THAT FOLLOWED the Senate hearing, Senator Donohue's reluctant involvement in the assassination attempt provoked a scandal. The secret militia arm of Earth First had been blackmailing her for decades over records they had of sums of money she should not have accepted. Of course, once one was subject to blackmail, the blackmailers could impose more and more onerous demands until the time came that Donohue had to let them into her hearing room as her personal visitors with far fewer screening requirements. Donohue herself had brought in the components of the crossbows separately and watched as they were put together right before her hearing. The attackers were to have knocked her out, maybe even shot her, on their escape from the room to give her plausible deniability. Indeed, who would ever have suspected her in the first place?

More came quickly to light as the conspirators all turned on each other. Donohue hadn't wanted them to kill the starship captains or the navigators. She'd had, according to a green-eyed man arrested in the hearing room, wanted him to kill Ray Hillman because she'd been spying on him and learned that he was about to spill the truth about the *Aeneid's* real orders and her involvement would have come to light. She had been the one who talked the president into signing the orders so long ago. Her new constituency wouldn't have liked that.

Aaron Ryder, the president of Earth First, looked like he might succeed in his efforts to convince the world that he had known nothing of the darker side of his organization. He had always dismissed such claims as fanciful. He continued to do so.

Two days after the Senate hearing that caused the entire world to pronounce Captain Paolina Nigmatullin, late of the USS *Aeneid*, innocent of mutiny, the U.S. Administration for Colonial Development announced it was dropping all charges against her. A careful review of the orders produced by Ray Hillman's granddaughter had proved them authentic, and USACD declined to further pursue the question of the legality of Captain Nigmatullin's actions. That this wise decision-making took only two days astonished all who worked for the government as well as those who used to. Calvin could not imagine how the review process had been expedited so hastily. He wondered if Ryle Feder had whiplash.

Other events that Ryle had put in motion did not go away so easily. Although Calvin had found it impossible to worry about his own ethics hearing in the lead-up to Polly's Senate testimony, its looming threat marred the lasting joy he should have felt at Babs Hillman's report on her grandfather.

Now that USACD had verified the credibility of the orders through the Pentagon, Calvin had to turn his attention to his own situation. He sat in the outer offices of the bar association's hearing room, waiting for his fate to be decided. He wore a sober suit, but one that fit his large shoulders well, and he had brushed his short brown hair within an inch of its life. Sara sat next to him in her role as his attorney.

She had assured him that she had been working hard on this, had filed a brief moving for dismissal, and had provided the board members all relevant pages from the hearing where he had gotten an inventor to testify to his role in the creation of the bubble drive when he worked for MarsCorp, which was a client of the firm Calvin worked at now. He had to admit it didn't look good, and asked himself again the question his father had asked him more than once in the past few months: with the most famous client on the planet to take wherever he wanted, why had he gone to the one place where he might look like he had traded a favor for a job?

One of the reasons—as he now grudgingly admitted to himself—

sat beside him, oblivious to how deeply stupid he was. It wasn't as if he could pursue a colleague, especially one who had turned him down once. Ruin lay in that direction as well. His had been a plan designed for self-torture. And now it looked like it had worked, in more ways than one.

To top it off, Sara's state of mind was entirely inappropriate. He had heard her chuckle to herself at least twice, and she had literally dimpled when he asked her what was up. Hers was not the best of bedside manners, and it was clear she was either drunk or in love, and a part of him very much hoped it was the former, even if she was about to act as his attorney for the next two hours or so, which was a task best accomplished sober.

He had read all of her filings, and had even reviewed them again the day before despite his own mild hangover. It had turned out that Nigmatullin believed in vodka as a celebratory device.

At ten of ten, Zeke Salisbury showed up immaculate in the dress greens of the *Aeneid*. He beamed at Sara, and Calvin pondered how he had the reach on the other man.

"What are you doing here?" Calvin asked in a friendly way.

"I've come to offer my moral support," Zeke said, and sat down on the other side of Sara. "Are we ready?" he said to her.

"I'm ready," she said. "Are you ready?"

"You bet," Zeke said with annoying good cheer. He wasn't the one scheduled for an ethics hearing. "How about you, Calvin?"

"I am ready, too," Calvin said stoutly. He wished Zeke hadn't come. "Where's Polly? Shouldn't you be guarding her?"

"She wouldn't let me in the restroom with her," Zeke said.

At that, Polly showed up, also in uniform. Maybe they meant to lend Calvin a little star power. It wasn't the worst thing, he decided.

She seated herself next to him and asked him if he was ready. It was getting annoying. "What do you think?"

She cocked her head. "If you aren't, Sara is. You're in good hands."

Calvin looked over at Sara, and she was laughing softly with Zeke, her golden head very close to his dark one. Calvin might have characterized it as giggling had he been feeling uncharitable. It was a good thing he wasn't. Nonetheless, he didn't find it appropriate to the circumstances.

Calvin turned back to his client. She was still his client, and he hadn't sent her his final bill. "I certainly hope so," he said calmly.

Polly grinned at him, as if she could read his mind or knew something he didn't. "How big is the room?" she asked.

He wished they would all stop talking to him. "I don't know. I don't come here very often."

She did not pursue that line of inquiry further. "I suppose that's good."

She tilted her head slightly to look at him. "I want you to know I feel a little cheated."

"By what?" he asked carefully. He couldn't believe she was going to talk about legal fees.

She didn't. "I didn't get to give my speech. It was going to be amazing."

He did not point out that he had warned her more than once she wouldn't get to give her speech. "I'm very sorry," he said.

"You told me so," Polly said, "but I didn't believe you. I wanted to win because I did the right thing, not because someone had set up a double blind of secret orders I didn't even know about. That's so—" she paused, as if unable to find the right words.

"So very ass covering, so very bureaucratic?" Calvin supplied helpfully.

"That's it. It's a cheat. I should have gotten off because I set up a colony against orders and it was self-sacrificing and brave."

"Subparagraph double little 'i' of the regulations doesn't have that exception," Calvin said. "I looked."

His client waved a hand dismissively. "That's not the point."

"It's the point for a mutiny hearing." He felt a little indignant. "You could have gone to jail. You should be much more grateful." He leaned back in his chair and laced his fingers around a crossed knee. His arm and hand no longer hurt. "I'm the one who should feel cheated. I didn't get to save you."

"You absolutely did," she said. They hadn't mentioned that, even during the vodka. "I watched the video. That arrow would have gone through my head."

"Not that," he said. He still didn't want it mentioned. It made him uncomfortable. "I didn't get to have my big trial and save you. It's kind of a let down it got cancelled."

They stared at each other for a long moment, and she snorted and he laughed at the same time.

"We're even, it looks like," Polly said.

The door into the hearing room opened, and a man of Calvin's age ushered them in. He looked like one of those people who ran for student council, all earnest and annoying. The space was wasteful. It looked like it could hold up to fifty people, and the Commission had had the nerve to arrange the seating like a courtroom, with two tables for counsel, a bench, and rows of seats in back of the bar.

Calvin followed Sara to counsel's table, and Polly and Zeke sat close behind them. Bart Locke from the firm came in one minute later and sat with them, likely to keep an eye on Calvin and Sara's representation. Ryle Feder showed up and seated himself behind the Commission's investigating attorney. Molly and some other print reporters showed up. Calvin was glad to see no casters with eye and voice. He preferred not to be in the public eye for this one.

Ryle sat there looking all serious, as if there was a real ethics charge against one Calvin Tondini. The man was utterly defeated and Calvin almost—but not quite—wished he could give him some joy. Maybe the investigating attorney would say something sarcastic about Calvin's choice of employers. That could make Ryle happy.

Sara moved for dismissal, with the transcript of the SPInc hearing as Exhibit A to demonstrate that Calvin had done nothing wrong and the observation that with Paolina Nigmatullin as his client he could have gone to any firm he wanted. She submitted a list of character witnesses by shortcast to the commissioners. Calvin idly wondered whom she had called, and whether it really mattered. Mostly, he wondered whether the commission was stacked with Ryle's friends, since the man seemed to know everyone or had at least met them over the course of his interminable life.

"This is a long list, Ms. Seastrom," said one of the commissioners, a woman with harlequin coloring and pale gold hair.

"Mr. Tondini has a lot of character," Calvin's lawyer said.

Sara put Calvin on the stand and began his questioning.

More people started to enter the courtroom. They were uniform in their clothing, the greens of the iconoclastic *Aeneid* uniforms. Calvin recognized several of them as they filed in and filled the room. He saw Bill Cannon, and a couple other xenos whose names he did not recall. He saw the *Aeneid*'s last surviving navigator, resplendent in unabashed body armor, and a number of other people he had seen at Polly's house from time to time.

He lost his train of thought and allowed his voice to trail away. He had been explaining that he'd had no intention of leaving the government until Captain Nigmatullin wanted to hire him. She had not shown up on Earth and been shot at or been charged with mutiny as of the SPInc hearing.

He couldn't help but wonder what the hell were all these people from the *Aeneid* doing in this room? They could not possibly have come to watch this most embarrassing moment in his career.

The commissioners appeared equally distracted, with the exception of the harlequin woman. "Mr. Tondini?" she prompted. "We are all waiting."

He blinked, and continued sharing his personal career plans with the judgmental strangers, and, now, apparently, a roomful of people who had breathed the air of another planet. He hardly noticed Ryle's stone face or his handsome head of hair.

It was hard to focus on what he was saying. He cared so very much that he not look a fool or a cheat in front of all these brave people, that he was likely not looking very intelligent in his responses.

Sara finished, the commission's lawyer had very few questions, and Calvin was allowed off the stand.

Once he was back at the little table allotted to him and counsel, Sara rose and addressed the panel. All gold, from skin to hair to painted nails, she shone with serenity. "The defense moves for dismissal, or, in the alternative, an opportunity to present character witnesses who will support a finding that he has committed no ethical breach."

The harlequin commissioner looked around the room with a dubious expression. She consulted a list. The harlequin patterning did not extend to her face, and her reluctance to ask her next question was obvious. "Are all the character witnesses present?"

"Yes, ma'am," Sara said. If a back could look happy, Sara's did.

"Would you mind asking them to stand?"

Sara turned to face the rows of seats behind Calvin, and there was considerable noise and rustling. Sara's face stopped Calvin from turning for a moment. Although she only barely smiled, because glee would have been inappropriate in this setting, she exuded a suppressed giddiness. He recognized the look. It was the one she had after talking to Zeke, but first she turned it on Calvin in a very doting way, and then she turned it on the crew of the *Aeneid* in the room.

The commissioners were whispering amongst themselves.

Calvin finally looked. Polly and Zeke stood behind him, and he realized what he had not noticed before. They were not only in uniform, but their shoulders and two rectangles above their hearts blazed with all the little holos they must have earned over the course of their careers in military service. They were very shiny. Behind them, solemn and equally resplendent, stood close to fifty people in the same colors. They were all staring at Calvin.

Where everyone else was serious, Zeke had a big, stupid grin on his face, and Calvin, who had finally realized what Sara must have been planning with the crewman over the past couple of weeks, decided that Zeke wasn't so terrible a guy after all.

He stopped himself from asking Sara how they could testify as to his character when he had never met most of them.

Sara turned back to the panel. "There are more outside, but there's no room for them."

Calvin felt his throat go tight. He swallowed.

"They're just grateful he got their captain off," Ryle said in the silent room.

"And saved her life," someone called from the back.

"More than once," said someone who stood right behind Ryle. There was laughter.

The lead commissioner banged a small gavel, and all attention returned to her. "Enough," she said. "You may stand, Mr. Tondini. The testimony of your many character witnesses will not be necessary. The investigation has unearthed no signs that there was any quid pro quo, any arrangement or expectation of an offer of employment in return for the series of questions, that, frankly, either side could have asked at that hearing."

Sara bit her lip.

The commissioner banged her little gavel again. "The investigation is closed."

Now Calvin let the air escape his lungs. He had not realized how long he had been holding his breath. He bowed his head briefly. "Thank you," he said.

Then he turned and hugged his lawyer and she hugged him back to the sound of cheering.

On the way back to the firm, because it was only the middle of the day and no one was suggesting the level of celebration that had followed the news about Polly, they were accompanied by a good number of the *Aeneid* personnel. The crewmembers all managed to shake Calvin's hand at some point along the way and thank him for his service to their captain and country, and he did likewise but threw in a bit about his gratitude to them for showing up at his ethics hearing. Everyone was very pleased with everyone else.

Most of them peeled off as they reached the tall office building painted in all the colors of the sunrise at 1776 K, but Polly and Zeke came upstairs to say their good-byes, with Zeke deciding he needed to talk to Sara for a minute.

Polly closed the door to Calvin's office and they stood facing each other. It didn't seem right to sit down and leave her on the other side of his desk. "I wanted to thank you for everything," she said. "If you ever need passage to Elysia, you know to come find me."

Happiness bounded through Calvin like a large Labrador puppy, and he grinned and stuck his hands in his pockets. She was free, and she could do what she wanted, go where she wanted. "Have you signed with MarsCorp?"

Polly smiled back. Her face no longer looked as stark as it had when he first met her. The horsetail had disappeared the day before, and someone had styled her hair in the segmented sheets now popular. She looked younger. "I have. There will be an announcement this afternoon."

"Just tell me when they start offering tickets." He still followed the news of the factories being built with great interest.

"Calvin," she said, her face now solemn, and she took his hand in both of hers. "I want to thank you. I haven't been able to think of how, but I really, really owe you."

He felt embarrassed. Part of him felt he owed her because she had let him be part of something important that mattered. "I think it's the other way around." Now he was really going to be embarrassed, but he had to say it. "I hope you never need me again, but it would be great to hear from you even if you don't."

"You bet, Calvin," she said, and the starship captain hugged her lawyer.

After Polly left, Calvin felt filled with a strange drifting weightlessness. It was all over, his great adventure, his huge ordeal. He wondered what he was supposed to do now. Bart would have told him he should seek more legal business, but he really couldn't think about regular work. Even the damned ethics hearing was done.

He was surprised, but he found himself outside again in the cold. The sky overhead was very blue, and that was as it should be. Even with the melting ice everywhere, the sun needed to be shining. He almost missed the sound of hurrying feet and Sara calling his name from the foyer of their building.

He stopped and waited on the sidewalk. He felt very still and empty, but not unhappy. Soon, he would need something else to come along, but right now he wanted to hold to the realization that something very good had happened and he had been part of it, even if it was over.

Sara walked toward him, her golden eyes warm. She stopped short, as if something showed in his face. "Where are you going?" she asked hesitantly. "Did you want to be alone?"

Calvin's long eyes narrowed, and he said, "No. I don't want to be alone." He tried not to think about what she might want. He was happy her victory had gone well, not only for himself, but because she seemed so very pleased, too.

She colored. "May I come with you?"

"I'm just walking," he said, and rounded the corner of 18th Street. He continued to try not to think about what she could be up to. He'd had such thoughts before, and they were never useful.

She took his arm, as if it were natural and maybe because it was cold. He found himself holding his breath. "I've been watching you," she confided.

That couldn't bode well. He said nothing.

Neither said anything, as if she had expected him to say something flippant, and he hadn't, and now she didn't know what to do. They kept walking. She plowed on. "It's been very educational for someone like me. You are very brave."

Just what one wanted to be for a woman—educational. He should have told her he wanted to be alone. She was destroying the serene quietude at the center of his being.

She continued. "You are brave with all that danger stuff, obviously."

He had to agree there, but only because there was no time to think. He wasn't sure he should get credit for it, but decided there was no need to say that out loud.

"You are also brave about putting yourself out there," she said.

He agreed, but kept silent. He wasn't so brave that he was going to risk distracting her from wherever she was heading with all of this.

They were up at the little park near Pennsylvania Avenue now, and he walked over to the empty fountain. Sara still clung to his arm. It was interesting.

"You're brave with your work," she said to the fountain. "With other people. You were brave with me." She swallowed. "And you have been a gentleman ever since."

Again, he had to agree.

"Which," she went on, "I stopped appreciating a while ago." Now she let go of his arm and looked up at him. The sun was bright on her golden skin, and the air crisp. She took a large breath. "And I realized that you had no way of knowing that, of course, but it took me a while. I also realized that I have to be brave, too, because for all I know you have lost interest in me, and I hope you haven't, but if you have I understand, but I have to ask anyway."

He couldn't help the big grin on his face. He really couldn't. "And what is it that you have to ask, Sara?"

For a moment it looked like she might explode. Her mouth dropped open, and then snapped closed. Then she laughed. She took his hand in both of hers and gazed at him very solemnly. "I was very much hoping, Mr. Tondini, that you might do me the honor of having dinner with me?"

"I would be very happy to, Ms. Seastrom," he said, equally solemn, and the serene happiness was back full force and on all fronts. "And I want you to know I think you are very brave, too."

ABOUT THE AUTHOR

Laura Montgomery began reading science fiction when she was thirteen, when the local U.S. Air Force base donated many amazing books to the school she attended in northern Thailand. Laura practices space law in Washington, D.C. She has worked on space tourism and launch safety regulations, which, honestly, are not science fiction. She lives outside Washington with her husband, children, and dogs.

You can sign up for her newsletter to hear about new releases at lauramontgomery.com.

If you enjoyed this book, please consider leaving a review. It may help someone else find an enjoyable read.

MORE FICTION BY LAURA MONTGOMERY

Waking Late Books
Sleeping Duty
Out of the Dell
Like a Continental Soldier

In the Ground Based Universe
Far Flung
Erawan
Manx Prize
No Longer A Mystery
The Sky Suspended
Mercenary Calling

Or, check her website at lauramontgomery.com

Made in the USA
Middletown, DE
30 January 2018